THE FUNERAL OWL

*A rare local sighting of a Boreal Owl heralds
a week of death and destruction for journalist
Philip Dryden*

When a reader contacts local newspaper *The
Crow* to report a rare sighting of the Boreal
or so-called 'Funeral' owl, the paper's editor
Philip Dryden has a sense of foreboding. For
the Funeral Owl is said to be an omen of death.

It's already proving to be one of the most
eventful weeks in *The Crow*'s history. The
body of a Chinese man has been discovered
hanging from a cross in a churchyard in Brimstone Hill in the West Fens. The inquest into
the deaths of two tramps found in a flooded
ditch has unearthed some shocking findings. A
series of metal thefts is plaguing the area. And
PC Stokely Powell has requested Dryden's
help in solving a ten-year-old cold case: a
series of violent art thefts culminating in a
horrifying murder.

As Dryden investigates, he uncovers some
curious links between the seemingly unrelated
cases: it would appear the sighting of the
Funeral Owl is proving prophetic in more
ways than one.

THE FUNERAL OWL

Jim Kelly

Severn House Large Print
London & New York

This first large print edition published 2014
in Great Britain and the USA by
SEVERN HOUSE PUBLISHERS LTD of
19 Cedar Road, Sutton, Surrey, England, SM2 5DA.
First world regular print edition published 2013 by
Crème de la Crime, an imprint of
Severn House Publishers Ltd., London and New York.

British Library Cataloguing in Publication Data

Kelly, Jim, 1957- author.
  The funeral owl.
  1. Dryden, Philip (Fictitious character)--Fiction.
  2. Journalists--England--Cambridgeshire--Fiction.
  3. Detective and mystery stories. 4. Large type books.
  I. Title
  823.9'2-dc23

  ISBN-13: 9780727896872

Severn House Publishers support the Forest Stewardship Council™
[FSC™], the leading international forest certification organisation. All
our titles that are printed on FSC certified paper carry the FSC logo.

MIX
Paper from
responsible sources
FSC
www.fsc.org   FSC® C013056

Printed and bound in Great Britain by
T J International, Padstow, Cornwall.

To Michael Kelly
Much-loved guardian of the family tree

ACKNOWLEDGEMENTS

I would like to thank my agent, Faith Evans, for her particular help in the writing of *The Funeral Owl*. The version which appears here is infinitely superior to the one she first read, largely due to her intervention and advice. My publisher at Severn House, Kate Lyall Grant, has been especially supportive of the final – ambitious – text. I would also like to thank my editor, Sara Porter, for her usual care and attention to detail. Here, in Ely, my thanks go to my established support team. Jenny Burgoyne read the text and provided an invaluable overview and a final, fine, edit. Rowan Haysom read the proofs to check the plot. Any surviving mistakes are all my own. My wife, Midge Gillies, found time amidst her own busy writing schedule to offer advice on a regular basis over morning toast. My daughter, Rosa, contributes her own share of ideas, and opinions.

I should point out that the township of Brimstone Hill does not exist. It may look like several fen villages and towns, but it is none of them. However, the Fen Motorway does exist, and all drivers should keep to the speed limit or risk death. The idea of building a plot around a painting hanging in a parish church came from Christ

7

Church, Christchurch, near Wisbech. I would like to thank the church warden for showing me around. All the characters in *The Funeral Owl* are entirely fictitious.

ONE

Monday

Philip Dryden gripped the fluffy wheel cover of the Capri and steered the car towards the broken white line in the middle of the road. To his left was an open grass verge, which quickly dropped away down a steep bank, ending fifteen feet below in the black waters of the Forty Foot Drain – one of the Cambridgeshire Fens' endless, arrow-straight, artificial rivers. The trench in which the Forty Foot lay was like a long, grassy coffin, often sunless, a trap for mists and fog. Whatever the season – and today promised to be the latest in a series of perfect summer days – the water looked like black ice. For Dryden that was the nightmare detail; white water held nothing of the sinister tension of its black counterpart. The fear of slipping down into the river, the spectre of an airless death in a submerged car, seemed to draw him like a magnet, not of iron, but of hydrogen and oxygen. He knew it was an illusion but the Capri seemed to be tugging them towards the brink. Droplets of sweat beaded his high forehead. His knuckles were white and numb.

They passed a sign on the left. It was blue, with white letters, as high as a house:

9

On this road in the
last two years:
35 INJURED
4 DEAD
KEEP TO THE LIMIT

The limit was thirty mph. Dryden was doing twenty mph. If he went any slower he'd stall. He was aware that driving was one of those skills that becomes almost subconscious, like riding a bicycle. Once you start thinking about it you fall off. He'd started thinking about it.

He tried to stretch out his legs to give his six-foot-two-inch frame some release from being cramped into the front of the Capri. He looked in the rear-view mirror and saw the fear in his own eyes, which were green, like the worn shards of glass you find on a beach. Dryden's face radiated a kind of intense stillness, but was handsome too beneath cropped jet-black hair; a strangely medieval face, architectural, as if fashioned by a series of mason's blows. A face that should have been looking down from a cathedral roof, or up from a crusader's tomb.

Another roadside sign:

RAMSEY FORTY FOOT
8 MILES

Eight miles. An eternity in tarmac, and slide-rule straight except for a single, obtuse, almost imperceptible kink to the left, halfway to the next village.

The road, known locally as the Fen Motorway,

was just wide enough for two cars to pass; a rat-run linking Ely and the Black Fens to the flatlands around Peterborough, the silty expanse known as the Great Soak, a vast plain of treeless fields and ditches. The shortcut was often clogged with HGVs saving mileage, taxis avoiding rush-hour snarl-ups on the main roads, and locals who knew how to thread their way through the network of lanes which zigzagged the wetlands, clinging to the flood banks.

The road had been built nearly four hundred years earlier on clay dredged from the river. Subsidence and slippage had wrecked the original flat surface. While it was straight in a two-dimensional plane, it was anything but in three dimensions. It undulated with an almost hypnotic rhythm, like a Möbius Strip. Dryden's ear canals, as prone to flights of fantasy as the rest of him, sent him impossible signals, appearing to indicate that the cab was about to corkscrew like a roller coaster.

The cab hit a dip and Boudicca, the greyhound, crouching in the back seat, howled once, then whimpered.

Dryden gripped the wheel harder because ahead he could see a lorry, one of the big agricultural HGVs, thundering towards him. It was getting bigger at an alarming rate which suggested a speed roughly double the maximum allowed. Streamers flew from its stovepipe.

'Hold on,' he said, to wet his mouth.

The HGV swept past, the wind nudging the cab another foot towards the edge of the bank. Dryden swerved back to the safety of the white

11

line. Then the wind, which had been a torment that summer, buffeted the cab further away from the water, so that for a moment he thought he was going to put them off the road on the far side, down a twenty-five-foot bank into a field – a descent which would have killed them just as surely as plunging into the Forty Foot.

His passenger rearranged his sixteen-stone carcass in the bucket seat. Humph was the cabbie who usually drove the Capri. Always drove the car. Never left the car. Lived in it, really, if the fetid truth were told. But today, just a few miles back, Humph had pulled over and announced he couldn't drive on.

'Stress,' he'd said. 'You drive. I can't see...' He'd waved one of his small, delicate hands in front of his face as if cleaning an invisible wind-screen.

It was a big favour to ask. Dryden had not driven for more than a decade, since the day he'd pitched his car into a drain just like the Forty Foot. The two-door Corsa had sunk. He'd been pulled to safety by another driver. His wife, Laura, had been trapped on the back seat, under-water, for nearly an hour, surviving in an air pocket. She'd lived through it, and so had he, but they'd never be the same again. Which was why he hadn't driven since, and why she always travelled in the front passenger seat.

Humph's mobile buzzed in his lap. He read the text. 'She's not at school,' he said, his high voice furred with fear. Humph's voice was like Humph, lighter than you'd expect, tiptoeing out of his small, round mouth.

12

The cabbie's eldest daughter, Grace, aged fifteen, was missing. The call had come that morning at 7.30 a.m. from Humph's ex-wife. Grace lived with her mother and stepfather in Witchford, a village on the edge of Ely, in the heart of the Fens. She'd gone to her room on Sunday night before ten o'clock, saying she wanted to revise for an exam in bed. Usually diligent and cheerful, she'd been moody and withdrawn. Her mother had put it down to being a teenager. But at breakfast time she'd found the bed empty, still made up. Grace wasn't at her best friend's. She wasn't with neighbours. Her mother rang Humph, who was sleeping in the Capri in a lay-by near Waterbeach, having spent the night ferrying clubbers home from Cambridge. Humph checked his house, a semi on Ely's Jubilee Estate, because Grace had her own key. No sign. So he'd rung the police.

Grace was level-headed, sensible, mature beyond her years, a kind of mezzanine mother to her younger sister Alice. And that's what scared Humph. The fact that they'd found Alice, asleep, untroubled, in the box room next to her sister's. The two were inseparable. Until now. Why had Grace gone? Where had she gone? Humph had a limited emotional range, so the signals he was getting from his brain, and from his heart, were overwhelming. The simple idea that he might lose Grace, that the last time he'd seen her might be the last time he'd ever see her, made his whole body ache. He had to make an effort to remember to breathe. It was as if he was trapped in a slow-motion accident, unable to escape

13

from this odd, echoey, world until Grace was found. And lurking in his subconscious was the alternative outcome. That the nightmare would begin *when* they found Grace.

Dryden wound his window down, aware that his body heat was misting the windscreen. The wind, which had blown from the east since the spring, filled the car with a blast of hot air. Boudicca sat up and stared at Dryden in the rearview mirror, panting.

The satnav told them to go straight on at the approaching junction. The electronic voice was a woman's, with a Blue Peter accent.

'Ignore her. Take a right here,' said Humph, pulling the cable out of the gadget.

The cabbie seemed to make a decision then, flipping down the glove compartment and taking out a miniature bottle of white wine. He collected them on his frequent trips to and from Stansted Airport. He looked at the label as if the vineyard made a difference. He checked his watch: 9.34 a.m. He put the bottle back unopened.

'Good call,' said Dryden.

He ran down through the gears, making a hash of slipping into first, then swung right, away from the lethal water. This road continued to run on a high bank, but there were fields on either side, which ran hedgeless to a hazy horizon. Dryden breathed out in a long shudder, letting tension bleed away. He flexed his neck and one of the bones in his spine cracked like a pistol shot.

They zigzagged on flood banks until they

14

reached a long stretch bounded on one side by a line of poplars – hundreds of them, running for a mile, thrashing in the wind, as if trying to break free of their roots. The breeze nudged the car too, like a giant boxing glove, jabbing from the east.

The sun was up, already hot, and they flashed from shade to light, from light to shade, as they passed the trees.

'She'll be fine,' said Dryden. 'She'll have gone for a secret sleepover with a friend. Kids do that these days.'

Dryden's own son was one year old. When it came to teenage girls he didn't know what he was talking about.

'Maybe,' said Humph, a slight lift in his spirits making the grip of his headache release just a notch.

A great change had come over the landscape within a few hundred yards. The black peat soil had gone, replaced by the silty fields of the Great Soak – pale, bleached, tinder dry. Some of the fields were dressed with fertiliser, a white powder which made it almost painful to let the light into the eye.

'Turn by the bins,' said Humph.

The bins stood at a corner of a turning, just a dusty track, set off at precisely ninety degrees, part of the mathematical grid which seemed to underpin the landscape.

Dryden noted the name of the lane: Euximoor Drove. 'Droves' were the narrow fen lanes, sometimes just dirt tracks, a network leading to a thousand dead ends. This one ran half a mile to the ruin of a farm. Beside it stood a 1950s bungalow, wooden window frames, double chimney pots, a pitched tiled roof. It must have been built on a concrete raft in the silt because the whole thing had tipped a few degrees from true, as if at any moment it might just slip beneath the soil.

Dryden turned off the drove towards the bungalow. Ahead the road ran on in an infinite straight line along which were strung a few more houses, a chapel, a farm. This was the hamlet of Euximoor Drove, thirty houses sprinkled along a straight line.

Dryden put the handbrake on and killed the engine, already telling himself he'd been fine driving, that he could keep the fear in check. But the air was heavy with the smell of anxiety – sweat and a hint of electricity, like a blown plug.

Humph struggled out of the Capri. The dog followed, bounding to the house.

A grey-haired woman was already on the doorstep. Overweight, fleshy, in boots and shapeless jeans. The sun caught the washing-up suds she was trying to shake from her hands.

'Mum,' said Humph, walking towards her on balletic feet. 'I've been ringing. You're not wearing your hearing aids, are you?' Humph's shoulders slumped and Dryden knew him well enough to sense that he was fighting the urge to blame her for the missing girl, her grandchild.

And for her, so much more than a grandchild. Humph's long and acrimonious divorce had meant his daughters had spent a lot of their childhoods out here on Euximoor Fen. Grace and her grandmother had shared tears over the

16

collapse of what had been a happy family. Most of all they'd shared the job of shielding young Alice from too much of the brutal truth: her mother's adultery and her father's inability to rebuild a life beyond the artificial confines of a 1985 Ford Capri coupé.

Meg smiled as she strained to hear.

He took her hands and spelt it out: 'Grace has run away from home. Is she here?'

She covered her small mouth with both of her hands, shaking her head, then looked back at the house.

'I'll check,' he said, brushing past. 'She might have snuck in.'

Dryden stood by the Capri.

Meg Humphries looked around her smallholding as if Grace would be there, so far unseen, amongst the beanpoles and rhubarb. 'Where could she be, Philip?' she asked. 'I don't understand – why? Why run away?'

Dryden shrugged. 'She'll turn up. I know she will. The police are looking too.'

'The police?' she echoed, drying her hands on her jeans.

Dryden was running the numbers through his head: the chances she'd turn up were falling sharply with each passing hour, each minute. A fifteen-year-old girl, missing for nearly twelve hours. Had she run away? Would she come back? There was a chance they'd never know where she'd gone. She'd been unhappy. She'd lied. She might hurt herself.

The cabbie appeared at the side of the house, pulling open an outhouse door, then walking to a

17

coal bunker, moving quickly, balancing his weight with an almost theatrical finesse. He left doors open behind him, each one a token of how important Grace was, and how unimportant the doors.

When Humph turned back towards the Capri Dryden could see that he'd begun to accept that it might happen: that his life might be defined by this day, the day his daughter was never seen again. This had been his last shot, the last place Grace might have gone for refuge and comfort. Now they were left with a chilling alternative. That she'd taken to the road. Despite the building heat of the day, Dryden shivered at the thought of those three words, which seemed to hang in the wide fen sky: *never seen again.*

'Can you make tea?' Dryden asked Meg. 'Humph needs to slow down. Just wait. We all need to wait.'

Suddenly Humph raised his arm, pointing past them, back down the drove they'd driven up.

The horizon had gone. In the mid-distance the water tower at the fen township of Brimstone Hill, and the little steeple of its church, were grey ghosts. Wind bent trees back like slingshots. Above it all broiled a cloud of dust, with a dark heart, almost black, but edged in what looked like ash. A soil storm – a 'fen blow'. The summer had been water-free and the wind had blown a constant stiff breeze, so that the telegraph wires sang all day. Dust storms wandered the Fens like giant spinning tops. Wind stripped tiny particles of dry silt off the fields and rolled them up into billowing, rolling clouds.

Meg Humphries was dragging in washing. 'Get inside,' she said. She'd spent a lifetime living with the wind and sky. The soil storms stung the flesh, blinded the eyes, and filled mouths and noses and ears. Farm workers wore hoods and face masks. The locals ran for the house, or found any shelter they could out on the land.

'And get the dog!' shouted Meg.

Dryden checked all the Capri's windows were up and locked the car. Humph helped his mother with the sheets, secured the bungalow's old sash windows and quickly laid three sandbags – set ready on the step – at the front door. Boudicca was last in before they shut it.

Then they stood in the bay window and watched the storm come. Dryden was aware immediately that this was unlike the 'blows' he'd seen around Ely that summer. They'd been benign by comparison, veils of amber dust in wide tornado-like funnels, dodging over the landscape. He'd been in one once on the train, the carriage plunging from sunlight to semi-darkness in a second. He'd always recalled the sound, a kind of sizzling, as if milk were boiling over.

This was different. The wind here was strong enough, steady enough, to lift the whole surface of the soil, blotting out the sun. The cloud wasn't see-through, or thin, but thick and churning, like a smoke bomb. And it seemed alive within, sudden billows erupting upwards and outwards, the heat in the air fuelling it, dragging in more heat, self-propelling; as violent as a volcano's pyroclastic wind, charged with energy, an

19

eruption of the earth into the sky.

'They're much worse this year,' said Meg Humphries. 'It's so dry, so...' She covered her mouth again. 'So violent. My God...'

Dryden knew that she was thinking about Grace, that she might be out there, alone.

'It'll be gone in a moment,' he said.

They watched as the forward wall of the cloud engulfed a pair of tied cottages a mile away, then a line of poplars, and a car parked on the drove. One second the trees stood in the grey polluted air ahead of the cloud, the next they were gone. The forward wall of the storm began to throw out debris – fence posts, pieces of roofing, up-rooted plants, farmyard litter.

Humph checked his mobile; the signal had gone.

They moved into the hall, away from the glass. The light faded; it was almost dark. The sun was eclipsed and there was an instant silence. Meg kept chickens and their constant clucking soundtrack died. Even the wind itself seemed silent. Boudicca lay by the fireplace as if she had been shot.

The front door had an art deco fanlight. The rainbow of colours faded away. Above them they heard the roof creak with the effort of staying on the house. The storm front hit with a muffled thud. They heard a tile fall, then others, and all the windows rattled. Then the noise of the wind returned, but they were inside it now, so the sound was circular, accelerating around them. From the backyard they heard splintering glass. Something hard hit the bay window and the glass cracked but held. In the chimney they heard the dust churning, a clatter as a dead bird fell into the fireplace, and finally a brick.

Then it was gone, as suddenly as it had come. Sunlight burst into the house.

Dryden hoped it was a parable; just like the storm, their fears for Grace would pass.

He ran to the back door and threw it open. Outside the world was grey – covered in a thin snow of soil the colour of school socks.

He heard a shout from the front room.

They were all looking out of the bay window. The air was still misty with dust but they could clearly see, lying on the path, the body of a girl, her head partly hidden by a holdall, her legs bare and white in the dust.

TWO

Grace was unconscious, caked in white dust, like the victim of some exotic earthquake, carried out of the ruins of a Mexican suburb, lit by TV floodlights. The silt had settled over her body and formed a crust, and there were no cracks in this carapace. Dryden got to her first and lifted her head. Her eyes were closed, her lips dusty and slightly parted to reveal her teeth. The thought that she might be injured, or even dead, made Dryden hold her very still so that he could look for signs of life. He searched her face and felt a second pass in slow motion.

She coughed, expelling a small cloud of dust.

'Thank God,' said Humph, kneeling down beside her. He wriggled an arm under her knees and they lifted her together.

They carried her into the front room and laid her on the sofa. Her limbs fell awkwardly, as if she was still unconscious. Opening her eyes, she tried to sit up, which sparked a bout of coughs. Meg arrived with water but the teenager pushed the glass aside. 'Don't fuss, Gran.'

Humph shook his head. 'You've given us a scare, Gracie. I'll ring your mum. She's in a state.'

'The holdall,' said Grace. Her voice was furred up. They gave her the bag and she put her hand in and fished out a can of Pepsi. She drank it all, coughed, then closed her eyes. Dryden thought that she had pressed them closed, to shut them all out.

'Thank God,' said Meg, her face wet with tears.

Instead of ringing Grace's mum, Humph pulled open the holdall. He found a few clothes, an iPod Touch, a hockey stick in its own carry-case, a copy of *The Catcher in the Rye*, a framed picture of a dog – a mongrel that had been run over the year before, a bath-bag the size of a football, a cuddly toy Humph recognized and a purse crammed with membership cards. And a portable draughts set in a little inlaid wooden box Humph had given her just before the divorce as a present. They played when they met because it meant they could spend time together without talking.

'What were you thinking?' asked Humph, sitting down opposite, as if he was preparing to interview his own daughter. The role of father inquisitor didn't suit him, overshadowed as it was by his real role as absentee father.

Meg told him to go and make eggs on toast and tea.

'I don't want tea,' said Grace. She brushed dust from her face and hands.

'Come on, you.' Meg took her granddaughter by the arm and led her into the bathroom. There was a shower only, a stand-up thing with a cord to pull, but she'd have to make do. And she had to pull the curtain on the bathroom window, because even though they were half a mile from the nearest neighbour, people had sharp eyes on Euximoor Fen.

'She's grown up,' said Meg when they could hear the buzz of the shower.

'You saw her a few weeks ago,' said Humph, worrying the eggs in the pan with a spatula. He'd driven Grace out to his mother's house on the Bank Holiday for a barbecue. Her little sister, too. The girls had made salad while he'd tended to a long line of sausages.

'A fortnight's a lifetime when you're fifteen,' said Meg. 'Leave her here for now, Humph. When she's eating, you go. I'll talk to her when she's ready to talk. Her mother can call.'

Always 'her mother'. Meg couldn't stand the sound of her name. She'd blamed her for the break-up of the family, although she had a pretty comprehensive grasp of her son's shortcomings.

'I'm all right,' Grace said, emerging in a dressing gown Humph recognized as one he had bought Meg twenty years ago.

'You passed out,' said Humph, by way of putting her right. 'You're not all right.' He led the way into the front room where he'd put a plate on the table. Two fried eggs, both yolks broken, the toast burnt. The dog came and sat under her chair.

Grace took her father's hand. 'I thought I'd never be able to breathe again. I panicked. Sorry.' She looked out of the window at the grey world, the air clearing now, as if after a snow-storm. 'I've not been in one like that. It's weird.'

'It's the dry summer. Global warming. Stuff,' offered Dryden.

She coughed. 'I'm not going back.' She attacked the eggs with apparent enthusiasm.

A tall girl, perhaps five foot seven, with narrow shoulders and an oval face, she reminded Humph of her mother. She prompted divergent emotions in the cabbie: he wanted to stand next to her and let his cheek touch hers, but just as urgently he wanted to leave the room, drive away, in case he was called on, suddenly, to protect her.

'I'm never going back,' she said. 'I want to live here with Nan.'

Meg said they'd talk about it, catching Humph's eye, glancing at the door. She didn't think now was the time for a cross-examination. If Grace wanted to tell them why she'd run away from home she'd do it in her own time.

'Last night,' said Humph, persisting. 'Mum

said you hadn't slept in your bed.'

She gave her father a one-shoulder shrug. 'There's a bench at the bus station in Ely. By the Indian. I was fine.' She didn't look at her father, or her grandmother, but chased a fried egg round the plate instead. 'I just wanted some space, OK?'

Humph covered his eyes with one small hand over the bridge of his nose. 'You've got my mobile number. Why didn't you ring?'

She took out her mobile and put it on the table, then pushed it away. The movement left a mark in the thin veneer of dust which had somehow settled on the interior of the house. 'Battery's flat. It's useless.'

His mother was right, thought Humph, Grace had grown up. On some extra mental plane he tried to work out when it was *he'd* last seen her. A week ago, maybe more. They talked every day, several times a day, on the mobile, by text, but he realized now that she could hide things from him if they didn't see each other, that if they relied on messages she could construct a version of her life that pleased him, and that he could do the same for her. It was a side effect of the modern world, he thought, that people could be who they wanted to be until you met them.

'Can I stay here?' She looked at her grand-mother. 'Please.'

'I'll talk to your mum,' said Humph, indulging in a huge sigh. 'It's her call.' The cabbie looked at his mobile and headed for the front door. 'I need a better signal.'

Outside it was very quiet, as if the landscape

was in shock.

Humph had a personal space slightly smaller than Norfolk, so Dryden said he'd find a better signal too, and wandered off down a path beside a field of leeks. Each of the plants had gathered soil in its leaves, grey and claggy, like the waste from a vacuum cleaner. If he took in a full lungful of air something in his throat would catch, making him cough.

Dryden had work to do. He was the editor – newly appointed – of *The Crow* newspaper, based in the small cathedral city of Ely, just ten miles east across the Fens. *The Crow* came out on Friday. Its sister paper, the free-sheet *Ely Express*, came out on Tuesday. One of the reasons Dryden had been made editor of *The Crow* was because he'd proposed increasing the paper's readership by launching new editions; the first of which was to be here, in the West Fens. He'd rented a new office for the paper in the fen township of Brimstone Hill, just a few miles from Euximoor Drove, and assigned himself to the new edition, at least for the first three months. He'd left his other two reporters to run head office in Ely.

News was scarce out on the Fens. So the dust storm was a gift from heaven – almost literally. The story was perfect for *The Crow*'s rural readership, and a strong West Fen story for the new edition. For the town-based *Ely Express* he'd stick to a picture. He'd got plenty of shots, and from the digital read-out on his phone they were decent ones. Each storm was bad news for local farmers because the wind picked up the

26

topsoil and moved it miles. Some farms lost crops, ruined and uprooted, while others saw seedlings and salad crops buried. Worst of all, some of the soil was lost forever, blown high enough to carry out to sea, or dumped in rivers and estuaries. And this had been a bad storm, much more violent than average, part of an emerging pattern of more extreme weather. There'd be plenty of damage out on the wind-swept land.

He rang the local rep for the National Farmers' Union and told him what had happened and said he wanted an update from his members. Also – a good trick he'd played before – he wanted an estimate of the damage on one, unnamed, farm in terms of insurance claims. Once he had that figure he'd multiply it by the number of holdings on the affected fens and get himself a nice big fat headline figure for *The Crow*: '£1m DUST STORM HITS WEST FENS'.

He called the local police station in Brimstone Hill. The township had a resident community constable and his house had a blue light and a front counter open every Monday, Tuesday and Friday between ten and two. Dryden tried his mobile and got the busy tone. Bad fen blows caused havoc on the roads, so he guessed the policeman was out somewhere at a traffic acci-dent. Then he rang the head of the primary school, a woman called Jan Riddle.

She answered her mobile: 'Dryden?'

'Sorry – just wanted to see if you're all OK. Did the dust get that far?'

'You're like the angel of death,' she said.

27

'Thanks a lot.' Dryden liked Riddle and had earmarked her as a key contact on an earlier visit. She was in her mid-forties, playful, one of those rare teachers who don't have to discipline the kids. Dryden had sneaked a story into the paper about her five-year-olds running a marathon by doing a hundred yards around the playground every day. So she was on his side.

'But yes, we're all fine, no one's dead, but we've had tears. They were out for break and I didn't see it coming. Those that aren't crying are too excited to sit down. The TA got them into the bike shed, so most of them only got a mouthful and their noses blocked. We dished out the milk early, so thank God for school milk.'

Dryden memorized the quote, thinking it would make a great top line for a sidebar on the main story:

'SCHOOL MILK
SAVES KIDS
AFTER DUST
STORM HITS
PLAYTIME'.

'Gagging, were they?'

'Have you tasted it? It's like a mouthful of cinders.'

He promised he'd pop in later, then ended the call. His mobile rang immediately.

It was Vee Hilgay, his chief reporter, calling in from head office in Ely. Dryden had recruited Vee in his first executive move as editor. Old money, a spinster, she'd spent nearly twenty

28

years running a charity which looked after the elderly in the fen winters. She wore a donkey jacket, CND lapel badge and Doc Martens. At the age of seventy-four, she was the coolest OAP in town.

'We've had a fen blow out here, a bad one,' said Dryden. 'I'll do you a hundred-word caption and send you some pics for the *Express*. What you got?' he asked, walking to the end of the path and catching sight of Humph, still standing by the Capri, his mobile to his ear. He could hear his high, tuneful voice, but the tone was odd, as if he was talking to a call centre in Bombay.

He heard Vee turning her notebook pages. Dryden operated without paper due to his indecipherable shorthand and the fact that people – especially in the Fens – always stopped talking if you started taking notes. He had an excellent short-term memory. He just needed to remember to make a note before the slate was wiped clean by a good night's sleep.

'One thing,' she said. He heard Vee sip tea. She lived on tannin, carting a thermos round with her the size of one of the shell cases from the Somme. 'Metal thieves struck again, out on your patch, Christ Church at Brimstone Hill. Last night, apparently, about thirty foot of lead off the roof and the odd lead angel from the graveyard. The vicar said she'd be on site at noon.'

'I'll get Humph to run me down to the church. If I can get a picture I will,' said Dryden.

'What about Humph's daughter?' asked Vee.

'She's here.'

29

'Thank God. Poor girl. It must be a nightmare being a fen teenager.'

'Why?'

'*Why!* She lives out in some godforsaken village where most people's idea of a good time is a smoke on the swings.'

'It's five miles from Ely.'

'The city that never wakes up,' said Vee. 'And five miles, Dryden. You know what the public transport system's like in the Fens. It doesn't exist. She might as well live in Timbuktu. Her Mum's on her case twenty-four-seven. Adolescence is horrible wherever you live. Imagine what it's like for her.'

'OK. I only asked.'

'And then there's her dad. If he's not actually working he's asleep in the cab in a lay-by. He might as well be in the Navy.'

Humph was Dryden's chauffeur during most daylight hours. Since the reporter's accident more than a decade earlier he'd needed someone with wheels. For nearly a year Dryden's wife had been in a coma so he'd had to live a strange, lonely life. He'd shared it, in part, with Humph, who in his turn was grieving for the loss of his marriage and children. Dryden gave him all his travel expenses by way of payment, which didn't amount to much, but that didn't bother Humph. The cabbie's core business was late-night trips from the Cambridge and Newmarket clubs, plus the Ely school run. In between times he was available to ferry Dryden around. The last thing Humph wanted was to go home, as home didn't really exist any more. So it suited the cabbie just

30

fine, and he slept when he could – feet up in a lay-by.

Vee ran through everything she had on her diary for the *Ely Express*. Then they went through what they thought they'd have for *The Crow* later in the week, earmarking the planning decision on a new southern bypass as the paper's potential lead story. The Ely edition could take a picture of the dust storm on its front page too, while the new West Fen edition could lead with the story and picture. Events might upset their news decisions – it was still a long time until the final deadline – but it was always good to have a plan.

Dryden was gratified that his hunch that Vee would make an excellent reporter had been vindicated. She was curious, organized and bloody-minded. He'd leave her to work up the by-pass story. He cut the line and walked back towards the Capri.

Humph was propped up against the side of the cab, finishing a call on his mobile. When he stood the suspension gave out a twang.

Back in the bungalow, Grace was swaddled in a huge duvet, still lying on the sofa. Her grandmother was reading snippets out loud from last week's paper. The girl's eyes looked heavy and she was still bloodless, with skin the colour of lard.

Humph waved the mobile at his daughter. 'Mum's on her way. She says you can stay here if you want, maybe till Sunday. So that's a week off school. Then it's back home. It's the best I could do. She wants to know why you left home.

31

Just so you know. So even if you won't tell me or Gran I'd recommend you tell her.'

Humph sat down and the kitchen chair he'd chosen disappeared entirely from sight.

'She said there'd been a fight, with Barrie's boys?' he asked.

Barrie was her stepfather. He had two teenage sons who lived at home.

'They went in my room,' said Grace. 'They didn't ask. He said I should forget it.'

'Barrie?'

'Yeah. Him.' She almost spat it out but Dryden felt she had faked the disgust in her voice, that she was play-acting, falling back on a cliché to portray her relationship with her stepfather.

She shivered and her grandmother tucked in the duvet under her feet. 'I bet she didn't tell you what happened, did she?' said Grace. 'Not all of it.'

Dryden noticed that she had a lazy left eye, which seemed to follow the right after a one-second delay.

'We had a barbie – we're always having barbies. There isn't even a real fire – it's gas. So this woman turns up by car, because that's the only way you can turn up at our house, and Barrie says – like out loud – that he'd lived with her after he left his first wife. This is out at Isleham. Wherever that is...'

Places like Isleham were mythical to Grace. Deep-Fen. Places where inbreeding led to webbed feet and IQs so low as to excite academic interest.

'"My common-law wife", that's actually what

32

he called her, like he was proud of it, and it hurt
Mum. I could see that because she started laughing about it. And then this woman starts telling
him how the kids are. *His* kids. *Other* kids. Kids
he had with this woman. And they were coming
too. Mum said later that she knew they were
invited, but I don't believe her.

'And then they were there too, in a souped-up
Vauxhall. A car again – it's like car city out at
our house. And the boy's just like Barrie, only I
don't think he's so cruel. And the girl didn't
want to be there so she just sat on the step with
a bottle of lager. She smoked too, one after the
other, like Barrie.

'So suddenly we're a fen joke. There's me,
there's Barrie's two boys, there's an extra boy
and an extra girl who came with the common-
law wife. Everyone's related to everyone else
but it takes you twenty minutes to work out
how.'

Humph laughed and then realized it wasn't
supposed to be funny.

'The party was Saturday night, right? Monday
I'm walking home from the college with Jilly.'

She looked at Dryden: 'She's my friend, right?
She lives in the village. And she says she heard
this joke in the canteen. How do teenagers in
Witchford say hello when they meet each other
in the street?' She left it a beat before providing
her own answer: 'Give me six.' She held up her
own hand to explain the joke. 'So I laughed, and
then I thought, that's me now. I'm a living fen
joke. So like, why's that funny? I hate them.'

There was no doubt in Dryden's mind that

33

Grace was telling the truth. But was it the whole truth? In an odd way it was what Humph and Meg wanted to hear, because it reflected badly on her stepfather and his family, not her father and his family. And if it wasn't the whole truth, then what was she hiding?

THREE

Christ Church, Brimstone Hill, was late Victorian, with a brick nave and no transepts, but a fine curved apse, and a single splinter spire in lead on the roofline, the pinnacle that Dryden had seen disappear in the advancing front of the fen dust storm. The building had a pleasing, smooth line, like a boat: another ship-like silhouette on the flat seas of the Fens, a tug perhaps, steaming towards the Ship-of-the-Fens itself: Ely Cathedral, which lay on the far horizon on clear days. There was a patch of missing lead on the roof over the apse, revealing wooden rafters. A pigeon clattered out of a gap as Dryden walked up the gravel path.

Christ Church was the heart of Brimstone Hill. But what *was* Brimstone Hill? Bigger than a village, smaller than a town, more like a Midwest township, with its buildings scattered along three unwinding roads which met at the church. The Victorians had founded these strange fen communities, draining the land, bringing machines on to the fields. Such places never seemed to have enough buildings to justify their streets, which occasionally just opened out, the gaps revealing a distant horizon. What was left was the bones of a town, but most of the flesh was missing.

The rectory was almost as imposing as the church, a rambling villa set back beyond the graveyard, now privately owned and screened from the road by a line of spruce. The rest of Brimstone Hill had most of the services expected of a town, but none of them was quite in the right place. The eye of the storm had missed it but the air was murky with dust, cutting visibility to a few hundred yards. Dryden could still see the village pub, The Brook, just off the junction, hidden behind a line of poplars. There was a mini-market corner shop along the March Road, but nothing actually on the corner where the roads all met. There was a memorial hall which everyone had forgotten, on a back street running out to the fen, and the stub of an original windmill behind a row of labourers' cottages. A row of shops stood down by the level crossing: a pet parlour, a video shop, a carpet shop which was never open, and a ladies' hairdressers called Curl Up And Dye. The social hub was a set of benches under a cypress tree by a bus stop, which was next to the automatic rail crossing. The train line was mostly freight, and services intermittent. Just beyond the crossing was the Brimstone Hill Café, its inappropriate neon sign flashing at all hours. Half a mile out of town was a wind turbine farm: seventeen gently turning windmills in antiseptic white.

Dryden loved the place, especially the church, which seemed to hold the far-flung elements of the town together like a magnet. Most of all he loved the name: Brimstone Hill, with its hint of sulphur. He'd found the story behind that name online, buried in one of the local history sites. One day back in the fourteenth century, the vicar of Upwell, ten miles away, had found the Devil in his church and chased him out, over the fields. When they got to this spot – a slight rise in the silt fens and marshes – the Devil gave up and fled, disappearing in a puff of his own smoke. So the vicar put up a cross to mark the victory of good over evil. And that was where the church was, and that was why they'd called it Brimstone Hill. The entrance to hell was here, the Devil's secret door to the underworld.

But there was another story. As he walked through the graveyard, Dryden spotted a single butterfly with sulphur-yellow wings. According to a friend at the nearby nature reserve at Welney, it was this butterfly which gave all other butterflies their name. It was an image of beauty to set against the Devil. The sight of it, dancing around a headstone, put a spring back in Dryden's step after the stress of tracking down Humph's missing daughter. He felt the day lighten, as if he'd been able to shake off the memory of a bad nightmare.

A clock struck noon.

Rev. Jennifer Temple-Wright stood by the war memorial waiting for the reporter. The stone, an Egyptian needle about ten feet high, was covered in names from the Great War, with those lost in the Second World War listed on a flat stone addition at its foot. Dryden had counted them one day, the dead of the two wars. There were thirty-one. The community of Brimstone

Hill, beyond the churchyard wall, looked pathetically small against such a death toll.

Temple-Wright was in her mid-forties with greying hair cut in a helmet-style which seemed to be CoE default for a certain class of female vicar. Even the steady, warm wind didn't put a hair out of place. Her husband made up another third of a team ministry which now cared for Brimstone Hill, Welney and Friday Bridge. She wanted people to call her Jen.

The churchyard was in shadow so that the screen of her iPhone glowed.

Greeting Dryden's arrival with an index finger held upright, she tip-tapped a message with her other thumb. Dryden's view was that a human being took priority over a digital communication of any kind. What really made such bad manners so infuriating was that people like Temple-Wright would have been stunned to discover they'd caused any offence.

'Right,' said Temple-Wright. 'What do you want to know?'

Again, the effortless bad manners in presuming it was up to her to indicate when their conversation could begin. Dryden had a leather satchel for his laptop which he swung round off his shoulder and laid at his feet, extracting a notebook. He rarely took notes, but it was a signal at least that the conversation to follow was firmly on the record.

She dusted silt from her hands and used her cuff to clean the screen of the iPhone. 'Dust storm was a bit biblical, wasn't it? I shouldn't really complain. It must be good for business.'

She meant *her* business: that was how she saw the Church of England, as a going concern.

She tried to brush the dust off her cassock, looking up at the roof where the lead had been stripped off. The vicar seemed preoccupied, but Dryden doubted it was the fate of her church that worried her. She'd made it clear to him, and anyone else who wanted to listen, that she had little time for the *church of bricks and mortar*. Her project was an internet church, centred around an online website for the three parishes that came under the ministry. She needed cash for website design, online sermons, upkeep of a Facebook page, Twitter and iPhones for all three vicars. She seemed to begrudge every minute spent under a roof, so it was hardly surprising that she was unmoved by the disappearance of one. Her own house was in another township, a modern sixties semi with a digital dish. God's message was delivered in person through the medium of a kind of ongoing tour. She travelled the Fens, like an ice-cream seller, in a converted VW camper she called her mobile church. A speaker broadcast the sound of bells. Her four-wheeled chapel had made frequent appearances on local radio stations, even regional TV. She was making a name for herself – a double-barrelled one. She was, for Dryden, the worst kind of English eccentric. A calculating one.

'How much will the lead cost to replace?' asked Dryden, getting back to *his* business.

'God knows.' She smiled. It was a joke she'd used on Dryden before. 'My last church we lost about the same one week, cost us about £4,000 to replace. But I'm not going to replace it. I'll take the insurance money, of course – but long term we're cutting our buildings' cover. I'm going to get something up there to keep out the water, maybe some plastic sheeting. We're already holding services in the apse. Take a look if you've got a sec – they're working on it now. For the winter I'm putting up a screen. Fewer draughts, and I can heat a smaller space. A stop-gap, of course – nothing more.'

Dryden looked up at the church. 'So long term the building's not got a future?'

'That's a fair comment.' She nodded rapidly. 'Absolutely fair. Long term.' She made eye contact with Dryden. 'Watch this space.'

'How did they get on the roof?'

'There's a spiral staircase which takes you up to the gutters; it's on the far side of the church. There's an exterior door, which they've just knocked off its hinges. I got a call this morning from the sexton. His grandson's made it secure but I'm going to get an iron grill with a lock. Which is more cost; more money we could better use.'

She took a step backwards and nearly fell over the corner of a grave. Like a lot of people who think they're smooth and efficient, she was oddly clumsy. The burial plot she'd stumbled over was marked by a marble plinth with its own lead angel, one foot raised, as if it was about to fly.

'What do the police say – any suspects?' asked Dryden.

'The thieves? The usual, I guess. You know,

40

metal theft is the flavour of the month. They're all at it. They didn't just take lead off the roof – they've prised it off graves as well – metal railings, sculptures, crosses. If it's not nailed down these days it's gone, and if it is nailed down it's gone too, with the nail! They muttered something about migrant workers: Poles, Portuguese, Irish from Lynn. If you ask me that's a default excuse for not catching anyone.'

Metal theft was like an outbreak of potato blight, not just across the Fens, but throughout most of rural England. The latest victims locally included the mothballed signal box up at Manea, several BT manhole covers, an entire street's worth of iron front gates from Euximoor Drove, and a three-foot-high copy of Eros from a front garden out on the Wisbech Road. Rising black market prices for metal were driving the crime rate up. Government attempts to crack down on licensed scrap metal merchants buying stolen goods off crooks didn't seem to be biting.

'Kids or a gang?'

'Getting up there isn't child's play. The stairs make it easier, but you've still got to get the stuff off the rafters and down. Then you've got to take it away. So, transport was organized. I'm sure our local constabulary can spin you some theories. I need to get on.'

'Increased security?'

'Think of the cost, Dryden. If they want to take metal they will. I'm sure they'll be back for more lead off the roof. What am I going to do? Mount a vigil? I lost an angel last week, off one of the Victorian graves at the back. I didn't even

41

report that.'

She turned and went, not bothering with a handshake, or a second look at the church. Dryden thought that summed her up beautifully: that she, the priestess of Brimstone Hill, could be untroubled by the loss of an angel.

FOUR

Dryden stood out in the road and watched the vicar drive away in her VW camper. The heat was building and the sun was high, so the image of the van buckled in the heat before Temple-Wright turned left at the T-junction a mile out of town. At the same moment a car turned into the road, heading for Brimstone Hill. As it got closer Dryden recognized the red Fiat 500 with white-wall tyres.

It came to a halt outside the church with a theatrical skid.

His wife Laura waved through the windscreen. He found it impossible not to mirror her wide Italian smile, which told him she'd got his text telling her Grace had been found and was fine. Laura retrieved their son, Eden, from the child seat and hoisted him expertly into a papoose.

'How's Humph?' she asked as he kissed her, one hand cupping the child's head.

'All over the shop, but what do you expect? He's angry, largely with himself, and guilty that he didn't make the marriage work. Guilty he doesn't see enough of his daughters. He's a sponge, soaking up guilt. He loves it really.'

She bounced Eden in the papoose. 'I rang the nursery; they'll take Eden after lunch.'

While Dryden was working at Brimstone Hill they'd put Eden in a crèche at the local school. Normally Dryden dropped him off by cab at eight but their routine had been shattered by Grace's disappearance. Usually Tuesday was a working day for Laura.

'Sorry – it's ruined your schedule,' said Dryden.

'I rang in and they sent a script over. I worked on the laptop; it's fine.' Laura had a job as a story-liner for a BBC soap opera called *Sky Farm*, an East Anglian rival to *Emmerdale*. Her job was to work with the scriptwriters, keeping them in line, making sure the 'big picture' made sense, monitoring continuity, helping develop consistent characters. Three days a week she had a fifty-mile commute to the BBC studios in Norwich.

'Well. Thanks, anyway,' said Dryden. 'It made a big difference to Humph. He was so stressed he had to stop driving.'

Laura's mouth fell open. She had large features, dominated by the curves which formed her lips, and the eyebrows above the luminous brown eyes. 'So *you* drove?'

'Yup.'

'Well done.' She hugged him, pressing her lips into his hair. For a moment they shared the memory of the ditched car, the darkness of the water,

43

the sudden pain.

The Fiat lacked air conditioning and Dryden could feel Laura's body heat. 'You're broiling. Let's get some shade.'

'This dust is horrible,' said Laura.

She ran a finger along her lips, then touched it to Dryden's. 'Pah!' she said. 'Look at Tano.'

'Tanooo,' echoed Eden, enjoying the sound of one of his favourite words.

Tano was the car, named for her father, Gaetano. It was covered in a silty film.

'I could write your name in the dust,' she said. 'I brought coffee.' She had a flask in the pocket of the papoose. She patted the other pocket. 'Sandwiches.'

The Brimstone Hill Café's menu was circa 1950s, and the only coffee you could get was instant, or a whipped-up confection from a vending machine that was meant to be espresso but was actually powder and hot water. They called it *fenspresso*.

Dryden lifted Eden out of the papoose and led the way into Christ Church. He'd visited before and the door was always open in daylight. Laura slipped into a pew and unscrewed the top of the thermos so that the delicious aroma escaped and seemed to overpower the usual scents of a lonely church – polish and candles. It smelt like a shrine to coffee. She had never been inside Christ Church. The chapels of her homeland, the Lunigiana, were baroque, gilded, crowded with statues and candles. Her local chapel in her home village was full of cherubs circling angels, looking down on the saints. The simplicity of this brick vessel took her breath away.

'So,' she said, nodding. 'Beautiful. You didn't tell me. You kept it secret so you could show it off now.'

Dryden set the child down on the narrow carpet in the aisle. Eden lay on his back, kicking. They were acutely aware that many of the children they knew from post-natal classes were walking already. Eden hadn't even shown an interest in crawling. He seemed to enjoy watching the world. A born observer, an outsider looking in. That there might be something wrong with his development was an anxiety which they had yet to share with each other.

Laura sat with her head back, looking at the roof. It was decorated with simple arts-and-craft designs in bright colours. Childlike, and beautifully executed. In the apse beyond the altar the decoration extended down over the brickwork, a riot of colour. A two-decked pulpit in stone and a brass lectern were gifts from benefactors and looked out of place. Dryden knew that the local congregation had been disappointed by Temple-Wright's refusal to preach from the lofty pulpit. She stood at the altar rail, on their level.

They were not alone in Christ Church. Workmen were constructing a wooden screen, to the vicar's orders, across the nave in front of the altar, creating a separate space beyond in the apse. A church within a church – somewhere cosy for the winter congregation. In many churches they'd have screened off a transept, but Christ Church had none. Its simplicity was like the living quarters on Noah's Ark. The builders

45

had a radio playing, tuned to one of the local commercial stations, but the volume died away as soon as the banging door marked their entry.

'So what's the plan with Grace – back to her mother's?' asked Laura, handing Dryden a thermos cap full of coffee and a bottle of fizzy water. The words of the question were slightly slurred. Laura had been in a coma for nearly a year after their car accident. The neurological damage had affected her speech so that the consonants were slightly dulled. It had been the one side effect of the coma which had got worse with time, and had put an end to her hopes of returning to acting.

Dryden was studying the hole in the roof directly above their heads where the thieves had taken the lead. Gaps showed between painted rafters.

'Philip,' Laura prompted. 'About Grace, what will they do?'

Dryden shook his head as if coming out of a trance. 'She doesn't want to go home. She's angry about something. I reckon two or three days out on Euximoor Drove will remind her of the comforts of home. Humph needs to make it clear to her that in a year she can do what she likes. Less, ten months. She can have a room at his house if she wants, right in town. He's hardly ever there. She wants to go to the local college for A-levels, which makes sense. She can see her mum. She can avoid her stepfather. It's her choice. She just has to put up with the way things are for a bit longer.'

'She must be unhappy, very unhappy, to

actually do it. Run away like that.' Laura brushed her hair back from her forehead and pinned it back with a clasp. Her face was exceptionally animated when she spoke, a mannerism which seemed to have deepened as the clarity of her speech had declined. She was like a heroine in a silent movie, each twist of emotion clearly broadcast for dramatic effect.

Dryden told her what Grace had said, about her ever-expanding fen family.

'So it's the Fens that are to blame,' said Laura, her eyes widening in mock horror.

'Maybe. I got the impression there was something else, something she wasn't telling her father, or her grandmother.'

'You think she's hiding a teenage secret?' Laura knelt down next to the baby and adjusted his jumper. Eden's eyes were focused on the dust they'd disturbed from the pews which was rising and catching the sunlight that raked across the nave.

Free, briefly, of the responsibility of the child, Laura let her gaze turn to a large painting which dominated the nave. 'That could be in a church at home,' she said.

A heavy, dark wood gilded frame surrounded a medieval Italian landscape which showed Golgotha in the foreground and the three crosses, with Christ crucified in the central role. The canvas itself was damaged: there was a diagonal scratch, two tears in the sky, and an old damp patch above Christ's head.

Dryden stood and went to the painting. 'I read about this on the village website. That's why it's called Christ Church, for this painting. Well, there were two originally – another one opposite. They were gifts from a local family of landowners.'

'What happened to the other one?'

'Destroyed by the damp and the cold. This one's not that much better.'

'That's unfair. It's beautiful still. Don't be so hard on old age.'

Dryden told her what he could remember from the website: that the works were nineteenth century, Italian, copies of two lost medieval masterpieces. In the manner of the time, the landscape was faithfully Italian, precisely of that between Rome and the sea, complete with ruins, rural scenes, villages and campanile. The background was inhabited by tiny figures acting out miniature dramas: a shepherd chasing his hat in the wind, a peasant chopping wood, children running after a horse.

Laura stood beside him, looking into the picture intently as if her own childhood was pictured there. She laughed, extending a finger towards the hatless running shepherd. 'I know him; he lived in our village.'

'Everyman,' said Dryden.

She shook her head, missing the reference. 'Stefano.' Laura studied the painting. 'So if it's a copy, who painted the original?'

'Masaccio.'

Laura whistled, recognizing the name. 'Yes, one of the masters. I think there's something in Parma in the cathedral – a vast nativity, with the magi on camels.'

'Shame this isn't the real thing,' said Dryden. 'Our delightful vicar could have her internet church and still have enough left over to cover that roof with gold leaf instead of lead.' He turned on his heels. 'Mind you, that really would get the thieves excited.'

As they left, Laura stole a glance back at Stefano and his flying hat.

FIVE

Dryden loved graveyards: there was something about their settled sadness, the sense in which they represented eternal rest, which in turn appealed to his own desire to step outside the day-to-day world of deadlines, appointments and rush. Laura had driven Eden away in Tano to the crèche, leaving him to eat his lunch. The headstones at the back of the church were older than those at the front – Victorian slabs of stone, etched with euphemism: *Asleep*, or *Gone Before*.

Laura had left him the coffee thermos so he sat on a box tomb and poured himself a shot of acrid espresso. He was surrounded by the graves of the rich, entwined by granite ivy and laurel, and adorned with carved wrens, robins, swords, urns and the occasional skull. It reminded him of one of his favourite cartoons, by the humourist James Thurber, depicting a street full of determined men and women striding to their next

49

appointments, against a background of a cemetery. The caption read simply: *Destinations*.

The churchyard ran to a fence, and then a ditch, beyond which was meadow and pasture, dotted with sheep – a recent innovation in fen farming, which had been largely devoid of livestock for a century, thanks to the cash value of salad crops and grain on the vast, rich, open fields. Right at the edge of the church land, up against the fence, was a striking memorial: a soldier carved in grey-green stone, in a boot-length cape. There was a plinth, in marble, with lead letters which read:

IN MEMORY OF THOSE
WHO FELL IN THE
KOREAN WAR
1933–1953
Peter Davenport
Paul Davenport
Brothers in Arms

It was the stone statue of the figure that dominated the memorial. Despite being a forgotten war, Korea did have this one potent symbol – the caped soldier. Dryden recalled pictures of the conflict in books, snippets of newsreel on the History Channel documentaries. A war of bloody attrition, with the Americans, Canadians and Australians dug in along a lonely front line with the South Koreans, facing the Russians, the Chinese and the North Koreans. Incessant, almost tropical rain had brought misery to thousands of troops in bitterly cold trenches. As a war it seemed to occupy a no-man's-land in Dryden's world-view of the twentieth century – lost between the bombed ruins of Hiroshima and Nagasaki and the tensions of the Cold War of the 1960s. Little had survived in the public memory other than this icon, the soldier in battlefield green, the cape big enough to cover his pack and rifle, and almost reaching down to the ground. The only part of the body to be revealed was usually the head in the helmet, and that was invariably held down, the chin on the chest, the face sheltered against the endless rain. Dryden ate his sandwich and wondered about the Davenport brothers. Twins, perhaps, given the identical dates, who had lived and died together. Perhaps both had been lost on the same day.

A clock chimed somewhere in Brimstone Hill. Glancing back at the church, he saw the small door that the metal thieves had ripped open to get to the staircase which corkscrewed up to the roof. The door was wooden, lancet-shaped, and hung out on its shattered iron hinges. A limp stretch of scene-of-crime tape hung across the opening. Dryden could just see the worn stone steps twisting upwards.

He walked over to investigate, carrying his coffee cup. The staircase was damp and smelt of leaves and dead birds. The thought of climbing up and looking down on the graveyard made his heartbeat pick up with a combination of fear and excitement. It was so rare to be able to look down on anything in the Fens. He looked up the spiral stairwell, trying to judge if he had the courage to face his fear of heights. The steps

51

were splashed with guano. The thought of climbing them made his legs go weak. He decided to stop himself doing anything stupid by closing the door. He put down his coffee and lifted the door up on its hinges, then brought it round and pushed it into place.

Which is when he saw what had been nailed to the outside.

The door kept falling open so he had to hold it back with one hand. He reached out his other hand to touch a small wooden sign carved to mimic the shape of a piece of paper or parchment, with curling gilded edges. His mouth ran dry, not from fear, but from an overwhelming memory. He'd been brought up a Catholic, and the iconography was still potent. Crucifixes in his childhood had always been replete with the broken figure of Christ, the bleeding stigmata, the crown of thorns, and above the head the sign that Pontius Pilate had dictated to the scribes to be written in Latin, Hebrew and Greek: *Iesus Nazarenus, Rex Iudaeorum* – shortened to INRI.

Jesus of Nazareth, King of the Jews.

And here was that sign. Nailed roughly to the door, so that the nail had split the wood. Had Temple-Wright seen this? He doubted it. Because it begged several questions: was this the work of the metal thieves, and if so, from which crucifix had it been ripped? Judging by the size of the plaque, about two feet by one foot, it was from a crucifix of some size. It was painted in gold, red and blue, and all the colours were weathered. There was something sacrilegious about the act of nailing it to the door. But the police had made no mention of it; or had they simply disregarded it as a mindless piece of vandalism? Or had the door just been discovered open, and no one had bothered to look?

Christ Church was named for the two Italian pictures of the crucifixion which had hung in the nave. Dryden had read on the local history website that this dedication had been further cemented with the erection of a crucifix in a stand of trees to the edge of the graveyard, a kind of miniature fenland Golgotha. A wood carver from Cambridge had won the commission for the figure of Christ. Dryden had always assumed that the crucifix had failed to survive the inter-vening century and a half of winters. It was certainly not visible in the churchyard.

He walked back to the box tomb he'd been sitting on by the Korean War Memorial and jumped lightly on top. He could see clearly over the headstones and memorials. There *was* a stand of trees in the north-east corner of the graveyard, a thick clutch of pines, set in a circle. He picked his way through the graveyard towards it, and saw immediately that a rough path led into the trees at an oblique angle. He stepped into the copse, from open sunlight to deep shadow in one stride, so that his eyes failed to make the transition. He had to stop, blinking. He heard an animal in the undergrowth scurry-ing for cover. Vision came to him slowly, reveal-ing that the path wound onwards around a very low mound, the borders of the way forward once marked with whitewashed stones. Now some

53

were missing, and those that remained were weathered and grey. The path itself was made of pavings set neatly in a slow curve, overgrown with weeds, cracked and uneven.

A wooden sign, in the same gold, red and blue as the vandalised INRI, said: VIA DOLOROSA. A black graffito obscured part of the lettering, but was itself indecipherable.

The air inside the ring of trees was still, but his arrival seemed to disturb it, so that he was surrounded by the pungent aroma of pine needles. It brought back memories of a summer holiday with Laura's parents in Italy and a Sunday spent circling a mountain above the village, climbing the spiral path towards the shrine at the top, where three crosses depicted the crucifixion. This secret Golgotha seemed oddly out of place in an English churchyard. Dryden could only think that when Christ Church had been founded the Anglo-Catholic movement had been running particularly strong in the Fens, its imagery coloured by that of the rituals of Rome.

He followed the spiral path, rising very slowly, inch by inch, but relentlessly, so that by the time he had described a full circle he could look down through the tree trunks and see the entrance to the thicket where he had walked out of the sunlight. He had climbed less than six feet, but in the two-dimensional world of the Fens it seemed as if he'd ascended a mountain. Another half circle brought him within sight of his goal. Through the trees he could see the clear shape of a large cross of the traditional design, with a small roof provided to shelter the figure of

Christ from the English weather, an apex added over the head of the dying man. Dryden's eyes were fixed on this shape, so that he did not see what lay on the path in the half-light until he tripped and fell. In the shock of the moment, he struggled to make sense of the image that was less than a foot from his face as he lay sprawled on the rough stones: a face, in agony, trickles of blood defying gravity by falling sideways, the eyes lifted upwards.

It was a face as familiar as his own: Christ's face.

He stifled a yell but the sound of his fall spooked a pair of crows which clattered out of the trees. Across the path lay the scattered wooden remnants of a figure of Christ. Dryden scrambled to his knees and looked around. The head had been lopped off the body, which lay in the shadows, one arm seeming to beckon him forwards. The other arm lay higher up the path, the severed joint showing as paler wood. One of the bare legs lay across the path and had caused him to stumble. Of the other there was no sign. The sculpture had not been painted for many years so that in places the original grain of the wood showed through the flesh. Standing, he peered through the branches at the crucifix and saw that the missing leg was still on the cross, because he could just see the pale foot.

He stumbled on quickly until the curve led into a small stone-flagged enclosure at the 'summit' of the mound. There were two beer cans lying in the grass, both Special Brew. A plastic Tesco bag was wrapped round the base of the cross. He looked at these items with an almost manic intensity because he had sensed – but not yet seen – what hung from the cross.

Not the severed wooden leg of the Christ figure, but a man, one of flesh and blood. Shirtless, the skin and muscle of the upper torso hanging down as if gravity had gained some special force within this circle of trees. In places, on the upper arms and around the neck, the skin was bruised, livid and swollen. A pair of jeans hung from the narrow waist, torn open at both knees, one of which was bloodied and caked with dust. The body sagged, only staying aloft thanks to knots of blue plastic rope at the right wrist and around the neck. The left arm hung down across the body. The head, too, was down, so that Dryden had to step forwards to see up into the face. The features seemed bloated, the skin holding a yellow tinge. The eyes were hooded with fleshy lids, the hair black and glossy. The upper lip was swollen and a trickle of blood had hardened as it fell across the chin.

In death no face can hold the likeness of life. Dryden knew only two things about this man. He was ethnic Chinese, and he knew how he had died. Blood had flowed from a wound in the left side where, traditionally, the Roman's lance had been thrust into Christ's body. Flies buzzed around the wound and made it shimmer in the slated light. At the centre of the wound was a black hole. Dryden had never seen one before in once living flesh, but he had no doubt it was a bullet hole, and even less doubt that the flesh was no longer living.

SIX

Constable Stokely Powell was Brimstone Hill's community policeman. Dryden had got to know him well in the few weeks he'd been in the township and found him relaxed and approachable, but it was clear he liked to preserve a certain formality: he was *Constable* Powell, and Dryden guessed that was because he was just a bit nervous of the Stokely. Powell was in his late twenties, early thirties – so he'd probably been named for *the* Stokely: the black civil rights activist Stokely Carmichael; the kind of black man a lot of white men didn't like. The Fens were a recruiting ground for racists, energised by the influx of East European migrants. But that didn't mean they wouldn't take time out to abuse a black man – and Powell was Caribbean black. He sat now in the last light of the sun, basking, immobile as a lizard on a stone wall. A still man, his limbs seemed effortlessly to be always at rest.

They sat together in the garden of Sexton Cottage, across the sheep field from the graveyard of Christ Church, Brimstone Hill. The house had been built in the same style as Christ Church, the rectory and the school – a playful Victorian confection of lancet windows and carved white-

57

washed guttering; further evidence that Brimstone Hill had a brick heart. It was early evening and the white light from the scene-of-crime lamps in the stand of pine trees around 'Golgotha' was growing brighter by the minute. The body of the victim had been taken down, but not yet taken away. Through the pine trees Dryden could see the neon shape of a forensic tent on the summit of the small hill. He'd been told the pathologist wished to see the body *in situ*. Dryden imagined it laid out beneath the brightly lit plastic, the bruises and bloody wounds stark on the white skin. He felt his mouth go dry each time the memory came back, reliving the first sight of the slumped and bloodied flesh. The simple charm of the English country garden around them seemed to make the reality of what lay amongst those pine trees all the more macabre. Sexton Cottage had been requisitioned as a murder incident room for the duration. A forensic unit was based in the kitchen, uniformed branch in the front room.

PC Powell had taken Dryden's statement several hours ago. A printed version lay in front of him now on a wooden table. Dryden had one hand spread out over it to keep it in place. Sudden gusts of wind, remnants of the earlier dust storm, still disturbed the evening air. The constable had a penchant for bling and wore a Rolex with a gold strap. He had a wrap-around set of Gucci reflective sunglasses in his shirt pocket and a gold chain round his neck, which Dryden could see because he had his first two shirt buttons open. And the panda car, parked in the narrow lane which led to the cottage from the road, was strictly for the job only. Powell's own car – a low-slung sports car – made occasional appearances when he was off duty but checking his patch.

Since Dryden had opened the Brimstone Hill office he'd seen Powell every few days. The policeman would bring snippets of local news to the office. Dryden, in return, had agreed to let *The Crow* back some of Powell's local projects: a new telephone-based neighbourhood watch scheme, an anti-vandalism campaign aimed at kids, and an amnesty on guns and knives. Dryden thought they had a good working relationship, because they both got something valuable out of talking to each other.

'So – to summarize,' said Powell, 'we need to be clear on three points: the lancet door to the roof was back on its hinges when you found it open just after thirteen-thirty hours today, the wooden sign was nailed to the *outside* of the door, and you believe the victim was dead when you found him?'

'Right on all counts,' said Dryden. Powell was a fan of logic and Dryden always enjoyed their conversations. 'Now. Can I make that call?'

'Sure,' said Powell, pushing the statement over for Dryden to sign.

They'd taken Dryden's mobile away and asked him to stay at the scene in order to give his statement and answer any questions when CID arrived from Ely. A message had been relayed to Laura that she had to come out and pick up Eden from the crèche. Beyond the church Dryden

59

could see a line of vehicles – an ambulance, two squad cars, several pool cars for CID, and now a van from BBC Radio Cambridgeshire. Parked in the distance he could see Humph's Capri.

Powell gave him his phone back in a plastic evidence bag. 'All yours. Mind you, I'm not promising there's any signal. That's why half of CID is inside using the landline...' He nodded at the kitchen window of Sexton Cottage. All the windows showed lights and they could hear the constant hum of conversation and the clatter of a digital printer.

Dryden stood on one of the garden tables to get a single reception bar on the phone. He called Vee Hilgay at *The Crow*'s office, knowing she'd have heard news on the radio and presumed he was on the case. With Powell in earshot he kept it short and to the point. He had the story; he'd write it overnight for the *Ely Express*. He had a few pictures on his phone of the police and scene-of-crime forensic officers with the church in the background. But Vee should get *The Crow*'s photographer, Josie Evans, to run out in case there were any better picture opportunities later.

'She left half an hour ago,' said Vee, sounding irritated. It was one of Dryden's failings, he knew: reminding his staff to do things before he knew they'd forgotten to do them. He struggled to believe anyone might be better at this job than he was.

'Great. Well done.' But the line was dead, the single signal bar flickering out of life.

A woman PC brought out a tray of tea and
60

biscuits, followed by DI George Friday, the doyen of Ely CID. Dryden had known him for five years. They had one of those sparring, tetchy relationships which can come very close to friendship. Friday sank his hands deep in his raincoat pockets. He was thirty-five but acted fifty and never complained of an injury which made him limp slightly with his left leg. He had three sons and spent Saturdays on windswept fields watching them play football, sipping coffee from a battered flask.

Friday was one of those smokers who appear to get no pleasure from their habit. He lit up now and threw the match away in disgust. 'Good job you found him,' he said. 'Mind you, this weather, we'd have got a whiff before long.'

Dryden felt something rise in his throat. The shock of finding the corpse might have receded but the sense of violation was still tangible. He felt that the world, certainly his world, had been despoiled. His first urge, kneeling there in front of the crucifix, had been to run to the village school and make sure Eden was safe. As he sipped his tea, the image of the figure draped on the cross flashed across his eye, reprinting itself on his retina when he blinked. 'I've got a story to write,' he said, trying to snap back to the present. 'Any theories? Arrests?'

Friday mimicked a laugh.

'Gang of Chinese migrants nick lead off a church roof then fall out, but over what?' asked Dryden. 'Who's set to get the most cash? Or did someone lose their nerve? But then there's the ritual element – the cross, the wooden sign nail-

61

ed to the church door. You must have some idea?'

'Must I?' asked Friday, letting cigarette smoke seep out of his mouth through his teeth. 'That all sounds good, but it didn't come from me. You found the victim, you know he was Chinese. You can go from there. That's where we're starting, too – Chinatown in Lynn.'

King's Lynn was eighteen miles north, an old seaport with a big migrant Chinese population who'd arrived in the town to meet local demand for cockle-pickers out in the Wash. They'd settled down by the docks in an area loosely known to the locals as Chinatown.

'And that's why we're not saying anything much today,' said Friday. 'Because, as far as is possible, I don't want them to know we're coming. Well, not all of them anyway. The ones who did this will be ready for it. Or they may have just gone to ground. Anyway, I'm not putting out any details until forensics have done their job. Not even a name – if we had one, which we don't. So it's all yours for twenty-four hours. I presume you aren't flogging this?'

Friday knew that Dryden made money as a stringer for Fleet Street, selling on news when it fell between his own newspaper deadlines. He also knew that he was fiercely proud of his own newspapers and would fight to keep a story a scoop.

'I'll put out a paragraph for the wire services, the bare details, but nothing that I can keep for the paper. That'll hit the streets tomorrow afternoon.'

Friday handed Dryden a piece of paper. 'That's the statement we're putting out.'

The body of a man was discovered in woodland near Christ Church, Brimstone Hill, at 1.30 p.m. today. Earlier, thieves had stolen lead from the roof of the church. Ely CID is treating the death as suspicious. The victim has not been identified. Anyone with information which might help the police in their inquiries should ring Ely 886345.

'So nobody heard a shot last night? You've done door-to-door; I've been watching.'

Friday's face glazed over. 'Like I said, just the statement. You know what you know; I can't do anything about that. Otherwise this investigation releases information when I'm ready for it to release information. Got it?'

On the road outside Christ Church a line of cars had now formed into a convoy, engines running. The buzz of police radios was like a distant swarm of bees.

'I'm off,' said Friday. 'Chinatown calls. The scene's all yours, Powell. Forensics are just finishing up. When the body's gone you've got a uniform from Wisbech to help keep the nosy parkers out.'

'Sir.'

'It was a warning, of course,' said Dryden. 'Why leave the wooden sign nailed up if they didn't want us to find the victim quickly? Takes some doing, getting a body up on a cross like that. Two people, at least, maybe three or four. Why go to all that trouble? Why not just hang him off a tree in the churchyard if you want to make a point?'

But Friday was gone, so he didn't get an answer.

SEVEN

They took the body away after the sun had set. Rigor mortis had passed, because the black body bag was sinuous, buckling as two forensics officers in white brought it out of the trees and laid it on a stretcher. A small crowd of villagers had gathered by the church, hemmed in by a long stretch of police tape. As the body was carried through the headstones a flashlight went off. When Dryden's eyes recovered he saw *The Crow*'s photographer, Josie Evans, up on top of one of the box tombs, weighed down with camera gear.

'I'll leave you to it,' said PC Powell. 'If you remember anything I need to know, ring the mobile, you've got the number.'

Dryden watched Powell walk across the field that led up to the edge of the graveyard and he thought he heard him whistling. Dryden recognized the melody – Bach, he thought, expertly tuneful. It occurred to him that, given the circumstances, Powell, a lowly PC, seemed particularly unfazed by a murder inquiry on his patch.

Dryden had his laptop on his knee and he

64

began to knock out the news story he'd have to file overnight. He thought that if he wrote it here and now, its principal virtue – that it was in part an eyewitness account – would shine through. The front page of the paper had to be designed and laid out in the morning, the presses would roll by noon, and the story would be out on the streets by teatime. The piece needed to read as if it had been written in the moment of discovery. That was the secret to reportage. Only tell the reader what you saw, heard, smelled and touched.

'Laptop's smart,' said a voice which made him jump.

It was the young man PC Powell had described as the grandson of the householder of Sexton Cottage. He'd been about all afternoon. He wore a grubby white T-shirt, splashed with paint and what looked like turps. His hair was fair and unruly, his frame spindly, and there was a tattoo on his right arm of an intricate Celtic design.

'Sorry,' said Dryden. 'Do you mind if I do this here? I've got a deadline.'

'Make yourself at home. Everyone else has.'

'Sorry. You're the owner's grandson?'

'He's upstairs resting. Yeah – Grandad was the sexton, best part of thirty years. House comes with the job, least it did. The last vicar said he could stay for life. That's the point of being sexton; you're the keeper of sacred things. It's a vocation. Not just a job.'

Dryden stood and offered his hand. 'I'm Philip Dryden, from *The Crow*.'

'Vincent Haig. People call me Vinnie.'

65

Dryden felt rings in the handshake – two, maybe three. Looking into Haig's eyes, he reassessed his age as being somewhere in the late thirties, maybe slightly older. The middle-aged trying to look young are never attractive.

'You spotted the lead missing off the roof?' asked Dryden, recalling his earlier conversation with the Rev. Temple-Wright.

'No. Grandad spotted it. Well, he heard them in the night. Not much he could do – he's blind, has been for five years now. Cataracts. He rang the nick at Wisbech and Powell's number; this was three o'clock in the morning. Left messages. They did fuck all.'

'I guess no one thought it was going to end in murder, did they? Hindsight's a wonderful thing,' said Dryden.

'Whatever,' said Haig. 'Grandad phoned me first thing to say he'd heard something in the night and I came over to check it out. I saw the lead had gone so I made it secure and rang the vicar. She rang Powell; he came round and bunged some tape over the doorway, said he'd report it, give us a crime number for the insurance claim. That should have been it, done and dusted. Like you said, none of us knew that poor sod was up in the trees on the cross.'

They heard a cat flap bang and a trail of three kittens ran out across the yard. Then the back door opened and an old man came out. Eighty years old, perhaps even more, with thin grey hair, outdoor skin and a wind tan, common in the Fens, which gave the face a leathery appearance. Both his eyes were clearly sightless, flat and dull, focused on a point out in the field. Dryden was troubled by the blind because he couldn't read character in their eyes. They could hide so much.

'I can hear your language inside. You might respect the dead,' he said, his eyes searching for his grandson.

A sneer disfigured Vincent Haig's face. Dryden disliked him immediately because he knew the calculation that lay behind it; that the old man couldn't see it, but that Dryden could.

The old man held a hand out into thin air. 'I'm Albe Haig,' he said, the first name pronounced to rhyme with bumblebee. Dryden introduced himself. Haig said he could stay as long as he liked and that he was making more tea and would bring the pot out.

Dryden sat with the grandson in silence. On the roof of Christ Church they could see lights moving in the dusk as the forensic team finished their work. A single PC stood at the entrance into the pine trees where they'd brought out the victim's body.

Haig licked his lips. 'See this field – the one between us and the church?'

Dryden counted twenty sheep still on the rough pasture.

'It's called the Clock Holt in the village, although there's nothing on the map. Story is that when they built the church, one of the local gentry gave this field to the parish on the understanding that any rents or income would go to the vicar to pay for the upkeep of the church clock. Back then a clock would have been rare in a place like this. Everything would have run by the bell: the working day, services, shops. That's the Victorians for you – they ran on clockwork.'

'I've never heard chimes,' said Dryden. In the dusk he could see a small exterior bell arch on the roof.

Haig leaned forward and looked into Dryden's face. 'That's because they decided it was more important to use the money for this cottage, a home for the sexton. So the rent covers all the costs. They promised Grandad, the last vicar did, that he could have it for life. Now she wants him out. She's gonna sell it, and the rent from the Clock Field's going to help meet costs. That's what she said to his face: help meet costs. Nice woman.'

There was something wheedling about Vincent Haig that set Dryden's nerves on edge. When he spoke his shoulders moved as if he was trying to flex an arthritic neck. His manner annoyed Dryden; he was like one of those charity workers who insist on shaking their collecting tin in your face.

'Was the promise made in writing?' asked Dryden.

Vincent Haig looked sideways. 'That's not how these things work. For Grandad's generation your word was good enough.'

Dryden's sympathies were with Albe, but he wondered what they would find if they could spool back to the moment the promise was made. What would they really hear? A cast-iron promise, or just a form of words? It was only human nature, after all, to hear what you wish to

68

hear, and to miss the get-out-clause.

But there was a story here. *Hard-hearted vicar evicts blind man from his home of thirty years.* What made Dryden uncomfortable was the feeling that Vincent Haig had fed him the information, like bait on a hook. It was also an oddly calculating thing to do as they sat surveying a murder scene. Was this really the right time to discuss a row over who paid the rent on Sexton Cottage?

The old man came back with a pot of tea on a tray with three mugs. His movements in the small garden were perfectly calibrated, shuffling between chairs and plant pots without error. As he set the mugs down, his free hand checked the flat surface.

Then he stood looking across the Clock Holt to the church. Dryden wondered what he could see in his mind: a jigsaw of memories, perhaps, in black and white.

'So you heard the thieves in the night?' asked Dryden.

'But I didn't hear a gunshot,' said Albe. He shook his head. 'That's not right, is it? I hear everything.'

Vincent Haig stiffened in his seat and set his hand on the table edge, the fingers splayed. Dryden saw that the top of his right index finger was missing – just a half-inch.

'What *did* you hear?' asked Dryden.

'They were good; I said to that copper they were professionals. I didn't hear a van, nothing on the road at all. But to get the lead off they needed to lever it off the rafters, where it's been pinned down. I heard that.' He pulled the lobe on his right ear.

'Did you look?'

It was the wrong thing to say but the old man was nodding. 'I went to the bedroom window. They were up and down in ten minutes. They tried to keep quiet, but there were a few words.'

'English?'

Albe Haig shook his head. 'Foreigners. People want easy lives now,' he added, and Dryden thought he was searching for his grandson's face. 'As if God owes them that. 'Specially foreigners.'

Dryden stiffened, hoping that this man who he liked – admired, even – wasn't going to reveal a bitter prejudice.

'You don't know that, Grandad,' said Haig, an easy, mocking swagger in his voice. 'Just because the one that died was ethnic Chinese, doesn't mean they all were.' Dryden noted Vincent Haig's careful political correctness.

'I heard them,' said his grandfather. 'The voices travel because they're light – like when we had a choir. Not English, something different.' He struggled to find the right word. 'Girlish. But men. Chinese, I reckon, like the copper said.'

'How many?' asked Dryden.

'Three, I think. Unless others didn't speak.'

'But no argument? You didn't hear shouting?'

Albe Haig sat down. 'No – just voices.' He pressed his hands to his ears as if he could hear them now. 'I can't believe someone is dead. Murdered. It's such a peaceful place.'

70

Dryden tried out a few of his own theories as to what had happened, hoping they'd share theirs, but they said they had none.

'I better get to work,' said Dryden eventually. He put a hand on the old man's shoulder. 'Good to meet you, Mr Haig. Hope this all quietens down. Gives you some peace.'

The grandson walked him to the edge of the Clock Holt.

'And Temple-Wright knows he's blind?' asked Dryden before they parted. 'I could do a story if your grandfather wants me to. Can you ask him? Not now. He's tired. But let me know.'

They swapped cards. Haig's said he was a picture restorer and framer. Dryden looked at his hands again, seeing this time that they were long, even elegant, with dry paint under the nails.

'I'll ask him. You know what I think? I think the vicar doesn't care about Grandad because he loves the place, the church, and because he was the guardian, the keeper. She hates that, hates the idea that we might love this place. *I know*.'

Something in the way Vincent Haig said it implied a darker knowledge.

'I'll talk to her if your grandad wants me to,' said Dryden. He felt a thrill for the power of his trade. If she backed down he could run a story anyway, saying the church had shown mercy. But something told him Temple-Wright didn't do backing down.

The ambulance into which they put the victim's body still stood on the road, the light flashing. Dryden thought they'd leave with the

71

forensic unit when the job was done. It was sad, poignant even, that they felt no need to hurry away with the body.

'You know the legend, about the Devil and Brimstone Hill?' asked Haig. He had a way of sharing information which Dryden found deeply annoying. First the question, then his own, pre-prepared and calibrated answer.

'Sure. He was chased here by the vicar and went up in a puff of smoke to hell.'

'Perhaps the Devil's back,' said Haig.

EIGHT

Tuesday

The Jolly Farmers had been closed for thirteen months, but it might as well have been thirteen years. It stood at a T-junction two miles from Christ Church, out on the fen. The smell of winter damp ran through it like the spreading fingers of dry rot. A single lavatory had been sluiced down with Domestos, adding an astringent note to the fetid air which had been trapped behind boarded windows and bricked up doorways. There was nothing quite as dispiriting, thought Dryden, as a dead pub. It was like an empty theatre; all the more desolate for the fact that it had once been so alive.

The atmosphere suited the occasion. The Ely coroner, Dr Digby Ryder, had decided to hold his court in the old pub – as was his right under the law – because the case he wanted to deal with was local, involving the deaths of two tramps earlier that year, whose bodies had been discovered in a flooded ditch. A local case, of local interest, so Dryden had put it in the diary a week earlier. But now the pub was crammed with journalists because Ryder was also due to formally open the inquest into the death of the man found in the churchyard at Christ Church. Given that the police had issued such a short statement the day before, and Dryden's eye-witness account had yet to hit the streets, the rest of the media were keen to cover the coroner's court, even if proceedings were limited to a few formalities.

The coroner's officer, DS Stan Cherry, had removed the boards over some of the windows so that indirect sunlight filled the old public bar. Dust didn't hang in the air – it clogged it, like cigarette smoke. Three darts stuck out of the dartboard, a handwritten Xmas Draw board hung on the wall beside a Pirelli calendar featuring Miss April 2010, and Dryden spotted four plastic rat-traps on the lino, each edged into a shadowy corner. A TV crew had set up in one corner at the back, and there were two radio reporters with microphones in the second row. The front row was reserved for local people who had an interest in the local case, which would now come on after the Christ Church killing. They looked bemused at the media circus around them.

DS Cherry was stout, in his early sixties, with

skin like the surface of a week-old party balloon. He was a northerner, from Bolton, with an affected air of continuous good humour which had survived his tenure as coroner's officer; a job designed to see him to retirement.

'Now then, Philip,' he said, handing Dryden a printed sheet. 'This one's nasty.' Dryden read a name and address on the sheet.

Sima Shuba
34B Erebus Street
King's Lynn

'This the victim?'

'Certainly is. Not a nice way to die, as you're about to hear.'

Dryden prayed that the coroner was not about to divulge too many of the details from the scene of the crime.

'Nice day out for you then,' he said. 'A bit of a change from Ely, plus a big fat expense claim?'

'You've got it,' said Cherry, straightening his back. 'It's the glamour, the poolside parties, the paparazzi. That's Brimstone Hill.'

Outside they heard a vehicle come to an abrupt halt on the pub gravel, followed by dogs barking. The coroner had two lurchers and Dryden had seen him hunting with a shotgun on the water meadows at Ely. He had that outdoor complexion which seems to be a hallmark of public schools; as if the skin has just been scrubbed with a wire brush. In court he affected green tweeds. In private his persona was less of a cartoon; the country-squire manners a screen for

74

extreme shyness. Dryden had once looked him up online. He was a member of the Royal Society, a medical doctor, with research interests in public health.

Ryder breezed in, concentrating on his brown brogues, not the court. He didn't once make eye contact with the public or the members of the press. The lurchers were on leads, their claws skittering on the boards. He sat at the bare table at the front and the dogs collapsed around his feet.

Cherry called for the court to be upstanding. There was a cacophony of chairs grating, repeated as everyone settled back down.

'Thank you,' said Ryder. 'I will now formally open the inquest into the death of Sima Shuba, aged thirty-two, of Erebus Street, King's Lynn. I can say Mr Shuba worked as a kitchen porter and that he was unmarried. The Foreign Office and UK Border Agency are examining his papers. I will adjourn the case itself while the police complete their inquiries. I do wish, however, to put on the record the results of an initial autopsy carried out last night at Wisbech. Mr Shuba died of a gunshot wound to the abdomen between one and five o'clock yesterday morning. The shot was fired at point-blank range. There would have been very little noise as a result. He was found at just after one thirty in the afternoon. His body was in the churchyard of Christ Church, here in Brimstone Hill. There are some indications that Mr Shuba died after a struggle. The immediate cause of death was loss of blood. Death took place at the scene. Mr

Shuba's family has been informed.'

Ryder shuffled some papers and the TV crew made moves to dismantle their camera.

Ryder tidied his papers into a neat pile. 'Once these facts are known I would encourage anyone who knows anything which might help the police find the killer, or killers, of Sima Shuba, to contact them immediately. I have been asked to stress that any information offered will be treated in confidence.'

The coroner smiled inappropriately. 'Case adjourned. There will now be a brief pause in proceedings before we move on to today's scheduled case. Thank you.'

Most of the journalists made a bolt for the door.

Dryden sat tight, opened his laptop, and wrote a fifty-word paragraph to email to the office so that they could add it to the story he'd already written for the *Ely Express*. It changed little of what they knew of the case.

The press pack had now been reduced to the usual suspects: two or three of the local dailies, and the weeklies. Dryden's instinct was to leave and follow up his own leads on the big story, the murder in Christ Church graveyard. But he had three clear days before the next front-page deadline. His immediate priority was the coroner's second case.

Sgt Cherry called for order and Ryder launched directly into a summary of the known facts concerning the sudden and unnatural deaths of Anthony James Russell and Archibald Donald McLeish.

A fen blow, nearly as bad, according to the coroner, as the one that had hit the area the day before, had struck Brimstone Hill one Sunday evening that spring. The next day, 8 April, the rain had fallen. A cloudburst had thundered down for two hours between 6.30 p.m. and 8.30 p.m. When the air cleared, the village's main drain, the Brim, was clogged, water lapping over and into the road beyond Christ Church. The problem was presumed to be a blocked culvert where the brook ran under the railway. The Fen Waterways Board turned up next day to dig out the silt. They expected to find something in the hole besides silt: a tree stump, a supermarket trolley, a dead badger. Instead they found the bodies of two men.

Identification was nearly instantaneous. The men were, in that telling phrase, 'well known to the police'. One was a thirty-two-year-old form-er land worker who had been born in the village. He'd been known, since school, as Spider Russell. He was six foot two inches tall.

'Spider for his long legs and arms, I think?' Ryder smiled at thin air.

Several heads in the front row nodded in agreement.

Russell began drinking at fourteen, said Ryder, starting with cider, usually in plastic bottles, consumed in private down by the railway line. By sixteen he was barred from both The Brook, the pub in the centre of Brimstone Hill, and The Jolly Farmers.

Ryder spread his hands out wide. 'The Jolly Farmers,' he repeated, as if they'd missed the

77

reference.

He took up his story again.

Spider Russell didn't let being barred stop him drinking. He'd walk the six miles into Friday Bridge on a Friday night with his agricultural wages and blow it all in the pubs there.

Two women in the front row began to discuss this fact and Ryder paused until they were embarrassed by the silence into which they were talking.

'Drink eventually cost young Russell his job,' said Ryder. 'Although it appears he'd tell anyone who listened that he'd been pushed out of the labour market by migrant workers who'd do the work for half the money.'

After becoming unemployed, Russell's life took a predictable route, continued Ryder. His mother moved to the East Midlands when he was nineteen to start a new life. There was no other family locally. Russell had a room above the mini-market in Brimstone Hill, paid for by his mother, using a banker's standing order. He smelt so badly they wouldn't let him in the shop, but they would sell him cans at the back door. He lived off benefit which he collected from Peterborough on a Monday.

'But for the most part he seems to have lived the life of an affable beggar,' concluded Ryder. He reached down under the table and ruffled the fur of one of the dogs.

Spider Russell's friend, whose body was found alongside his in the ditch, was called Archie Mc-Leish. Ryder said Russell met him in Wisbech on market day and brought him back to Brimstone Hill. He was from Ayr, Scotland. McLeish was nineteen, a former heroin addict, who'd switched back to alcohol. Russell let McLeish sleep on his floor. The Scot was clean, almost fanatically so, and he washed his clothes in the laundrette at Friday Bridge once a month. He didn't claim benefit, but he did have a debit card, which he used in the hole-in-the-wall in Wisbech. The coroner's officer had been able to get his bank records and they showed McLeish had a current account credit of £13,800 – the remainder of the estate of his father, a solicitor, who had died when he was just sixteen. His mother had remarried and did not wish to attend the inquest. Ryder's lip curled slightly, perhaps indicating what he thought of the absentee mother. McLeish, he added, had no siblings.

McLeish's and Russell's bodies were found together in the flooded culvert with two empty vodka bottles and some food wrappers from the corner shop: pork pies, pasties, and apples. McLeish had three twenty-pound notes in his pocket; Russell thirty-eight pence in coppers.

'This is a very unusual case,' said Ryder, with a hint of the intellectual curiosity that he so often concealed.

'The cause of death in both cases was drowning. McLeish had sustained a head wound before he died. It was late evening when the cloudburst struck the area. Witnesses had seen them both out on the fen, drinking, apparently in good humour. This was on the Wisbech Road, near the bus stop. They were sitting on the grass verge. What happened when the rain fell and the ditches filled with water? It is easy to speculate, but we will almost certainly never know the truth.

'It is not difficult to imagine the scene. When I say that the ditch was full of water, I mean – of course – the Brim. Hardly a ditch. A river, running in a deep culvert, and on this day probably churning with water. I think that the most likely scenario is that McLeish fell into the floodwater, possibly sustaining the head injury, and that Russell tried to save his friend. There is a chance that they argued, possibly blows were exchanged, but none of the evidence supports that view and there is not a single recorded instance of either man using violence. So, I am happy to speculate that they were both the victims of an accident. But it is speculation. Once they fell in the water they had very little chance of survival due to their general physical condition, which is the real point of calling this inquest at this time, and in this place.'

Ryder tidied his notes. 'Each day of our lives we all move closer to our deaths,' he said. 'But these young men were moving very quickly towards an early death when they had their accident. I doubt either would have lived for more than a few months longer. Both were being poisoned by drinking contaminated illicit alcohol. "Moonshine" is a euphemism – especially in this case.'

DS Cherry came forward and put three vodka bottles on the table. Two were empty, one full of a golden liquid. They had yellow labels, with a picture of what looked like wheat or reeds on the

80

front. The brand name was *Zabrowka*.

Dryden was pleased by the thought that the national newspapers had quit the court and missed the story. A much better story than anyone could have predicted from the bare details of the case.

'Zabrowka is a type of vodka made widely in Eastern Europe,' said Ryder. 'Usually at eighty per cent proof. The key, distinguishing ingredient is Buffalo Grass. This contains coumarin, and that's the secret, because it gives it an extraordinary scent and taste. These two empty bottles were found in the ditch with the victims. This third bottle has been obtained by Trading Standards officials.'

Dryden raised a hand and asked the coroner to spell the 'secret' ingredient.

He spelt out COUMARIN letter by letter.

'It flavours the vodka, as I say, so you get this amazing...' Ryder unscrewed the cap on the full bottle and flourished his fingers under his nose. 'Coumarin is what makes new-mown hay smell sweet. Plus there's vanilla, coconut, almonds. And there's the colour. The gold, like living gold. It is rather beautiful, isn't it?

'Unfortunately this is bootleg Zabrowka. The smell is reproduced, but little else. The label may fool some, and provide assurance for many, but the contents, when imbibed, are redolent of anything but new-mown grass.'

The coroner wandered into some arcane detail, but Dryden tracked the central thread of relevant facts: the autopsies revealed that both the victims had been ingesting two toxic substances

81

over a long period of time. One was lead; the other was methanol, or wood alcohol. Both were present in the empty bottles in minute traces, detected with a spectrometer in the forensic lab. The full bottle was tainted with both.

'Methanol is produced by using wood chippings to distil alcohol. It is cheap and dangerous. One of the symptoms of poisoning is disturbed vision, even blindness, and I think this should be kept in mind given the circumstances of the deaths. Other symptoms include stomach pains and seizures. Lead is a common by-product of illicit stills because bootleggers often use old machinery to help in the distilling process. The most common, in rural areas, being old tractor radiators. Lead poisoning brings about headaches, delirium and convulsions.'

Ryder nodded to Cherry, who handed a further statement to the coroner which he read out: 'It is clear that the victims had access to a source of illicit alcohol in the West Fens which is severely contaminated and is a threat to public health. I have notified the police of my findings in advance. No one should buy alcohol which is not sold through licensed outlets and properly branded. Drinking so-called "moonshine" can seriously harm your health, precipitate mental health problems and eventually lead to death. I am also releasing pictures of the Zabrowka brand label. Consumers should avoid bottles with this label at all costs. Genuine bottles do not have these yellow labels.'

Ryder moved a foot and one of the dogs yelped.

'Given the complexities of this case, and the poor health of the victims prior to the events which led to their deaths, I am going to record an open verdict in both instances. I have passed the files to the West Cambridgeshire Police and I have asked them to identify the source of the poison in this case; for poison it most certainly was.'

He looked up from the prepared statement.

'I have asked them to treat this issue as a priority and I shall be monitoring the investigation.' He looked straight at Dryden when he read out this final sentence. There was an unmissable inference that the police had so far not been giving the case the attention it deserved. It crossed Dryden's mind that PC Powell, his local friendly contact in the constabulary, had failed to give him any hint of the story.

Later, walking back along the arrow-straight road which led back into town, Dryden looked down into the Brim. A trickle-line of damp earth ran along the bottom of the ditch. He imagined the flood on that day, the water churning, powering its way towards the culvert by Christ Church, carrying the bodies of Russell and McLeish. Given the evil nature of the drug they were addicted to, he couldn't help thinking they'd been given a gift that day by the gods of the sky: a swift and tumultuous death.

NINE

Dryden walked through the centre of Brimstone Hill, past Christ Church, heading for his office – a modest single room with a landline, over the little parade of shops hidden in a cul-de-sac by the level crossing. When he'd gone for the job of editor of *The Crow*, he'd told the interview panel that they needed to expand the circulation area. Stop trying to change the paper to make more people buy it in Ely, and take the same paper wider afield. Create new editions, gather more news, make *The Crow* something people couldn't live without. Customize it. Print separate editions for local areas. Then put it all up on the web on publication day, a few hours after the paper hits the streets. The West Fens was a prime area for expansion: small Victorian towns dotted on the silty, flat landscape all the way to Peterborough and Wisbech. Towns just like Brimstone Hill, right bang in the middle of nowhere, but in the middle nonetheless. And if you were going to move in to a new area you had to have a presence on the ground; you couldn't do it from a desk twenty miles away. They needed a new office, and he was prepared to run it for the first three months.

The mini-market above which Spider Russell

had lived was in the same parade of shops as Dryden's office. It sold *The Crow* and the *Ely Express* and, despite the fact the paper wasn't yet out, a billboard outside carried the splash headline:

GUNSHOT MURDER
IN BRIMSTONE HILL

Dryden thought if that didn't flog a few copies then nothing would.

On the roof of the parade of shops Dryden had rented a space to set up a neon advertising sign which read:

The Crow – YOUR local newspaper

The Fens had a lot in common with the American Midwest: the wide open fenceless farms, the love affair with the motor car, a certain taciturn mistrust of outsiders *and* a fascination with lights. At Christmas time some of the drove roads looked like Blackpool's Golden Mile, each house supporting jiggling Santas and prancing Rudolphs. It was the flat landscape that was the key, because any half-decent display of illuminations could be seen for miles. Dryden had checked out *The Crow*'s new flashing sign and had made Humph drive nearly three miles before it fell entirely out of sight in the cab's rear-view mirror.

He let himself into the office at the top of a short flight of steps from the pavement. There was a certain frontier simplicity to the interior:

two phones, a desk, a table with a kettle on it, a window with blinds. Dryden thought briefly of the newsroom on Fleet Street he'd worked in for a decade: 200 desktop screens flickering, flat screen TVs showing twenty-four-hour news, and that buzz – a hypnotic brew of tension and excitement. He'd chucked all that in after his accident, to be closer to Laura as she fought to recover in hospital in Ely. Oddly, he'd never missed the buzz, or the noise. The only sound here was a bee caught behind a pane of glass. He edged it to freedom with a rolled up copy of the paper.

Then he sat down, put his hands behind his head, his feet on the desk, and looked out of the window. This was what he really loved about the life he'd chosen for himself: that he was in charge, and that nobody told him what to do or think.

He sent a text to Humph asking how Grace was. Humph had ferried him to the coroner's court first thing that morning but then sped off towards Euximoor Drove and his mother's bungalow.

The cabbie was a swift and expert thumb-texter. The answer was with Dryden in less than fifteen seconds: SHES NOT TELLING ME SOMETHING.

Dryden, irritated by the missing apostrophe, made himself compose a reassuring response. SPEND SOME TIME WITH HER. YOU ARE IMPORTANT. PICK ME UP ABOUT SIX? Then he attacked the post with a letter-opener in the shape of a silver eel. It consisted almost entirely of advertising flyers, except for a single brown envelope marked *newspapa* in a child's hand. He tore it open and found six photographs. They were of an owl, a species of the bird Dryden had never seen before. This one was chocolate brown, with white speckles, the traditional 'surprised' expression, and huge yellow eyes. Small, slightly huddled, and faintly exotic.

Only one picture carried any information, in the same crude hand, on the back of the shot.

Funeral Owl (Aegolius funereus) is very rare so you should put this in yore paper. I got this picture from my hide. I sore two – a pair – so maybe they are breeding hear.

There was no name, and no address. But the first shot, the one taken with the least magnification, showed some fencing by a road and a sign which read THIRD DROVE. He knew the spot, out on Euximoor Fen, in a grid of back roads simply named by number.

He had a scanner attached to the desktop iMac. Once he had the best shot in digital form he sent it to his mobile and forwarded it to a friend at the bird reserve at Welney on the edge of the Bedford Levels, just half-a-dozen miles from where he sat. The Levels, a wide area of grassland between two of the Fens' artificial rivers, provided Europe's biggest freshwater reserve for birds. When the sluices were opened a man-made lake twenty-five miles long was formed. Welney offered a huge hide for visitors and he'd already picked up several stories for the paper in the months running up to the launch of the new edition. They were experts in wetland birds at

Welney – but it was a good place to start, if he wanted to know more about the owl.

He added a text message to the picture. *Reader picture – claims it is the FUNERAL OWL. Is it rare? Is it possible? Or is he mad like rest out here? D*

The office clock said it was fifteen minutes past noon. The *Ely Express* would be on the streets soon. He'd then file the same copy to the Fleet Street papers. His eyewitness stuff might make the story strong enough to run nationally. In the meantime he did a quick round of calls, picking up some facts and figures he could use in *The Crow* when they reran the story on the dust storm. The emergency services had dealt with eight calls from Euximoor Fen and the immediate area. Two cars had collided head-on at a junction but they'd been crawling in the gloom at under ten mph. Five calls simply reported the storm's arrival. Two people had used mobiles to call for medical assistance; a woman pushing a pram and an elderly man who'd been on his smallholding when the cloud hit. Both had been treated on the spot by an ambulance crew from Wisbech. The storm itself had been short-lived, rising about ten miles east, dying out immediately after it had passed over Brimstone Hill. The NFU man had some insurance claim figures for one of the farms. Dryden used the desk blotter to conjure up a headline figure of £400,000. Disappointed, he redid the maths until he got to £500,000.

He heard footsteps on the stairs. A sign on the outer door invited members of the public to drop in with news snippets, advertising copy, or just to talk to a reporter. Dryden always felt a newspaper that hid behind bricks and mortar was doomed to be irrelevant. At his first evening paper, in York, the front counter at street-level had been linked to the newsroom by an internal – public – telephone. Anyone could walk in off the street and ring the newsroom and ask for a reporter to pop down for a chat. It had been an archaic system but it had brought in a steady stream of decent news stories. In modern newspapers reporters hid behind their computer screens. Dryden was determined to be the real-life 'face' of *The Crow* in Brimstone Hill, even if that meant the occasional twenty minutes spent discussing a prize-winning turnip with an allotment gardener.

A man appeared at the door with a raincoat over his arm, neatly folded. Around his neck hung a pair of expensive high-powered binoculars. Dryden had seen him about in Brimstone Hill but they'd never talked.

The first thing Dryden noted was the aftershave. Something expensive and subtle but very distinctive, which strangely zigzagged in his mind so that he thought of coumarin, the extract of Buffalo Grass which held the aroma of new-mown hay.

'Jock Donovan,' he said. If he'd ever had a Scottish accent it was gone now. The voice was mid-Atlantic, oddly state-less. 'Someone said it was OK just to walk in?'

'Of course,' said Dryden, offering him the seat. Rather than walking to it, Donovan grabbed it

89

by the back and swung it round behind him with an easy grace. Despite his age, and Dryden estimated he was at least in his late seventies, he somehow retained the echo of a youthful physical power. Perhaps it was in the steady gaze, the ability to hold the head still and meet Dryden eye-to-eye.

'Tea?'

Donovan nodded, then produced from a rucksack a hefty black machine, like a CD player or tape deck, with a microphone attached.

They swapped mindless banter about sugar, milk and Earl Grey. Then they talked about the murder in the churchyard. Donovan said he'd heard it was triads – Chinese criminal gangs – fighting a war. Dryden noted that his skin was tanned, and very clean – that kind of steam-blasted clean which comes from taking two showers a day in a wet room. He asked him whether he was a birdwatcher. Was that why he carried the binoculars?

'Birds? Sometimes. I'm interested in whatever I can see.'

'Catch the storm?' asked Dryden, pouring boiling water into mugs.

'I watched it come in,' he said. And then Dryden did see an echo of those Scottish roots. Not in the voice, but in the face: asymmetrical eyes, one higher, wider open, and the mouth, down on the right side, up on the left – both indicative of a dip into the Northern gene pool. Or were they cultural attributes? The result of generations of hard, rational Scottish inquiry?

Donovan leaned forward and picked up a

framed picture of Eden on the desktop. 'How old?'

'Fifteen months; he's not walking yet. He's lazy – like me.'

'Don't worry. He will; he's just a slow starter.'

Dryden didn't think he was worried. But then why had he said it? As a child he'd been tearing about at ten months, according to family legend. Perhaps he should mention that to Laura, by way of contrast. When did she take her first steps? They could compare notes.

A train ran past over the level crossing outside, the bass rumble of the freight trucks set against the high treble of couplings squealing. Donovan turned his head aside, as if the noise upset him. He wore a white shirt, crisp, linen and ironed, and a tie – a rarity in Brimstone Hill. This tie was blue with a crest featuring an elephant over a motto.

'How can I help?' asked Dryden, giving him the tea in his best mug with the Ipswich Town crest.

Donovan lived a few hundred yards up the Ely Road, at Brimstone House, a white, Artexed 1920s gem with a flat roof. Perhaps Dryden knew it? It was difficult to miss. Dryden recalled Crittall ironwork, and those corner windows which look two ways.

'It must be great,' said Dryden. 'Having light from two sides in a room.'

'It is,' said Donovan. 'There are fourteen rooms.'

So far their conversation had been easy, relaxed, but now it seemed to have come to a sudden stop. Part of the journalist's trade was an ability to keep people talking.

'Is there a story behind the tie?' he asked.

Donovan touched it, running the material between finger and thumb. 'Duke of Wellington's Regiment. I signed up in nineteen fifty-two. Just in time for Korea. The Battle of the Hook, that was all ours. I was just a soldier, a rifleman. I ended up in a trench one night with two of my mates. The Chinese sent over five thousand shells. By morning I was the only one left alive.'

His voice was very smooth, and there appeared to be absolutely no emotion in it at all. Dryden was struck by two thoughts: first that a simple question about a tie could lead within a few words to a scene of literal carnage; and second that only yesterday he'd stood in front of that oddly moving memorial to two brothers who'd died in that very same forgotten war.

'That's what they told me but I don't remember,' said Donovan. 'Never have. I count my blessings.'

Outside they heard an ice-cream van jingle as it parked outside the school for break time.

'There's a memorial in the local churchyard for the Korean War, two brothers.'

'That's it. The Davenport brothers – they were my mates. They were in my trench. They didn't make it.'

'I'm sorry,' said Dryden.

In 1954 he'd been demobbed, said Donovan, and he'd come to Brimstone Hill to see the parents of his dead comrades. Army procedure: visit the relatives, tell them it all happened very

92

quickly, that they felt nothing, that they were heroes. 'Heroes,' said Donovan with glittering eyes.

The father of the brothers had died. There was a sister; just a girl of ten or eleven. The mother made him welcome, gave him tea.

He sniffed the brew Dryden had given him, then looked round the room as if suddenly aware of where he was.

'For her, for the mother, I was a link to the boys she'd lost. She offered me a job there and then – just labouring. There's a tied cottage down by the road and I had a room there. It was what I needed because I was in a mess. They've got fancy names for it now. Which way up you look at it doesn't really matter – I was a bag of nerves, so working on the land was good for me. I stayed for two summers. It's always been home, this place, since then.'

Dryden drank his own tea and tried not to look at the strange machine with its microphone.

Donovan was still thinking about his two lost comrades. Dryden could see it in his eyes, that 'living-in-the-past' stare. Not quite the 'thousand-yard stare' of the traumatized soldier, but only a few yards short.

'I tried to get the boys' name on the war memorial, the one by the church. They wouldn't do it, the powers-that-be; it was just for the world wars, they said. As if we didn't fight for our country. So I paid for a wooden plaque which went up inside the church. That was in the sixties. When I came back here to retire, after my wife died, I thought even more that they'd

93

been treated like second-class soldiers. All of us had. So I paid for a memorial myself. Just for them: granite, with lead lettering. Born in nineteen thirty-three – both of them. Which is rare, of course – they weren't twins, you see, just born in the same year. One in January, one in November. But they wouldn't tell anyone who was younger, who was older. That would have been like breaking ranks.'

'Do you visit the grave?'

'Couple of times a week, usually at dusk. I don't leave flowers. I don't take anything. I bear witness. It's not a big deal. No one else goes, not even the sister; she says she'd rather forget. That's fine. She doesn't even shoot any more because it reminds her of them. And she was a fine shot, as good as them. I don't go out there to remember. In fact, it's the opposite. It helps me not to remember. I've never remembered...'

His Adam's apple bobbed in his throat.

'As I say, I can't remember. Not that night. It's a cliché, I know; my generation, we don't seek to deal with our problems. We just get on with life. Touching the memorial stone helps. I can live another day.' He smiled. 'I've bought the plot next to the memorial, so one day I'll stop out there.'

He'd gone too far, Dryden could see that, as he watched him suddenly gulp.

'Do you want me to write a story about them? Is there an anniversary, of the battle, of the day they died? Is that why you're here?'

'No. I don't want a story about that.' He looked appalled that Dryden could be so stupid. 'No. I came about the noise.'

He pressed a button on the machine. A noise played. A kind of whistling crackle. It brought an image to Dryden's mind of a beach, empty of people, but dotted with miniature toy windmills turning. 'Kites,' said Donovan. 'The farmers use 'em to keep birds off the fields when they've sowed seed. They're shaped like birds of prey and they keep the pigeons off. They're all round my place. There's a factory out on Euximoor Fen that makes the things, tests them as well. They'll fly twenty-four-seven now, cos they're so light. It's all high-tech.'

'Where is this factory exactly?'

'Coupla miles to the west. The old airfield at Barrowby. There's a line of industrial units and they've got one of those. But the kites are all over the place. They make that crackling noise a lot, the one you can hear, but that's OK, I can live with that. I'm not some nutter. It's the other noise. A kind of high-pitched call. I can't sleep through it; I can't think through it either. It's a torment.'

'Tell me more about the noise. What kind of high-pitched call?'

'Like the squeak from a rusty gate – but higher – and pulsing, at a set interval of two or three seconds.'

'I can't hear it,' said Dryden.

Donovan turned off the machine. 'I know, but I can. I complained to the council and they gave me this machine to monitor the noise but it doesn't show up. I think the frequency is too high. It picks up the crackling, but that's all.

See?'

He gave Dryden a paper printout which had, presumably, rolled out of the machine. It was like the record of an earthquake produced by a seismograph. It showed a jittery line, but there were no real peaks.

'Tractors, combines, all the heavy stuff, that's no bother to me. I live in the country; I don't expect silence, especially at harvest. But this, this is in *here*.' He poked a finger at his temple, and when he took his finger away the pressure left a mark.

'Perhaps it's tinnitus?'

'Doctor says my hearing's perfect. He thinks maybe I can hear higher frequencies than normal people. That I'm sensitive to the higher spectrum because of damage to my ears in the war. That's possible, isn't it?'

'What about the kite company, did you try them?' countered Dryden.

'Answerphone. I left a message, and they never got back. I thought you could help. I have to do something because it's very difficult to live with. In fact, it's not possible to live with it. It can't go on.'

There was a tremble in Donovan's neck which was making his skull shake very slightly.

Dryden thought that it took a lot for a man like Donovan to admit he couldn't live with something.

'The military doctor back when I was demobbed said my startle reaction was bad, on account of the shells. I don't remember the shells. But they must have made a noise and they said at the

96

time, in the field hospital, that I would be hyper-sensitive to noise for a while. Maybe six months. That was more than sixty years ago.'

He looked around the room, waiting for something to make a noise. Dryden thought about Brimstone House and its fourteen empty rooms. Shell shock, he thought. It was the summer of 2014 and he was sitting opposite a man with shell shock.

TEN

Dryden's eyewitness account of finding the body of Sima Shuba was running on the Press Association wires by early evening; lifted word-for-word from the paper but credited in full to the *Ely Express*. Then the calls started: Fleet Street news desks checking if it was safe to lift the story. Dryden gave them carte blanche but asked, nicely, if they'd squeeze in a mention of the source. A few would, most wouldn't. Journalism was a tough trade, so the majority would lift the facts and run it straight. The 'crucifixion' angle, plus the link into the Chinese gangs, was enough to guarantee the story what reporters liked to call 'legs': it would run and run. The BBC rang from Cambridge and said they were on their way out to do a 'day two' story from the scene. They too would lift Dryden's copy, but in the blur and buzz of TV he'd just become an eyewitness who found the body.

At five he shut up the office and headed for the mini-market. There was a bench outside where young mothers gathered with pushchairs to talk and smoke. Two of them were reading the first edition. Dryden bought a paper but then made himself pause on the way out and read the notices up in the window, the board advertising old beds for sale, lost cats, or offering baby-sitting services. His first paper, in Bedford, had once sent him to a one-horse town for a week to gather stories. The increasingly desperate efforts to find anything newsworthy had driven him to despair. A car had backfired on his last day and he'd seriously considered interviewing the driver. Then he'd stopped and read a postcard in a newsagent's window:

LOST: pet rattlesnake called Charlie.
Venomous. If seen please ring 01235 778778.
Do not pick it up.

It wasn't a Pulitzer prize-winning tale, but it was a story, and it had made a page lead in the paper and nearly £300 in lineage to the national tabloids. The hunt for Charlie had lasted ten days and by the climax, when Charlie was cornered in a local back-garden paddling pool, there were two TV crews there to capture the historic moment.

Dryden's eye flitted over the notices now but there was nothing new.

As he was about to leave he looked back at the counter. The woman who had sold him his paper

98

was engaged in a text conversation and hadn't looked up when she took his money. Above her head a CCTV screen showed a picture of the shop's alcohol aisle. The coroner had said that the late Spider Russell had bought cans of beer from the shop, not over the counter, but out the back. He wondered how and where Spider and his mate Archie had got the moonshine to supplement the cans.

There was a spotless white-and-blue panda car at the kerb, the passenger door open. At the wheel was PC Stokely Powell, one arm swinging out the driver's window, the Rolex catching the light.

'Your friend the cab driver's sitting outside The Brook with a pint,' said Powell. 'Shall we join him?' The request was unhurried and friendly, although Dryden could see that he had a copy of the *Ely Express* folded into the glove compartment. One of Powell's eyes seemed to be permanently watery, and he brushed a tear away now, with the heel of his palm.

Dryden got in and let the law drive him the 200 yards to the pub. They passed Christ Church and saw a single squad car parked outside, police tape still looped over the gates. Dryden thought how quickly the excitement drains from the scene of a crime once the body has been removed.

Humph was sitting at a picnic table with a book open in front of him. The cabbie had taken to the I-SPY series with enthusiasm and had just bought himself the edition on British trees.

Powell went inside to get drinks. As the policeman opened the bar door Dryden heard the buzz of talk from within and guessed that the single topic of conversation would be the murder at Christ Church. Powell's entrance killed the noise level dead.

The pub was run by two Portuguese men, both ex-migrant pickers. They'd been seen holding hands during long country walks. The locals were willing to overlook this scandal as long as they kept the pub open.

Humph studied his book. 'How's the runaway?' asked Dryden.

The cabbie shrugged. 'She wants to stay with her grandma till Sunday. She's got what she wants. She won't say why she doesn't want to go home. Apparently she's happy here, although you could have fooled me.'

'So you don't believe her?' he asked, sitting down.

'Not really. I spoke to her mother. This barbie when she fell out with her stepfather and his boys was weeks ago. It's something else that's spooked her. Maybe she'll tell her mum, but she's taking her time.'

'She might tell you,' offered Dryden. 'If you asked nicely.'

Humph produced a small pair of field glasses and looked east. 'She should go home to her little sister and her mum. That's where she belongs.'

'You don't go home; why should she?' said Dryden. The cabbie had lived alone since his divorce, in a rented house, yet he slept most nights in the cab. It was one of the things he shared with Dryden: a fear of domesticity.

Humph scratched his Ipswich Town top. 'I'm a grown-up. I'm allowed to do what I like.'

'Where's Boudicca?'

'I left her with Mum. Grace likes taking care of her. It's something to worry about that's not her, that's outside her.' He pointed across the fen at a distant lonely tree. '*Sorbus Aria* – The White-beam.'

Dryden followed his eyes. 'Right. You can walk about and look for trees, you know. They don't run away if you get near. It's not a Big Game hunt.'

Humph had the glasses up to his eyes again, whistling.

Powell came back with a pint of orange squash for himself and a half of cider for Dryden. The Brook had access to a local apple press. The resulting liquid was milky and so dry it seemed to suck every particle of moisture from the body of the drinker. If Dryden held it to his ear he was just able to detect a slight effervescence. The brewers had no idea of its alcoholic strength but wrote six per cent on the label. Dryden judged they were out by a factor of at least two.

The three drank in companionable silence. The pub looked out on the open fen from a deck, which held a gas-fired barbecue machine. In the distance they could see lorries on the high bank of the road to Wisbech. A train trundled over the level crossing carrying sand. Humph counted the forty-one trucks out loud, then lifted his legs out from under the picnic table. 'Back to work.'

They watched him walk to the cab and lower

himself into the front of the Capri, set the seat back, and close his eyes.

'Life in the fast lane,' said Dryden.

Powell had brought his copy of the *Ely Express* with him. 'Just an update,' he said, laying a palm across the paper. 'There'll be some arrests tonight in King's Lynn. A bit of a sweep through the vice industry. CID's pretty certain this is gang warfare, probably one gang falling out with itself. At the moment that means it's strictly limited gang warfare, which is where everybody wants it to stop.'

'What's at stake?' asked Dryden. 'What were they fighting over? It's not a few hundred quids' worth of lead off the church roof, is it?'

Powell licked his upper lip. 'No.' The policeman seemed to deliberately relax his muscles, sinking slightly, his shoulders dropping, and Dryden wondered if it was a tactic to dissipate stress: 'But the scrap metal trade is big money. Our information, and this is off the record for now, is that one of the triad gangs in Lynn had this trade sewn up. We're talking about bulk sales of stolen metal. Iron, steel, aluminium, lead, zinc, copper. Ten years ago the legal copper price was a thousand dollars a tonne. Now you'd get eleven thousand a tonne, and more. The current thinking is that this triad gang sent a foot soldier up here to discourage some members of the gang branching out on their own.'

'And the crew on the roof didn't take kindly to this discouragement?'

'Right. They clearly felt that Brimstone Hill, the West Fens, was *their* patch and they had a right to defend it. They made their point, pretty graphically.' He drained his orange juice, pivoting his hand to tip the glass, his elbow anchored to the picnic table top.

'One thing,' said Dryden. 'I went to the coroner's court this morning. Second case up after our victim on the cross was the bodies they found in the culvert earlier this year.'

'McLeish and Russell.'

'Ryder says it's moonshine that was killing them and that the floodwater simply intervened. He said it's your job to find the illicit still that's producing the stuff. Maybe it was my imagination, but he seemed to suggest you'd not been as interested as you should be in the case?'

'Me?'

'Well. The police.' Dryden spread his arms, indicating the deserted streets of downtown Brimstone Hill. 'That looks like you for now.'

Powell laughed, and for the first time Dryden thought it wasn't a genuine response. There was something wary in the eyes, too, as if he'd really like to talk about something else.

'It's a turf war,' said Powell. 'Health and safety, trading standards, CID in Wisbech, us on the ground. Interpol. Everyone's just a little bit responsible. Which means nobody is. It's sorted now – we'll find the coroner his illicit still. We're close enough. It just needs a few pieces of the jigsaw to complete the picture.'

PC Stokely Powell had just told a lie, thought Dryden. He didn't know why, but he was pretty sure a copper of his calibre wouldn't let bureaucracy stand in the way of closing down a poison-

103

ous distillery on his own patch. There was a subtext to what he'd said, and Dryden had no idea what it might be.

Dryden deliberately let the silence stretch out, wondering if Powell had sensed he sounded less than convincing. The sun was just setting beyond the roof of Christ Church. Dryden half-closed his eyes so that diamonds sparkled in his eyelashes.

'Before all this blew up I was planning to ask for a favour,' said Powell. He covered his face with both hands, then drew them away, stretching his skin. 'This is incredibly bad timing for you and me. The last thing I need is to be caught up in another case when I've got a gang war on my patch. The last thing you need is another story. This *can* keep – but not for long, Dryden. I need publicity, and I need it quickly. It's a cold case. Interested?'

'Sure,' said Dryden, although he couldn't help feeling that this new story had been introduced, in part, to divert attention from further conversation on the subject of the illicit still. The police manipulated the press, that was a fact of life, but that didn't mean Dryden had to enjoy the experience. 'I'll get us a refill,' he said.

At the bar Dryden stood looking at a large framed black-and-white picture of Brimstone Hill taken, according to a scrawled whitewash note, in 1889. He admitted to himself that he had an almost unhealthy interest in cold cases, so for now he was prepared to let drop the subject of the trade in lethal moonshine. There was something about an unsolved crime which seemed to intensify with the passing years, as if it became more vivid, less mundane. For the victim, time simply replaced the fear and trauma of the moment with an accumulation of bitterness, or a determination for revenge.

Back at the picnic table Powell had a briefcase open: worn, light leather, classy. He took out a newspaper cutting from *The Daily Telegraph*, Friday, 13 June 1999. The headline read:

US-STYLE 'HOT' BURGLARY LEAVES ONE DEAD IN FENLAND ART SPREE

'"Hot burglary" was what they called it back then. I guess they'd go for house invasion now. Breaking in when the owners are home, and using violence to intimidate. It's almost always a gang crime; they go mob-handed to maximise the threat. You've read *In Cold Blood*?'

Powell shook his wrist so that the gold watchstrap jangled, a mannerism Dryden had noted before. He couldn't decide if it betrayed stress or a need to draw attention to the bling.

'Sure,' said Dryden. Although brought up in the Fens, Dryden had spent most of his working life in London, which was where he'd have been in June, 1999. Dimly he recalled this cold case, and as Powell had pointed out, the echoes of Truman Capote's classic true-life crime novel *In Cold Blood*, which told the story of the brutal killing of a Kansas farmer called Herbert Cutter and his wife, and two of their children, by two armed robbers.

'That left four dead, of course,' said Powell.

105

'This could have been as bad. They did four properties in one day, a gang of three. First one was at Welney, a cottage. I've been down the lane to take a look and you can see why they chose it. There's nothing else for miles, just the reed beds, the fields, the river. Owner was a widow in her sixties. They just burst in, tied her up. Then they searched the place, every room, clearly looking for something specific. It could have turned nasty because they couldn't find it, so they asked her straight. She talked. It was right there, in the kitchen, hanging on the wall, so small they'd missed it. And that was all they took, an oil painting eight inches by six.'

'Experts then, art thieves?'

'You'd think.' Powell used the heel of his palm to clear the watery eye. Dryden wondered how long he'd gone without sleep. With a murder on his patch he must be under pressure to give CID as much of his local knowledge as possible.

'The painting was by an artist called Louis Grimshaw,' said Powell. 'His father is more famous – I think Louis was Atkinson's son. The two of them specialized in nineteenth-century scenes of industrial cities. This one was of Liverpool docks by moonlight. Worth fifteen thousand pounds.'

Dryden whistled. 'Not bad in nineteen ninety-nine. A decent's day's work by anyone's standards. How was the woman?'

'They left her tied to the chair. Neighbours found her the next day. She said she'd been screaming for help for six hours. So she wasn't great. Hospitalized, then released. She never

106

went back to the house, not even to pack her things.'

One of the Portuguese owners came out to clear their drinks. He talked them through the menu, even though they said they hadn't come for food. They said they'd think about it.

Once he was out of earshot Powell took up his story once again.

'Second one was at Friday Bridge. One elderly resident, a man this time, wheelchair bound. A terraced cottage, but the houses on both sides were empty in the day, which is when they called. This time they were after a watercolour. A moonlit scene of the Coliseum in Rome, half-buried in ivy and ancient trees. Victorian artist called Pether. Very collectible. Twenty thousand pounds.'

'So they always recce the house, and they know their art market,' said Dryden.

'Turns out they'd got hold of an auction room catalogue plus the names and addresses of the owners of each item. Neat trick. So in each case they had the address and then the description of the item. Needless to say, a major breach of security on the part of the auction house. And yes, there was – in retrospect – evidence that they'd visited the scene before the day of the crime.

'Third one was a farmhouse at Upwell. Owners were out but their daughter was upstairs. She panicked when she heard them coming up the stairs so they coshed her, broke her skull. Then they took six paintings, all by an Italian artist of the nineteenth century, a series of rural scenes.

Insurance cover was for two thousand pounds.'

'What age was the girl they coshed?' he asked.

Powell checked his notes. 'Fifteen.'

Dryden pushed the cutting aside and covered his eyes. Sometimes crime crept under his radar, brought a darkness into his life. He looked down the street towards the school and the crèche.

'Last call of the day was here, out at Barrowby Drove. A big Georgian farmhouse set on its own in a stand of pines. This time things really turned nasty. Broad daylight, Friday evening. The couple – the Calders – were at home. They'd planned to auction one picture, a miniature portrait of the Duchess of Bedford by a Regency artist named Hargreaves. The estimated sale price was thirty-five thousand pounds. They were selling to meet the costs of running the house, which had been in the wife's family for three generations. He wouldn't tell them where it was. Point-blank refusal. Our robbers didn't take it well. They knocked him down with a length of iron piping and then dragged him into the kitchen. He was sixty-eight.

'The wife, she was younger, by ten years or more. She passed out when the violence started. Lucky she did. So that left him. They got his hand and put it on the kitchen table and drove a nine-inch kitchen knife through it, pinned him to the top.'

Powell left that image to linger for a second.

'I guess they wanted him to talk. But he still wouldn't tell them where it was. It was a miniature, and the house was a rambling maze of rooms and cupboards. So there was no way they were going to find it. So they did the other hand. Then he passed out. They must have left then, cutting their losses. When the wife came round her husband was dead. There was a lot of blood under the kitchen table. Coroner said heart failure got him before the blood loss, which was probably a blessing.'

There was a look in Powell's eyes which reminded Dryden that it took guts to be a copper in the Fens, a black copper even more so. A rarity in West Cambridgeshire, Powell could look forward to rapid promotion. All he needed was to get noticed. Maybe that was what this was about. Solving an infamous cold case after a decade would earn him valuable career points. Playing second-fiddle on a murder investigation which was likely to lead to organized crime looked less promising.

'The wife's never spoken about what happened,' he said, draining the squash. 'In fact, she always said she couldn't remember anything after the thieves got through the front door. They knocked the lock out, by the way – one blow with a hand-held pile driver. Doctors said she'd developed protective amnesia. We had descriptions from the other victims, at the other houses. Problem is, the gang wore stockings over their heads, so what we got was minimal. All three were dark, very dark. Heads shaved. Only one spoke and he had an accent which was consistently described as heavy east European. Remember, this was nineteen ninety-nine, so EU migration was kicking off. The presumption was they were Poles.'

'Anything since?'

'Not really. It's still on the books. They kept tabs on migrant gangs but never heard a whisper.'

'The paintings?'

'Only thing that ever turned up was the Pether, at an auction in Cork, Ireland. Forged papers. Trail was cold, so we never got anywhere.'

'But now?'

'The wife, Muriel Calder, still lives at the house. A week ago she was sitting on the bench by the level crossing when a car pulled up. In the back was a man, his head against the glass, asleep. Seeing that face triggered a memory she'd suppressed for years. When the thieves were in the kitchen she must have regained consciousness for a few seconds lying on the floor. She saw one of the robbers roll up the stocking over his face and drink some of her husband's malt whisky from a decanter. That was the face she said she recognized. A few seconds, then the train went through, and the car drove off at speed. She's willing to swear the man in the back of the car was the man in her kitchen that day. We got a forensic artist up from Cambridge to try and produce a likeness, but it's pretty hopeless.'

He slid a glossy reproduction of a pencil drawing of a face out of the briefcase. Dark hair, glossy and unkempt, over a pale face, with dark eyes and a heavy brow.

'Could be anyone, to be fair,' said Powell. 'The thing is, she remembered something about the car he was in. A Ford, she thinks, two doors, blue. In the back passenger-side window where

110

this man leaned his head there was a sticker. A round white disc, about six inches across, with a black dragon in the middle belching red fire. Question is can we track down the car using the sticker? It's the kind of detail people notice. A neighbour, perhaps – someone who parks next to it every day, the garage where the car gets an MOT, the petrol station they use.'

Powell stretched his arms out. 'This is about speed, Dryden. It's possible the killer knew Calder had spotted him. She says the car drove off at high speed. If that's true, he'll dump the car or hide it, then disappear. Memories fade. So this needs to run next week at the very latest.'

Powell edged closer, his dark eyes shining. 'If we find this car, Dryden, we find the killer.'

ELEVEN

In a narrow inlet off the river two miles south of Ely lay *PK 122*, a former inshore naval patrol vessel converted to a houseboat. Barham's Dock was overgrown with reeds, the water ink-green with algae. Dryden had bought the boat for the small wooden plaque in the wheelhouse which read with heart-breaking simplicity: *Dunkirk 1940*. It had a panelled cabin, portholed sleeping berths, and a shower and bathroom he'd had adapted for Laura when she'd first come out of hospital after the accident. The paintwork was still naval grey, the letters and numbers of *PK 122* three-foot high on the prow.

Eden's birth had prompted them to abandon the boat and experiment with a more domestic life. They'd lived for a year in an old tied cottage on Feltwell Anchor, a vast expanse of dry fen to the north of Ely. The landscape had been an inspiration to them both: huge skies over vast fields, ingrained with a sense of isolation. They'd been happy, but only despite the house. The dull predictability of rooms and doors and windows seemed to weigh them down under the wide fen sky. It had, wonderfully for Dryden, been Laura who had come up with a solution. They'd decided to buy a narrowboat, named the *Rosa Jane*, and moor it alongside *PK 122*. Within hours of its purchase, Laura had set to work to re-christen it the *Lunigiana* after her native Italian province, the land of the moon-worshippers. A series of moons, from crescent to full, decorated the woodwork around the name. The two vessels, side-by-side, fitted snugly between the banks of the grassy dock. They slept in the narrowboat, lived in the naval launch; a chaotic existence which they both found thrilling. There were downsides: the naval launch was damp, they had to keep an eye on Eden, the ducks kept Laura awake, and Dryden had nightmares about waking up underwater. But overall, on balance, it beat domesticity.

In the wardroom below the deck of *PK 122* Dryden could hear Laura working, the dull tap-tap of the computer keyboard resonating through the steel deck. Eden was asleep in a child seat at his feet. The sun was touching the horizon, the red light interrupted every few seconds by the turning blades of the thirty-foot wind turbine they'd had erected on the bankside to supply power to the boats. The blades created a stroboscopic effect at sunset, a hypnotic light show, which Dryden enjoyed.

He had a glass of cider in his hand, his third of the day, and he was making a physical effort to let the memory of the last twenty-four hours fade with the light. The image of the murder victim hanging from the cross in the churchyard at Christ Church was still vivid, but it no longer flashed, unbidden, across his mind. According to Powell there would be arrests tonight in Lynn, as CID looked for the killers amongst the migrant Chinese community. Dryden would pick up the details in the morning, but if the arrests led to charges he'd only be able to print the bare details in *The Crow* – although the story would still make the 'splash' on the front page. After that all he had to do was to wait for the defendants to appear in the magistrates' court. Then there'd be the long wait while the case edged its way towards the Crown Court in Peterborough.

Not for the first time since DI Friday had made it clear his prime suspects were members of organized crime, Dryden wondered if the police were taking the path of least resistance. There was a danger that in the rush to label the crime the product of a gang war they might overlook possibilities closer to home. He resolved to keep his own reporting rigidly objective until the police came up with hard evidence for their theories. There was nothing as unedifying as a newspaper trying to perform a three-point turn in a murder hunt just because the police had switched suspects.

He tried to wipe such anxieties from his mind. Letting his head flop back, he studied the sky. Despite the heat, the air was now very clear over the Isle of Ely, the stretched-blue of dusk, and he hoped he could spot the first pinprick of light which was the Evening Star.

Laura came up on deck with a glass of white wine. She put her mobile on the bulwark.

'Still no word,' she said.

She had a crisis. Working for a TV company, thought Dryden, seemed to consist only of crises, as if the theory of creative tension had been elevated into a business plan. In the next episode of *Sky Farm*, Laura and the BBC script-writers had planned to show a demonstration against a land-based wind farm by local villagers trying to stop new giant turbines being added to the existing ones. The scene would show vil-lagers tussling with security guards. The planned action scene, where the mob would tear down a fence and break in, occupying an old abandoned farmhouse close to one of the turbines, was due to be filmed the next day at a spot on the North Norfolk coast near Cromer.

But the company which ran the site, a Nor-wegian multi-national, had not cleared the issue with the trade unions covering its workforce and engineers. Industrial action had been called. The shoot was off, unless the dispute could be settled tonight. Otherwise the series storyline was in

114

tatters. Laura would have to organise a new episode, and get it scripted, or she would have to find an alternative site, preferably one that was non-unionized, and a long way from Cromer.

The mobile buzzed and she grabbed it so fast she nearly dropped it in the river.

She walked to the pointed prow of *PK 122*, talking quickly, acknowledging only that she could hear her caller, and understood what was being said.

The call was brief. 'Disaster,' she said, turning to face what was left of the sunlight. 'Full industrial dispute, no prospect of a deal, so the shoot's off.'

'What do you need?'

She took an inch off the wine in her glass. 'I need a wind farm, in East Anglia, with a farmhouse inside the perimeter, so that we can film scenes with the house amongst the turbines. It took me six months to find this place.' She covered her eyes. Under stress the voice disability was worse, the sharpness of the consonants dulled, so that Dryden had to see her lips to be sure he'd heard her right.

An echo of his own day came back to him. As Humph had driven to Euximoor Drove they'd seen the wind turbines at Coldham's Farm in the distance. Coldham had seventeen turbines, most of them 100-foot plus. He'd driven past a few times – was there a house amongst the turbine shafts?

Dryden had his laptop under his seat and the boats had Wi-Fi. He went to Google and fed in Coldham's Farm. The turbines were run by a company in Cornwall. Their website had a picture gallery. He offered the laptop to Laura.

Fifteen of the turbines were clustered in a three-row 'peloton' at one end of the common. At the edge of the site stood a farmhouse. It wasn't perfect, but even Dryden, who knew little about filming for TV, could see how cameras could be placed to shoot through the forest of turbines and catch the image of the farmhouse.

Laura's eyes bored into the picture on the screen. The outside film shoot had been her idea. If it collapsed it might cost her the job. She was on a six months' probation period which had been described as a 'formality'.

Taking a telephone number off the site, she walked away with her mobile to the prow.

Dryden's laptop chimed to register an incoming email. Vincent Haig, the old sexton's grandson, had sent him an email earlier in the day saying his grandfather was happy for Dryden to take up his case with the Rev. Temple-Wright. So Dryden had sent the vicar an email containing several pertinent questions: principally, why did the church feel it was no longer obliged to keep the promise the former vicar had made: that Albe Haig could live out the last years of his life in the house he knew so well? Here was Temple-Wright's response:

Dryden,
Aren't there more important issues?
Albe Haig has paid a peppercorn rent of £10 A YEAR! Did his grandson mention that? There are plenty of pensioners in the

116

parish paying that A DAY for rented accommodation. The sale of Sexton Cottage will go ahead by auction. I've given the Haig family the date. It's Friday, by the way, the evening land sale at Dacey's in Ely.

I'm not sure Haig's blindness alters much. I would have thought – and this is purely advice, I'm not an expert – that he might be more at home with others sharing his disability. I've attached links to relevant charities in my correspondence with his grandson. In many ways the fact that he's blind makes it all the more important that he moves from the cottage. Technically the insurance position is very disadvantageous for the church. Much better, surely, that he spends his last years in a secure environment.

I'm happy for you to use any of this in a story if you feel you must write one. I can't imagine anyone will be interested.

I've organized an action day for world peace on Sunday; there will be a service at the mobile church at Coldham's Cross at noon. I have no doubt you won't find space for THAT in the paper.

I don't think it's very helpful the press becoming involved in this. It will only raise false hopes. I will speak to Vincent Haig about his grandfather. I'm sure we can help him find the best place available. The church itself has almshouses in Whittlesea. But there is no possibility that I can stop the sale of Sexton Cottage.

Yours, etc.

'I can't imagine anyone will be interested,' Dryden said out loud, shaking his head. He detected weakness in the email. The offer to help find Albe Haig an almshouse was veiled but significant. He'd need to talk to Vincent Haig first thing in the morning. He checked the address on his business card: The Old Forge, Barrowby Drove.

Laura was back. 'Got it,' she said. Her face was a decade younger. 'The company uses a spin-off for maintenance and they're non-union. There's a charge, a couple of grand, but that's birdseed for us. And the farmhouse is currently empty. It's been on the market for rental, has been for three years.' She looked at her glass. 'Refills?'

He was alone when a new email landed. It was from his contact at Welney, the bird expert to whom he'd sent the picture of the Funeral Owl.

Hi. Rare? Very. My last reference for a sighting in UK is 2001. Last sighting in Cambridgeshire was 1903! Great pic. I know you'll ask derivation of the bird's name. Simple – the owl as omen of bad news, principally death. It's more commonly known as the Boreal Owl. If you find a location I'd love to know – obviously we won't alert the twitchers. They'd be down like a flock of starlings.

TWELVE

Wednesday

They were a mile short of Brimstone Hill in Humph's Capri when Dryden finally got through to the West Cambridgeshire Police press office. CID had made thirteen arrests in King's Lynn overnight in connection with the murder of Sima Shuba in the graveyard of Christ Church. Charges were imminent. Dryden still had two days to go before *The Crow* was out, so he just listened to the details and rang off. He'd be able to pick up the story later from the news agencies online.

He tossed the mobile into the glove compartment of the cab.

'That's that,' he said. 'CID have arrested half of Chinatown, King's Lynn. They must have some decent forensic evidence from the scene. Blood, DNA, fingerprints. They'll have lifted something they can take to court. Charges expected later today. So that's a good story dead as a doornail for six months.'

The sun was high already, the day's heat building, despite the fact they had the Capri's windows down.

Dryden fished out Vincent Haig's business card from his wallet. The Rev. Temple-Wright's

119

email had made the church's position on Albe Haig's tied cottage very clear: he needed to find a new home, fast, as the property was being sold by auction this week. Dryden knew he couldn't stop the sale, but he might be able to help swing Albe Haig a decent new home care of the Church of England. All he needed was a few more details off his grandson. And while he was about it he had a job for a picture framer. He rummaged in the door compartment of the cab, extracting half-a-dozen Ordnance Survey maps for the West Fens.

They drove past The Jolly Farmers and turned down Barrowby Drove. A wooden sign for The Old Forge appeared after half a mile. Humph parked the Capri and settled down for a nap with his headphones clamped to his small, round head. Each year the cabbie chose a different, obscure European language to learn off CDs in the Capri. For Christmas he'd buy a cheap ticket to the country in question for a two-week escape from a family Christmas, without family. For that brief period he'd speak the language as best he could. Then he'd forget it and choose a new one. It was typical of him that he sought some measure of fluency in languages that he was hardly ever likely to speak again. This year it was Albanian.

Dryden trudged up the drove, an avenue of shadow thanks to a double wall of poplars which shared a constant stream of whispers. He heard a dog bark and felt his guts tighten. On the list of scenarios he feared this was in his personal top ten: a lonely fen farm, no fences, no gates, and the sound of a mastiff slobbering. He imagined the mouth open, wet and soft, like a red orchid with teeth.

The Old Forge, a wooden barn on stone footings, stood by a single tied cottage; mean, brick-built, with ugly modern PVC windows. Double doors stood open, emitting a chemical smell and the sound of air-pressure venting. The scene inside explained everything: Vincent Haig was using a blowtorch to lift paint off a heavy gilt frame. Not an industrial blowtorch, but a small, delicate hand-held model Dryden thought more suitable for putting a crisp sugar topping on a crème brulée.

But the noise was loud enough for Haig to wear ear protectors, so he hadn't heard Dryden approach. The barn was part workshop, part studio. At the far end stood the original forge, a massive iron range, set in brick, but long cold.

The whole barn was lit by neon, which made the pictures which covered one wall look stark. There was a vast swagger portrait of landed gentry showing a family, with two children cursed by the artist with the faces of adults. Three landscapes, a set perhaps, looked Dutch and were dominated by sky. And half a dozen portraits in heavy dark-wood frames, nineteenth-century Victorian patrons, founders, perhaps, of Cambridge colleges, or fenland workhouses.

The blowtorch died and Haig pushed the ear protectors back. But it wasn't quiet; Star Radio was playing, dominated by the morning-show frenzy of a fast-talking DJ.

Dryden scratched his shoe over the concrete

floor and Haig swung round. He wore goggles, but they were up in his hair. There was something in the startled eyes that was close to fear, before it faded away.

He cut the radio. 'Dryden.'

'Sorry. I have a job I'd like you to look at.' He held up the clutch of Ordnance Survey maps. They had to clear the metal workbench to get all six open and spread out. Then Dryden manoeuvred them until they all matched at the edges. Together they made a single cartographic picture of the West Fens, with Brimstone Hill at the centre.

'It's for the office,' said Dryden, but in truth it was for him, because he saw the world in spatial terms, as if he was sitting at the centre of a compass, in *The Crow*'s office in Brimstone Hill, with the world spread out around him. It made him recall the Mappa Mundi, the ancient map of the known world. That was vaguely round as well, with the lairs of dragons at its edge.

They did a deal: a simple frame, the maps mounted on board, with a thin Perspex cover: thirty-five quid cash.

Haig took a note while a kettle boiled. He spread out the maps again, weighting the corners, and Dryden noticed again the missing fingertip.

'How'd that happen?' he asked, holding up his own fingers.

'Art school. I had an argument with a paper guillotine.'

Dryden winced in sympathy, then switched on his phone and paraphrased the email he'd got

122

from Temple-Wright about Sexton Cottage. 'She won't budge,' he said. 'I'll run a story. I can't stop the sale but she might make an offer to rehouse your grandfather. It's the best I can do. Has she spoken to you?'

'Sure. I think all this stuff about a place in an almshouse is a distraction. She can't promise that, it's not in her gift.' Haig's eyes flooded with what looked like tears. 'Christ. It'll kill him, moving out. Not this year, maybe not next, but it'll kill him. Sure as poison.'

'What're your options?'

'The rich have options,' said Haig. 'We rent this place and the lease controls the number of people we can have. I could try and get it changed. There's a spare room, but we are planning a family, and he knows that, so I don't think he'd come.'

Dryden tried to imagine a partner for Haig but the image wouldn't come.

'There's a council home in Peterborough for the blind. I've got the paperwork in the house.' He looked Dryden in the eye. 'It's down a back street near the ring road. There's a big waste-burning plant planned, that'll be opposite.' He laughed. 'But that's OK – it's a home for the blind.' He shook his head. 'We've looked at other places but he doesn't want to go too far away. There's St Dunstan's at Cromer – he went there for occupational therapy, and they take people on a residential basis.'

He was talking quickly now, and he slurred the word 'Dunstan's' and repeated it.

'I drove him over with Kath. It's brilliant, on a

123

cliff top, best view on the Norfolk coast. And that's right, cos you don't need eyes to feel the space. And if you tell him what's there, paint a picture, he *can* see. He knows what he's lost. But he won't go there. Brimstone Hill is his home. Why should he leave?' He gave Dryden a tin mug of tea. 'So you'll run a story?'

'Yes. I think so. We need to go up the chain of command. I've lobbed in a question to the media desk at Church House in London. Let's see what ripples that creates. They won't comment but they might ask her what the hell's going on. They might even tell her to stop the sale, but as I say, that's a very long shot.'

Smiling and nodding, Haig put his tea down on the workbench beside an etched glass which held a yellow liquid. The contents must have been viscous, because the inch of glass above the level of the liquid was blurred.

Dryden turned away as Haig went to drink from it but he caught the definite edge of alcohol on the air.

The opposite wall to the framed pictures was covered in canvases, unframed, on stretchers, mostly landscapes of the Fens. They were all by the same artist, there was no doubt of that: blocks of colour deliberately using a limited palette, but one perfectly matched to the Fens – russet, and several greens, from iceberg lettuce to leek tops. The skies were extraordinary, each one embellished with violent clouds. The lines in each picture were mathematical, lattice-works of ditches and drains, wind turbines, droves. And in each there was a constant small symbol, like a

124

signature, in one corner or another: the unmistakable shape of Christ Church, in three dimensions, in jet black.

Haig was looking too, his body moving less erratically than when he'd first met Dryden at Sexton Cottage. The shoulders still circled in that wheedling way, but now the motion was oily, almost sensuous. It occurred to Dryden that he might be high, or drunk. It was nine thirty in the morning.

'I work at night – through the night,' said Haig. It was as if he'd answered Dryden's unspoken accusation. He picked up the glass with the yellow liquid and swilled it round before downing it in one swallow.

'These pictures are by you?'

Haig nodded, kept nodding, walking towards the nearest picture until it must have filled his vision. 'They don't sell,' he said.

They talked about art. Haig had been to Ruskin College, Oxford. He'd won a scholarship, from one of the Wisbech grammar schools. And that helped paint *his* picture. A gilded youth, but an under-achiever.

'Now I put frames round other people's work instead,' he said.

He seemed to try and shake himself free of the note of self-pity. 'That's where I met Kath. Ruskin. She did art too, then after graduation she went into graphic design.' He turned towards Dryden and the contempt he clearly felt for that decision actually curled his lip. 'She's out all day. She works for an advertising firm in Peterborough. It's a tough world.'

125

He shrugged, clearly happy to let her struggle with her own life.

'Does that stuff help?' Dryden pointed at the yellow liquid in the etched glass.

'Sure.' He took the glass up and drained a drop, as if daring Dryden to find fault. 'Like I said, I've been up since midnight. I sleep after lunch.'

He reached under the table for a bottle. It had a beautiful label, a yellow woodprint of reeds, exactly the same as the three the coroner had produced in evidence at the inquest into the deaths of Spider Russell and Archie McLeish.

He held it to the neon light. The yellow was, thought Dryden, reminiscent of urine.

'Where'd you get the vodka?' he asked.

Haig's eyes dimmed, literally faded. It was extraordinary but Dryden had an image then of him as a cat, with a translucent third eyelid, which could act like a shutter.

'A gift,' he said, pleased with himself to have found an answer that simply asked more questions.

'Be careful. Bottles like that have been turning up in the West Fens contaminated with methanol and lead. If you drink a lot it's going to make you ill. I mean, really ill.'

The paper-thin confidence in Haig's face bled away. As if to divert attention from his discomfort, he picked up the blowtorch and with a Zippo lighter sparked it back into noisy life.

As Dryden left the barn he noticed an easel by the door, so he paused and eased the dustsheet off a corner to look. It was a shock to find a portrait, not a landscape. Haig's work again, there was no doubt, given the same mathematical style. The picture made Dryden's skin cool in the shock of recognition. A woman, the face made up of colour blocks again, but this time the palette was violent – red, and black, and a kind of sickly pale cream. The eyes reflected the rust-brown background. It was the vicar of Christ Church, Jennifer Temple-Wright. He thought that if Haig had done it from memory then what a dark memory it must be. She held out a hand, palm flat, and on it was a miniature three-dimensional model of Christ Church, Brimstone Hill.

THIRTEEN

The farmhouse was Georgian, its facade as balanced as a beautiful face: four windows, and a fine door under a simple portico. Dryden found it difficult to imagine that it was here, a decade ago, that a man had bled to death in his own kitchen, his hands pinioned to the table top by knives. The crime had a ritualistic flavour which made it hard to imagine it happening anywhere, let alone within this idyllic farmhouse, sheltered by a ring of pines. A vine had recently been cleared from the facade of the house and he could see still the intricate pattern of the leaves, tendrils and branches. There was an original gas lamp over the door, inside of which was a light bulb, which was on, but only just visible in the sunshine. No electric bell was on offer, a sign, he always felt, of old money. There was a knocker, instead, in brass, of the Lincoln Imp.

Dryden rapped twice and turned his back on the door. In the distance, through a gap in the pines where the drive snaked in from the fen, he could see Humph's Capri heading back towards Ely along a bank-top, the cab's long rear aerial making it look like a radio-controlled car, which, in an odd way, it was.

Muriel Calder opened the door with a polite smile lodged in place. PC Stokely Powell had said she was now sixty-eight, but Dryden thought she looked to be in her late fifties. Another victory then, and this time over time itself. She wore a stylish dress in grey, stud earrings in lapis lazuli, and a watch with a tan leather strap.

Dryden showed his press pass and said that he'd spoken to PC Powell and she might be expecting him?

Calder invited him in, but as he crossed the threshold she delivered what sounded like a prepared statement. She'd agreed to help, in fact she *wanted* to help, but she didn't think it would do any good: all this as he followed her down the hall towards the kitchen. She moved with a sinuous elegance, and her footsteps were silent on the polished floorboards.

The house wasn't grand, just comfortable, but with one grandiose feature: a polished wooden staircase, in a hard wood, which rose to a landing, then turned back on itself beneath a large multi-paned window. A red patterned carpet

128

climbed the stairs, held down by brass runners.

There was one portrait on the landing wall, in a military style, of two young men standing in profile together, rifles held vertical. There was a regimental badge in wood mounted above, an Indian elephant, identical to the one on Jock Donovan's tie.

'The Duke of Wellington's Regiment,' said Dryden, making connections, recalling Donovan's haunted recollections of the night he survived the Battle of the Hook.

Muriel Calder came back from the kitchen door to stand beside him. 'Yes. That's very clever of you. They're my brothers; they died when I was very young. Dad had that painted from a photograph.'

'I'm sorry,' said Dryden. 'There's a memorial in the churchyard. They died in Korea?'

Muriel's slender fingers adjusted one of her earrings. 'Yes. They were very young. As I say, I was younger – just a kid. They've rather over-shadowed my life, I'm afraid. Well, that's not fair, is it? Their deaths have, not their lives. I remember them both very clearly. I was their favourite. We played together.'

Dryden noted a display cabinet on the landing. He could see medals, cups and military caps. Also a gun, with a wooden stock, polished so that it drank in the sunlight, and then radiated it back out.

'I met Jock Donovan – he told me the story. The Davenport brothers. That was your maiden name?'

She nodded, studying Dryden's face. 'Yes.

129

There's no one better than Jock to tell that story. How is he? He doesn't visit any more. I think it upsets him. He worked here – did he say? That was immediately after the war when he was trying to get back on his feet. He had problems sleeping, just being still. Nerves were shot, I suppose.

'Mum couldn't hide what she felt. Jock was a reminder of the boys, her boys. That's the curse of the survivor, isn't it? A living token of those who are not here. That must be a terrible burden. So Jock left us in the end, and I don't blame him. And he did well, ran his own business, quite the jet-set entrepreneur.' Her eyes widened in mock surprise. 'Then he came back to retire. I'm glad he did. I'd like to think he feels that he's come home in a way. And he visits the grave every week, which is a comfort really, because I can't. It brings too much back.'

She walked on down the corridor to the kitchen.

Dryden followed her and took a seat at the large old deal table which stood in the middle of the quarry-tiled floor. He tried not to examine the surface of the wood. On the way to the house he'd reasoned that she'd have got rid of the table. Now he'd met Muriel Calder, he thought that wasn't right. He guessed instead that she'd made a point of keeping it, denying the killers who'd broken into her home that day in 1999 an additional victory. So it was still here, old and weathered, a kind of family hearth, and a symbol that she could live with the memory.

He sat down and the moment passed in which

she might have offered him tea.

'Three men killed my husband in this room,' she said.

Dryden tried to say something but the words didn't get past his tongue. For the first time he wondered if this woman's outward serenity was an elegant facade as thin as the one on the house.

'I saw one of them last week. In a car in Brimstone Hill.'

Dryden slipped out his notebook. 'Constable Powell said that back then, after the murder, you couldn't remember anything?' He flipped through the pages, not to find the facts, but to remind her this was for real, that her words would appear in print.

'Would you like a drink?' The way she said it made it clear she meant a *real* drink.

No decent reporter turns down a drink. Alcohol loosens the tongue. And it was noon, so just about acceptable in polite circles.

She uncorked an open bottle of white wine from the fridge. While her back was turned he ran a hand over the table, but stopped when he thought he'd felt a narrow slit-like hole.

'It's not nice out – but shall we?'

So perhaps, for her, the kitchen did still harbour a ghost.

A line of poplars screened the garden on two sides but the third was open to the south. In the far distance he could see the industrial estate on the old airfield at Barrowby, on the edge of Euximoor Fen. Over the fields several kites hung on the wind – two or three were 'hawk' shaped; one looked like a miniature airship with extra-sized

131

owl eyes painted on the fabric. Two or three of the kites trailed tails which fluttered. Dryden strained his ears but he couldn't catch a note of Jock Donovan's mysterious high-pitched wail. He'd promised the old soldier he'd take up the issue but he'd yet to find the time for the call, which made him feel guilty, so he made a promise to himself he'd ring that day.

They sat on metal chairs at a round metal table. Dryden explained that while he'd heard the story of her husband's murder from PC Powell, it would be a great help if she could tell him in her own words.

'It was June the first, nineteen ninety-nine,' she said, sipping the wine. 'The first thing I could recall was the hospital ward at Wisbech. It's still there, isn't it, the General? Dreadful Dickensian place, blackened bricks, and those awful narrow windows. They were ashamed of illness. Or were the patients ashamed of taking charity, perhaps?'

Dryden just held her gaze.

'Yes. Well. I woke up in the hospital but I didn't open my eyes; something told me I shouldn't, that there was something there I would regret seeing. But I felt this hand, holding mine, and I thought it would be Ronald's. That was my husband, Ronald. I just lay there, they said it was for hours, and every time I came round I could feel his hand. Then I heard my son's voice by my ear. He works in Brussels, he's a linguist, and he'd had to fly in to Stansted. He's very clever. I heard the word "Mum". And then he said that Ronald was dead. So I opened my eyes and I was holding his hand. But he'd only just arrived.'

She sipped her wine and let him consider this small miracle. Dryden was trying to assess just how reliable this woman's memory might be. If PC Powell was so interested in the cold case, why didn't he release an official statement? Why use Dryden as a cat's paw? Did Powell doubt her testimony? And then there was his initial suspicion that Powell had conjured up the cold case at precisely the moment when his own performance in tracking down the West Fen illicit still had come under scrutiny.

The wine was very light, almost colourless, crisp and cold.

'It's local,' she said. 'From the vineyard at Ely, the one the monks founded before the Conquest. It's wonderful, isn't it?'

'And that was all you remembered until now?' prompted Dryden.

'Yes. All these years. They, the family, insisted I went to a counsellor. She tried to get me to remember but I couldn't, and to be frank, I didn't want to. I know what happened. They killed Ronald. I asked and they told me how they killed him. I live in the real world. I have accepted that it happened. Why do I need to relive it? I've got on with my life.'

She touched one of the earrings. 'A week ago I was sitting on the bench by the level crossing in town.'

'My son's in the crèche there,' said Dryden, nodding, wondering why she sat on the bench in town. He didn't see her as a gossip. Perhaps it was for the company, or just to see the trains go by, the faces at the windows. Had she, subconsciously, always been searching for that face?

'A goods train came through – there's a lot more now; they've upgraded the line to Ely so they send trains through for Felixstowe and the docks. They're endless. That's an odd illusion I've experienced before, that it's a circular railway, and it's going to go on going past and that eventually I'll start seeing trucks again.'

She sipped at her glass but Dryden noticed the glass was empty.

'The barriers were down and this car drew up. A Ford, I think, small, a bit battered, in blue. There was a driver in the front, a passenger in the back – which is a bit odd, isn't it? Why wasn't he in the passenger seat? I think, while the barrier was down, he was asleep, or resting. Anyway, that's supposition. I wouldn't do very well in the witness box, would I? Let's stick to the facts. He had his eyes closed.' She smiled and Dryden mirrored the facial expression exactly.

'And I knew instantly that it was one of those three men who killed Ronald.'

'But they wore stockings over their heads?'

'Yes. I remember them coming into the house, I've always recalled that bit of what happened, and yes, they wore stockings over their faces. But as soon as I saw this man in the car, with his eyes closed, I saw him in my memory too. It's just a few seconds long, the memory, but very clear. It's like one of those little films on You-Tube. My grandson shows me the funny ones.

Just a clip. And in this clip in my head he's standing in the kitchen alone, my kitchen. I can hear Ronald's voice, but I can't see him. And this man has rolled the stocking up over his face and he's drinking from Ronald's whisky decanter. It was Edinburgh crystal, and he was very fond of it. And this...' Her mouth, for the first time, took on an ugly straight line. 'This lout just drank from the mouth of it. I don't think he could see me. Or at least, at that moment, he wasn't bothered about me. Constable Powell said that according to the case notes when they found me I was on the floor. So perhaps that's where I am in this memory, and it's just a fleeting moment of consciousness. It's not just the sounds. I can smell something, too, iron, like rust. That's the blood, of course, I know that now.'

Dryden wondered if she'd stopped breathing while she relived the memory, because she took a very sharp intake of air which nearly made her cough.

'As I say, I knew, immediately, that it was him. And then the last truck went through, which is always a shock, like the surprise when a noise stops that's been going all day. It only takes a few seconds before the barrier goes up. I think the noise of the all-clear signal, the beeping, woke him up. He opened his eyes and we were looking at each other. One second, then he looked away. The car drove off very quickly, and it got faster because I watched it along the straight past Christ Church and it swerved and clipped the kerb and there was a cloud of dust. So I'm

135

sure, really, that he recognized me too.'

'It must have been frightening,' said Dryden. 'If he did recognize you...'

'He might come back,' she said. 'But I don't think so, do you? It's much simpler to just keep away, which is what he's done, because if I'd seen him once in the last ten years I'd have known, instantly. So he doesn't live here, or work here, or if he does he keeps himself hidden away. I don't think he knew I'd seen him that day in nineteen ninety-nine, so he'd have been oblivious of the danger of being recognized. But he'd still keep away, wouldn't he? That's human nature.'

A dove clattered out of the tree above them.

'I'm not very good at descriptions. I went in to the police station at Peterborough and we tried to make one of those ID pictures, but it was useless.'

'PC Powell said you tried your best.'

'It wasn't good enough,' she said. 'I do recall his expression. He had plump lips. I suppose, in another place and at another time I'd have said he was handsome, but it was a face with something missing. Does that make any kind of sense? He looked lost. Not geographically, but emotionally. That might be daft.' She laughed again. 'Best not mention that.' She poured herself more wine.

'PC Powell did give me some details about the car. There was a sticker, wasn't there, in the rear window? A black dragon, on a white circle, belching red flame. That's unusual, and he thinks that if we get that description out to people,

136

someone is bound to recognize it.'

'Yes, yes, that's true. I'd never seen it before, anywhere. It was quite...' She made a waving action with her hand, '...worn out. As if it had been there a long time and had been rubbed out almost. But I saw it, very clearly. A black dragon.'

She smiled, a carbon copy of all the other smiles she'd given Dryden, and then sipped her Elysian wine. 'Do you know why I'm doing this?' she asked, and something in Dryden didn't want to hear the answer, but he had to shake his head.

'I thought that just for a day, or a week, I could make him feel as anxious as I've felt all these years. Afraid of what might happen next. Afraid of the world, and everything in it. If I can do that, I'll feel that Ronald has been given a little of the justice he deserves.'

FOURTEEN

Dryden was three steps from the door of *The Crow*'s Brimstone Hill office when his phone buzzed with an incoming text.

It was from Laura. *Story at wind farm. Urgent. Bring camera.*

He opened the office, grabbed a set of three old press cameras, and set out for Coldham's Farm. Laura had left home that morning at 5.30 a.m. in

Tano to meet the BBC film crew on site. They'd paid for just one day's access to the site for filming and she was determined the shoot would be a success. Dryden knew her well enough to know she'd have thought carefully before using that key word: *urgent*.

The wind farm lay a mile on the far side of town. Dryden decided to jog the distance, which wasn't too bad once the stitch went and his heartbeat began to flatten out. He was aware that the sensation of blood coursing through his veins was unfamiliar and he made a mental note to do more exercise. One of the downsides of Humph's ability to be on hand with the Capri at almost all hours was that he rarely had to walk anywhere.

Once he'd cleared the old council estate on the edge of Brimstone Hill, the wind farm came into view: seventeen turbines, all over 100 feet high, fifteen in one pattern, two outlying to the south. White, streamlined, strangely alien, Dryden liked them because they reminded him of the windmills he'd played with on the beach as a child, but with the added quality of elegance. The speed of the turning blades was unhurried, unlike the frantic flutter and whiz of the toys. Here the combination of scale and the stately speed was beautiful.

Coldham's was an open site, with each turbine enclosed by a security fence at the base, but with open grassland between them, and a road snaking past from east to west. From half a mile away it was clear something was wrong. He stopped running to massage his stitch and took the opportunity to try and memorise what he could see. The way to write a decent news story when you were short on facts, and you never knew when that might happen, was to take pictures with your eyes. At all costs, remember detail.

Usually all the turbines in a wind farm were angled in precisely the same direction to catch the wind, and most turned at the same gentle pace. But today several were pointing in random directions, half a dozen were motionless despite the wind, and one was revolving at high speed. It was clear that the computer-controlled system which operated the unmanned facility was either malfunctioning or inoperative.

He ran on a further hundred yards and stopped again. Close enough now, he could pick out the sound of that one fast-spinning turbine, the blades slicing through the air. The road that led through the wind farm had been closed off with an emergency barrier. Beyond, parked in a circle like a Wild West wagon train, was the BBC film unit: several caravans, a mobile editing suite, two outside broadcast camera units, a canteen, plus all the cars for the production staff, and a luxury coach, presumably laid on to link the site to the BBC offices in Norwich. It was, almost literally, a media circus.

Dryden's eye found Laura instantly, walking from one of the make-up caravans towards the mobile café. He had that ability, to spot her in a crowd amongst hundreds. He knew her walk, the slight hesitation before each footfall, and the set of the head, chin up, and fixed, never scanning from side to side. Coldham's Farm itself, the old house, was the backdrop to the scene, beyond the turbines. Dryden noticed that the BBC had imported some livestock to bring the landscape alive; a flock of geese were penned in by one of the vans.

A man in a linen suit was walking briskly to meet Dryden as he approached, the thin cloth of the trouser legs flapping furiously in the wind. Occasionally a gust would edge him off the beeline he was making for the reporter, because the wind had picked up, and now they were clear of town, it was strong enough to flatten out the grass in random patches, as if an invisible giant was putting down footprints. There was something about the relaxed shoulders of the approaching figure, the easy smile, the sober suit, that shouted public relations.

'Hi. I'm Dominic Slater, I do press and media for Aeolian.' He nodded at Dryden's cameras. 'Press?'

Laura had filled Dryden in on the background to Aeolian the night before. The company owned several wind farms in the Fens. Its green credentials were impressive. It ran a workers' co-op based in Cornwall, and liaised closely with the RSPB to reduce bird kill in the turbines at sea.

'Problem?' asked Dryden.

'You are?'

'Sorry. Philip Dryden, from *The Crow*.' The light of battle went out of Slater's eyes. Dryden could imagine what he was thinking: local press, small impact, who cares what he writes? Which was why most decent press officers were ex-national newspaper reporters. They knew that Fleet Street relied on people like Dryden, reliable local stringers who could alert them to stories. The good news was that if Slater was stupid enough to think Dryden didn't matter, he'd be off his guard.

The PR spread his arms wide. 'It's early days. We've got technicians on their way, but it looks like we've been targeted by metal thieves. Cables have been lifted, and some bits of machinery in some of the turbines. They've got into eight of them, right up into the gondolas. Just walked in, as well, because the security doors don't seem to have been a problem. Which is a bit worrying.'

Dryden tried to calculate rapidly what this fresh bout of metal theft meant for the inquiry into the murder at Christ Church. If there was a violent gang war going on in the West Fens, then one side still had, apparently, the time and nerve to pick off a wind farm. It was possibly an indication of the cash that they could generate by selling rare metals on the open scrap market. There was another possibility. The raid may have been long planned. The thieves could have decided to strike quickly before moving out of the area. Whoever they were, they weren't amateurs: Slater had made it clear they'd used considerable expertise to get through the turbine security systems.

'What about that one?' asked Dryden, nodding at the turbine now revolving at a speed just short of becoming a blur.

'Yeah. Not sure. They're all fitted with default

safety systems, so that if there's no control they should feather so they don't turn, and there's a braking system, too. But that one's just running wild.'

Dryden had his hands in his pockets but that didn't mean he wouldn't use the quote.

He let Slater talk for a while, got his card and mobile number, and then left him to deal with incoming calls on his phone.

While he was on the site, Dryden thought he'd get a snap of the star of *Sky Farm,* an actor who'd just been nominated for a Bafta for an earlier role in an ITV drama.

But Laura found Dryden first. 'The turbines are bust,' she said.

'I can see. What about the shoot?'

'Fine. We're done. We just lined up the cameras to catch the ones that were working. We're fine.' Dryden could see how the stress was stretching her skin across her cheekbones. 'And we can come back and do a few long shots when it's all fixed.'

'Where's your male lead? I could take a snap.'

Laura led him over and introduced him to the star, whom Dryden didn't recognize. After three minutes Dryden was reminded why he hated interviewing actors. He prided himself on being able to get under an interviewee's skin, to capture something about his subject's real motivation. He always forgot that most actors didn't have a real character, being merely a collection of facades. Having concocted ten good questions, he was exasperated to discover that the actor didn't have one good answer.

He was halfway through a dozen portrait shots with the wind farm in the background when he heard a shout. Everyone turned to look north: the out-of-control turbine was trailing smoke from its gondola. Slater stood at its base, looking up, on a mobile.

Dryden took some still shots, then used his phone to get video footage.

As the first yellow flame appeared, the PR started running. By the time he got to his silky-black BMW the gondola was fully alight. It crossed Dryden's mind that he didn't know what was actually burning – not metal, so what? Perhaps the gondolas were plastic, or fibreglass.

'Can you film it?' he asked Laura. 'I can try with the mobile but the quality's poor.'

The turbine gondola was ablaze now, like a struck match. One of the turbine blades sheared at the base within a minute, falling, a dead weight, less than fifty yards from the turbine shaft. The fire above spurted, like a faulty firework, pieces of machinery flying out, but landing well short of the crowd.

It struck Dryden then that the thieves had made an error of judgement in targeting the wind farm. Their other sources of precious and semi-precious metal were low profile: water pipes, manhole covers, church roofs. This was high impact, visible, and would make the local, if not the national news. The police would respond by rapidly switching resources into hunting them down. Coupled with the murder at Christ Church, it had turned a series of petty thefts into a major news story.

Then a windscreen broke on one of the parked cars beyond the unit. Dryden imagined a nut or bolt, a screw, thrown clear of the revolving hub of the turbine. He grabbed Laura and they ran with the rest of the crew to the perimeter of the farm, two hundred yards upwind of the turbine.

A crewman had brought his gear with him, a hand-held equipoise camera, plus telephoto lens. He set up a tripod and continued filming. One of the two remaining blades sheared and flew downwind, striking the blades of the next turbine and wrapping around it, like a sweet wrapper in the wind.

Laura was watching, fascinated, but smiling. 'I can write this in. It's great stuff.'

'It's an ill-wind...' said Dryden.

Laura shook her head. 'The cynical press.'

The police arrived in the form of PC Powell's blue panda. Dryden borrowed binoculars off one of the crew and focused on the base of the burning turbine. A set of steps led up to a circular gallery, and a single door. Rather than a conventional lock, it had an electronic keypad. So not keys at all but coded numerical passwords, presumably unique to each turbine.

As he tried to focus on the security pad, the door itself blew open, blasted out by the pressure within, and a gout of flame licked out like a dragon's tongue.

FIFTEEN

Dryden left the front door of the office open and took the stairs in sets of two, leaving the inner door ajar. A breeze blew through the window, once he had it propped open, but the heat was still unbearable. He thought he could hear tar bubbling on the flat roof above his head. A thermometer he'd put up on the wall in the heatwave of early summer now read eight-five degrees Fahrenheit, which just made him feel hotter. He stood on a chair so he could catch the breeze in his face. In the distance he could see the stricken wind turbine, smoke trailing away to the south. Its damaged neighbour was motionless, one blade broken.

The landline was ringing but he ignored it.

Switching on the laptop, he found BBC News 24. And there it was: Turbine 13, Coldham's Farm, burning like a giant sparkler. The TV crew had got the footage straight to the newsroom in Norwich via Wi-Fi, and from there it had gone national in minutes. Which was why his landline was ringing.

The BBC would sell on the footage. The media world was dominated by an insatiable demand for moving pictures. He imagined people watching it in some deadbeat Midwest town, or a South African township, or a petrol station in the outback. The BBC would sell words, too, a 'fat caption' as it was called in the trade. But Dryden could provide more: he'd collected quotes out at the site. And he could write in a reference to the metal thieves and the murder hunt, all of which added to the picture's media shelf-life. He needed to bash it all out and get it to the Press Association, the main UK-based wire service, making sure they credited *The Crow.* Brimstone Hill was always going to be world famous for a day. This was that day.

He cut the ringing phone and rang out, clipping on headphones so he could lean back in his chair.

Vee Hilgay picked up on the first ring in *The Crow*'s main office in Ely. 'Hi,' she said. 'Philip. You're famous. Well – Brimstone Hill is. I didn't call because I knew you'd be out there.' She was the only person left in the world who called him Philip, other than Laura.

They talked through the newslist for the Friday edition. By the end of the week there was every chance there would be charges in the Christ Church murder case, so that would give them a lead story, even if it was dry as dust due to legal restrictions on what they could print.

'Let's build up the whole metal theft story, the wider picture,' said Dryden. 'Anything you've got, let me have. If a nut and bolt goes missing, chuck it in. We need to throw the story forward. Check out other wind farms in the area. There's that huge one out towards Chatteris – ring them. Then there's the pylons. Do they ever get target-

146

ed? Ring the power companies for me, will you – increased security around pylons, et cetera, risk of death. You know the score.

'There's one thing on this story we might have over the competition,' he went on. 'The thieves got the doors open on the turbines without forcing them. They're controlled by security touchpads, a numerical square, ten numbers, two symbols, I think. So that suggests this might be an inside job, or at the very least it suggests they had someone on the inside. Let's keep that to ourselves. The police might withhold that, too, while they check the staff, suppliers, security guards. Let's keep our fingers crossed.'

He heard Vee scratching out a note and reminded himself she'd only been a journalist for just over eight months. He should slow down, give her time, let her learn.

He took a deep breath and tried to release the stress in his neck. 'This time next week we'll be desperate for stuff, so anything that can keep – keep.'

But there were some stories that had to run. The coroner's warning on the illicit moonshine being top of the list. All the competition would run with it, and it was right on their doorstep: *hell*, it *was* their doorstep.

'One other thing,' said Vee. 'A child's gone missing from the Cromwell.'

The Cromwell was one of Ely's two comprehensives: a big, brutal, concrete campus on the far side of the ring road. Dryden had done a story there only a week earlier on a sixth former winning a national maths competition – a story he'd got off Humph, who'd heard it from Grace, who was in the same school.

'All a bit weird,' said Vee. 'And sad. I don't know if you'll want this in the paper.'

Dryden's spirits flagged. While Vee had taken to the trade of journalism with alacrity, she was never going to develop the necessary mindset that went with it – not cynicism exactly, but a kind of brutal scepticism. If she felt it was worth telling Dryden the story, it was worth putting in the paper.

'He got into one of the chemistry labs,' continued Vee. 'I rang the head and it seems the boy was a scholar. Head was willing to talk, but off the record. He was studying chemistry, maths and double maths. Apparently he just wrote in chemical symbols all day. Brilliant with it, predicted A-star grades across the board. Reading between the lines, he had personality issues. Anyway, he applied for Cambridge and they turned him down after interview. Head says *he* wasn't surprised. On the other hand the boy was devastated.'

'What did he do?'

'Made himself a cocktail. Barium and tonic. Mixed it up himself after stealing the key to the fume cupboard. Then he sat down and wrote emails to his parents, friends, a girl. Left them on his laptop screen filed under LAST MESSAGES. Then he drank the barium. The cleaning woman found him, unconscious, and when she sat him up he vomited the poison. He was carried off to the sick bay while they got a doctor in. When they got back he was gone.'

'Shit. Name?'

'Julian Amhurst. But everyone called him Stinks, because of the chemistry. Children, they don't really have that much imagination, do they? Everyone's really worried he'll try again. The head told the school assembly that they were looking for him and everyone was worried. So they're all looking. Parents have split up, by the way – the boy lives with the mother in Ely and the father's out your way. Welney Reach.'

Dryden had done a Golden Wedding there, a hamlet of half-a-dozen interwar houses, with bank-top views of Ely.

There was something in Vee's tone of voice which suggested Julian's plight had affected her personally. 'Are you OK with this, Vee? I can write it.'

'No, no. Sorry, I knew the family years ago. Julian's dad was in the Labour Party. He used to bring him to meetings and he'd play on the floor while we talked nonsense about trade union rights. I suspect the interest in politics was a cover for a lack of interest in being at home with Julian's mum. The child was just obsessed with whatever he had: Meccano, Lego. I suppose that's the root of numbers – shapes. A nice, pre-dictable, safe world to escape to.'

'Is there a picture?' asked Dryden.

'From the school magazine, in a white coat. He's smiling, of course – why is that? The tragic ones are always smiling.'

'OK. Here's what we do, Vee. Boil it down to one par, no more, but put it on the front with the picture. Don't mention the suicide attempt, just

149

plain missing teenager, parents worried, et cetera. Get Josie to blow up the face so we can see him.'

Dryden thought of what the kid must have been through to drink barium, to actually feel the poison flowing down his throat. The sun shone in through the window of his office, and a brimstone fluttered into the room. Somehow it gave Dryden hope. He thought of young Julian out on the fen, perhaps, battling with demons. The wandering scholar.

He had an idea. 'And add this, Vee – *The Crow* will pay one hundred pounds to any reader assisting police to find Julian Amhurst. Cash.'

Sometimes, he thought, it was fun being editor.

SIXTEEN

Humph parked the Capri on the verge 100 yards beyond the school. The cabbie had a packed lunch which he picked up every day from the Brimstone Café: full English breakfast bap, a pork pie, an avocado pear, and a packet of cheese and onion crisps with a pickled egg in it – a fen delicacy. Lunchtime for Humph was three o'clock, allowing time for two (occasionally three) breakfasts in the run-up to the midday meal. He had a thermos which the café staff filled for him with the soup of the day. Today it was cabbage and kale, so he'd given it to Dryden. Eating inside the cab, Humph left only the passenger-side window open, as the wind was still blowing a hot gale.

The cabbie had parked facing directly west so that they had a clear view of the seventeen turbines of Coldham's Farm, now effectively reduced to fifteen. A thin wisp of smoke still rose from the stump of the burnt-out turbine. Humph had expressed the hope, having missed the blaze, that it might spread to the others. But they were all now stationary, locked still, blades feathered to offer no resistance to the wind. So the cabbie put a draughts board on the passenger seat and set out the counters, remembering precisely the latest position in the game he was playing with Grace. A game he was losing.

Dryden sat on the hood of the cab, partly blocking Humph's view. He swigged from a bottle of water. The laptop on his knees was set at an angle so that he could see the screen. He'd managed to do a quick bit of research on agricultural kites, the object of Jock Donovan's noise complaint. He'd promised himself he'd make that call to the kite factory at Barrowby Drove. It wasn't the biggest story on his list but it was only Wednesday. He had time, especially for an old soldier.

And there was something about the story, or rather Jock Donovan, which intrigued him. He'd once written a piece for the daily paper in York about noise pollution which had helped get him the job on *The News*, on Fleet Street. The paper had printed a stream of complaints from residents in a certain area of the city known as

151

Huntington Road about a mysterious night-time noise which became known as the 'Huntington Hum'. The usual suspects had all been set aside: power lines, local businesses, aircraft. Then they'd got the Department for the Environment in to do a study. Dryden had been given a sneak preview of the final report, which concluded that the problem wasn't a noise at all, but the *lack* of noise.

York was just too quiet. No motorways, no twenty-four-hour factories, no all-night clubs or bars, no high-rise buildings brimming with heating systems, no multi-storey car parks, no subways, no all-night transport. After midnight it was pretty much devoid of noise. So there was no background sound at all, no so-called 'white noise', to drown out deep-rooted vibrations that in most towns and cities nobody ever heard: water mains, power lines, the river flowing, a single HGV on a distant road.

The real fascination for Dryden had been the psychological factors identified in the report. The authors had reviewed the science on human hearing. Once the brain found a noise, it could lock on to it like a self-tuning radio, then amplify it, so that the victim's mind became a giant receiver, a dish taking incoming signals. A large minority of those suffering from tinnitus, for example, were simply amplifying their own body noises: blood flowing, the heart beating. It terrified Dryden, the discovery that you could bring that nightmare upon yourself. So much for the sound of silence.

He had sympathy for Jock Donovan whichever

way the story played out: either he was being tormented by a real noise, or his brain was searching out some tiny, insignificant sound and then relaying it back to his over-sensitive brain. Or, perhaps the worst outcome of all – he had tinnitus. Which meant he had a noise in his head which would torment him forever.

Agricultural kites were, according to his twenty minutes of online research, big business. Fact: a kite in the shape of a hawk keeps pigeons and other birds off the fields. The government estimate for bird damage to UK crops was £450m a year. Several high-tech companies were trying to develop kites that would stay up in very low wind speeds. Mostly kites were silent, but those with 'tails' did flutter. The biggest operator was Helikites, specializing in kites built round small helium balloons. The company on Barrowby Airfield was a newcomer, a Cambridge Silicon Fen spin-off called Silent Hawk.

Clearly, for Jock Donovan, not silent enough.

Dryden looked up. Above him, a hundred feet high, was a kite. Hawk-shaped, silent, almost stationary. One in the field to the north had several 'tails', each one twisting, emitting a crackling like fire. That wasn't Donovan's problem: he could live with the tail fluttering, it was the high-pitched wailing call that was robbing him of sleep.

Whatever their sonic qualities, there was little doubt the kites worked. The field on the far side of the road was weedless, studded with lines of green shoots, salad crops just appearing. There

153

wasn't a real bird in sight.

There was a landline number on the Silent Hawk website, plus a mobile number and an email address. Dryden ran into a message service on the landline, so he switched to the mobile. A man answered and Dryden said quickly he was press, and that he was following up a complaint of noise pollution. There was a pause, then: 'I'm Doctor James Barnard. I'm in charge of research and development. The kites are silent, Mr Dryden. A few have the tails which crackle, but that's supposed to happen.'

'I know. The man who's complaining is fine with the tails. As I said, it's a high-pitched note that's the problem. And I admit it is a note I can't hear. I'm about a couple of miles away from your unit on Barrowby Drove and there are lots of kites flying and they're silent. But Mr Donovan isn't making it up – at least I don't believe he is. I think he may be picking up a specific high-frequency noise from another source. But it is causing him a lot of distress. He's an old soldier, from the Korean War, and I said I'd help. It would give him some peace of mind to rule the kites out.'

Dr Barnard asked Dryden to write a letter or send an email. He added that the fluttering tail noise came from some experimental kites and would not be a long-term feature of Silent Hawk's test programme. Dryden got the impression Dr Barnard wasn't listening very carefully to what was being said.

'The fluttering isn't the problem. This is a high-pitched, intermittent, but regular call.'

154

'Well, that's not possible,' said Dr Barnard, which was an interesting response. Not *impossible*.

'He's highly sensitive to noise,' offered Dryden.

'That's interesting.'

'Why?'

'We do have experimental kites aloft at the moment which emit a noise pitched well beyond the range of human hearing – hence our brand name, Silent Hawk. That's our USP: we scare birds with a silent noise. It's designed to mimic the call of several raptors. But as I say, it's not audible to humans.'

'Mr Donovan's from Scotland, not Alpha Centauri. He can hear something, believe me.'

'How far away from Barrowby Airfield does he live?'

'Just under two miles, according to my OS map. But that's from the factory unit, and some of the kites are much nearer.'

Dryden could hear paperwork being shuffled. 'We've had no complaints from anyone else in Brimstone Hill.'

Again, he'd moved on from the possible/impossible issue, without actually addressing it.

'The kites are silent,' repeated Dr Barnard.

'Mr Donovan lives in the large art deco house near Christ Church. Perhaps you know it?' That was a detail which would work in his favour, thought Dryden, because it implied Donovan had money, and influence, and couldn't just be dismissed. Most of all, it meant he could afford a lawyer. 'I can't just ignore him,' said Dryden.

155

'I'll probably do a story. I thought it was only fair to touch base.'

Dryden heard a slight inhalation. It was an effective tactic, telling people the story was inevitable, giving them the stark choice between being part of that story or being part of the follow-up.

'Look,' said Dr Barnard. 'I'm out at Barrowby now on a regular site visit. We could test fly a few of the kites and see if he can pick out the experimental ones, the ones emitting the ultra-sound call. He won't, which will prove my point. But I'm willing to give him the chance.'

Dryden checked his watch: 'OK. Well, I'm here, you're there. If he's about, then why not now?'

Dr Barnard said yes, but that he'd have to contact Silent Hawk's owners in Cambridge, although he was ninety-nine per cent certain they'd be relaxed about a test. It was an issue, it needed dealing with. They were either *Silent Hawk* or they weren't. If there were any problems he'd text Dryden, but otherwise he'd expect him at Barrowby Airfield within the hour.

Humph tapped on the windscreen and offered him another cup of the cabbage and kale soup. It was hot, tasted of iron, and made Dryden feel instantly nourished.

He rang Jock Donovan. According to one of Dryden's OS maps, there was a footpath to Barrowby Airfield from the back of Donovan's house. They could walk there together. Dryden didn't give him time to make any other arrangement, because he wanted to see where he lived.

156

He said he'd be round in thirty minutes and cut the line.

Dryden scanned the horizon and watched the smoke rising from the gutted wind turbine, catching the wind. It made him think of a battlefield and of Donovan's traumatic time as a rifleman in Korea. He tapped 'Battle of the Hook' into Google on the laptop.

What had Donovan called it: the Forgotten War? The casualty figures made Dryden's skin go cold even under the baking sky: 180,000 dead on the UN side, up to 750,000 Russians, Chinese and North Koreans, plus more than two million civilians. It occurred to Dryden just how bitter he'd be if he'd fought in such a war and come home to find that hardly anyone knew it had been waged. It seemed to be a war without a timeslot, buried somewhere in the pages of modern history. His disorientation only increased when he found a description of the battle on a military history site. It sounded like the First World War: trenches, artillery bombardments, hand-to-hand fighting. The 'Dukes' had repelled a force five times superior in numbers during the battle. They were given the battle honour: *The Hook*. He thought of Jock Donovan's mundane description of what he could recall of the battle. The 5,000 shells that had rained down on his section of the front line. And the realization that came with the dawn: *I was the only one alive.*

SEVENTEEN

Brimstone House was alabaster white, a curved wing with long Crittall windows, and a two-storey central entrance with tapering vertical lines which reminded Dryden of an Odeon cinema. The paintwork around windows and doors and along a balcony rail was a very light green. The garden, full of flowering bushes, stood in relief against the building itself. Over the door was the name of the house, stencilled in the concrete, with the date: 1931.

Donovan was at the door before Dryden got up the path. 'Come through. Excuse, you know, the mess. I live alone.'

The hallway, wooden floored, ran straight ahead. The amount of light funnelling down and through the house was blinding. There was nothing on the white walls, nothing on the floors; no rugs, no carpets.

They passed two rooms off the hall. Both were almost entirely devoid of furniture, but both had obvious practical uses. One was a toilet, all steel and enamel, with a bidet. The second was an office: one desk, a wide-screen computer, a printer, and a clock which appeared to show the time in New York, London and Sydney. Dryden saw the word ORIENTO in blue letters on the face. And under that word in smaller letters: Established 1962.

The main room had a sofa, a flat-screen TV, and speakers. Floor-to-ceiling windows looked out across the Fens.

'I watch sport,' said Donovan, as if he needed to explain the presence of anything in the house that wasn't wall or floorboard. 'I've got Sky One, Two, Three and Four. The disc is on the roof but you can't see it from the street. The council wouldn't let me put it up anywhere on the front because the house is listed. Grade two.'

'It's quite something,' said Dryden. 'I've never seen so much light indoors.'

'I like space. I've lived a lot in Japan, Korea, with work. They do the light thing really well, but we're rubbish. Dark and dingy, that's our forte.'

The main wall held a single picture, a photograph of an eastern city full of pagodas and lakes, Buddhas and intricate willow-pattern bridges, all in a startling Technicolor photograph.

'Kyongju,' said Donovan. The twisted syllables seemed to fall easily from his mouth. 'They call it the museum without walls. South Korea's a great country. Great people.'

'You visited the city in the war?'

'There was a battle there, fighting on the outskirts. We were held in reserve miles back, so we didn't see any action. I've been back many times, always for work. It's an incredible city. You been?' Donovan didn't wait for an answer to his question. There was a boot room at the back of the house and he led the way in.

'You didn't say what kind of work you did,' said Dryden, as Donovan selected a pair of heavy shoes, then a hat.

'Just business,' he said. 'You do what you know. I picked up some Korean in the war, so I built on that. I can speak the language pretty well now. So: I was in trade, import export. Boring, really. Too boring to talk about.'

The boot room was ultra-modern, more in keeping with the Chelsea-on-Sea set of the north Norfolk coast than the Fens. Wooden benches, a shower-room, lots of expensive outdoor wear, a rack of binoculars. This room, of all those he'd seen, felt lived-in.

The house itself wasn't a surprise to Dryden; it was the fact that it was the house of a man who must be nearly eighty years of age. Because what was missing was the past – his past, any hint that he'd accrued objects, or mementoes, or tokens; anything that might spark a memory.

'I spend most of my time out. Walking. Watching. The skics are good,' said Donovan, standing, a hand to the small of his back.

The garden was all grass and mowed in those neat alternate strips which drove Dryden to despair, as if someone had some demented scheme to tame nature. He wondered if that was why Donovan liked the Fens, because it was man-made, and appeared to be a mathematical landscape.

They set off along a well-worn path. It was two miles to the old airfield and the industrial units at Barrowby Airfield where Silent Hawk had its factory. It took them forty minutes, zigzagging over the fields, quickly finding themselves under some of the flying kites.

They reached a rare fen stile where the old man stopped. He took the step up and listened. 'I can hear it, the noise. Actually, it's not bad here. Less piercing than usual. But it's there. Can you hear it?'

Dryden shook his head.

'I remembered something, too – that I'd heard something like it before. When I was a kid in Glasgow we had a doctor come to the school. Like the nurse that looked for nits, but more scary. They had a machine for testing hearing. They played these notes into your ear and you had to say what you could hear. He'd start low, then gradually rise. In the end there'd be just these tiny, high-pitched, fleeting notes. It's just like one of those notes. One of the top ones, almost beyond range.'

Donovan strode ahead until they got close to the old airfield. The water tower was still standing, and the ruin of the control tower. Access to the site was by an old road which ran off the airfield, crossing the Twenty-Foot Drain by a low humped bridge. At the junction with the road there was a set of automated barriers.

The old runway was just close-cropped grass until you got to the concrete apron where they'd built the industrial units, six of them, each with a roll-up door, single storey, with a long aluminium roof which radiated heat, so that the air above buckled as if gently simmering.

The kite maker's was the first unit, marked by

161

an outline of a hawk on the roll-up door. Outside the next were parked four old grey Rovers, one of them up on blocks. At the far end from Silent Hawk there was a unit with a butter-yellow painted door and a large white van parked alongside. The noise of machinery running came from inside, and a complex sound of glass tinkling, like a milk float.

The roll-up door of Silent Hawk rose to the sound of an electric motor. Inside they could see steel racking, kits packed into shelves, spools of guideline on the wall.

A man Dryden presumed to be Dr James Barnard came out to meet them. He didn't look like a scientist, or more accurately, he didn't look like the scientist who'd spoken to Dryden on the phone. He was in his twenties, wearing designer shorts and a T-shirt which said 'CAPTURE THE WIND' and featured a picture of a kite which looked like a cross between a zeppelin and a giant jet engine.

Barnard did the small talk well, thanking Donovan for his time, Dryden for making contact. 'A lot of journalists wouldn't have bothered. I appreciate it.'

Which was bullshit, thought Dryden, because he'd never met a journalist who wouldn't have rung the company to get their side of the story. They might not have printed their side of the story, but they'd have rung.

'OK. A quick test, Mr Donovan,' said Barnard. 'If you're ready.'

Donovan hadn't said a word but he gave Barnard his Scottish eyebrow. 'They make a noise,

162

your kites. Like a squeaky trolley wheel. I can hear it now.'

Barnard held up both hands as if for silence. 'I'm not saying you don't hear *something*. But we need to do the science. So I've set up an experiment. There are eight kites flying in the far field, do you see? The field by the road.' He turned on his heel and pointed along the access road, over the bridge, towards the B-road which ran between Brimstone Hill and Wisbech. 'I've lowered all the rest we're testing today. One of these eight kites emits an intermittent high-pitched ultrasound note inaudible to humans.' He smiled at Donovan. 'The field is dry and there's no crop on it at the moment, so it's OK to wander around. If you can hear this noise, try and identify which kite is responsible, and count the interval between the pulses of sound. None of them have crackling tails – so there should be no confusion.' He smiled again, even more broadly this time.

'The noise is excruciating,' said Donovan. 'It's not a joke. I made a complaint to you, by phone, and email. I got nothing back. I've been in business most of my life. Treating the public like that isn't very smart. Or very nice.'

Barnard had the decency to blush slightly under his academic tan. 'Yes. Sorry about that. You're right, we haven't covered ourselves in glory, have we? We do get complaints about the fluttering noise with the tail models. Our people in Cambridge must have assumed it was that which was making the noise. I'm sorry.' Barnard made himself stand up straight. 'We're all sorry.'

163

'Let's do this,' said Donovan, setting off.

They walked with him to the bridge. Dryden was surprised by the size of the Twenty-Foot Drain beneath. Sunk between banks, it held a large, flat-bottomed Dutch barge, moored to one bank. The boat looked abandoned, but Dryden noticed a fresh oil stain on the water surface seeping from the engine cowling, and in the half-open wheelhouse a bright red plastic thermos flask. The bridge gave them ten feet of height in a flat landscape, so that suddenly they could see for miles.

Barnard looked east towards Coldham's Farm. 'Quite a show earlier on the wind farm, flames and everything.'

'I know. I was there.' Dryden gave him a quick run-down on the story. Barnard said he'd have to get security checked on the lock-up.

'Who's in the other units?' asked Dryden.

'Number two's a garage. Owner specializes in Rovers, as you can see, but he's only open weekends, rest of the time he works for one of the petrol companies on a forecourt. Number three is storage – I think. But I never see anyone. Number four's empty. So is number five. Number six is Barrowby Oilseed; they make oil from rapeseed. It's the new olive oil.'

Barnard laughed, shaking his head, as if it couldn't happen. But there were several rapeseed oil producers on the Fens, Dryden knew, including one near Ely which had carved itself a niche in the 'extra virgin' market.

They heard a door slam, and looking back saw two men come out of the back of the Barrowby

Oilseed unit and get in the white van. A minute later they swept past, taking the bridge at speed, both driver and passenger looking the other way.

'Friendly,' said Dryden.

'They're OK. I guess they're trying to make a living like everyone else.'

Donovan watched the van pull out and drive away, as focused as a hawk himself. Then he completed one more round of the field under the kites and marched back to the bridge.

He brought his shoes together as if coming to attention. 'Eight kites,' he said. 'From your left – one, two, three and four along the road, then five, six, seven and eight. It's number three.' He pointed back. 'Hawk shape, black and brown. Pulses are every three seconds.'

'That's not possible,' said Barnard, visibly shocked.

'Why not?' asked Dryden.

Barnard's shoulders slumped. 'That's the one, the experimental model. It emits a note every three and a half seconds. No one should be able to hear it.'

'I can,' said Donovan.

Barnard looked at his shoes. 'Yes. Sorry. It appears that you can, Mr Donovan.' He wiped a hand across his lips. 'We'll have to do more tests. There's a chance you got it right by accident, a fluke, a coincidence. It would be bad science not to check. But there's not much doubt, is there? The real question is, how rare are *you*? We need to know why you can hear it.'

'The real question, if you don't mind me saying, is when can I get some peace?' said

165

Donovan.

They talked it through inside the unit. Barnard set up an electric fan and gave them coffee and biscuits, then made Donovan an offer on behalf of Silent Hawk. They'd pay him to do a series of tests once they'd modified the sonics on the kite. Fifty pounds an hour was the lab rate for volunteers. They'd pay for an audiologist from Addenbrooke's Hospital at Cambridge to test Donovan's ears. In the meantime, they'd take the kite down.

And there was a deal for Dryden, too. If he'd hold off on the story until they had the test results, he could have all the details on an exclusive basis. Given the logjam with news on *The Crow*, this was, for Dryden, the perfect outcome. He swapped business cards with Barnard and said he'd call in a week.

Dryden said he'd walk Donovan back to his house. As they passed the industrial units they saw a man outside Barrowby Oilseed smoking a cigarette: central casting east European, with a full stubble set, a shaved head, and at his feet a small fighting dog, one of that breed which seems muscle-bound to the point of being unable to walk. Inside they could hear the machinery running, a bottling plant, presumably, for the Fens' answer to olive oil. The man chain-lit a new cigarette and looked at Dryden, not at him at all, but through him: a genuine thousand-yard stare.

EIGHTEEN

Humph picked Dryden up at *The Crow*'s office in Brimstone Hill at five. The reporter had collected his son from the crèche and installed him now in the child seat in the back of the Capri. Then he got in the front and asked the question he was determined to keep asking until he got a satisfactory answer: 'How's Grace?'

'Fine.' Humph pretended to monitor a car behind them in the rear-view mirror as they swung past Christ Church and up the Ely Road towards The Jolly Farmers.

'Seen her today then?'

'Sure. We played draughts out on the lawn. Three games. Her mum's agreed to a couple more days at her nan's. She'll have to go to school, but I can ferry her in and out. And she can go back at weekends if she wants.'

'What did you talk about?'

'Stuff. The dog mainly. She's smitten.'

Dryden checked Eden. The child was already asleep, his lips creating a perfect rosebud.

'You could just ask her why she ran away from home,' he said. 'Tell her you don't believe it's just about the stepfather, or the stepsisters and stepbrothers. That she can tell you anything she likes and that you'll still love her.'

167

Humph nodded. 'Eden walking yet?'

'No, not yet. If the crèche thought there was a problem they'd say something, right?'

They'd reached the T-junction by the pub. Humph swung the cab left towards Ely, the distant silhouette of the cathedral appearing on the horizon dead ahead.

'I'm not worried,' said Dryden. 'Laura's not worried. He'll walk when he's ready.'

Dryden opened up his laptop bag and pulled out the black-and-white print of the Funeral Owl which had been sent in by an anonymous reader. The Boreal Owl had been haunting him: it was an omen of death, but he'd been sent the picture *after* he'd found the body of Sima Shuba hanging from the cross in Christ Church graveyard. He couldn't dislodge the anxiety that this owl presaged another death.

If he could publish the picture perhaps he could exorcise the omen.

The OS maps were still in the door compartment and it took him just a few seconds to find his destination.

'Detour,' he announced. 'Next left down Second Drove.'

The black-and-white print clearly showed a hedgerow beyond the owl, and set amongst the hawthorn a road sign reading THIRD DROVE. This area was known locally as 'the Droves'; a mathematical network of dirt lanes numbered one to six from east to west, seven to ten from north to south. They found the sign six hundred yards from a junction by a telephone box.

Humph didn't say a word once he'd brought

168

the cab to a stop. He just closed his eyes and pitched his seat back into the reclining position. Dryden wondered, fleetingly, if the cabbie was missing Boudicca. Leaving the dog with Grace had been a kindness she would probably never appreciate.

Dryden winched himself out of the Capri, wincing at the familiar screech of the rusted hinges of the passenger-side door. Beside the sign for Third Drove was the entrance to a field, left to rough pasture, scattered with the burnt marks of old fires, scrap metal hauled into one corner, with a set of Portaloos in another. A sign on the gate said it was the Euximoor Fen Travellers' Site.

It was midsummer, so most of the travellers were out on the road, leaving just one caravan. Dryden knew the routine: this would be home to a single family left behind to keep the plot for the rest. And not so much a caravan as a silver and white mobile home, nestling in the lee of a hedge, curtains drawn, a small awning over the door, with three steps up made of loose bricks.

Had he imagined a single dog bark? It released a flood of adrenaline into his bloodstream. That was the problem with travellers' sites: the absence of dog leads.

He thought about the picture he'd been sent of the owl: it was a fine piece of camera work, sharp, of stunning quality. He could do with it in the paper – not this week perhaps, but next. But it needed a proper caption. It was hardly pro-fessional to use it with the limp addition of 'photo by a local reader'. If it was that rare a sighting, one of the national papers would demand more words, and if his reply was that he hadn't spoken to the photographer they'd think he was a hack from the sticks. Which was the last thing he was, or wanted to become.

So he squared his shoulders and walked across the field towards the mobile home, trying not to think about dogs. There was still no sight of the standard travellers' Alsatian, but he'd never been on a site without one. So where was it? Its absence was infinitely more terrifying than its presence. He had time to imagine what it would look like. There was one variation to the Alsatian norm; a sleek Doberman, perhaps, with fur like a slug's skin.

Within the mobile home he could see a high shelf, china on display, and a spotless stainless-steel galley. There was a large bookcase but no novels; just textbooks and pamphlets. He could read two spines: *Frozen Planet* and *A History of the Crusades*.

To one side of the caravan was a brick bar-becue, the ashes of a fire and a table upon which had been left a single dirty plate, smeared with ketchup. Beside it were some sheets of paper covered in numbers, split into four-digit groups.

'Who are you?'

He swung round and would have looked at the face of the young man if he hadn't been holding a dog lead.

'Where's the dog?' asked Dryden.

The man nodded across the field to a gap in the hedge. The dog was on a long rope attached to a fence post. A Doberman, with canines visible,

170

and a lolling tongue.

'Who are you?' The question was repeated in exactly the same tone of voice. Dryden got the fleeting impression that the young man didn't know he'd asked already, and that he might just go on asking in the same monotone voice until he got an answer.

'Philip Dryden. With *The Crow*, the local newspaper.'

'*Corvus Corvidae.*'

'Sorry?'

'The crow. That's the family, the genus. A lot of crows are a murder.'

'Someone sent me a wonderful picture of an owl. That was you, then?'

Dryden realized that he'd subconsciously altered his speech pattern and vocabulary to match that of a child. The man before him was at least twenty-five, maybe thirty. Cheap jeans, an old checked shirt, binoculars around his neck that must be worth around £1,000. Dark hair, almost handsome, with full lips. He had one of those home-made haircuts that looks as though it's been stolen from someone else's head.

'I don't want my name in the paper.'

'That's OK. I just wanted to ask when you took the picture, and have you seen the bird again?'

'Promise about the name?'

'I promise.'

The young man waited.

'I promise not to put your name in the paper,' said Dryden. 'We can just say a local ornithologist, how's that? But perhaps I can give your name to the bird experts at Welney? And a number. They're keen to try and see the owl. And I need a few details about the sighting.'

'The eighth of August, seventeen-thirty hours. By the fence. No. Not again. I've looked, all night once, but no. Is that it?'

'Just your name to pass to Welney, not for the paper.'

'Brinks is the name.' He ran a hand back through his hair. 'Will.' He had a strangely immobile face, but Dryden got the very strong impression that his mind was racing, computing, trying to solve some arcane puzzle. He glanced down once at the numbers written on the sheets of paper. 'Just Will Brinks.'

'The experts are very excited. They said the last time one had been seen in this region was a century ago. So well done.'

'Everyone calls me Brinks. I talk to other people who like birds. On this.' He slipped a mobile out of his pocket: an iPhone, in a green case. He gave Dryden the number.

Everyone? Dryden looked round the empty field.

'In winter there's twenty units,' said Brinks. 'They're on the road now. My stepdad, he keeps birds of prey. Raptors.'

'That's the word, is it? For birds of prey?'

'Yes. But that isn't why I said it. It's what my dad's business is called: Raptors. They do a show. My half-brothers, my sister, they all help. They hire the birds out too. But I don't do that. I stay here, because it's my job to stay here.'

'Did he teach you about birds, your dad?'

'Stepdad. Yes. I haven't been to school. I can't

172

read. Not because it's difficult, but because I can't.'

Dryden turned to go.

'They leave me here to look after the field.'

'You said.'

Nobody moved.

'Have you seen the new kites?' said Dryden. 'They're shaped like raptors too.'

'I can tell the difference very easily between the fake ones and the real ones,' said Brinks. 'A hundred yards away, five hundred even. No problem. They move too much, they don't feather their wings, so they don't hold their hunting position. It's a giveaway. That's what Dad says, and he's right.'

Dryden went to speak but his question had somehow unleashed Brinks' voice.

'They're getting better, the kites. In the old days we used to do it, scare birds, with our hawks. It was well paid, and in cash, no banks or chequcs or nothing. That's where the business started. Now, we can't compete. But we're better, just ask a farmer. It's that people won't pay for quality any more, will they?'

The last sentence was delivered with a different cadence and Dryden guessed he was copying his absent stepfather.

'I should go now, let you get on. But I need to get past the dog,' added Dryden. 'That rope is very long.'

Brinks looked at the dog and smiled. There was something innocent in the man's face, but something cruel as well; which was, after all, a childlike combination. Brinks walked over and

173

pulled the dog in on the rope.

'What's his name?' called Dryden.

'Lolly. It's our word for money.'

'Mine, too,' said Dryden.

Dryden was going to try for another quote about birds but he could see that Brinks' anxiety levels had risen sharply. He was visibly shaking, the loose hand not holding the lead turning back and forth on the wrist.

'Thanks,' Dryden said. 'Picture should be in next Friday's paper. Not this week. I could drop one by.'

Brinks wouldn't meet his eye. 'Don't bother, thank you. Don't.'

So Dryden went, the fear making his own hackles rise.

NINETEEN

Thursday

Dryden had a dream riddled with images of the Funeral Owl. He was walking by the river, and it was *his* river, south of Ely, although he'd been overcome by the sense that he'd never been on the path before. It was both somewhere that didn't exist, and also the most familiar place in his memory: a bend in the river, slow and to the left, and then a pool overhung with willow trees. The pool, and the grotto, were dominated by colour, although he knew that in dreams you don't see colour. He sensed a deep green, a mixture of water reed and shadow. And inside the depths of the shadows there was the owl, on a branch, looking out at him. Yellow eyes, slow blinking, and drawing him in despite the effort he was making not to walk that way on the towpath, but to turn round and walk away. He'd lift a foot and go to set it down as if to turn back, only to find that in its downward fall the foot would be drawn round, and back, towards the waiting owl.

The dream, at least this remembered sequence of it, had begun in the sunlight. A brimstone butterfly darted above the cowslips. Each step took Dryden further into the shadow, the green-black, cool, shadow, and into an almost under-water world beneath the willows. Briefly, he found himself in a dappled place between the sun and the shadow, but then the light and heat were gone, and he was in the grotto, alone with the owl. From the outside the green-black world under the willow had been impenetrable, but now he could see the surface of the river turning slowly in a circle where the pool had worn away the bank. On the surface was a reflection of the owl on its branch. His eyes penetrated beneath the surface and he discerned the shape of a pike, hung in the water, holding its position in the current as precisely as a hawk in the sky. And beneath the pike a hubcap, still silver, glinting dully. And a sudden shoal of tiddlers, synchronized, moving as one in a three-dimensional design of layers and rows.

And then he saw Grace's face: Humph's

175

daughter, the white flesh somehow lit within.

He screamed in his sleep. But the muscles of his face wouldn't respond and he couldn't wake himself out of the nightmare. She lay on the muddy bottom of the river, eyes closed, tinted green.

He seemed to get closer without moving his feet. Closer; falling down towards the face, through the water but not feeling its touch, until he was very close, and the whole of her face filled his vision. And at the last moment, just before their faces touched, she opened her eyes, and they were the eyes of the owl.

And then her lips moved and she said one word: 'ORIENTO.'

He screamed, and this time the muscles did work, so that he was jolted awake and heard an echo of his shout in the narrowboat cabin where he lay.

'Go back to sleep, it's just a dream. It's not real,' said Laura, finding his head with one hand and laying the palm of it across his forehead.

He got up instead and climbed into the small outside cabin area. In summer he always kept a small gas stove here, so he lit the flame and boiled water in the kettle, standing by it to make sure the whistle didn't sound.

It was an hour before sunrise and there would have been light in the sky but for a deep mist. There were few trees out here at Barham's Dock, no willows, no riverside pool possible, because the river ran between high man-made banks, so that the water was above the fields. There was no echo here of his dream, but the image lingered, and he shivered as he made his tea.

Flipping open his laptop, he took comfort from the blue glow. He conjured up a memory of the clock in Jock Donovan's house, over his desk, the word ORIENTO printed in light blue script: stylish, vague in a way that suggested concealment. He should have checked it out before. He fed the word into Google but got nothing intelligible. So he wrote an email to a friend who had worked with him on *The News* and moved on to the *Financial Times*:

Clay,

Hi. A favour. I'm writing a story and a company has come up – at least I think it's a company. The name is ORIENTO and it was established in 1962. If you need to go to a company search I'm happy to pay the fee. Sorry to call in a favour without prior notice. Hope all is well.

Dryden

PS I need it quick.

He sent it, and listened for the bong that signalled it had flown into the ether. Perched in the bow of the narrowboat, he looked north towards Ely. The effect of the featureless mist, the straight line of the near bank, the oily, motionless water, was to play tricks with the eye, which searched for something, anything, upon which to fix. He found himself at the centre of a grey world, and the feeling of floating within it made him feel nauseous.

Then he heard a voice. A word was said,

something banal, like 'plastic'.

A figure appeared almost immediately, on the far bank, swishing a stick through the grass, rhythmically. A policeman, caped, like one of the Korean heroes, with a peaked cap.

And then an identical figure on his side of the river.

A burst of radio static confirmed the identification, as another sound intruded on the landscape: an outboard motor. It sounded as if the boat was downstream coming up, but Dryden knew that the mist was a bizarre and baffling reflector of noise. And then it appeared, to prove him right, upstream going down. A rubber rescue craft, two divers aboard, ten to fifteen knots, leaving a wide V-shaped wake.

The boat went past. Dryden stepped off the narrowboat and walked quickly along the dockside to the junction with the river. He must have loomed out of the phlegm-coloured mist, because the policeman jumped.

'Jesus. Where did you come from?'

Dryden laughed and they heard dogs barking. 'I live here,' he answered, by way of explanation. 'I couldn't sleep. You'll need to go in along the dock, there's a footbridge.'

'Thanks. You're awake early. Hear something?'

'No. Just your boat. What's up?'

This policeman was cap-less and had black hair which was saturated with tiny drops of mist. He shook his head, like a dog, and water flew off. 'Just routine,' he lied.

Dryden knew they didn't search the riverbanks, or the river itself, as routine. 'You're looking for the missing boy – Julian Amhurst?'

'Why would it be him, sir? Did you know him?'

'No, no. I'm a reporter. *The Crow*. I remembered the name.' He looked at the river. 'He tried to kill himself once. It's only logical that you might think he'd try again...'

'And you've seen nothing?'

'No.'

'Good. No news is good news,' he said, delighted at the joke, in a cruel way. 'If you do see anything, ring us, please. Right away.'

'Do they know why he tried to kill himself? Drinking poison is a bit more than a cry for help.' Dryden was determined not to be intimidated. It was one of the police methods he despised the most, this inference, that if you weren't with them, trying to save the desperate life of young Julian, then in some malign way you were against them, obstructing justice.

'I suppose that's private,' said the copper, putting a cap on at last.

'This isn't very private is it, dragging the river?'

'We're not dragging it. Sir.'

And then he was gone.

Dryden followed him over the wooden bridge across the dock and looked down into the water. There was more light now. He could see green weed and looked away before he could conjure up the white face of his nightmare.

TWENTY

Dryden sat behind the editor's desk in the main newsroom of *The Crow* in Ely. Through the open bay window he could hear the sound of market day. The West Tower of the cathedral was just visible over the shop roofs opposite, circled by wheeling crows. A man who always played the accordion under the arch which led to the shopping precinct struck up 'Alexander's Ragtime Band'. He had a repertoire of two tunes. One was 'Alexander's Ragtime Band', the other was not, but was otherwise unrecognizable.

Dryden's editorial staff sat at their desks, and for the first time he was struck by the fact they were all women, and that he'd chosen each for the job. Vee, chief reporter, led them through the newslist. She wore her reading glasses on little coloured threads which looped from behind her ears. Her T-shirt called for TROOPS OUT. Between each expert summary of an item, she sipped at a cup of tea.

It was a first-class newslist.

SPLASH: murder at Brimstone Hill. Police throw dragnet over Lynn Chinatown.
LINK TO TURBINE EXPLODES: metal

180

thieves steal cables and start blaze at Coldham's Farm.

BYPASS LATEST: county council faces
mass demo over plans for flyover close to
cathedral.

ELY TEENAGER MISSING: latest on
search for Julian Amhurst.

DUST STORM: picture special (on front for
West Fen edition).

Miriam Barkham, junior reporter, took notes.
She was that rarity, a sexy nerd. She'd picked up
three A-levels in maths, computing, and physics
and she'd built *The Crow* a website in less than
two weeks. Miriam was one of those people who
always feels hot. Dryden's degree had been in
geography and he'd been taught how to estimate
cloud coverage in an open sky in terms of
eighths: so 8/8 was overcast, 0/8 a perfect summer's day. He always judged what Miriam was
wearing, or rather what she wasn't wearing, in
the same way: today was 2/8 – shorts, a midriff-
revealing top, and sandals, one kicked off.

Josie Evans, photographer, completed the
staff. Josie had sent in pictures to *The Crow* for
use on the sports page since the age of eleven;
mainly football and rugby, under the name Jo
Evans. Her work was first rate because she
understood the golden rule of press photo-
graphy: get close, then get closer. She was well
built, just short of solid. A long line of boy-
friends were referred to only by the name of
their favoured football club. She'd gone out with
Norwich for a year, but he'd just been dumped

181

for Fulham.

Vee Hilgay finished her run-down on the stories for that week's paper. It was still only Thursday, so nobody wanted to set anything in stone, but Dryden thought it was important that they all knew what was planned.

Miriam had a wide-screen iMac on her desk and she called up the website to talk them through the digital edition. All the stories would go up on the website on Friday night, giving the actual newspaper several hours' advantage. So the *first* edition you could read was always the paper one – a bonus for those prepared to pay the cover price: the loyal, if dwindling, readership.

'A reader out beyond Brimstone sent us a link to some video of the storm,' said Miriam. 'So I've put the link in. Plus all your pictures. And a link to the Met Office and the NFU site.'

She listed websites, using the exotic codes of the internet as casually as Dryden used words. She then hit a series of keystrokes without looking at her laptop and wheeled it round so they could see a 'hit' counter on the site for last week's paper. Total: 263,567. More keystrokes. Week 13 – 21,450. *The Crow* only sold 17,500 copies. The website was the future, even if it made Dryden weep for the days of hot metal and newsprint.

'I'm gonna tweet on the missing boy, description only,' added Miriam. 'We'll use the Facebook site for the fêtes this week: Wilburton, Isleham and Little Thetford. Nice pics. That should work.'

'Talking of pictures,' said Dryden. 'Josie?'

'This for the front,' she said. 'Best I could get off your phone. I've increased the contrast and cleared up some of the pixel wash and all the colour is artificial, but then all colour is.'

It was the Coldham's Farm turbine alight, in colour. A bright flame, the white turbine, a blue sky. It looked sharp as a pin.

'Terrific. OK, we'll go with that. And the splash?'

Josie had a set of black-and-white stills taken in Christ Church graveyard. The best showed the body bag being carried past the headstones of the dead.

'That's it,' said Dryden. 'So for Ely we'll take the churchyard with the splash, a pocket version of the wind-farm turbine in the masthead, and the storm on page three. Great stuff. For Brimstone Hill and the West Fens we'll stick with the splash, but use a nice big pic of the dust storm. The bypass story can go inside. Right, I'm out of here.'

It was all over. The only scheduled meeting of the week and only one rule was sacrosanct: that it had to be over in under twenty minutes. That was one of the great things about being a newspaper editor. It was like being captain of a ship. You were a dictator, never questioned. Dryden's career had shown him good editors at close range, and bad ones. Good ones took decisions fast – lots of them, even if a percentage were wrong.

TWENTY-ONE

Humph had the Capri bowling along the Fen Motorway beside the Forty Foot Drain heading for Brimstone Hill when they hit a traffic jam. The memory of Dryden driving the cab along the same terrifying stretch of road seemed to belong to another life. The cab came to a stop behind an HGV, brake lights flashing, at the tail-end of a line which seemed to stretch ahead unbroken towards the village of Ramsey Forty Foot; the water on one side, the open fen fields on the other. Dryden, keen to get back on his patch and check in with the police on the murder inquiry, was in no mood to sit and swelter on a back road for hours. Jumping out, he ran down the side of the lorry to the cab at the front.

The window was down, revealing the driver wreathed in cigarette smoke and tattoos.

'What's up?' Dryden asked, realizing only then that he was talking to a woman.

'Level crossing gates are down at Ramsey, have been for twenty minutes. So, no idea. If I could turn round I would.' She lit a fresh cigarette from the butt of the last, which she lobbed out the window.

Humph, anxious to spend an hour with Grace while Dryden worked, had a better idea than sitting tight in a line of traffic. They'd been stationary for seven or eight minutes and not a single vehicle had come past them the other way. So he pulled out on to the right-hand carriageway and hit sixty, then seventy, making the junction in a minute.

The road was now clear to Brimstone Hill, but across country, towards the western horizon, Dryden could see a goods train, a big one, standing still. He counted fifty wagons before he gave up.

His mobile buzzed with an incoming email. The sender was the Rev. Temple-Wright.

Dryden,

Busy week. Made busier by your unnecessary inquiry about Sexton Cottage to the press office at Church House, Lambeth. They simply passed it on to me. So back to square one. You know what I think.

So, can we move on?

A story. You'll hear gossip because the church is going to be locked, so you might as well know the facts.

Christ Church was named for two oil paintings which hung in the nave. Copies of originals by the Italian master Masaccio. One was taken down about fifteen years ago, by which time it was disfigured by damp. It sat in the vestry until Christmas this year when the church council agreed to destroy it, although we sold the frame. The remaining picture – The Crucifixion – is insured for £1,000. The insurance premiums are an annual drain on our meagre resources. And

185

the damp is getting to it. I asked Conways, the auctioneers, to see if we could put the picture up for sale. They did some preparatory work, and someone came to have a look, and they now inform me that there is a small chance – well, a very small chance – that the picture is original. Clearly, this is the opinion of their local expert only. They are prepared to take on the costs of having the picture taken down for a proper examination in London in their laboratory. (I think this tells us all we need to know about what they think of their local expert!) Apparently they have an Italian agent and he's over next month. So they will rope him in as well. They'll also cover the short-term insurance cover to the tune of £100,000 as long as they can write it off against their fee if the picture is genuine and they sell it. I have taken the precaution of having the church locked at all times until the painting is taken away. Albe Haig at Sexton Cottage has a key in case anyone wants access for prayer. I haven't given this to anyone else. I'd be grateful if you could delay publication for a week. That way, by the time the paper is out the picture will be gone. Perhaps you could make that clear.

Can I pre-empt one question? This makes no difference to my decision on Sexton Cottage. The church estate must be rationalised. We can do so much of real VALUE in the community with the cash liberated from the sales.

Best, etc.

They were passing Christ Church. Dryden let his eyes play on the brickwork, baking in the sun, and thought of Christ on the Cross within. Opposite was Jock Donovan's snow-white house. The sun, low now in the sky, glinted off the rounded corner windows.

Humph hit the brakes and they executed an unnecessary skid, coming to rest at the tail of another line of cars going nowhere. Dryden got out and strolled forward. A goods train was stationary on the level crossing, blocking the road. A group of drivers had gathered by the lowered barrier. They seemed to agree that there had been a derailment.

The goods train had come through at just before four o'clock. One of the HGV drivers said he always counted the wagons through and that he'd got to sixty-three when there was a screeching noise from the wheels and the train's speed diminished rapidly; another ten wagons went past, but then the whole thing ground to a halt.

Dryden looked down the track and could see the line of trucks bending away from him so that the distant engine was out of sight. Each truck was identical – a hopper, emblazoned with the word HARDCORE. Paper stickers on the truck nearest to Dryden carried a series of numbers and the word FELIXSTOWE. The train had been stationary for an hour and was emitting heat, and that distinct aroma of baking metal and paint.

Dryden ducked under the barrier, climbed over

the couplings between two trucks, and reached the far side. Now he could see the engine, a half-mile distant; the long curve of the stranded trucks revealed to the eye. In the mid-distance he could see three men in Day-Glo jackets beside a series of trucks which appeared to be tilting over, angled away, out of the curve, about to tip from the embankment, but held in place by the wagons coupled on either side.

Dryden jogged to join them, trying to keep his footing on the gravel.

'Stop there,' said one of them, when he was fifty feet away. 'It's dangerous. One of these goes over it could take the rest with it.'

'Local paper,' said Dryden. 'Just wondered what had happened? A word?'

One of the two men who hadn't shouted walked forward to meet him.

As he picked his way over the gravel Dryden saw the rail beneath the nearest truck had shifted about three feet out, so that the wheels were sunk in the stones.

'Derailed?' asked Dryden.

'My name's Henderson. You are?' He had a suit beneath the Day-Glo jacket.

'Philip Dryden, editor of *The Crow*, Ely.'

'Right. I'm chief engineer for Railtrack Peterborough. Nothing on the record – OK?'

'Sure. I just need to know what's happening.'

'Some oik's nicked the holding pins. Half a mile of 'em. Hundreds missing. Maybe a thousand.'

'Metal pins? So thieves, then?'

'Yes – metal thieves, again. Usually they target

188

signal boxes, points and stations. But the holding pins are steel. Worth bugger all unless you go for bulk. You know what they say, if it's not nailed down ... Well, this time they were nailed down, and they've nicked them anyway.'

'Anyone hurt?'

'Nope. But it's a mess.'

'How long till the track's open, and the road?'

Henderson rubbed a hand over his face. 'I'd be amazed if we're clear in a week.'

'A *week*?'

Anger flashed in Henderson's eyes. 'Well. You work the fucker out.' He spread his arms out to encompass the stranded train.

'Fair point,' said Dryden, stepping back, trying to look sympathetic. He'd always found that just shutting up was as good a tactic as any when people were under stress.

Henderson actually gritted his teeth. 'We can't just uncouple the train into three sections because then these trucks in the middle will spill over and then we'll have to drag them back up a ten-foot embankment. We'll need to get some heavy gear in to lift them off the rails. Problem is we're in the middle of a field of sodding cabbages...'

'It's kohlrabi,' said Dryden.

Dryden never heard Henderson's reply.

He was looking directly west. Living in the Fens, surrounded by US airbases and military hardware, he'd often imagined the worst: a nuclear strike, perhaps, or an accident in a bomb bay. He'd see the sudden ripping light, a horizontal glare, like a crack in the sky, and then the mushroom cloud appearing like a watermark from hell. It would be the last thing he'd ever see. No time, even, to run to the crèche. So now his body reacted instantly: his pulse raced, his breath held.

Light travels faster than sound so he'd seen that first: a very bright yellow flame on the horizon, and it had a very precise shape, which stayed on his retina. It formed a narrow vertical bar, like the letter I. And then the yellow turned red, with just a flash of purple between, like some bizarre set of traffic lights from a nightmare.

Then the shock hit him. Not an explosion at all. Not even a proper sound, but simply the sound waves, hitting his eardrums. It was the noise that a pressure cylinder would make as the gauge hits DANGER, just a second before it blows. It was the sound of splitting, as if the fabric of something metallic had been torn in two.

The blast actually knocked him down, in a kind of slow-motion collapse. It wasn't so much the force of the explosion as the surprise of it. Everything was glacial for that few seconds. Everything seemed inevitable, and inescapable, as if they were all trapped in the moment.

When Dryden got to his feet he was deaf, which confused him as he'd heard no bang, and there was blood running from a gash in his cords. He started to walk towards one of the other men, but his knees went. Henderson had kept his feet and was shouting, his mouth distorted but producing no sound.

They were all looking back to where they'd seen the explosion. Henderson took out his mobile. One of the other men was taking pictures with an iPhone. The point of fire had gone. In the sky, over Barrowby Airfield, there was a single black cloud shaped like an exclamation mark. Dryden's ears switched back on and he heard alarms: car alarms, fire alarms, the school bell, and, intermittent, but distinctive, the bell of Christ Church itself, ringing out a ragged tocsin.

TWENTY-TWO

Dryden ran because it was a kind of release, a way to turn the fear into movement, and dissipate the tension. The air was still ringing with bells and klaxons. On the horizon the strange, black, vertical cloud still hung over Barrowby Airfield.

Humph had brought the Capri forward to the level crossing barriers on the wrong side of the road, executing a swift U-turn, so that he was ready to escape the traffic. The passenger-side door was open.

'What is it?' said the cabbie, already accelerating away.

'No idea.' Voices still sounded odd, so Dryden tried to pop his ears, swallowing hard. 'Something over on the old airfield, an explosion. Maybe fuel? Could that be it? A long-forgotten dump for aviation fuel? Or petrol stored in the unit that renovated cars?

'I felt it through the tyres, the shock,' said Humph. 'Barrowby's two miles away. That's one hell of a bang.'

As they took the sharp bend by Christ Church the random sound of the bell grew louder. Dryden looked up and saw it still swinging wildly in its small brick arch on the roof. Opposite, outside Brimstone House, Jock Donovan stood in the road, his hands pressed to his ears.

Somewhere they heard a fire engine siren, but it was behind them, beyond the level crossing, and Dryden realized they'd be trapped there and that they'd have to drive back, taking the long way round to Barrowby Airfield.

The cab took the T-junction by The Jolly Farmers at fifty mph. The entrance barriers to Barrowby Airfield were up.

When Humph killed the engine there was total silence. Not a bird, not a grasshopper, not a bee. It was as if the landscape was in shock. The airfield itself, usually dotted with rabbits, was deserted. Not even a butterfly moved. Not even a brimstone.

There had been no sound, and now there was no smoke. It was as if the force of the blast had blown out the fire. But the location of the explosion was obvious. The roll-up door to Barrowby Oilseed's industrial unit was buckled but still in place; the roof, low-pitched corrugated iron, was twisted and blackened, revealing rafters of charred timber. Fifty yards away the large white van lay on its side, wheels towards the blast, but the paintwork untouched.

There was something moving on the ground, in front of the burnt-out lock-up.

Dryden ran to the spot and knelt by the head of a man who lay spreadeagled, face down, on the concrete. Most of his clothes had been blown off, leaving him with torn boxers, a sleeve of a shirt and a single shoe. An odd detail, the laces were undone. In one hand he still held a dog lead. The other, naked foot trembled slightly, and the man's hands were clawing at the concrete, but only slowly, as if in a dream. His white skin was dotted with tattoos.

Dryden turned him on to his back. It was Will Brinks, the man who'd photographed the Funeral Owl. Dryden had last seen him standing in the travellers' field at Third Drove with a dog on the lead. Now he kept shaking his head as if trying to dislodge something in an ear. Then he went to scream, his mouth stretching wide.

'There's an ambulance coming,' said Dryden quickly, holding the young man's head in his hands, a palm to each cheek. Brinks watched his lips but didn't seem to understand. Dryden was horrified to see a thin trickle of bright red blood leave the corner of his mouth.

Humph arrived. 'Ambulance is at Coldham's Cross. It'll be a minute, maybe five. The derailment's screwed up the roads.'

The cabbie held a plastic bottle of water but he didn't offer it because he was looking around Brinks' body, his mouth hanging open.

'Jesus,' he said. There were fifty-pound notes everywhere. If the wind had been the slightest zephyr they'd have been gone. But they just lay there, as if pinned to the dry grass. Dryden thought then how odd it was, that the wind had gone, as if the blast had blown it out too, like a candle.

Dryden picked up one note: it was crisp, flat, new issue.

He took the bottle from Humph and pressed it to Brinks' lips but the water just brimmed over his chin.

Brinks seemed to pass out then, laying his head back on the concrete, his eyes shut. The blast had revealed parts of his skin that were usually covered up, and turning him over Dryden had noted bird tattoos: owls, eagles, hawks. But the most daring had been the long-necked swan in flight on his back, which stretched from his left hip up until the outstretched bill reached his hairline, the only inch of design that would have shown if he'd been clothed.

Dryden left Humph pressing the bottle to Brinks' lips and walked away to the Barrowby Oilseed lock-up.

Ten feet from the metal roll-up door he could feel the heat and smell ash. He had to lift the side door to the lock-up off its buckled hinges to get it open a few inches. If there was someone inside could they have survived? He pulled the door out with his full weight and it fell down, so that he had to stand quickly aside. Waiting a moment for the ash to settle, he stepped into a strange, viscous darkness like velvet. Something kept brushing his skin and he dabbed at it, realizing it was ash in the air.

He stood for a moment waiting for his eyes to penetrate the scene, with the help of a little light creeping in through the burnt rafters. The first thing that materialized was a stretch of black concrete wall which seemed to sparkle like quartz. Touching the surface, running his fingers back and forth, he looked at traces of blood on the tips. His blood. The wall was embedded with tiny shards of shattered glass.

A metal bench ran down the middle of the unit with machinery on top: iron, aluminium, steel. But all of it was partly melted, even the table itself, sagging and distorted. Dryden could feel the heat now, still radiating, almost burning his skin, and when he held a hand near the edge of the table, just an inch away, he had to whip it back as the pain pulsed in his arm.

He walked to the back wall of the unit and looked up. There was a small gap in the ruptured roof so that he could see sky framed by wooden rafters, each of which was charcoal black, and smoking very slightly. Light was fading from the clouds above, the sunset approaching. Under his feet the broken glass was a foot deep, a silica snowdrift, sucking in the light, so that the rest of the room seemed darker.

One more step and he was on the far side of the bench.

Two things happened quickly, in surreal succession. First he was blinded by a direct ray of sunlight. There must have been a hole in the metal roll-up door, because the setting sun was shining straight into his eyes from the west; the light beam, unbroken, was like a searchlight seeking him out. It was the last few seconds of the day, concentrated like a laser beam, preternaturally bright.

He put up a hand to block it out and then he saw what was on the floor at his feet: a scene from the museum at Pompeii. Three bodies, frozen in melodramatic poses on the floor: one leaning back against the wall, a hand up to shield his eyes, echoing Dryden; another, back turned, hunched forward so that the head was between the knees; the third flat out, arms straight up as if about to enter the water in an Olympic dive. Each one frozen stiff, as if in black ice.

Each was dead. Of that there was not a doubt.

Where he could see skin it was charred, ridged like wood which has smouldered all night in the grate. There were clothes but it was difficult to see where they ended and the skin began. The brunt of the heat had caught their faces, at least the two faces he could see. Flesh had burnt away leaving full sets of teeth, the incisors too long, stretching down where they should have been veiled by lips and cheeks. He looked for eyes but there were none. The Olympic diver had his mouth open; jaw-breakingly wide, and Dryden saw that he had no throat.

He could feel adrenaline in his blood and realized he hadn't breathed since he'd seen them. A second? A minute? At that his knees buckled and he knelt in the glass, ignoring the pain. One breath wasn't enough; he tried to suck in another, then another, but nothing seemed to fill his lungs. The slimmest strand of smoke rose from the victim with his hand up before his face.

196

It circled the victim's fingers as if he was smoking the butt end of an unseen cigarette.

Dryden's vision buckled and he had to reach out for the edge of the bench and only remembered at the last second not to grip its red-hot surface so that he fell sideways, under the bench, into more glass. Scrabbling in the glass, he felt panic rising in his throat. His feet, kicking out, made no noise, even though he felt them striking the wall, and the metal stanchions of the workbench.

Then two hands, gloved, stiff, grasped him under the armpits and dragged him away, out through the door, his feet trailing, into the evening light. Air rushed into his lungs as if there had been none inside the lock-up. Sweet air, unblemished by the sickly smell.

He must have passed out, because when he came round a fire officer was beside him, kneeling on the grass, his face sooty where the visor had not protected it. His name was Bevan, a senior officer from Ely. A walkie-talkie cackled in his front pocket.

Dryden's head was supported on a rolled-up blanket. He guessed Humph had given them the dog rug from the back of the Capri because it smelt of Boudicca.

A paramedic appeared and gave Dryden a sweet drink in a bottle.

'Sorry,' said Dryden. 'I went in. I thought someone might be alive.'

Bevan nodded. 'Me too.'

'I saw the explosion. It didn't make a noise. And the smoke just stopped, like it was a bomb.

197

And...'

Bevan put a hand on his shoulder to stop the words. 'It *was* a bomb,' he said. 'Sort of. The perfect explosion, like your Christmas pudding. All the fuel is used up in the ignition, there's nothing left for the sound. That's what the bang is, the energy left over after the explosion. There was nothing left after this one; well, very little. As I said, the perfect blast.'

'The oil, they made oil, from rapeseed?' asked Dryden, trying to sit up.

'Not in there they didn't.'

The fireman offered him an empty bottle to sniff. The yellow label showed reeds in a woodcut design.

'Best fuel in the world,' said Bevan. 'One-hundred-and-twenty per cent proof alcohol. It's moonshine. Once the fumes build up to more than three per cent of the air by volume, it can just explode. Delicious, I'm sure, but lethal.'

Dryden saw only the back-stretched corpse, the throat burnt away.

TWENTY-THREE

By midnight the old airfield was floodlit, a ring of scene-of-crime lamps around the industrial units, a helicopter circling above with a searchlight. The intensity of the beam was blinding, so that the distant fen beyond looked featureless and bleak. Emergency vehicles, including a set of vans from the police forensic unit at Wisbech, a single fire engine, a brace of police squad cars, and several CID estates, were dotted around the old runway. The judder of a digital printer came from a mobile incident room. The fire engine was drawing water from the Twenty Foot, two hoses snaking off behind the lock-ups.

The whole site had been sealed off. A TV crew was at the barrier gates, and a clutch of reporters, but no statement had been issued beyond a terse 100 words on a single sheet of A4 handed round by a uniformed PC. They'd given Dryden a copy: four victims, three dead, one in intensive care at Wisbech Hospital, an ongoing investigation. Nothing more. A second helicopter appeared, a commercial one, with a camera fixed in the open door. It was quickly grounded, according to the medic who kept checking on Dryden's condition, in order to leave the airspace clear for emergency services.

The three bodies had been taken away at ten o'clock. Forensic officers had completed the *in situ* examination of the corpses; Dryden watched them bring the victims out of the side door. A detail haunted him: the body bags had hinted at the stiff death poses within – one almost a ball, one the fully stretched diver, another triangular, perhaps the kneeling man, shielding his eyes. It was as if he could see through the mask of the black material to what lay beneath.

The medic who tended Dryden told him the survivor was gravely ill. Both of his lungs had collapsed, and he referred to him – twice – in the past tense, which indicated that the professionals didn't expect him to last the night. The shock wave had also broken three ribs, dislocated a shoulder, and ruptured his spleen.

'Does that hurt?' asked Dryden, and was relieved to see the medic smile. He could only imagine what it had been like. He'd felt the shock wave two miles away. Will Brinks had been fifty yards from the explosion.

Dryden's own condition was curious. He'd suffered shock, and a brief period of unconsciousness, which had left him elated and desperately tired, so that intermittently he would wake up, to discover he'd been asleep. His eyelids were scratchy and painful. While he tried hard to arrange his thoughts in a logical sequence, nothing quite seemed to make sense. He noted with a strange objectivity that the little finger on his left hand was vibrating like a tuning fork. Every time he thought about the scene inside the lockup he felt his throat constrict.

A uniformed constable gave him a blanket and asked him to stay at the scene to give a statement. Dryden told the constable he knew the name of the man who was in intensive care, and his address, but he was told to include that in the statement. A somewhat obvious instruction. Dryden added that the man had a dog, and had been holding the lead. It was, he thought, a mongrel, but mainly Doberman Pinscher.

The constable left him with a renewed instruction to stay put. They gave him a folding chair to sit on. He felt like an idiot, sitting wrapped in a blanket, bathed in halogen lights. But sticking around was what he wanted to do; because this was where the story was. Three dead, one dying, made an exploding wind turbine look like an outbreak of fly-tipping, even if the fatal blast proved to be an accident. Soon it would be mid-night, press day would dawn, and *The Crow* would have the inside story.

A familiar figure dragged a lame foot towards him across the grass. DI George Friday carried two cups of coffee in plastic beakers.

'Accident, then?' asked Dryden. 'It's a still, right? For making alcohol?'

Friday put the coffee cups down on the grass and sank his hands deep in his raincoat pockets. Dryden guessed that he wasn't allowed to smoke at a crime scene, which was unlikely to improve his mood. 'You've seen the statement. Forensics will take twenty-four hours. I'm going to wait for the results; I suggest you do the same.' Friday studied the reporter's face. 'And I'd look after yourself. You've had a shock. You look like death warmed up.'

Dryden searched in his pocket and produced one of the fifty-pound notes they'd found near the body of Will Brinks. 'You better have this.'

'It's touch and go whether our survivor will make it, by the way,' said Friday. 'Nasty internal injuries.'

'The kid's called Brinks – Will Brinks,' said Dryden. 'Lives over on the travellers' site at Third Drove.'

'Who?'

'The survivor.'

'Christ.' Friday flapped his arms inside his

raincoat. 'We've spent the last hour trying to get something off what's left of his wallet. Why didn't you fucking well tell us you knew who he was?'

'I did. I told the constable who asked me to stick around and give a statement.'

Friday threw his head back, looking up at the stars, which had started to pop out in the sky. He kept that pose for about thirty seconds and Dryden guessed he was counting, slowly, trying to keep his temper in check, his anxiety levels under control.

'Anything *else*?' he asked eventually.

'Strange kid. Learning difficulties, maybe Asperger's, but I'm no expert. A keen bird-watcher. The travellers left him behind each summer to look after the site on Third Drove while they went off flogging stuff. Maybe they sold one-hundred-and-twenty per cent proof vodka on their travels? That would work.'

Friday patted his raincoat against his thighs. 'Anything *else*?'

He was joking, but the smile fell off his face as Dryden stood. 'Yes. But I need to show you. In there.' Nodding at the burnt out lock-up, he felt something tighten in his throat. It was the last place on earth he wanted to see again. It was the first circle of hell.

For a moment Dryden's world spun round in a circle and he thought he was going to keel over.

Friday stepped in and took his arm: 'Steady, soldier. It can wait.'

'No, it can't. Believe me.'

It took ten minutes to get clearance from the

forensic team, and then get togged out in the forensic overshoes and hairnet.

A few minutes later, standing in the unit by the metal bench, where the petrified corpses had lain in their shroud of broken glass, Dryden thought he could detect a smell, something which reminded him of a kitchen. He closed his eyes and tried to think of clear water, the smell of ozone.

'Don't throw up,' said Friday. 'Not in here, anyway.'

'Can they cut the lights in here? I want darkness.'

They got a forensic officer in and he pulled a set of plugs off a lead. Dryden noted a strange effect: that as soon as he was deprived of sight his other senses were sharper. That smell was meat, specifically pork. Saliva flooded his mouth.

He forced himself to try and recall precisely his movements when he'd first entered the unit. 'Here,' he said, walking round the bench. 'I was right on this spot. Just by the corner. That's when I saw them on the floor.' He stood at the point. 'There!' He didn't mean to shout but he was relieved that it hadn't been an illusion. 'And I saw that too.'

Electric light leaked in through cracks and gaps where the blast had distorted the roll-up door. But there was one clean, crisp hole. Dryden walked forward to put his finger close to the edge. This was where the dying sunlight had glinted in his eyes in the second before he'd seen the bodies.

The hole was at the centre of a pit in the metal

which had bent the door inwards. Friday got his nose up close and sniffed.

'It's a bullet hole, right?' asked Dryden. 'Something triggered the explosion. This would do it. One shot – then the place explodes.'

Friday didn't say a word. One of the forensic officers came through the side door and stood at the detective's shoulder.

'Thoughts?' asked the detective.

'We'd have got it in daylight.' He had the honesty to look away. 'Sorry. Looks like a bullet hole, and it looks fresh, but we'll have to do tests. But it all fits.'

'Get a floodlight round the back and see if there's an exit hole,' said Friday.

The detective's eyes had narrowed and something in his calm, suppressed anxiety told Dryden that the discovery of the bullet hole wasn't the surprise it should have been.

'I guess this changes things,' said Dryden.

'Maybe, maybe not. It could be a year old, five years. Last week.' Friday eased his leg, lifting his bad foot off the ground for a second of relief. For the first time Dryden wondered if he lived in pain. It would explain a lot.

They went back outside.

'I owe you one,' said Friday.

'OK. Answer me one question, then. Your mate from forensics said something interesting. *But it all fits*. Fits what?'

Friday looked at his feet. 'Three dead men. If you asked me what we knew about them I'd have to tell you that two of them are ethnic Chinese, one a Pole. No names yet.'

204

Dryden made a series of connections in half a second. 'So the gun that put a bullet through that lock-up door could have been the gun that put a bullet in the guts of Sima Shuba, the man I found hanging from the cross in Christ Church grave-yard? It's a gang war.'

'That's not an inexpert summary,' said Friday. 'We found a gun. Over on the grass. It could have been blown out of Brinks' hand. In fact we rather thought it had been blown out of his hand. So maybe he was the shooter. Another job for forensics.' Friday slipped off his forensic gloves. 'Now, if you don't mind me saying so, you and I are quits. And everything you've heard is off the record. Just stick to what you saw.'

Friday walked off without another word.

Dryden took his seat again while the medic gauged his blood pressure. A final check, he said, and then the reporter could go, although he should see his GP in twenty-four hours to check there were no long-term effects from the shock of finding the bodies. Dryden hated the feeling of the rubber band around his arm, the way it seemed to create pressure in his blood vessels, as if they might burst. To distract himself, he tried to imagine what had happened in those few seconds before the blast. Friday's theory that this was all about a gang war made sense, but for a few loose ends. How could the single gunshot have been *designed* to produce the fatal explo-sion? Why was Will Brinks, the principal sus-pect, carrying a holdall packed with fifty-pound notes? Why was he holding a dog lead? Where was the dog?

TWENTY-FOUR

Friday

The first hour after midnight brought a mist creeping out of the ditches and drains of Barrow-by Fen. It seemed to boil up, spilling out over the black peat. Even in the dark Dryden could see its pale fingers spreading out on the fen. The forensic teams were working through the night beneath the unforgiving lights. Dryden wondered how the story was playing in the outside world, so he rang Laura. Humph had rung her earlier, to reassure her that Philip was not seriously injured, but she had been worried nonetheless. She was obviously relieved to hear his voice now. She told him that the local radio was running the news of the explosion, as had regional TV. Both mentioned the current police theory that the blast was due to an exploding illicit still. The news had just made the late-night bulletin on Radio Four. All the reports said there were three dead, one in intensive care. She said the shock wave of the explosion had reached Ely, nearly fourteen miles to the east. A single stone gargoyle had fallen from the North Transept, according to BBC Radio Cambridgeshire, and car and shop alarms had been set off in their hundreds. But no sound: just the silent shock

206

through the earth, like the distant echo of an earthquake.

Dryden said he'd be home in a few hours and he'd try not to wake her or Eden. It occurred to him that he might walk back into Brimstone Hill and ring Humph for a lift. The cab wasn't in sight, but he suspected it would be in a lay-by in the area. Walking might clear his mind, expunge the corrosive images from within the lock-up. On the way he could check on Jock Donovan. The last time he'd seen the old soldier he'd been standing outside his house just after the explosion, hands to his ears. The blast must have been a terrible shock: traumatic for a man sensitive to sound.

Strolling across the grass runway, he came to the gap in the hawthorn hedge where the path began. The Fens at night defied logic. By daylight they seemed empty and lifeless: no sheep, no cows, no serried rows of pig styes. But above all no people. A chimney pot here and there amongst a windbreak of trees, but no one moving. At night the darkness pulsated with lights. Every house had a security light, every farm building was lit, cars crept at all hours along zigzag droves. He could see a blinking neon light in Brimstone Hill, probably on the roof of the café. The light pollution was appalling, staining the clouds, creating an ambient orange glow.

Ahead Dryden could see a path crossing a field of sweetcorn, picking out the track he'd walked along only the day before with Donovan. The moon had risen and its pale light lit the way forward. There was something theatrical about

207

the scene, and as that thought formed in his mind a muntjac – one of the small fenland deer – sauntered out of the corn and stood in the light. A ghost, in silver grey, so pale that Dryden thought he could see right through it. It turned and walked a few steps away, then bolted, diminishing to a vanishing point.

It seemed like an invitation to follow, so Dryden did.

The moon rose quickly over the crops. It was to the north, low in the sky, like a headlamp, and Dryden experienced the odd illusion that he could feel its heat. He wondered what a moon tan would be like: he imagined a pale, silvery spider web on his skin. Beyond the fields of sweetcorn he saw a horse standing stock still on grassland, its legs in the mist up to its forelocks. Then, after twenty minutes' steady plodding, he saw Brimstone House, the white Artex vivid in the moon shadows.

A ditch ran along the boundary between Donovan's garden and the open fen. Dryden crossed it using a wooden bridge shaped like a leaping horse. He could just see Donovan standing on the far side of the plate-glass window, holding field glasses.

By the time Dryden reached the back door Donovan was there to meet him, clutching the lapels of a greatcoat to his thin neck: 'I've been safe,' he said, a thin echo of a Glaswegian accent polluting the mid-Atlantic vowels. Dryden saw that he was holding on to the doorframe and that when he took his hand away it was shaking violently.

Dryden took him by the arm. The kitchen was in darkness so Dryden searched for a light switch, but the neon was movement-sensitive and flickered on by itself. Donovan's face was bloodless and he looked his age, as if the bones beneath the skin were working their way out.

Dryden put the kettle on, then helped Donovan through to an armchair in the main room, lit by the half-light from the kitchen. There was a crack in the window, cutting diagonally right across from top left to bottom right, a brilliant diamond-white line.

'The blast did that,' said Donovan. 'It rocked the house.'

Outside, two miles away, they could see the helicopter still spiralling over the scene.

'What was it?' asked the old man. 'The radio said an illegal still?'

Dryden told him what he knew, and a hint of what he'd seen.

Despite the overcoat the old man was clearly shivering.

There was an open fireplace, a basket with logs and kindling, and newspaper. Dryden knelt down and conjured up a blaze, borrowing a lighter from Donovan, so that the room was full of the noise and flickering of flames. The kettle whistled. Dryden searched neat cupboards for tea bags and sugar, and found milk from the fridge, which was stocked up with pak choi, chicken livers, white fish, fresh prawns, white wine and a bottle of saki.

He put a mug of tea before Donovan on a low table.

Donovan hauled himself up out of the chair and went to a small inlaid wooden cabinet in the corner of the room and retrieved a bottle of malt whisky: Tallisker.

He shot some into his tea, then Dryden's, without asking.

Dryden watched him sip the liquid, the hands curiously steady, before a single jolt spilt an inch of the brew down his shirt. He didn't seem to feel the hot water on his skin.

Dryden sat and took a gulp of the fortified tea. For a minute they were both silent, watching the fire burn, the alcohol warming them from the inside out. For the first time since he'd found the corpses in the lock-up, Dryden felt alive; he could feel the blood in his cheeks and the exquisite pain of stress seeping out of his muscles.

'I went to ground,' said Donovan. 'If a shell lands, that's what you do, you go to ground. I ran out to the ditch by the bridge.'

Dryden guessed that the shock had disrupted the old man's memory, because he hadn't gone to ground at all – at least, not at first – because he'd seen him outside in the road just after the blast.

'See anything?' asked Dryden.

He shook his head. 'I kept my head down. An hour, two, or three. I got cold; now I can't warm up. Can't stop shivering.'

Then the eyes dimmed and it was there, as palpable as the heat from the fire, the thousand-yard stare. They weren't here, in Brimstone Hill, they were in Donovan's memory.

'I remembered,' he said. 'That night in the

210

trench in Korea. For the first time in half a century. I couldn't stop it. It just came back to me, the whole thing, perfect, like some terrible jewel.'

He gulped tea and whisky. Dryden thought what a striking metaphor that was: the *terrible jewel*. The last thing he wanted to hear, given what he'd just had to live through out on Barrowby Airfield, was a story of carnage from the past. But he was powerless to move. Whisky and delayed shock were making his limbs heavier, as if his whole body was sinking under a crushing gravity.

'I remembered what happened the night my friends died,' said Donovan.

'The Davenport brothers?' prompted Dryden.

'We'd built trenches,' he said. 'Ours was a crescent, the tails of the crescent facing away from the Chinese lines. We dug it that day, our company, because we knew they'd use the night. And they did. I've read the books and they've got the numbers – five thousand five-inch shells. Like I said before: five thousand.'

Dryden turned away to add a log to the burning fire. 'The Battle of the Hook?' he said.

'It didn't have a name then.'

'You're safe now, in here.'

A blue light flashed out on the fen as an emergency vehicle left Barrowby Airfield.

'Before it started we talked, me and the boys,' said Donovan. 'They were a mile away, the Chinese. So it didn't matter if we raised our voices. And the moon was up like a light. So Pete read a letter from home, for his brother, and for me. It was from his mum. She hadn't met me but they'd talked about me in their letters home. So I got a mention. Like family. And Paulie read another, about the farm, from his dad. About kale, and beet, and chickens and ditches to clear. And I listened. And then the first shell came. Just like the one today. At evening time. No noise – just the impact. I was scared.' He forced his hand across his mouth.

Dryden waited.

The air flooded out of Donovan's lungs as if he'd been winded. 'This is why I go to the churchyard. To stop this memory coming back. If I go there and touch the stone I don't have to relive it. But tonight I couldn't stop it. I was a coward.' Both hands to his mouth now. 'Tonight, again. I couldn't move. I didn't look over the edge. I tried to get under the earth. I clawed at it. I dug down. I went back along the crescent and left them at the front.'

In his mind he seemed to be reliving both nights at the same time.

He held out a free hand, dark with peat and smeared green with weed, where he'd been in the ditch. 'Again, tonight.'

Dryden reached out and refilled his own mug with whisky.

'I closed my eyes because that's like being under the earth,' said Donovan. 'The guns stopped at dawn. The first thing I saw was my own hands.' He looked at them now, clutching the tin mug. 'And then I saw the bodies of the rest around me. All dead. I looked along the trench we'd dug, but because it was crescent-shaped I couldn't see the boys. I knew they were there because I'd heard *them* firing in the night. And talking, to each other, and to me. I remember my name – hearing my name, in their voices.

'So I stood up, and then I fell down because my legs wouldn't work. I crawled down that trench. And within a few yards it became a shell hole, full of water and blood, but I kept going, calling out their names, until I came round the corner of the crescent to the front of the trench. And standing there was a Chinese soldier. Just one. He'd got forward to loot the bodies. He was smoking a cigarette and he'd got Pete's wallet and was flicking through the pictures, of his dad, his mum, his sister. I raised the gun I'd never fired but I was shaking so badly I couldn't aim it. I couldn't pull the trigger. He laughed. Then he just dropped the wallet and the pictures into the water and the blood, climbed the face of the trench, and ran back.'

Donovan's eyes were fixed on the distant lights of Barrowby Airfield.

'An officer arrived, one of ours. He said the Chinese had run. Later I went forward and we found their trenches. The Chinese dead, hundreds dead, thousands. Dead in their capes. I never said what had really happened. I got a medal.'

The helicopter approached the house and flew low over the rooftop, forcing Donovan to pause and grip the arms of his chair.

'They made me write the letter home to the boys' mother.'

He leaned his head back in the chair and closed

213

his eyes.

'I said in the letter there'd been no pain. I said they'd died like heroes, and that's what their memorial should read. And it does.'

He opened his eyes at that, suddenly. He wasn't in the past any more, it seemed, because his eyes were focused, but Dryden thought he was living through something even more terrible than that blood-filled trench.

TWENTY-FIVE

The smell of death clung to Dryden. More than twelve hours after the moment he'd stepped into the burnt-out lock-up it was still there when he got home to the boat. He arrived at dawn; the mist gone, a wide barge carrying gravel slipping past on the river towards Cambridge. Laura made him shower in the narrowboat and bagged his clothes for the laundrette. She pushed her face into his black hair and said he smelt of lemon, and strawberries. But something lingered in his nose and throat, that sweetness, a ripeness. He drank orange juice and black coffee, ate toast with marmite; tasted the malty meatiness, then left the rest.

'You OK?' she asked. They were sitting on deck. He'd been looking out over the fen for twenty minutes without saying a word. 'They said three dead on the radio?'

'I found them,' he said. 'It was as if they'd been in a furnace.'

'Take a day off. Sleep, you're out on your feet, Philip.' She had a script on her knee and she flicked through the pages, pretending not to care if he took her advice. Eden lay on a blanket on the deck, trying to close his fist round a wooden eel suspended over him on an arch. He said a word which might have been *fish*.

'It's press day,' said Dryden.

He was so tired he forgot that Eden's failure to walk had become a taboo subject. 'Why do you think he doesn't want to walk? He doesn't even want to crawl, does he?'

'I think he's happy. And he's like you, he looks at the world, weighs it up. He doesn't need to walk yet so he's not bothered. He can talk. He thinks the world will just pass him by, like a parade, and he's happy with that.'

'You're not worried?'

She gave Dryden a cool look. 'I wasn't.'

'Sorry.' He filled an awkward moment by checking his phone.

His powers of simple concentration had abandoned him. Cotton wool seemed to be crammed into his skull. Humph, who'd slept in the Capri up by Barham's Farm after running him home, rolled up at quarter to eight. They went straight to the railway station because it had a decent coffee bar. Dryden got takeaway cappuccinos and a sausage sandwich for Humph.

Jean, *The Crow*'s long-serving receptionist, was just opening the front office as Humph parked outside. She adjusted one of her hearing aids,

215

eager for gossip. 'Eden?' she asked.

'He's fine, thanks,' said Dryden, remembering to look at her, and to let her see his lips. 'Anyone here?'

'Vee's in. Does she sleep?' Jean's speech was slightly dulled by her hearing disability. The syrupy consonants reminded Dryden of Laura.

This was the best time to work with Vee. She was a morning person, and so was Dryden. Getting up, getting ahead of the world, was important to them both. She had the papers spread over the news desk and the radio on – BBC Radio Cambridgeshire. Dryden switched on another radio by the coffee machine which was always set to KLFM in Lynn.

Over the newsdesk a flat-screen TV showed BBC 24 News. Dryden turned the sound up so that they had three voices speaking at once. It was like a real newsroom.

'How's the blast story running?' asked Dryden. Splash, the office cat, came and sat on his lap.

'Top item on all local broadcasts, third on Radio Four. Three dead, one still critical, after illicit still explodes. Two ethnic Chinese, one Pole. Everyone is drawing the obvious conclusion, that it's linked to the Christ Church murder, although the police are playing it straight for now. They're waiting for forensic reports and autopsies.'

Dryden told her what had been found at the scene: the bullet hole in the lock-up door, and a gun, on the grass near Will Brinks. 'It means we've got a scoop as long as CID don't blow it in the next six hours. Friday wants to wait until he's got forensic back-up on the gunshot, so there's a chance we'll make it. Even if they release it we'll be the first out with a paper. If anything, a bullet makes it more likely there's a link to Christ Church. It also means the traveller – Brinks – is the prime suspect. Gun crime's pretty rare in the Fens. And lightning never strikes twice, especially in a backwater like Brimstone Hill. There has to be a link. So we'll print an extra thousand, get digital copies of the front page to TV and radio.'

Drinking his coffee, Dryden felt a wave of nausea. He closed his eyes and the turning, falling sensation continued.

'You all right?' asked Vee.

'Not really. But I might as well be here as anywhere.'

Vee gave him a bottle of mineral water which he drank in one go.

'Right,' he said. 'That's better. So – we'll lead with the story in Ely and Brimstone Hill. All editions. There's a press conference this morning at Christ Church; if there's anything to add I'll send a few paragraphs. If not, go with the story I've filed. When's Miriam in?'

'Due any minute. She's doing police calls, touching base at the magistrates' court.'

'Get her to do a feature for the page-three slot about migrant workers and illicit trade. Vodka, dope, tainted food, the lot. I want the words *black market* and *gang* in the headline. Then she can do the website. But don't let her put anything live until I say so. Let's sell plenty of

217

papers first.'

A cab beeped its horn outside and Dryden went to the bay window, the glass emblazoned with *The Crow*'s motto: *Never Weary Of Doing Good*. Outside the Capri was at the kerb, engine running.

'I better go,' he told Vee. *The Crow*'s deadline was eleven. On the streets by two. 'If you've heard nothing from me by ten forty-five, go with the story as it stands.' He began to close down his laptop. 'Of course the big story of the week will just make a picture caption,' said Dryden. 'Dust storm near Brimstone Hill. Now we'll have to run it inside.'

That was the plan: an eight-column pic of the broiling fen blow on page three with a cross-reference to a page later in the run where they could carry the full story. In an ideal world he'd have slipped the story and pictures into his top drawer and used it the following week, but there was no way it could keep. That was the trouble with real news.

Vee smiled. This was the sort of moment when she enjoyed Dryden's company. 'You're the editor. You can do what you like. How would you make the fen blow the lead story, given it's up against a triple violent killing? Possibly five violent killings in time, if they prove a link to the church and the survivor doesn't make it.'

'I talked to the NFU yesterday, Vee – farmer over to the east lost an inch of soil. An inch. In one go. A square mile of it, straight up in the air. OK, some of it comes down, but most of it is lost for good. Out to sea, into the rivers.'

He pulled a report out of the pile on his desk. 'Cranfield University study, came out this week. It estimates the average soil loss across the Fens is two centimetres a year.' He got a ruler off the subs bench and showed her what two centimetres looked like. 'And that's the average. It'll be far worse where the fen blows run. There's corridors for them, like tornado alley in the US. The land's too dry, and it costs money to irrigate. We've grubbed up trees, orchards, the few hedgerows there were left on the land. And there's no spring rain to hold the soil down. People want to know what global warming looks like. This is what it looks like...'

He used Vee's computer to scroll to the pictures he'd taken of the cloud approaching Euximoor Drove.

'It's like the Dust Bowl, 1933. Remember *The Wizard of Oz*, or *The Grapes of Wrath*? A fifth of the agricultural land in this county is officially classed as desert. Every winter's drier, every summer's winds are stronger.'

'Pictures are good, too,' said Vee, daring him to put it on the front of the paper.

'Nah. Can't do it. Hard news is hard news. We're a weekly newspaper, not a quarterly academic review. We want people to read, not study. Three dead in fen blast, you can't beat that. Plus murder, gangs, illicit booze. There's enough news here for a year's worth of papers.'

'Picture for the front?' asked Vee.

They skipped through the pictures he'd downloaded from his mobile phone, taken out at Barrowby Airfield the night before.

219

They showed the burnt-out lock-up, the buckled roll-up door, a police guard behind a scene-of-crime tape. One showed the three body bags being removed by paramedics. 'Black bag' was one of those euphemisms which seemed to be worse than the reality they sought to obscure. There was an echo here of the shot taken at Christ Church, of Sima Shuba's body being taken away. Four victims, four black bags. Dryden hoped the death toll would stop there.

TWENTY-SIX

Christ Church, packed for the press conference on the Barrowby Airfield deaths, was full of the earthy stench of over-brewed tea. A uniformed female PC was behind a trestle table doling out beverages in paper cups, suggesting that the West Cambridgeshire constabulary was no further ahead on women's issues than it was on twenty-first-century catering. Several plates of biscuits had been reduced to crumbs. The cream of the East Anglian press corps was in attendance, plus a camera team from Anglia, and a BBC radio unit.

DI Friday was sitting up at the altar behind a heavy table, the wood almost black, the legs carved with the heads of Biblical figures. He had a digital projector and laptop set up on the table, currently displaying the West Cambridgeshire Constabulary's crest on a whitewashed wall above the arch of the chancel.

Dryden checked his watch: he could get copy into the paper after eleven but it meant they had to stop the presses. Each interruption in the print run cost about £200. Given *The Crow*'s narrow profit margins, any such decision had to be carefully offset against the benefits of keeping the paper up with its competition: the *Cambridge News*, the *Peterborough Evening Telegraph*, the BBC website. Dryden had the splash he'd written on his laptop ready to edit if anything needed changing. He could send it digitally with a single push of a button. He'd also sent Vee some headline suggestions from the cab en route to Brimstone Hill. His favourite:

BULLET HOLE RIDDLE AS
THREE DIE IN FEN BLAST

He wanted two 'strap' secondary headlines to run under the splash headline:

POLICE PROBE LINK TO CHURCHYARD
MURDER
DETECTIVES WAIT TO QUESTION
SURVIVOR

Dryden strolled down the aisle, trying to look relaxed, pausing by the picture of Christ's passion in its gilt frame. The figure of Christ had been depicted in agony, the ugly angles of the elbows and knees reminding Dryden of the horrific scene he'd stumbled on in the lock-up at Barrowby Airfield.

His eye found a cottage in the background he hadn't noticed before, washing on a line, crisp white linen against the green fields of the Roman countryside. The scene raised his spirits. And there was always the joyful figure of the peasant Stefano, chasing his hat.

Dryden took a pew beside Alf Roberts from the Press Association. Alf was neat, in his sixties, teetotal. He had the most beautiful shorthand Dryden had ever seen: an elegant, sinuous text which could easily accommodate 150 words a minute. That took up the right-hand side of each page. On the left-hand side were small sketches. Usually he concentrated on local wildlife and fauna, birds, butterflies, flowers. This morning he'd chosen the carved leg of the altar table, focusing on a detail of Noah's Ark, pairs of lions, with pairs of gazelle, tripping up the gangplank.

'Film show then?' asked Dryden, nodding up at the laptop projection.

'It's Rocky Five,' said Alf.

DI Friday called order and outlined the facts of the case. The three dead were Jia Jun and Cai Xiaogang of Erebus Street, King's Lynn, and Daniel Fangor of London Road, Wisbech. The first two were ethnic Chinese from Hong Kong, the third was a Pole; all immigration documents were in order.

Evidence at the scene suggested the dead men had operated an illicit still producing vodka. The still was unlicensed. An explosion was the im-

222

mediate cause of death. One survivor, still unconscious, was at Wisbech General Hospital. Friday said he would be unable to answer questions until an interview had been completed with this man, whom he could now name as Will Brinks, a member of the traveller community of Third Drove, Euximoor Fen, Brimstone Hill. Meanwhile inquiries would continue within the Chinese community in King's Lynn.

'These three aren't the only victims in this story,' said Friday. 'Some of you will know that this week the Ely coroner highlighted the case of two men from this very parish who had clearly been imbibing tainted alcohol from an illicit still over a long period of time. It's all part of the same bigger picture. All I would add at this stage is that while drinking this stuff can kill you, the tragic events of the last twenty-four hours illustrate that trying to distil it can kill you too. One-hundred-and-twenty per cent alcohol is as dangerous as nitroglycerine.'

Dryden leaned over to Alf. 'But twice as much fun at parties.'

'What I did want to share with you was some pictures of what we found earlier this morning when the key holder was able to open up the industrial units at Barrowby Airfield. The estate is managed by Artoro Real Estate of Croydon, although the owner is the MOD. Barrowby Oilseed is based in unit six, the site of the explosion, which contained the still and a bottling plant. A connecting door led into unit five, where we found what I'm reliably informed is a rapeseed oil press.'

223

He put a bottle of Barrowby rapeseed oil on the altar: an elegant, slim-necked bottle with an artisan black-and-white label showing a farmer.

'So – two products, rapeseed oil and vodka. One bottling plant. This is what is referred to in *Dragon's Den* as a business plan.'

He let the laughter die away.

'It wasn't their only business. This is unit four, access to which was via another internal door.'

The digital slides showed the interior of the next unit. It was crammed with scrap metal.

'Just here,' said Friday, using a light 'arrow' to indicate a pile of dull grey metal. 'You can see roof lead. It's Victorian, and almost certainly came from above our very heads. We're confident the rest of the metal in the lock-up is stolen goods.'

Several reporters looked up, and the BBC swung a camera round to pan across the rafters.

'Clearly we have a potential link between the explosion at Barrowby Airfield and the murder earlier this week of Sima Shuba, whose body was found here in the churchyard at Christ Church, following the overnight theft of lead from the roof. We have to consider the possibility that the explosion at Barrowby Airfield was not an accident and might be related to the illegal trade in stolen metal. Was the survivor, Will Brinks, involved? Before we can begin to answer these questions we need to complete and consider forensic evidence collected at both scenes, and autopsies on the dead. And we need to speak to Brinks when we get the all-clear from medical staff at Wisbech.'

Friday's reluctance to speculate further in public on gang warfare was admirable, thought Dryden. But in private Friday's views had been clear: this was an underworld spat between vicious ethnic gangs, or a civil war within one of them. Was this view based on the evidence, or a series of presumptions – even prejudices? It was certainly a neat solution. Dryden reminded himself that the truth might be less obvious. Perhaps the odd mix of ethnic backgrounds, Chinese, Polish and Irish traveller, hid a more subtle story.

A few hands went up amongst the pews.

'I'm sorry. No questions today,' said Friday. 'I'm sure we'll have plenty to say soon enough. For the record, we have also recovered from unit four several hundred yards of electrical cabling which we believe was taken from Coldham's Farm wind turbine facility, Brimstone Hill, and nearly two-hundred-and-eighty steel bolts lifted from the goods railway line here the night before last – the immediate cause, I believe, of a goods train derailment. The line is still closed. Industrious bunch, and reckless too, because these thefts put innocent lives at risk. In the case of the railway line, hundreds of innocent lives.'

A new shot showed various pieces of ornamental ironware taken from gardens and houses, and several items of graveyard sculpture, including a small angel with one foot raised, and a figure of death in a shroud, which hid the face.

'This is now a major criminal inquiry involving three police authorities,' said Friday.

He put up pictures of the two Chinese men and the Pole.

'We need to link these men into the wider criminal community. If anyone has information which could be of assistance to the police there are email addresses, telephone numbers and website addresses on the press release. We'd appreciate it if the media circulated this information. Also, the injured man owned a vehicle, a silver Ford Fiesta.' He flashed up the registration number on the screen. 'We need to find this vehicle.'

There were no pictures of the survivor, said Friday. Will Brinks was a member of a travellers' community which was out on the road. There were no documents in his caravan at Third Drove – no passport, medical card or driving licence. The police were keen to track down the family. Brinks himself had suffered second-degree burns to his face, which was heavily bandaged. When he regained consciousness he would be interviewed.

The screen held the three pictures of the dead men. Why did they always look like this? thought Dryden. Haunted, hunted, desperate. The blank passport stare. These shots always seemed to suck any virtue out of a face, and leave it swollen with vice. Then he recalled the faces he'd seen on the incinerated corpses in the Barrowby Oilseed lock-up and thought that even this ugly, brutal flesh was better than those black ghosts.

Dryden walked out into the churchyard, leaving Friday to stonewall questions, and perched himself on a toppled tomb. Flipping open his laptop, he reread the splash, made a few changes, then hit the SEND button. It was pretty much the perfect story – but for one, annoying omission – a picture of the chief suspect, Will Brinks.

TWENTY-SEVEN

The story flew from Dryden's laptop with an audible *ping!* The moment was one of strange liberation. Unlike his former colleagues on Fleet Street, he didn't have to worry about tomorrow's story. His next paper was several days away. What he needed was to get ahead of the pack so that he had something to say in Tuesday's paper. Something to say, or something to show. Within hours CID would interview Will Brinks. An arrest might follow. What Dryden and CID knew – that a gun had been found at the scene and there was a bullet-hole in the lock-up door – put Brinks firmly in the frame as prime suspect. If Dryden could track down a picture of him, it would be a scoop in itself. Which was why he asked Humph to drive him to Rick's Tattoo Parlour.

Rick's stood at the heart of the village of Rings End – no apostrophe – two miles out of Brimstone Hill to the east. If you left Brimstone by any other direction you'd be heading for civilization: north, south or east. But west took you into the Great Soak, a silty fen wilderness which seemed to peter out into nothing. Once, a great mere had stretched over the land. Now, two hundred years after they'd drained the water, the roads still didn't bother to reach across it to where the far shore had once stood. The dwindling country droves reminded Dryden of trickles of water, wandering into a saltpan, drying out under the sun.

Rings End had a sign, but it wasn't twinned with anywhere, so there was nothing fancy, just the name. An apostrophe wasn't the only thing it lacked. Dryden had always sensed it had battled all its life to even be itself, to be a place at all. A road, a narrow carriageway of mind-numbing straights and sudden double-turns, cut through it, passing a single chapel, a row of farmers' cottages disfigured by double-glazing, and Rick's shabby lock-up.

Humph pulled off the road into a lay-by. An HGV crashed its gears and swept past, back towards Brimstone Hill. The road was so narrow that the big wagons seemed to lean over with the camber as they threaded the turn by the chapel, a building almost obscured by a billboard offering DISCOUNT CARPETS. It was a typical fen village, devoid of thatched charm, more like a deserted castaway fragment of the city than the country at all. Or all that was left of a city, perhaps, after civilization had left.

Humph slipped one of his language tapes into a CD player and clamped on his earphones.

Dryden checked his mobile; a text from Vee informed him that *The Crow* had gone to press.

Rick's door was always open but the view was obscured by a flyscreen made of beaded string.

A customer lay back in the reclining dentist's chair: a woman, in trousers and a blouse, maybe thirteen stone, with a lot of pale skin showing at her neck and arms.

Jazz played on a CD player – Brubeck or Parker.

Rick looked up from under his green eyeshade. He was thirty, neat, an ex-jockey from Newmarket who'd run to fat after his teenage years. All that suppleness, and latent speed, seemed wasted in this box of a shop, with its single window. Dryden had done a feature on the tattoo parlour for *The Crow* five years ago. His own preconceptions of the 'art' had not been positive. But his interview with Rick had at least tackled the issues, and there was little doubt it had brought him some new customers. Dryden often dropped by for a cup of tea and to pick up gossip. That was the real magic of the tattoo parlour: the chair. It seemed to be a modern-day equivalent of the confessional box. Once seated, the customers needed little encouragement to tell Rick secrets they'd die to keep hidden at home.

Rick took in Dryden with a sad smile. 'Kettle's just boiled.' He'd been hoping, thought Dryden, for a paying customer. As he made tea Dryden thought, not for the first time, that he could never live a life like Rick's, always waiting for his livelihood to walk in the door.

The window of Rick's was full of painted designs, and through it Dryden saw a car pull up. A smart family hatchback with a taxi sign on top, it disgorged two kids in neat grey uniforms from one of Ely's private schools. That was where

Rick's money went, on school fees, school trips, extra tuition. The kids came in, took chairs, and immediately began homework. The car drove off. Mrs Rick – she'd never been introduced by name – ran a cab based on the station rank. Humph called her Union Jack, which was her radio call sign.

Rick's tattoo gun whirled and Dryden told himself it was an illusion that he could smell burning flesh. The gun buzzed for two minutes with all the excruciating edge of a dentist's drill. In the sudden silence the customer asked if she could smoke and Rick said she could but she'd have to go outside. As she left, Dryden saw the blood on her neck, a thin dribble down her clavicle, as if her skin had split.

There were design books on a low counter and Dryden was flicking through.

'You after a tattoo at last?' joked Rick. 'If you can get Humph interested I do cheap rates for landscapes.'

'I was looking for a flying swan, starts down here...' Dryden touched his hip. 'But reaches up to the back of the neck.'

Rick found it instantly – £240 in black, white, yellow and that dash of red on the beak.

'Handsome,' said Rick.

'Handsome when you're twenty. Looks pretty weird when you're sixty,' said Dryden.

Rick looked at his kids then and something darker crossed his face, a sadness, maybe even a regret, that he couldn't give them what he thought was the best in life without them seeing where the money came from.

'You heard about the explosion out at the airfield?' asked Dryden. 'I found the bodies. Not a pretty sight.' He felt a lump in his throat. It didn't seem to matter how often he tried to treat his discovery of the victims as a coldly journalistic coup; the personal reality of the moment refused to fade. 'The survivor's got one of these tattoos. Can I look at the wall?'

The customer came back in, alternately hauling her thighs, like coal sacks.

Rick said Dryden could go on through. At the back of the lock-up was a door and a corridor to a loo – spotless, clinical, because the council checked the place out, and controlled the licence. The corridor ran twenty feet and the whole of one side was pictures, snapshots of customers displaying tattoos.

Dryden sipped his tea and began, methodically, to work his way along. He didn't really have any hopes of finding Brinks but he thought he'd kick himself if he didn't check. There were a dozen tattoo joints within twenty miles of Brimstone Hill, but Rick's was the only one with a wall like this. It was like Facebook, in bricks and mortar. Or the *News of the World*. That had been the paper's slogan: *All Of Human Life Is Here*. And it was: a naked woman covered in a vine, grapes in bunches on her breasts. A man in a suit, white shirt, and tie, holding his tongue out to reveal a dragon in green; a teenager with his eyelids closed but blue eyes drawn on the lids. Each tattoo seemed to be designed to unsettle, distract, shock.

Even the humdrum made Dryden feel uneasy –

231

the anchors on forearms, mythical birds on biceps, Union flags on shoulders, little miniature crowns and roses at the waistline. It wasn't as if he had some hang-up about skin being unblemished, forever young. He liked the process of ageing, as he liked old wood, because it showed the passage of time. Old age could have dignity. It wasn't the pictures that grew old, it was the canvas, and there was something unnatural about the contrast.

Under a snap of a woman with tattooed toes, he saw the edge of another picture, just a fan of white feathers. He edged it out, then pulled the pin that held it in place. It was Will Brinks, naked but for briefs, the eyes bright with something, maybe 120 per cent proof hooch. With his back to the camera, he tried to look over his own shoulder at the tattoo. He looked exultant, as if he'd been able to outsmart, for once, a world that probably seemed, for most of his life, too complicated to understand.

Back in the shop the customer was out for another smoke and the kids had moved on to their laptops.

'That him?' asked Rick, looking at the snap Dryden had in his hand.

'Yeah. That's him.'

'Name?'

'Will Brinks.'

Rick shrugged. 'Tinker?'

Dryden looked at the picture again: bad teeth, slightly swollen face, jet-black hair worn long and cut at home, pale blue eyes. He did look like a traveller out of central casting. Rick would have had him in the confessional chair for an hour; maybe three.

'Site's a mile from Brimstone Hill,' said Dryden.

Rick reached down behind the counter. 'He dropped this off by way of thanks. He liked the work.'

It was a bottle of vodka, identical to the one the coroner had produced at the inquest.

The liquid inside was yellow. The label was the same as the others Dryden had seen, illustrated with the amber hay field.

Dryden put his hand on Rick's shoulder. 'Just don't drink it, OK?'

Rick laughed. 'Drink it? You crazy? I've been washing the needles in it; it's one-hundred-and-twenty per cent proof.'

'One bottle?'

'A crate.'

'What do you reckon on Brinks? A bit simple?'

'Sure.' He looked at his kids. 'Damaged, I thought about saying no...'

Dryden held up a hand. He wasn't there to judge.

'You know what those tinkers are up to?' said Rick. 'This is Third Drove we're talking about? Rumour is they're pulling together the cash to buy the land, then get planning permission for mobile homes. Maybe they saw moonshine as a useful source of cash to finance the purchase.'

It was a trend in the Fens. A big travellers' site at Smithy Fen, north of Cambridge, had become a national *cause célèbre*. They weren't Romany – they were Irish, and in the winter they went

233

home to the Republic, to a village outside Cork, where they had smallholdings. They'd bought the land in Cambridgeshire off the local farmer and were trying to get planning permission for homes, against the opposition of nearby villagers. Local house prices had plummeted.

The idea of the Irish running the illicit still – and the scrap metal trade – upset DI Friday's neat picture of inter-Chinese community warfare.

'So what are we saying?' asked Dryden. 'That the Irish set up the still to generate the cash to buy land and put down roots? And they got the Chinese and the Pole to do the work. So this kid, Brinks, was like the overseer?'

'Maybe. He might have been simple but he wasn't stupid.'

It was a thought that seemed to transform the story: the idea that Will Brinks might have been in control. In a perverse way it meant the dead men were victims too, exploited workers, not criminal entrepreneurs. But if he'd been in charge, why had he taken that shot? Had the travellers decided to pull out of the business after the murder of Sima Shuba in the graveyard at Christ Church? Was Brinks leaving the site with his investment reclaimed in fifty-pound notes?

Dryden held the picture of Will Brinks out at arm's length. He realized then that the yellow in the vodka bottle was a perfect match for the light he'd seen when the still had blown up. Electric yellow, like the hottest part of a flame, the eye of the storm which had knocked Brinks down so hard he might never get up. Whatever Brinks was doing that day at Barrowby Airfield, he held the key to the mystery of the triple killing. If he died in Wisbech General, they might never know the truth.

TWENTY-EIGHT

It was a journalistic ritual that Dryden found hypnotic. A kind of newspaperman's tai chi. He'd buy a beer from the Fenman bar behind the Lamb Hotel and then wander out into the old coaching inn's yard. They'd put out dusty picnic tables on the cobbles, which had been colonised by smokers. He could see the cathedral's West Tower, and *The Crow*, across Market Street, and there would always be a small queue at this time: four p.m. Not waiting to get into the newspaper offices, but lined up on the pavement, apparently going nowhere. Then the van would arrive from the printers and the driver would throw open the back doors to reveal the piles of papers, and heave one on to the pavement, then two, then go.

Jean, *The Crow*'s resident receptionist, would come out and clip the plastic bindings with scissors. It was 'right money' only, and everyone knew, so she just had a box for the coins.

Dryden would leave his pint, saunter over, and Jean would give him two papers off the top of the pile and take no money. The rest of the punters would give him a curious, mildly antagonistic glare.

Back at the table he'd stand up, put one of the papers on the seat, and judge the front page.

BULLET HOLE RIDDLE AS
THREE DIE IN FEN BLAST
POLICE PROBE LINK TO CHURCHYARD
MURDER
DETECTIVES WAIT TO SPEAK TO
SURVIVOR
By Philip Dryden

Dryden felt his world tilt just a few degrees. The ritual was supposed to make him feel centred, secure. During the long months of Laura's coma after their car accident he'd needed something to hold on to, a career, a purpose. But this headline made him see again the petrified bodies of the dead and he drained an inch off his pint, struggling to keep the horror of the scene at a safe distance. And there was a sliver of guilt too, in that he always felt the frisson of excitement in seeing his byline, even attached to such bleak news.

Now there was a new satisfaction: as editor he could admire the whole paper, and feel that it was in some way all his work. It looked good: newsy, and the gunshot scoop put them one step ahead of the morning papers and TV and radio. He'd let the story tell itself, and it proved to be a powerful narrative. The gun at the scene, the bullet hole being tested, Will Brinks guarded in hospital, the police keen to interview the sur-

236

vivor. The wire services were already running the story, with *The Crow* getting an upfront credit.

Page three carried the shots he'd snapped at Euximoor Fen as the storm had blown through, plus the cross-reference to the story on page seven. He ran a finger over the table top and picked up a smudge of peat dust.

Humph pulled up in the cab, finding a space in the Lamb's rank of reserved guest spots, so that if he sat with the door open he could chat. Dryden went and got him his usual, a pint of Electric Pig cider at eight-point-five per cent.

'How's Grace?' asked Dryden, after ten minutes of silence.

'I've just dropped her in town. She wants to shop.' He shook his head and extended his upper lip to the edge of the pint pot. 'She's up to something.'

'Boyfriend trouble?' suggested Dryden.

'Christ.' Humph spilt cider on his Ipswich Town top. 'She's fifteen. Last time I took her out she wanted to see the latest Walt Disney. She ran away with a cuddly toy. I don't think so...'

Dryden's phone buzzed on the picnic table top with an incoming text. It was Vee Hilgay. *Dacey auction rooms – police raid. Now.*

Dacey's stood beside Ely's old cattle yard at the back of Market Square. There was a single Victorian wrought-iron and glass structure, effectively an ornate shed, which could have easily accommodated a small zeppelin. The cattle yard was now a car park. Friday evening was viewing time ahead of the main sale on a

Saturday morning. Everything from bicycles and furniture to tools and antiques. With the pubs open, and the working week at an end, the auction rooms always drew a big, high-spirited crowd.

The police and trading standards kept an eye on the goods for sale. What intrigued Dryden was why the West Cambridgeshire Constabulary would divert scarce resources to raiding the auction rooms on a day when they were still struggling with what might be an outbreak of violent gang warfare in the Fens.

There were four police vans parked in front of the auction hall, which was surrounded by a crowd. Dryden spotted one of the local trading standards officers pushing his way in.

An unmarked police squad car arrived and DI Friday got out.

Dryden gave him a copy of *The Crow*.

'Thanks. I can't talk,' said Friday. 'Go away.'

'What's this got to do with the explosion?' asked Dryden, tracking the detective as he walked.

But Friday had said all he was saying.

Dacey's main hall was packed, flooded with light through the frosted glass panels in the walls and roof. It was like a miniature Crystal Palace. There was a café in one corner, a cash office in another. All the goods for the main Saturday auction were on show like a modern-day Aladdin's Cave. Except it was mostly tat, not gold. There was a crowd around one pen reserved for ironware: ornamental garden objects, a fountain, a sundial, gnomes. Each item was being listed,

238

bagged up, taken away by uniformed constables.

A hand touched his shoulder and he turned to find Vee, notebook open.

'They've taken a load of stuff from outside too, metal castings, cabling, some railings. Looks like they're trying to find out how the Chinese fenced the stuff once they'd nicked it.'

'What do the auctioneers say?'

'They say the stuff's all come from legit sources. I can't get to the boss; he's doing a property auction in the hall at the back. That's on now.'

The auction hall had been founded by a local estate agency, which occupied a 1920s building tacked on to the main shed, and still ran occasional property auctions on a Friday evening.

'There's not much we can do here tonight,' said Dryden. 'Pics?'

Vee pointed to a raised platform by the auctioneer's dais. Josie Evans was perched on one of the iron girders taking snaps of the crowd below. She was being held securely in place by a young man Dryden recognized as the Fulham supporter she'd brought to the office summer party. Dryden doubted she needed quite that much support.

'I'll hang about,' said Dryden. 'I'd knock off if I was you. Paper's terrific, by the way. Well done.'

Dryden got a coffee and sat watching the milling crowd. The police had caused a stir but they hadn't diverted the regulars from their Friday night entertainment, checking out the lots. The sellers swelled the crowd, keeping an eagle eye

239

on their goods. He saw Grace Humphries, Humph's daughter, wandering with the rest, until she came to a display of framed old maps of the Isle of Ely. She studied one, a map of the new waterways built in the seventeenth century, a network of straight drains and cuts, drawn together at the centre by Denver Sluice, the beating heart of the whole, living, watery system. She seemed drawn to it, and stood staring for several minutes. Then a clutch of girls her own age surrounded her, hugging, holding hands, whispering. There was something subdued about the group, with not a giggle heard. They moved off towards the café, towing Grace along.

Dryden flicked through an auction catalogue. At the back was a list of the properties to be sold by auction. There were six in all, a pair of derelict cottages on farmland in Manea, two lots of agricultural land with planning permission for homes, three rented houses in Ely being sold by a single landlord, and one sale from the Church Commissioners: Sexton Cottage, Christ Church, Brimstone Hill.

The Rev. Temple-Wright had said nothing would stop the sale. She always kept her word.

The door to the property auction room was manned by a flunky for Dacey's. The atmosphere beyond was very different from the main shed. Here there was an intense silence, broken only by the auctioneer's clipped commentary. The room was packed with about 200 people.

The auctioneer stood at an ornate wooden lectern. He wore a spangled waistcoat and was in the middle of selling one of the parcels of land with planning permission attached.

'I have one hundred and forty-five thousand pounds with number sixty-seven.'

Dryden was standing at the side of the room. Looking across the ranks of punters sitting down, he could see one man holding a wooden panel, the number sixty-seven painted in black.

He'd covered a property auction before for the paper; the sale of an old Methodist Church in Ely which went to a family who planned to open a curry house. Only registered customers could bid, those who'd given their details to the auctioneers beforehand and had proved they had adequate finances to complete a sale. They would also have agreed to pay a fifteen per cent deposit, non-returnable, if they won the bidding. A lot of institutions used auctions because they were fast, sure and above board, with no chance of gazumping, or backhand deals.

Sexton Cottage was next up.

'Very nice property,' said the auctioneer. 'An acre of land. Needs a little work done to modernise, but plenty of period Gothic detail. Leasehold tenant in situ who requires only one month's notice. There's a surveyor's report with the papers. So I don't see why we can't start at eighty-five thousand.'

There was silence in the room.

The auctioneer knew his business. He let it last three seconds. 'Fifty thousand, then. Let's get this started, please.'

A paddle rose at the back of the room.

'Thank you.' He pointed a pen at the bidder.

241

'Sir. Number eighty-one leads the bidding.'

Dryden scanned the room and spotted Temple-Wright, her brittle grey hair catching his eye in the back row. Even from a distance he could see her steely glint fixed on the auctioneer.

'So. Do I see fifty-five thousand?'

Beside the auctioneer stood two 'spotters', assistants who'd also note the number of whoever came second in the auction in case the winner couldn't meet the price.

Another paddle rose. And a third bidder outbid him. A buzz seemed to bring the room alive.

Dryden leaned back against the wall and closed his eyes, listening to the hypnotic rise of the bids. The three raced to ninety-five thousand in under a minute. He thought of the blind old man in Sexton Cottage at that moment, sightless eyes turned to the light of the window, with its view of Christ Church.

'So. With number eighty-one, where we started, we have ninety-five thousand. Any more?'

Two seconds' silence.

'Thank you, sir. Number thirty-one. A new bidder at one hundred thousand pounds? Thank you. One hundred thousand it is.'

There was a rustle in the room as heads turned. The new bidder was standing on the same side of the room as Dryden, and so he couldn't see him, as the side aisle was crowded with people.

The bidders edged to one hundred and twenty-five thousand pounds.

'So. With our new bidder, number thirty-one. Any more for any more? The last time of asking. Sir? No? OK. And...'

242

A sharp, untheatrical tap of the gavel and the house was sold.

The crowd dispersed, while a buzz of gossip filled the room, and Dryden saw the winning bidder being approached by one of the spotters with a clipboard. The bidder was Vincent Haig: the poor, struggling picture framer whose grandfather faced eviction from Sexton Cottage.

Dryden hung around outside by the exit. He was angry, confused, but most of all he felt like a fool. But for the fact that the Barrowby Airfield blast had wiped most other stories off the newslist, he'd have run the story of Sexton Cottage in *The Crow*: how a heartless vicar threatened to evict a blind man from his home. Now it turned out the victim's family had the cash to buy the house. It seemed Dryden had merely offered Haig a useful option: if he'd failed to win the auction, the newspaper story would have applied some pressure on Temple-Wright to find his grandfather a decent home.

Haig appeared about twenty minutes later and worked his way around the large shed towards the pen reserved for a special sale of antique pictures. Dryden followed at a distance, deciding to watch rather than seek an immediate confrontation. A rope was slung across the entrance to the stall to keep idle punters back from the canvases. Haig slipped easily underneath it and chatted with one of Dacey's officials, a man with white hair, in one of those overalls that's exactly the same colour as a brown envelope. There was a third man, who looked like the stall-holder, in a suit. As they talked Haig ran a finger around an

243

ornate gilt frame which held an English landscape in oils. He smiled, touching the carved
wood, caressing the gold.

TWENTY-NINE

Saturday
Dryden woke at dawn with a single word echoing in his head: 'Raptor.' Perhaps it had surfaced
from a nightmare, because the last time he'd
heard it had been at Third Drove, talking to Will
Brinks, the travellers' guard dog straining on its
rope leash. They'd talked about the kites farmers
flew to keep birds off the crops, and how they'd
once used real birds of prey. Brinks had reminded him that the proper word for them was
raptors. *It's what my dad's business is called:*
Raptors.

Dryden always slept on the outside of the
double bunk in the narrowboat, so he was able to
slide his left leg over until the knee could bend,
allowing his foot to fall silently to the boards.
Laura turned away at the movement with prac-
tised ease. Eden lay in his cot, on his back, limbs
loose, as if in parachute freefall.

He went out on deck and stepped across to *PK*
122, into the wheelhouse. The sun was a pale
circle in a thin mist and devoid of all heat. But
the laptop glowed and made him feel warmer.
He put 'raptor' and 'Brinks' into Google while

the kettle boiled, thinking that nothing was ever that simple; but there, ridiculously, was what he was after.

It was the third item down, under English Hen Harriers Right On The Brink and About Us: Raptor Research Association. It read: Raptors to Star in Village Fête. From the *Lincoln Echo*. RAPTORS – a travelling display of birds of prey, was to provide the finale to the festivities at the village of Seawall, twenty miles south of Lincoln. The village lay in the heart of the Lincolnshire Fens, the distant flatlands which stretched south from the chalk hills on which stood Lincoln Cathedral. Flatlands which would blend, seamlessly, into the Great Soak, and then on – as if the world was indeed flat – to the Black Fens, and to Ely Cathedral on its low hill.

According to the *Echo*, Seawall's annual fête was today. The finale was at two. It was eight o'clock in the morning. Normally he'd spend a Saturday with Laura and Eden. The weekend beckoned, with maybe a trip to one of north Norfolk's deserted golden beaches. But Will Brinks held the key to what had really happened out at Barrowby Airfield. Dryden knew nothing about his life, his family, his background. The explosion was a big story: *The Crow*'s lead had been followed up widely on TV and radio, and surfing now on his laptop he found it in all the nationals, tabloids and broadsheets. The vast majority cited *The Crow* as the source.

All of which would enhance Dryden's Fleet Street reputation, and make it much more likely that in the future he could sell stories, and in the

245

long term attract talented youngsters, looking for a good start to a career in newspapers, to sign up as a trainee in Ely. So this wasn't just any old story. It could begin to make *The Crow*'s reputation. Dryden had given up a Fleet Street career after the accident to be at Laura's side. It was a decision he had never regretted. But he still had ambitions, and one of them was to build something in Ely that would mark his editorship of *The Crow* as a turning point in the paper's history.

So he wrote Laura a note, cut himself some bread and cheese from the galley, and rang Humph, telling him to wait up by the farm, and to be ready for a long trip, starting at nine.

The Capri arrived ten minutes early, with a full tank. It was an extraordinary journey: 124 miles in two dimensions. But for the slight eighty-foot rise of the Isle of Ely, the rest of the route was either at, or below, sea level. After fifteen miles he lost sight of the cathedral's West Tower in the rear window. From the top of the embankment on the Fosse Way he glimpsed distant waves out in the Wash. Turning north, they hugged the coast past Skegness and then turned inland through wide, empty farmland. It was flat, but there the parallels with the Cambridgeshire and Norfolk fens came to an end: this was a different world, of old farmsteads, lonely but mighty trees, wealthy houses, hedgerows, the patterns of the past set down on a living map, not the brutal mathematical grids of the drained south fens.

The village of Seawall was fifteen miles inland, behind its eponymous bank, built to keep

246

the distant sea from overwhelming the land in the eighteenth century. There was a church, a few cottages in a red northern brick, and a redundant railway halt. From the top of the sea defences Dryden could see Boston Stump, the tower of the parish church, the highest in England, fifteen miles to the north. The fête was out on a field, the stalls set in a rough circle round the cricket pitch. There was a car park for the day on grass, and Dryden left Humph parked beside a vast barbecue grid, upon which sausages sizzled.

The raptors were displayed on wooden tree stumps. Owls, hawks and falcons, each masked, all with leather straps. One of the owls was huge – the size of a child, with a head that moved like a turret on a gun. There was something dusty and sad about the birds; tethered, robbed of the beauty they held in flight. Behind the raptors was a cloth backdrop, and behind that a mobile home, beside which a man sat chopping raw meat on a breadboard. He had blond hair, in long locks, and was smoking, a roll-up stuck to his bottom lip. A peregrine falcon perched on the edge of the table, the bird's gyres wrapped round the sturdy wooden table leg.

'Sorry to bother you,' said Dryden. 'I know you're busy. I've driven up from Ely. It's about Will Brinks. He'd be family?' He put the snapshot he'd taken from Rick's Tattoo parlour on the table.

The falcon blinked, looking at Dryden with one eye.

The traveller studied the photograph. There was dried blood under his nails, which were long and neatly trimmed. Dryden thought that there was an indefinable stillness about people who spent most of their lives in the open air. This man had that: as if he had a right just to be here, in his own skin, under the sky.

The man looked at him then. Blue eyes, as piercing as the falcon's beak.

'I'm sorry,' said Dryden quickly. 'But there's been an accident and I don't think the police have been able to make contact?' Dryden held up both hands. 'Will's in hospital – injured. He's clearly very ill but he's got the best care. I thought you should know. I talked to him a few days ago about a picture he took of an owl and he mentioned the name of your business so I tracked you down.'

The traveller stood, letting the plastic chair fall back on the grass. 'Let's walk,' he said, plunging the knife into the chopping board. The voice was much higher than Dryden had expected, almost singsong, suggesting an ability to hit a note at will.

There was a beer tent and the man bought two halves of cider and set them on a table in the sun and wind.

'How did this happen?' he asked, draining half the glass.

'You hadn't heard? It's been in the papers, radio, TV.'

'We keep apart. That's why we live like this. And I try not to read the papers. They don't really seem that concerned with our world.'

'There was an explosion, on Barrowby Airfield,' said Dryden. 'Three men, two of them

248

Chinese, were brewing illicit alcohol. The still exploded. Will was standing outside; the blast knocked him down. He's suffered some burns, internal injuries. The other men were killed.'

For the first time Dryden had been able to describe what had happened at the old airfield as if he hadn't been there. He let his shoulders relax, tension bleeding out of his neck muscles.

The traveller's face was immobile, but Dryden noted a sudden dilation of the blue eyes.

'I'm sorry to bring such bad news. Another man, Chinese too, died earlier in the week at Christ Church in Brimstone Hill. He'd been shot. Thieves had taken lead off the roof. The police think it's a war between gangs, or within a gang. Will may have been holding a gun at the time of the blast. The detective leading the investigation believes Will might be responsible, for the explosion, and the murder at Christ Church.'

'They think *Will* did all this?'

Dryden didn't see any reason why he should lie. 'Yes. They need to interview him. But I think they'll charge him whatever he says if the forensics fit. So maybe murder, on three counts.'

The man looked back at the mobile home and the raptor stall.

'You're his father?' asked Dryden.

'Stepfather. I'm John Brinks. His mother, Mary, she's in the caravan. She'll want to go to the hospital. I'll go too. After the show.'

'I found him, your stepson, after the blast. I was the first on the scene. It's a mystery why he was there at all. The police can't find his car, or any documents in the caravan at Third Drove, and his dog's missing. When I found him there were fifty-pound notes lying scattered around him. He had a holdall full of cash, as if he'd been carrying the money when the blast knocked him down.'

'He did security for Barrowby Oilseed,' said John Brinks. 'That was his job, to keep an eye on the place, day and night. They paid well. It all looked above board. Will wouldn't have done anything he knew to be illegal. I know you won't believe that. We're travellers. We break the law. Flout it. That's a word I hear a lot. Flout.'

'Maybe he didn't know it was illegal, at least at the start,' offered Dryden.

'I said. He's afraid of the law. Of breaking rules. When he was a teenager he fell in with a bad crowd. Not travellers; foreigners, field-workers. Once, he was held overnight in a cell at Wisbech. He'd have been fifteen. They'd all got pissed up and in a fight. He couldn't take that, the cell. It wasn't just a fear of it, it was a phobia. They had to let him out during the night because he was harming himself, hitting his head against the wall. Summers he won't even sleep in the caravan. So he never broke the law, absolutely never, because he couldn't take the thought of gaol. That was part of him, the way he was.'

'I don't doubt you,' said Dryden. 'What if he found out what they were doing? That it wasn't just rapeseed they were bottling. Perhaps they wanted him to help, to work with the still. And they stole metal as well. They could have tried to use him to flog it, to find a fence. Then he'd be in a tight corner. Trapped. So maybe that's why he planned to run away.'

Brinks gave him a despairing look. For the first time there was doubt in his eyes.

Dryden always got the impression, talking to travellers, that he was seeing into the past when he looked in their eyes. As if there were several lifetimes' worth of experience inside, behind the oddly colourless eyes. A strange, troubled depth. He thought that most cultures carried the past in books. These people seemed to carry it within themselves.

'I think he was leaving Barrowby,' said Dryden. 'For good.'

'The airfield?'

'No. Brimstone. The Fens. The site. That's what it looks like, doesn't it? The cash, the car, the paperwork, even the dog. He was clearing out.'

Brinks drained the cider and Dryden got refills.

The bar was full, voices raised; a few glanced sideways at the traveller in the leather jerkin, the scars on his hands, of claws and beaks.

Dryden ferried ciders to the table. 'Why was Will left behind at Third Drove?'

'He was a loner. He used to come with us when he was younger, he was part of the show, he's good with the birds. Better than me. But we don't need him. So he stayed. He's reliable. Always. He has his problems, but he likes to fight them alone. I'm proud of him.'

There was a sudden glare of the eyes, daring Dryden to suggest Will Brinks had done anything to sully that pride.

A woman appeared at John Brinks' elbow. Thin, petite, with auburn hair, in a suede jacket and smart green corduroy trousers and leather boots, she could have been County Set – a solicitor's wife, or an accountant's.

Her eyes searched Dryden's face.

John Brinks stood. 'It's Will. There's been an accident; we need to go back after the show.'

'Is he alive?' The voice was perfectly under control.

'Yes,' said Dryden. 'But he's ill. There was an explosion on the old airfield, at the unit he guarded. They were running an illicit still; it exploded. He's in Wisbech General in intensive care. The police are at his bedside.'

Her lips buckled. 'Is he dying?'

'Everyone hopes he'll pull through.' Dryden had tried to be honest in his reply and she was smart enough to pick up the inference: sometimes, hope wasn't enough.

'We'll go back now,' she said.

THIRTY

At first they formed a convoy: Humph leading in the Capri, Brinks' four by four and caravan behind. But once they hit the main road Brinks went past at eighty-five mph on a straight stretch. The Capri got to Wisbech forty-five minutes later.

'What we doing?' asked Humph. 'Hospital or home?'

As the cabbie waited for a reply, the Capri circled what was now officially known as rabbit roundabout. Several years previously residents had noticed rabbits appearing amongst the civic greenery on the central island. They responded by chucking any spare salad on to the grass as they drove past. It's not difficult to find spare salad in the Fens: sixty per cent of all carrots eaten in England are grown within twenty miles of rabbit roundabout. The rabbits thrived. They did what rabbits do. The council dug them a brick warren, copying the practice of the Romans of a millennium earlier, although they didn't go on to harvest the animals for food. The council put up a sign that said Rabbit Round-about, and then everyone lost interest. Everyone except Humph, who liked to try and count the rabbits whenever he drove past, and always allowed himself three circuits to complete the census.

'Forty-two,' he said, as they swung round for the third time. He offered Dryden a biro so that he could add the number to a list inscribed on the dashboard. It was the kind of meaningless ritual that made them both happy.

The record, of seventy-three, was circled.

'Let's go home,' said Dryden. He saw little point in hanging around the hospital. The Brinkses would be by Will's bedside, as would the police. What was Dryden going to do? Best to go home and wait for news. He had enough background from John Brinks to use for a feature if his stepson turned out to be Friday's prime suspect. Plus, he'd surreptitiously taken a few pictures of the family home and the raptors while the Brinkses had packed up.

Dryden yawned, his jawbone cracking. 'Home,' he said again. And closed his eyes. The sleepless night of his nightmare was beginning to affect his nervous system. A micro-muscle ticked under his left eye. The broken bucket seat of the Capri felt ridiculously comfortable. He needed to blank out the world behind his eyelids, which was odd, because usually Wisbech perked him up. It was an oddity, Cambridgeshire's secret seaport, just six miles from the coast of the Wash along its muddy tidal estuary. It was a place which had gone on a strange journey in the last ten years, from being voted the 'typical' English town to the place in Britain with the highest percentage of migrant workers. *Wisbechistan* to the locals, a red rag to the BNP, a melting pot which could boil over any Saturday night.

Humph's radio crackled. Hardly crystal clear when the cab was fifty yards from the control room in Ely, the reception here, thirty-five miles north, sounded like fifty full English breakfasts cooking at once.

A thin, reedy voice could just be heard through the static: the cab controller announcing that all West Norfolk mobile police units had been called to Erebus Street, King's Lynn. Cause: civil disturbance. Fire and ambulance alerted.

'Let's go,' said Dryden. Erebus Street was

home to the two Chinese workers who'd died in the lock-up unit at Barrowby Airfield. He didn't believe in coincidences. Whatever was going on down Erebus Street – and civil disturbance covered a multitude of crimes from domestic doorstep tiff to a full-scale riot – it had to be linked to the Barrowby Airfield explosion.

They took the Lynn road across the Fens. The journey promised mile after mile of flat farm-land stretching away from the road on its high bank, the only break in this horizontal world the occasional medieval churches which marked the line of the old coast. Dryden drifted into sleep, lulled by the onward motion of the cab, follow-ing the Roman road east. Humph tuned into KLFM to pick up the latest news, as if he had to fill the silence as Dryden slept, although it was no different from the silence when he was awake.

Dryden opened his eyes as the cab reached town, troubled by a series of zigzag turns, as it threaded its way through the grey overspill suburbs. Erebus Street was in the town's dock-lands, down near the giant grain silo which towered over the fishing wharf. The street was short, terraced, a cul-de-sac, running down to a dock, with the view ahead open-ended, but for the locked gates. The rusting hulk of a container ship stood twice as high as the houses.

The street looked like a set for a disaster movie. There were barriers across it at the junc-tion with the main road, plus two police cars swathed with bulletproof padded shields. A crowd of about a hundred and fifty people stood

255

watching a house burn. Gouts of flame roared from the two windows in the upper storey, like jet engine flares. Water played into the flames from three fire engines. The windows on the lower floors were burnt out, smouldering. Dryden caught the sad smell of soaked bedding through the cab's open window.

Up close Dryden realized this was no ordinary street. Lynn's local economy was as tough as Wisbech's, powered by a volatile mix of ex-Londoners who had moved north for cheap council housing, and migrant workers, both legal and illegal. The sign reading Erebus Street had been painted over with Chinese characters. There were three Chinese restaurants: one on each corner and one in the distance at the bottom of the street by the wharf. A church on the corner boasted MARTIAL ARTS on a banner strung across its stained-glass window. One of the terraced houses had a pub-style sign which read MASSAGE. A Chinese lantern hung from a lamppost.

Dryden approached a uniformed PC he didn't recognize on the barrier and showed his press card and ID for *The Crow*.

'What's up?' he asked.

'You're a bit far from home,' said the copper. He was young, slight, with a poor attempt at a moustache under his nose.

'Can I go through?'

'No, you can't. It's not a ride at the fair. You can talk to him, though, if you're desperate.' He pointed along the barrier to a man decked in cameras. 'He's from the local rag.'

Gary Merton introduced himself. He was with the *Lynn Herald,* the town's own weekly. He was the chief photographer. They didn't have a reporter on the scene because it was a Saturday, and the editorial staff was all on leave, or off shift.

'So it's all down to me, not for the last time.' He smelt of applewood, quite distinctly, and of carbolic. His skin looked incredibly clean, as if it was about to be featured in an advert for cosmetics. 'I was in the club.' He nodded at the MASSAGE sign, and his eyes widened. 'It's good. The girls know their stuff. By the time I'd got me kit on the place was alight. There'd been a fight in the street, apparently, loads of 'em. That's the story. A "pitched battle" – that's the quote. Soldier on soldier.'

He'd used the words deliberately, but when Dryden didn't bite, he explained himself: 'That's what they call 'em. It's a Triad thing. *Soldiers.* Everyone's got a number in the gang; soldiers are forty-nine. Every one of them. They're the muscle. Whereas, say, four-one-five is White Paper Fan; that's the moneyman – finance and advice. You'd be surprised what you need to know to stay safe in this town.'

He hitched up a badly fitting pair of jeans.

'So I asked one of the women what was up, and she says the soldiers that were fighting each other are from the same gang, that the gang that runs the street is breaking up, like in a civil war. Some of the soldiers have set up a rival gang; they've joined up with some Poles. That's what she said. This breakaway lot are Christians. I

257

told her that was crap, that there aren't any Chinky Christians, but she says it's the big thing now. What d'you reckon?'

'Where do these Christians worship?' asked Dryden.

'Church of the Nativity, that's on the other side of the docks. That's where the Poles go, and she's right there, because I've done some weddings and they've been Poles.'

Dryden thought of Sima Shuba's dead body draped over the crucifix in the graveyard of Christ Church, surrounded by the shattered wooden body of Christ. Had that been a deliberate defilement of the Christian religion? Had Sima Shuba been a member of the breakaway gang? And had his 'crucifixion' been a message to them to fall back in line, or at least keep off disputed turf?

Merton stopped talking long enough to take some shots as the fire gutted the top storey, then began to billow smoke, as a roof beam snapped and cartwheeled out into the street.

'Hey up,' he said. A plain-clothed CID man was walking towards them up Erebus Street. He carried a megaphone and a radio. 'Gary.' He nodded at Merton. 'Someone said you wanted to get closer. I'm taking it we get prints, as usual?'

Merton nodded. 'You will indeed, Mr Talbot.'

'Come on then. But stay with me. This is turning out to be a bit more serious than we first thought. Can't have you trampling all over the place in your size tens.' He lifted the tape of the barrier.

Gary gave Dryden a kitbag of camera gear and

a tripod and told him to follow.

They walked past a small group of women and children talking to two women PCs. One of the women, tall, with a Western haircut, was crying, held upright by the rest, her hands pressed against her face, which was flushed and shiny with tears.

A second barrier had been set up opposite the house. The fire was almost out now, white smoke drifting from the upper windows. The fire brigade had a video camera on a tripod set up and running on automatic. Scene-of-crime officers were entering the house.

'You can take some snaps from here – no closer,' said Talbot. The CID man was short, muscular, with the slightly knuckled face of a rugby player. His suit jacket was tight across his shoulders.

They could hear the sizzle of steam and foam now from the gutted house. A forensic officer came out of the ground floor with a plastic evidence bag, which he gave to Talbot.

Dryden noted that the number 426 had been painted on the wall of the burnt-out house, four foot high, in red.

'What does that number mean?' asked Dryden.

'And who are you?' asked Talbot, but not unkindly.

Dryden gave him his card. As he read it, flicking it over, Dryden tried to work out what Talbot had in the forensic bag. It looked like a piece of metal plumbing.

'The four-two-six denotes Red Pole,' said Talbot. 'That's the master. The head of the gang.

It's all bollocks. They're crooks, small-time hoods; it's just all dressed up as something else. Underneath all the shite it's still drugs, vice, protection.' He pointed across the street. 'And massage parlours.'

'Where is he, this master?' asked Dryden.

'He's dead. In that front room,' said Talbot.

Dryden stopped breathing because the moment took him back to Barrowby Airfield, and the three incinerated victims in the ash of the lock-up. There was smoke here, and flame, and blackened timbers; and now there was another body, this time unseen. But that didn't make it any easier. He wanted to turn away, maybe run away, and find clean air to fill his lungs.

Merton's camera whirred as he took picture after picture, zooming in through the downstairs window. They could see a mirror, bare walls with old wallpaper, white-suited forensic officers reflected in the silvered glass.

Dryden took a deep, calming, breath. 'Dead? How?' The questions came out as a whisper.

'There'll be a statement later from headquarters. Use that. We've never spoken. Got it?'

Dryden nodded, both hands held out in compliance.

Talbot held up the evidence bag. 'Murder weapon,' he said. 'One of them, anyway. The cans are scattered around. Looks like there were three of them, each armed with one of these.'

And then Dryden saw what it was: the head and nozzle of a hand-held blowtorch, the kind you can use for DIY, peeling paint off woodwork.

'They used them on his face,' said Talbot. 'Let's just say that we're not going to be able to get a visual ID on the victim. Get the picture?'

The detective pressed the back of his hand against his mouth as if overcome by the moment. The hard-bitten copper seemed momentarily unable to carry on. 'Come to think of it, we're not going to be able to use his teeth either.'

THIRTY-ONE

Sunday
Dryden hoped that with the dusk would come some respite from the drama on Erebus Street. The fire, and the fate of the unseen victim within the burnt-out house, had added a fresh circle to the hell he'd first glimpsed in the ash of the lock-up at Barrowby Airfield. Entangled in this tale of fire and flesh, he was struggling to maintain his role as the natural outsider, watching, and then reporting, on the lives of others.

It was very quiet on board *PK 122*. The winds always died at sunset. This summer the pheno-menon had been striking because it was the only time the blades of the turbine were at rest. The old boat appeared at its most haunted in this daily silence. The wooden plaque that read *Dunkirk 1940* seemed to radiate its own soundtrack; very faintly, the voices of men, calling from the water. Dryden's imagination provided the

261

pictures: the boat nosing its way forward in the surf off the Normandy Beaches, ack-ack clouds above, the dead in the water, survivors struggling towards *PK 122*.

Normally such echoes were a comfort to him. Today they seemed to mingle with the images he was trying to suppress. He tried to keep himself busy, fixing one of the pumps on *Lunigiana*, making tea for Humph, joining Laura on a walk by the river, Eden in the papoose. It was the kind of Sunday he loved in many ways: domestic, but without the deadening central weight of a house. But still a black cloud hovered, dampening his mood. He wondered if the shock for which he'd been treated at Barrowby might have an echo, returning at intervals, creating that strange sense of separation from the real world.

DI Friday's black Ford purred down the drove road from Barham's Farm. Dryden had seen him on Sundays before, but always up in the town park, watching his sons play football. The detective parked his car on the narrow wharf beside the boats. As he got out he lit a cigarette and the effort of inhaling raised his shoulders.

'Social call?' asked Dryden.

'Yeah, right.'

Dryden realized with a shock that, despite his natural antipathy to authority, he liked George Friday.

The detective's damaged foot was hardly noticeable in the mornings, but by the close of the day he always seemed tired, wrapped in a raincoat despite the heat of the day, halting with the limp.

'Can we talk?' asked Friday, without enthusi-asm.

The car had woken Laura from an afternoon sleep. She appeared on deck with Eden. The day of filming at Coldham's Farm had been a triumph for her, and ever since her eyes had held a visible spark. 'I'll make tea,' she said, disappearing below deck.

Friday came aboard and took a seat in the stern of *PK 122*. Dryden wondered if he'd been home since getting the call to Barrowby Airfield three days earlier. He seemed to radiate a profound exhaustion. Producing a small plastic envelope from his pocket, he held it up to the light. There was a bullet inside.'I thought you should know sooner rather than later.'

The sun caught the object in the bag so that it glowed, as if emitting its own light.

'Is that...?'

'The bullet fired at Barrowby,' said Friday.

Dryden thought that this small, almost beautiful object had caused a great deal of grief. It had almost certainly sparked the explosion which snuffed out the lives of three men in a few devastating seconds.

'It was embedded in the breeze blocks in the back wall,' continued Friday. 'Soft enough to slow it down – didn't do a lot of damage to the bullet, did it? Forensics have just filed a report. It took a deflection off an iron girder before hitting the wall, so that's probably what ignited the gas vapour. Anyway, the metal around the hole in the door was rust-free. Totally. Apparently metal scratched like that will begin to alter, chemically, within twenty-four hours. But this was newly exposed metal, no sign of rust, so the bullet was fired that day. Given the explosion, we have to presume it triggered the blast.'

'So it all fits,' said Dryden.

'Not quite. This bullet didn't come out of the gun we found by Brinks. That gun had not been fired for some time, maybe years.'

All the images Dryden had in his head seemed to pixilate, like a dodgy DVD, gradually breaking apart.

'This bullet was fired down a rifled barrel. Brinks had a handgun, no rifling. The bullet's got a ballistic signature, so we know, broadly, the type of gun used. A very classy model, apparently – probably military. Kind of weapon that starts its life in Eastern Europe.'

'So Brinks is no longer your prime suspect. He's a victim too.'

Friday dug his hands in the raincoat pockets. 'Indeed. What we need now is a new prime suspect. Let's say we're taking a keen interest in the events on Erebus Street yesterday. My spies tell me you were there?'

'You think that was payback? That this is all gang warfare – killing the triad master was retribution for the deaths at Barrowby?'

Friday continued to stare at the river.

'Arrests?'

'Eight. No charges. The main triad organisation in Lynn, and indeed in the UK, is called 14K. The two Chinese men at Barrowby were members of a breakaway group. These new kids on the block are called Sun Yee On. It's got links

264

with migrant Polish workers.'

'They're Christians,' said Dryden.

'Indeed. Well, they go to a Catholic church. Is that the same thing? Having just come from the autopsy on the victim found in the house on Erebus Street, I would doubt it very much. Let's just say the breakaway group likes to see itself as different on a point of religious belief. It's all part of the brand image – they're the future, not the stuffy old past. They believe in the religion of the West – not Taoism, or Buddhism.'

Friday accepted a mug of tea from Laura. 'Sun Yee On tried to make the metal trade their own, apparently, and they'd clearly branched out into illicit booze too.'

'And this turf war started with Sima Shuba's murder,' said Dryden.

'Looks like it. But it's complicated, and we don't really know what happened that night at Christ Church. Sima Shuba used to be an enforcer for 14K. But we're told he'd changed sides and was working out at Barrowby. We think 14K sent someone up to put the frighteners on Sun Yee On. I reckon they followed them to Christ Church and then struck. Looks like they chose to make an example of Sima Shuba. Maybe he was the newest recruit. Anyway, he ended up on the cross. I think that was a message, don't you? This is where the Christians end up. Don't mess with us any more. This is what happens.'

Friday slurped tea. 'So that's where we are,' he concluded. 'All I need to do is find some forensics to link 14K to Barrowby. The gun would be nice. Am I going to find it? Not unless I am very lucky.'

Dryden stretched his legs out. 'So what are we saying? That 14K turned up at Barrowby, took a pot shot, got lucky, and the place blew up? Doesn't sound very likely.'

Friday drained the nicotine from a fresh cigarette. 'Nope. It isn't. What if they just got close and waited to pick someone off. Or waited to pick all of them off. So they take a shot at Brinks and hit the lock-up. Then the lot goes up. Maybe they didn't set out to wipe 'em out.'

'But that would mean they missed Brinks, right? Do these guys miss?'

'Always a first time.'

A swan went by on the river, its wings set like icing.

'One thing,' said Dryden. 'A few days before the blast, Brinks took a picture of a Funeral Owl. He's a twitcher, a bird nerd. But the Funeral Owl is rare, and it was a terrific picture. He sent it in for us to print, although when I went out to see him he was pretty terrified I'd print his name, or his picture. Anyway – my point is that outside his caravan was a table. There were sheets of paper covered in number grids, four-by-four grids, all the digits from nought to nine inclusive, plus two blanks. Those turbines at Coldham's, they have identical security keypads. If he got that shot of the owl he's got cameras, telephoto lenses, the lot. I think he watched the maintenance crews getting into the turbines with the field glasses and noted down the codes. He got some right, some wrong. I think he was on the inside, not the outside. I talked to his stepfather.'

Friday nodded. 'I know. He's by the kid's bedside with one of my uniforms.'

'He reckons he's terrified of breaking the law, all goes back to some traumatic night in the cells when he was a tearaway,' said Dryden.

'He's got previous. We're on to that.'

'But has he talked?'

'Not yet.'

'I think he got drawn in to the gang, then took fright and decided to do a runner. I'm just saying, I think he was more than an innocent bystander.'

Laura joined them with Eden, so they talked about the river, about the boats, about not having a house.

'Thanks for coming by,' said Dryden.

'A favour,' said Friday. 'My one chance is the gun. I'll have the spec and a picture soon. Can you run it in *The Crow*? These gangs bring their guns in, but there's a chance it's local.'

'OK, sure. Thanks for the update.'

'I had to come down anyway; there's a body in the river, up at Ely. They'll have the details at control in the morning. Looks like the missing teenager, Julian Amhurst. He had chemical symbols in ink on his arm.'

Laura took Eden up in her arms. 'God, how awful. Do the parents know?'

Friday looked at his shoes. 'Not yet.'

THIRTY-TWO

Monday
Dryden opened the gate into Christ Church
graveyard. He paused in a splash of sunshine
shaped like a star and looked up at the roof. The
Rev. Temple-Wright had been as good as her
word. The missing lead had been replaced with
black plastic sheeting. It was as if the building
had been wounded. Like many simple, beautiful
objects, the blemish destroyed its symmetry,
blurred its simple lines.

The sheep on the Clock Holt were crowded in
one corner, in a patch of shade, and bleated as he
walked towards Sexton Cottage. A white van
was parked in the lane, artwork on the side in a
decorative style.

Vincent Haig
Pictures framed and restored.

But it was Albe Haig who opened the door. His
eyes were focused on a point over Dryden's left
shoulder. 'Come in,' he said, shuffling back. He
looked at his feet, which were in slippers.
'Vinnie's here,' he said. 'You'll want to speak to
him.'

There was music in the house: 1940s big band

sounds. Vincent Haig appeared holding an iPhone, using the thumb to text. In his other hand he had a mug of tea. 'Hi. Come through.'

They'd locked eyes and Dryden was struck again by the pink sclera, the cracked blood vessels around the irises.

They went into the cottage's front room. Miniature again, hardly ten foot square, with a small Victorian iron-grate fire, a pair of arm-chairs, a bookcase full of audio tapes, a side-board too big for the house, let alone the room; and an easel holding a canvas half finished. It was a portrait of the house, in thick dollops of oil. The light from the window played across the surface of the painting so that Dryden could see the furrows and ridges of the brushwork.

Haig had propped Dryden's collage of OS maps up on one of the chairs, neatly framed, Perspex covered, showing the whole of the Brimstone Hill area in impeccable detail, the individual charts beautifully dovetailed to pro-duce a single map.

'This is perfect,' said Dryden. He gave him three ten-pound notes and a fiver.

Haig slipped them in his wallet. A tradesman's wallet – leather, worn, and thick with notes. 'I was at Dacey's auction rooms on Friday,' said Dryden. 'The police raided some of the stalls, looking for stolen metalwork mainly. That's what the crooks out at Barrowby Airfield were up to when they weren't distilling gut rot in bottles. Police and trade descriptions have been watching the sales for some time in case any stolen metal turned up. After the explosion at

269

Barrowby they decided to cut their losses and swoop, to see what they could find. But you had other interests at Dacey's on Friday night...'

'So?'

'Congratulations on buying the house,' said Dryden. 'Were you going to mention it, or was I supposed to run the story anyway? If I hadn't kept it for next week I'd look like a prize fool. I don't need help to achieve that status. Or was the idea just to put Temple-Wright under pressure, see if you could get it for nothing? And if that failed, which it did, you had the cash all the time.'

'I didn't know.' It was the old man, talking from the doorway. He crossed the threshold, his eyes searching for Dryden's.

'I didn't know,' he said again. 'I don't approve.'

'Not going to stop you living here, though, is it?' said his grandson. There was a cruel note in the voice and it made the old man cower. 'Just leave it,' he told his grandfather. 'We don't need to apologise to anyone.'

Vincent Haig squared his shoulders, forcing himself to meet Dryden's eyes. 'I was going to tell you if we were successful at the auction. It was a public auction. We've done nothing wrong. The house is ours now. The fact we had to buy it to make sure Grandad can go on living here is still a scandal. He was promised. There was a bargain.'

The old man's hand moved to the doorjamb, finding it with just the slightest of spatial errors, so that it looked like he was grabbing it for

270

support.

'The question is, how did you buy it?' said Dryden. 'Where did the money come from?'

'That's none of your business, is it?'

'Mortgaged his own home,' said the old man. 'Went to the bank, too. I said he was a fool.' The old man had raised one hand as if he expected a blow. But then Dryden saw that he was trying to put his hand between his own, unseeing eyes, and those of his grandson, as if he didn't want a connection to exist between them.

'I need to talk to Grandad,' said Haig to Dryden, as if the old man was a child.

And Dryden thought: *You might like to tell him the truth. Because you told me that both the Old Forge, and the cottage you live in, were rented.*

'Zabrowka,' said Dryden. 'The moonshine vodka. I know you're partial. But you told me, when I asked, that the bottle you had was a present. You've told me lots of lies, but do you know what, I *believed* that.'

'That stuff you drink,' said the old man, almost spitting it out.

'Christ, will you shut up, old man,' said Haig. The profanity, Dryden guessed, crossed a boundary which had perhaps been rarely crossed in this house. And a calculated insult, because of all the words he could have used, he'd chosen that one, in the shadow of the church which bore Christ's name.

'Why did you deserve that particular present, a crate of hooch?' asked Dryden.

Haig's face was a picture now, one of his own pictures. Slabs of colour, the lines of the face

271

inhuman, as if he'd been assembled by a com-
mittee.

'What did you do for them?' asked Dryden.
'Did you buy and sell, perhaps? It's your world,
I think, auctions, fairs. You buy and sell frames
– pictures too? Did they want you to link them
up to the trade? Is that what they needed, Vinnie,
a fence?'

'Vinnie?' asked the old man. 'Is this true?'

'I'd like you to leave. This is family business.'

Dryden clicked his fingers. 'Business. I'm
really hoping you didn't do business with the
men from Barrowby Oilseed.' He took a step
closer to Haig and was delighted to see him back
off in response. 'You didn't do *that*? You didn't
borrow the money from them, did you?'

Haig struggled to keep an impassive face.

'That's a really stupid thing to do, Vinnie,' said
Dryden. 'I don't think they do tracker mort-
gages. We're talking triad gangs here. By the
time you pay them back you'll have paid twice,
three times. That's the good news. The bad news
is what happens if you don't pay them back.
Barrowby wasn't an accident, you know. It was
murder. That's business, triad-style.'

'Does Kathleen know?' asked the old man. He
turned to where he'd last heard Dryden's voice.
'That's my daughter-in-law. She's a wonderful
girl. Works hard.'

The implication was clear.

'Shut up,' said Vincent Haig, but something of
his authority had gone. He sounded like what he
was: a bully, losing ground.

'I've always worked hard, too,' said Albe
272

Haig. 'So did your mother. We were a decent family. I don't need charity.'

Vincent Haig laughed. 'Yes, you do. You've needed charity all your life. For the last ten years you've needed me. Want to know why I stuck by you all these years? It was for Grandma.'

The old man actually flinched at the word.

'I promised her that I'd always be here for you. Always.'

He pulled at the loose shirt at his throat and Dryden saw where the loss of temper had blotched the skin.

'And, yes, Kath does know. Nice of you to ask, for once. And it is *Kath*, by the way. She hates Kathleen; she hates anyone calling her Kathleen. She just can't face telling you not to do it. Ten years of not telling you to shut up and call her by her real name. Do you know what that is? It's pity.'

Dryden couldn't look at the old man's face. His grandson's was flushed, the eyes full of tears. Dryden took the map and let himself out.

The sheep on Clock Holt had fanned out over the field to munch at the grass, but his arrival sent them all off into the shadowy corner again, where they bleated in a huddle.

Jock Donovan was at the gate out of Christ Church graveyard. Dryden was immediately aware that the old soldier had been waiting for him.

'I saw you arrive,' said Donovan. Beyond him, on the far side of the road, was Brimstone House, the old man's home. In the morning sunshine the Artex-white facade was almost pain-

273

fully bright. 'I wanted to thank you for sorting out the kites. I've been sleeping. It's made a real difference to my life. This is for your son. I'm sorry, I've forgotten his name?' Donovan had a plastic bag and from it he took a ball.

'Eden,' said Dryden.

'He'll walk when he wants to, of course,' said Donovan. 'But I thought this might help. He can hold it, but if it rolls away he'll have to go after it, and it's too big to swallow.'

Dryden accepted the ball. It felt like leather, but with a textured surface, and was about twenty centimetres across. The colours were very bright, reds and blues and whites, and there was a circular script in a language which looked to Dryden's eye like Japanese.

'It's a *jokgu* ball. The South Koreans invented it in the sixties to keep the army conscripts fit. It's like volleyball, but you use your feet, and the net's low, like tennis. Great to watch.'

'Thanks. That's a really good idea,' said Dryden. 'Thank you. I'll run a story on the kites when they've finished the tests. Local man's super hearing solves mystery of singing kites. That kind of thing. I might need a picture.'

'Yes, that's fine, that's what we agreed. Good luck with the ball.' With that Donovan turned on his heels, still holding the empty plastic bag, and walked stiffly back towards the house.

That left Dryden holding the ball. If he bounced it he'd scuff it, and it was brand new, so he just balanced it on one hand. Presents always took him aback, especially unexpected ones. He knew what he ought to feel: gratitude, a link with the giver, especially when so much thought had gone into the choice of the gift. Instead, he was left with a sense of unease, and he had to admit – if only to himself – that he often mistrusted the good intentions of others.

THIRTY-THREE

The Brimstone Café's All-Day Super Breakfast came on its own oval plate. Dryden had ordered one for Humph, but only a cup of tea with toast for himself. Grace said she wasn't hungry. They sat outside at the café's only table, under the shade of the London plane tree. Dryden thought Grace looked ill: pale, her face puffy, her narrow fingers clutching at her hair. She'd asked for coke when pushed. Humph sat opposite his daughter, trying to get her to talk. Grace was spending her time trying not to cry.

Then the all-day breakfast arrived and Humph concentrated on that.

Dryden had his laptop open and was looking at a digital image of the proposed page layouts for the next day's edition of the *Ely Express*. The front was reserved for the latest on the Barrowby Airfield killings, with the exclusive picture of Will Brinks taken from Rick's Tattoo Parlour. Brinks had switched from the CID's prime suspect to the last remaining victim of the Barrowby explosion, but the photograph was still worth its place on the front.

Page three featured the sad story of Julian Amhurst.

STAR PUPIL'S BODY FOUND IN
RIVER AT ELY

The news had been running on the local radio bulletins since dawn. He read all the copy on the front and page three and then sent Vee Hilgay a text at *The Crow* telling her it all looked good. Any late news could be added in the morning. The advertisers liked the free-sheet to be out early, and on time, to be delivered to households and businesses in the town. Dryden didn't like the free newspaper business, but by putting his own version out on the streets, he had effectively stopped a competitor muscling in on his patch.

Humph had his knife and fork in his small hands, both pointing skywards, when he finally seemed to summon the energy to stop eating and talk. 'I spoke to Mum on the mobile,' he said to Grace.

His daughter drained her coke, then looked away.

Dryden examined the ball Donovan had given him, trying to see order in the chaos of the Korean hieroglyphs.

'She said a policeman called at the house,' said Humph. 'From Ely. She said he wanted to talk to you. Why's that?'

Humph was aware that every time he spoke to Grace he was somehow adding to that centrifugal force, the one that was throwing her out,

276

away from the centre, away from him; but he couldn't stop himself.

There was a magazine on the table and Grace had found a page with a puzzle on it, a grid. She toyed with it, trying out numbers in each square with a pencil on a length of string attached to the table leg, keeping her eyes down.

'Grace,' said Humph. 'I don't care what you've done. Just tell me. I can help. We can all help.'

She pressed down with the pencil until the lead broke.

Humph chased a button mushroom round his plate with his knife. 'Mum told the copper you were staying with Grandma. So they'll be round.' Immediately he regretted the threat, realizing he'd given his daughter a watertight reason to run away again. 'Don't even think about it,' he said, waving a fork with which he had previously skewered a kidney. Two drops of watery blood fell on the plastic white tabletop.

'I'm getting more tea,' said Dryden. 'Anyone?'

He left them to it for a minute. Grace's crimes were likely to be trivial. Dryden imagined a spectrum of possibilities, from mindless shoplifting at Boots to some elegant graffiti in one of the ring-road subways.

He ordered tea and turned down a third attempt by the woman behind the counter to sell him an all-day breakfast. She was ethnic Chinese, married to a Fenman who sweltered in the kitchen. The Brimstone Café had once been a butcher's shop and the walls were still tiled. A little frieze of glazed farm animals ran round the room at eye level – cows, pigs, chickens, ducks and hares. He never ate in the Brimstone because there was a strange echo even now of its past: the iron smell of blood, the coldness of the metal hooks, a raw saltiness.

Outside the Humphries family had lapsed into silence.

Dryden dunked his tea bag in his mug – 'mashing' his father would have called it, a northern word, from the factory floor. It was a comforting ritual that reminded him of what had been a happy family.

Since his confrontation with Vincent Haig, his mind had been circling Christ Church. He couldn't shift the idea that the key to the explosion at Barrowby Oilseed didn't lie in the vicious underworld of Wisbech's triads, at least not entirely. He felt it lay here, in Brimstone Hill. Had Vincent Haig borrowed money off the triads? Dryden thought of the fifty-pound notes lying around Will Brinks' body. Had there been more cash? Had Haig, perhaps, decided to solve his problems with a single bullet? And then there was Jock Donovan. He'd been miles away from Barrowby at the moment the illicit still exploded. Dryden had seen him just after the blast in the street outside Christ Church. But images of the old man's forgotten war seemed to echo still. It hadn't been North Koreans, at least not North Koreans alone, who had sent those thousands of five-inch shells into Jock Donovan's crescent-shaped trench. It had been the Chinese, the People's Army. Had that eaten away at Donovan's soul? Was he really the forgiving man he seemed to be, free, until the moment of the Barrowby Oilseed blast, of the memory of blood and water?

The drops of kidney juice on the table were drying in the sun. Dryden's mobile buzzed, indicating an incoming text. It was from Vee at *The Crow*. *Will Brinks does runner from hosp. Manhunt.*

THIRTY-FOUR

There were three people and a dog in the Capri but none of them had made a noise for an hour. Humph was asleep, despite the large fluffy earphones clamped to his head. Dryden, in the back seat, had spent the time following a zigzag chain of thought which worried away at a single question: why was Will Brinks on the run – *again*? If the lethal bullet was the result of a gang war, why was the lowly security man afraid for his life? Had he, perhaps, seen the gunman just before the fatal blast? In the front passenger seat sat John Brinks, Will's stepfather. What he was thinking was hidden behind those remarkable blue, raptor-like eyes. The cab was parked in a clump of trees on the edge of a field so large that its distant edge was lost in a buckling mirage of midday heat.

They'd found John Brinks at his stepson's

caravan at Third Drove. The police had run him out there from the hospital. Mary Brinks was due to make an emotional appeal for her son to turn himself in on TV news later that evening. John Brinks, taciturn at best, did tell Dryden what had happened at the hospital. He'd been maintaining a bedside vigil but had slipped away to the canteen to get a cup of tea. The uniformed PC on duty had chosen the same moment to test the fire exit, and have a swift cigarette, in the process. When Brinks got back there'd been a warm, empty bed. His stepson had been on medication, and was in no condition to be on his feet, let alone on the road. He had to be found quickly, for his own health if nothing else.

The police manhunt was in top gear. A description of Brinks' car had gone to all units and a watch was being kept on all arterial roads out of the Fens. The ports were on alert, as were regional airports at Cambridge, Norwich and Peterborough. The police had dropped John Brinks at Third Drove with instructions to sit tight in case his stepson appeared. There was still no sign of Will's car, his dog, or most of his personal belongings – clothes, books, passport, driving licence, and field glasses. He hadn't had any of these at the hospital, so unless he picked them up from somewhere he couldn't run far.

Dryden had told Humph to drive straight to Third Drove so that he could get pictures of the caravan and the site for *The Crow*. He'd phoned Vee and told her he'd update the story for the paper overnight. John Brinks had needed little persuading to abandon his vigil at Third Drove.

His stepson might have learning difficulties but he wasn't stupid. He was unlikely to turn up at the site where the police knew he lived, which was why they were parked in a clump of black-thorn trees at the entrance to a field of leeks. Across that field was a wood, scattered birch mostly, sparse enough to let light pick out each tree trunk. Inside the thicket was a bird hide, young Brinks' private hideaway since child-hood. He'd taken his stepfather there once, a few years back, to show him a cygnet he was raising by hand. It had been no more than a shed built of branches, a plastic-sheeting roof, and some rough bedding, but young Will had treated it like a teenager's bedroom. Bird-spotting books and a journal of sightings were kept in a waterproof tin, a collection of feathers and hatched egg-shells arranged on a shelf built of bricks.

The sun was high above the trees, Tizer-red, so that the black peat of the field was tinged orange. They'd decided to give it an hour and then investigate the hide, see if Brinks had used it to stash his valuables.

Dryden could see John Brinks' eyes in the rear-view mirror, fixed unblinkingly on the distant wood. 'He's scared, isn't he?' said Dryden, final-ly breaking the spell of the silence. He thought the chances of Will Brinks turning up here were 1 in a 1000. The chances of him turning up at the caravan site had been 1 in a million, so they were still playing the odds.

'He is now,' said John. He had a fuzzy voice and Dryden guessed he'd not long ago given up smoking. 'Problem with the kid is he's half

281

stupid, half genius. If I said I understood him I'd be lying. He's my son just as much as the other two, but how he thinks? Forget it.'

Humph shifted in the driver's seat and the suspension gave out a resonant twang.

'How did he get the job at Barrowby Oilseed?' It was a question that had been worrying Dryden. He couldn't see the shy, awkward, Will Brinks just doorstepping potential employers.

'He had an eye for picking up bits of work. We all do. It's how you make a living without a full-time job. Without a house to live in. Contacts are important, a personal link. He'd have got a tip from Dan.'

'Daniel Fangor?'

'Yup.'

The Pole who died in the explosion, alongside the two Chinese.

'How'd he know him?'

Brinks' eyes flicked from the view across the field to Dryden's reflection in the rear-view. Being a Capri it was a back seat without a door. Dryden didn't like that look, and he found himself wondering if he could get his bony frame out of the open window in a hurry. His question had clearly crossed an unseen line.

He tried another. 'It's not full time then, a job like that?'

Brinks was very still. 'No. It's called pluralism. The holding of many jobs at the same time. It used to be standard practice in the church, the state. It was one of the reasons everyone hated the church so much before the Reformation. It's one of the ways the rich stay rich. They get paid

282

for doing two things at the same time. If you're poor it's seen as a swindle, moonlighting. Will had other jobs. Most were casual, paid in cash, no paperwork.'

It was such a surprising answer Dryden just nodded. He wondered then if they had time to find out John Brinks' life story. Dryden had thought of him as a born tinker. But perhaps he'd married into the family. Where had the education come from – teachers or study? He sensed the almost manic focus of the autodidact, and recalled the bookcase in the caravan at Third Drove, with its volumes on history and natural history.

Brinks took a deep breath. He had a barrel chest, almost a deformity, as if his spine was curved. 'He met Fangor in Wisbech. There was a crowd of them, mainly Poles. If they'd been middle-class kids you'd say they were friends; these kids, on the other hand, were a gang. He was out of his depth so he chucked them in, kept to his bird-watching. With being the caretaker at the site in the summer, it meant he was on his own a lot, but he liked that. That was his role, his position. It's important, and he took it seriously. When Fangor turned up on the old airfield he offered Will the job at Barrowby Oilseed. He couldn't afford to turn it down.'

Across the field of leeks Dryden could see the hide in the trees, but so well camouflaged it looked like a dense thicket of branches and dead wood. When they'd parked the Capri they'd all agreed they'd keep watch for an hour. Dryden's watch said fifty-seven minutes. He thought again about finding Brinks at Barrowby Airfield, the fifty-pound notes scattered on the grass around him. He was sure Brinks had been about to disappear. If so, he'd have packed a bag. And the car? Where was that? Parked in Ely or Wisbech perhaps, on a backstreet, with a full tank.

'Where will he go?' asked Dryden.

'It's going to be tough. He might be the son of travellers but he doesn't travel well. Maybe Ireland. He could find the village. But the coppers here'll have contacted the Garda. So perhaps he'll just watch and wait. That's the smart thing to do. He can sleep rough – he's done it before. If he does that we might lose him for good. That's Mary's nightmare, so it's my nightmare too.'

On his lap John Brinks had a cardboard box with a decorated top which said RAINBOW PHOTOGRAPHIC STUDIOS. The police had taken it from the caravan to try and find a picture of his stepson, but had returned it now, having drawn a blank. Each snap had a caption in capitals on the back. Brinks had explained that Will was shy, almost manic in his desire to avoid being captured on film, but he'd always been keen to get behind the camera. He'd taken many of the pictures, but was shown in none.

Brinks took the top off the box now and shuffled through the snaps. He passed one over his shoulder to Dryden. A teenager, perhaps nineteen. Very dark hair, sallow skin, dark eyes, something cynical in the look to camera.

'That's Dan Fangor,' said Brinks. 'He had wheels.'

284

It was a Ford, blue. The rear window held a round sticker, white, with a black dragon, breathing red flames. The legend read: The Wavel Dragon. Krakow. Krakow, ancient capital of Poland. *A Black Dragon*.

Dryden saw the scene: the level crossing at Brimstone Hill. Muriel Calder locking eyes with one of her husband's killers. The brief communion, then the barriers rising, the klaxon sounding, and the Ford disappearing in a mirage of speed. Fangor at the wheel. The killer in the back. A white face, black hair, European features. Had it been Will Brinks? Was that why he was on the run now?

Humph woke at that moment and the sudden jolt of his limbs made them all look up, and out, across the field.

They saw a pheasant clattering up into the trees from the field, and then a figure running, breaking cover for a second on a bank top by the ditch, then down almost below the leeks, the head bobbing. John Brinks slipped out of the car and pulled the seat forward for Dryden. They knelt on a grass bank next to the car with some brush at their backs to blur their silhouettes.

They could see the figure now, moving against the background of the tree boles. The sprint had winded him so that he stopped, doubled over, shoulders heaving.

'It's Will,' said Brinks. 'He's in pain.'

And then they heard a dog bark.

'That's Lolly,' said Brinks.

The sun had gone, so that the red light was diffused and soft. Will Brinks disappeared into the muddle of wood and branches which obscured the hide. When he came out they could see the shape of a rucksack on his back, and the lead stiff in his hand, the dog jumping up, overjoyed.

Brinks fought his way through the criss-cross mesh of trees and branches towards the western end of the copse, which was denser, but without trees, just hawthorn, and yellow-dotted whin. A car door creaked, then an engine came to life.

They were back in the Capri when they saw him pull out on the drove road behind them, creeping out from the edge of the wood on a track: a silver Ford Fiesta, Will Brinks at the wheel.

Humph waited till the car was almost out of sight, then followed, while John Brinks rang a number DI Friday had given him for emergencies. He gave someone details: a description of the vehicle and the direction and speed of travel: forty-five mph, east along Siberia Belt, a long drove road that led out into the zigzag maze of dead-end fields and farms towards the unbridgeable barrier of the New Bedford River: a wide fen waterway sunk in a trench. Beyond it stretched the fresh-water marshes of the Welney Bird Reserve.

The Capri stayed half a mile back but the long straights would have given Brinks time to spot the cab in the rear-view mirror. After the second right-hand turn they regained the straight to find Brinks nearly a mile distant, a cloud of dust rising from the rear wheels.

'He's seen us,' said John Brinks. 'Don't push him.'

Humph's foot was down on the accelerator but the Capri couldn't break sixty mph. Ahead, they'd lost him, the car turning away to the left, directly towards the New Bedford River.

Despite the tinder-dry fields Dryden could smell fresh water through the open windows of the cab. The idea of the river-filled ditch that lay ahead filled him with an immediate unease. He took in a lungful of the weedy, stagnant smell; trying to quell his anxiety by meeting it head on. But the scent of water was on his tongue now, and the fear almost fully formed: the fear of water that had haunted him since childhood.

Ahead, without warning, Brinks' car appeared again as they took a left turn. Humph had closed the gap to 200 yards but as they came in line they saw the Ford jump, a zigzag skid almost putting Brinks in the roadside ditch, as the car leapt forwards.

'Steady, kid,' said Dryden.

'Back off,' said Brinks. 'Give him more room.'

Dryden wondered what shape Brinks was in. Had he, somehow, managed to avoid taking the sedatives and drugs the nursing staff would have given him in hospital? If he hadn't he was taking his life in his hands driving at more than ten mph, let alone seventy on back roads. At least now Dryden understood why he might take such a risk. If he was one of the burglars who had watched Ronald Calder bleed to death that day in 1999, pinioned with knives, he faced a life sentence if caught.

The horizon for which they were now heading was absolutely straight, and slightly elevated,

287

and Dryden realized it was the distant bank of the New Bedford River, twenty feet above the level of the surrounding fields. At its western extremity, he saw a yellow school bus, double-decked, cracking eastwards at what looked like a steady fifty mph. Such buses were common in the Fens, where distances were large, population small, and schools distant. One of the slit windows on the upper deck was open and a blue and white Ipswich Town scarf flapped in the wind.

Brinks and the bus approached the distant T-junction on what looked like a collision course. At the last moment the Ford seemed to swerve, as if Brinks had only just seen the bus, but he couldn't brake in time to let it pass across the junction; instead he seemed to accelerate, trying to get ahead of it, swinging out, cutting sharply to the left. They heard the distant thunder of the bus horn, the tearing of rubber on tarmac of the skid.

Dryden had his head out of the Capri because the windscreen was smeared with dead insects. He thought Brinks had made it, but the swerve had started a lethal chain-reaction of adjustment and over-adjustment, so that although he was now travelling in front of the bus, the car was out of control.

It clipped one verge, then the opposite one, finally climbing the bank.

It flipped once as the wheels locked and then, for a single second, they saw it against the sky, free of the bank, spinning out over the unseen river. The sound of the car hitting the water

288

beyond was unexpected: a collision of solids, like the slamming of a door.

Humph slowed the cab and swung it easily left at the T-junction to come to rest behind the bus, which had backed down the road. The driver was out, already up the bank, but he'd left the doors closed so that the kids were trapped, but they'd all crowded upstairs, their faces filling the windows, fingers thrust through the slits that opened for air.

Dryden ran to the top of the bank. The river, in its culvert, was as blue as the sky, carrying in its mirror-like surface the reflection of a single storm cloud. Concentric circles marked the spot where Brinks' car had punched a hole through the surface.

The bus driver joined him, keying numbers into a mobile phone.

Dryden was untying his own shoelaces, sitting on the bank, but he wasn't sure why.

John Brinks stood beside him. 'I can't swim,' he said. 'None of us can.'

Dryden unhitched his belt. In another dimension of time and space he was a child of ten, trapped beneath the ice on the river by his parents' farm. It had been the beginning of his fear, although he'd always suspected that he'd inherited it in part as well. He'd never seen his father swim, or paddle at the sea, or take to a boat. It was only after his death that he'd found out the truth: that he'd taken a group of boys to the Scottish mountains from the comprehensive where he taught in London, and one of them had died in an icy tarn. Jack Dryden, a poor swimmer, had been unable to stay afloat long enough to reach the body.

But Dryden's own fear had begun as a child that Christmas Day on Burnt Fen. He'd been trying out his best new present, skates. He hadn't seen the thin patch where the ducks had slept. Once he was in the water, looking up, he'd found a glassy ceiling of ice above his head. He could recall no panic, only a sense of loss, for the warm kitchen at home, his presents, a fire of bog oak. His life. A minute, or three, he lay beneath the surface. His father had found him and cracked the ice with his boot, hauling him back into the world, kicking, screaming, as if newborn. New born with this fear. His birthmark.

He stood up on the grass and began to throw off his jacket and trousers. He looked at the water and back at the top of the bus: the faces pressed to the glass, the fingers reaching for air. John Brinks was holding his clothes. Each of his feet seemed to be pinned to the grass. He was no better a swimmer than his father had ever been. But if he didn't move, if he didn't take a step, he'd be doomed to wait until they hauled the car out of the water, the limp body at the wheel.

For the first time in his life, looking at the surface of the water, he thought that his life might be a failure. He could feel his heartbeat in his skin. His brain felt disengaged, floating.

Beside him he was aware of John Brinks speaking: 'It's OK. I'd wait, there's an ambulance on its way. What can you do?'

He jumped.

THIRTY-FIVE

Panic would have engulfed him once his head was below the surface but for the shock of the image before him: clear water, so that he could see the opposite bank, and the car on its roof in the silt of the river bed. His subconscious had been ready for a green, reedy slime; for white bubbles trailing slow-motion arms. But this was surreal: a kind of calm, green-tinted edition of the world above. Time had slowed down so he was able to wonder if he'd actually passed out when he'd jumped and missed the splash as he hit the water. He didn't appear to need air. His lungs didn't scream, there was no pain. In fact he didn't think he could remember what it felt like to draw in oxygen. One explanation, that he was dead, or dying, seemed frivolous, so he pushed it aside.

The only sound was of liquid mechanics: a kind of thudding watery heartbeat, the percussion of being *inside* the moving river. It told him that he was alive after all; that and the fact there *was* movement, even though it was glacial. The impact of the car on the riverbed had raised a circular wave of silt which was even now spreading upwards and outwards, as ponderous as a flower opening in a slow-motion film. Through the silt, beyond this silent explosion, *through* this explosion, he could see the car. Its headlights had come on, and he thought he could detect the dull pulse of an alarm as if it, too, had a heartbeat.

He floated, air trickling from his nose and mouth, the current gently creasing and uncreasing his boxers.

Despite endless childhood hours of trying, he always struggled to move forward with any speed in water. But down here, away from the surface, that didn't seem to matter. He realized now that for all those years his fear had not been so much of water at all, but of the *boundary* between water and air. Down here, in the green world, there was no ambiguity, no borderland. Fish-like, he wriggled his body, and was exhilarated by the sudden forward movement, the sense of power which came with the kick of his right leg, the onward momentum imparted by the matching push with his left. He slid through the water as if his body had been oiled, a part of the machine.

Kicking out he was within touching distance of the car in a few seconds. Will Brinks sat in the driver's seat. His head was up, his chin raised, snaking slightly on his neck with the current circling the interior of the car, his forehead marked by a jagged, bloodied wound. The dog floated in the water in the back of the car, its narrow back bent at an angle, its eyes open and lifeless, a trail of blood leaking from the mouth.

Dryden knew, despite the absence of any pain in his lungs, that he might die if he wasted a second in thought. Not because it would use up time, but because it might lead to other thoughts, to his fears, and to the reasons behind the fears. The sense of being outside this moment, as if watching himself, was so powerful that he felt he might just separate from his real body and float up to watch it from the surface above; which appeared as a shimmering white and blue plane, a mirrored ceiling, made of mercury.

Locking a hand on a door handle, bringing the other round, to mesh with the first, he pulled. The door came free with a deep, visceral clunk which he felt as well as heard: and then the lights shorted out and the alarm stopped ringing in its faraway place. The door had come open so easily because Brinks had been driving with the windows open and the car had flooded, although Dryden could see a single bubble of air, trapped in the back, up against the window.

Brinks had been able to spring his seat belt before passing out, so that now Dryden had the door open, he seemed to simply *flow* out of the car, rising slightly, so that his head brushed the roof-edge as he came out into the green light. Buoyant, his lungs still holding some air, Brinks rose quickly, his arms coming away from his body in an awkward arc, his legs trailing like sand bags from the basket of some strange, aquatic balloon.

Dryden feared that if he touched him he'd weigh him down. So he rose with him, the two of them like underwater dancers, corkscrewing slightly, but not touching at all.

The surface above threatened a return to

thrashing arms, to panic, to the fear that Dryden would find himself again on the edge of life. So six feet below the surface he reached out and took Brinks' forearm, reeling him in, so that he could hold him round the chest, taking him towards the bank through the green water. The liquid world seemed thicker here at the edges, as if it might just suddenly solidify, and they'd be trapped, like insects in green jade.

The spell broke when Dryden's head came up out of the water.

He would have panicked then but the bus driver was half in, half out of the river, and he reached out to grab his arm. Humph was in the water too, just his head clear, one hand holding a clump of reed on the bank with bone-white knuckles. They took him under both arms, then grabbed at Brinks' sodden shirt, hauling them both on to the steep grass bank.

The sounds around him made Dryden realize he was back in the real world: the hiss of wind, the call of birds, the rumble of the bus engine; and from Humph, words without a meaning. And a strange, unidentified noise like the wings of birds flapping. Dryden was on his knees, looking up the bank away from the water, so that he could see the top deck of the bus. The children had their hands out of the slit windows, clapping.

THIRTY-SIX

Tuesday

The shivering, at first continuous, slowed after midnight but sleep was impossible. He'd been five hours in A&E. They'd given him drugs and told him to go home and sleep. If only. He lay in the narrow bunk of the *Lunigiana* and thought how bizarre it was, in retrospect, that he'd chosen this place to lie each night, separated from his greatest fear, the river water, by the thin steel hull of the boat. He splayed his hand against the cool metal and tried to feel the water beyond. This sudden awareness came without fear or anxiety; it was simply that, an awareness – a bolt of self-knowledge, the idea that each night he'd put himself this close to his fear. Dragging Will Brinks out of the New Bedford River had been a genuine victory. He could see the world more clearly now.

But he still couldn't sleep. Lying awake, he'd had time to consider the old photograph Brinks' stepfather had shown him of Daniel Fangor, and the blue Ford with the distinctive window sticker of a black dragon belching red flame. If it was the car Muriel Calder had seen at the level crossing in Brimstone Hill, then the man she'd recognized in the back seat could well be Will Brinks.

The description fitted, and Brinks was the only European – other than Fangor – working out at Barrowby Oilseed. All of which would explain Brinks' sudden decision to leave home, and keep running.

Laura sensed Dryden was awake so she got up and made coffee in the small galley in the *Lunigiana*. She suggested they drink it up on deck. A sense of peace enveloped Dryden as he climbed aloft because he knew that when he went back to his bunk he would sleep. He just needed to see the dawn. A glimpse of sunlight and he'd give up on the day.

A satellite sped across the sky above. He watched it orbit, sitting, head back, scanning the stars. Laura went back to bed. Dawn spread, a light electric blue bleeding across the darkness. He checked his mobile and rang Vee Hilgay's number, leaving a message that he'd be out of action for a day on doctor's orders. He'd filed a story on Will Brinks' escape and capture – minus his own heroics. When Eden cried he brought the boy up to see the sky. He made one more call. The duty officer at West Cambs Police HQ confirmed that Will Brinks' current condition was 'improving' in intensive care at Wisbech General Hospital. Dryden hoped that this time they'd put two coppers by the bed.

A sunbeam swept the fen. He rang Humph. The cabbie picked up quickly, no trace of sleep in his voice. Dryden imagined the Capri in a lay-by somewhere.

'Usual?' asked Humph.

'No. I need to sleep. Six tonight, if you can

296

make it. Sharp. Bring me a paper.'

'Right.'

The cabbie hung up, displaying, again, an almost autistic ability to use conversation solely to transmit information.

Then Dryden went below, put a sleeping Eden in his cot, and crawled into the bunk and experienced that rare pleasure of falling asleep limb, by limb, by limb, so that by the time his mind slipped away it represented his entire disembodied consciousness.

Sleep was a dark tunnel in which a black dragon slept.

THIRTY-SEVEN

When he saw the light next it was the evening sun, bouncing off the water outside the porthole window of the *Lunigiana*. Humph was parked on the riverbank. Despite the change of time, the cabbie had seen no reason to alter any other detail of his daily routine. He'd brought two double espressos from the shop at the station and a round of bacon sandwiches.

Just under twenty minutes later the cabbie swung the Capri over the gravel in front of Muriel Calder's house.

Dryden kicked open the cab door, so that the rusted hinges squealed. He felt a bone creak in his foot, and a pain ran down his spine into his thigh. His whole body ached, as if it had been shaken until the tendons and ligaments had snapped and frayed. It was astonishing to him that his entire time beneath the water had passed in a painless trance. Since waking his pain levels had risen progressively, as if he was feeling the effects in reverse. From his pocket he took a bottle of pills he'd been given in A&E and popped three.

'I don't know why there's pain at all,' he'd told a nurse, who'd relayed the question to the doctor, who'd come by with an answer, putting an unnaturally clean hand on Dryden's knee as he sat in a wheelchair. According to an eye-witness – the bus driver, also admitted for shock – he'd been below the water for nearly three minutes.

'That puts an enormous pressure on your whole body, like you're a submarine, forced down to the ocean bed. It's as if your rivets are creaking. They didn't fail, and that hurts. But it's a good pain.'

Dryden walked stiffly towards Muriel Calder's front door. His iPhone chimed to indicate an in-coming message from Vee: Will Brinks was now 'comfortable' and in a private room under police surveillance. The official statement on Brinks' escape and recapture had been, in part, agreed with Dryden: Brinks had been apprehended after a brief chase on Euximoor Fen near his home on Third Drove. No mention of the river rescue. Dryden loved words, but of the few he hated, 'hero' was top of the list.

The electric light in the porch of the house was

298

still on. The Georgian facade, defaced by the scars of ivy hacked back from the ashlar stone, gave him a blank stare.

He knocked, stood back. The snapshot of the blue Ford, and the black dragon, had given birth overnight to an idea, a suspicion, which seemed so outlandish he'd not allowed it to form in his mind, even in the shape of those shadow words that are just thoughts. He hoped with a genuine passion that DI George Friday was right and that the Barrowby Airfield deaths were down to a vicious gang war. But there were other options.

The door opened. Muriel Calder stood, blinking.

In her eyes he thought he could see something that made him think he was right. There was a pulse of fear, like a dash of electric light, but then it was gone. She saw the single bulb burning and reached to the side to turn it off, then, noticing, perhaps, the approaching sunset, she left it on. 'Is the story in the paper?' she asked, pointing at the rolled-up copy of the *Ely Express* he had in his jacket pocket.

It took a moment for him to realize she was talking about the story they'd planned: the hunt for the Ford with the dragon stickcr. 'Oh. No – no. I was planning to use it in *The Crow*, Friday's paper.'

She was in jeans and a burgundy corduroy shirt, but the trousers were stylishly drawn in at her waist with a rainbow belt, and the shirt matched two stud earrings which showed beneath the neat, short hair. 'Come through,' she said, too well mannered to ask why he'd called.

At the bottom of the mahogany steps he looked up at the rifle box under the military portrait. It was empty, the wooden-stocked rifle gone. He thought then that this wasn't a game, and given what had happened in the kitchen ten years ago, the house held deadly possibilities.

He made himself climb the stairs to the gun cabinet. There was a brass plate in the green velvet under the empty gun case:

Peter Davenport
Lee Enfield Rifle No. 1 Mk 6.
The Appleton Cup
Catterick Cadet Camp
1952.
First Prize.

Did a 'Lee Enfield Rifle No. 1 Mk 6' count as a 'classy military' weapon? That was how DI Friday had described the ballistic experts' description of the gun that had fired the fatal bullet at the lock-up on the airfield.

Muriel Calder had gone, and he could hear the sound of water running in the kitchen. He had an urge to run then, so strong it made one of his legs twitch. But he walked down the stairs, as slowly as he could, and pushed the kitchen door open. The back door was hooked back so he could look out over the fen, and that seemed to dissipate the fear he felt.

The first time he'd been in this room the sunlight had been veiled by the aftermath of the dust storm. Now the sunset lit it vividly, and he could see the knifepoint holes where the burglars had pinned her husband's hands to the wood.

He threw the paper on to the table, splash headline showing. 'Seen that?' he asked.

'I heard the radio news. The survivor from the airfield tried to get away. How is he?'

'As well as you'd expect. He'll live.'

She poured boiling water into the pot, sluiced it, tipped it out, then refilled, adding loose tea from a caddy. She set a cosy on the top and put the pot in the middle of the table. 'Is there something wrong?'

The clock ticked and he suddenly had a vivid insight into what her life had been like since the day she'd opened the front door and seen the man with the shotgun, his face obscenely streamlined by the stocking. Every time there was a knock at the door, did she relive that moment? Did she think, perhaps, that one day she'd open the door and somehow time would loop backwards, and she'd bring her innocent caller in here, to the kitchen, and her husband would be sitting at an unblemished table?

'His name was Will Brinks, did you know that?' he said, trying to load his voice with authority.

For the first time he thought that the years alone in this house had taken her mind, because her face just seemed to freeze. 'Who?'

'The man you saw in this kitchen on the day your husband died. And the man you saw at the level crossing in the blue Ford. Will Brinks, almost certainly. The Black Dragon is the symbol of Krakow, the owner of the car is a Pole called Fangor. There's a castle with a cave under

301

it, and in the cave there lives a dragon. Fangor was probably here in this kitchen that day as well. In this room.' He smiled, looking at the teapot.

'Does this man Brinks live close?' she asked.

It was an odd thing to ask and it made Dryden question his suspicions for the first time.

'He lived – lives – at Third Drove, on Euximoor Fen. A mile away, maybe a little bit more. He worked out at Barrowby Airfield, in one of the units. I don't think you knew that when you saw him that first time, by the level crossing, but I think you saw him again.'

Dryden flipped over the newspaper. There was the picture of Brinks. Calder licked her lips. She reached out for the paper, her fingers shaking, but then she pulled back, clutching both hands together at her heart.

'He survived the explosion at Barrowby,' said Dryden. 'Fangor, the Pole, didn't. I saw the body. He was...' He searched for the right word because he did want to give her that satisfaction, a clear picture of his death. 'Burnt-up. A cinder.'

Her lips set in a thin horizontal line. 'Good. But the other one – this Brinks – is going to live, you said. This one?' She pointed at the picture.

'The explosion was caused by a gunshot,' said Dryden. 'It produced a spark which ignited fumes in the lock-up from the still. I think that whoever pulled the trigger wanted to kill Brinks. Easy, if you're a good shot. And you're better than a good shot, at least that's what Jock Donovan tells me.'

She looked him in the face, her eyes very cold,

302

even hurt.

'Was it you?' he asked. 'Did you try to kill Will Brinks?'

'How could I?'

'The rifle. Peter's rifle. Did you go out to the airfield and wait for your moment? A rifle like that, with a telescopic sight, it can't be difficult if you know how to handle the weapon. And you do know how to handle it – don't you? Where's the rifle now?'

'I think you should leave.' She touched the table as if it was a talisman.

Dryden stood up. 'You'll tell the police?' she asked.

He walked out into the hallway, in no hurry to answer the question. 'Of course. They'll want you to identify Brinks, at the very least.'

'I can do that. Tell them I'll do that. But I didn't try to kill him. I didn't know he worked out at the airfield. I didn't know he lived on Third Drove. Believe me. I gave the rifle in to the police on Wednesday, the day before the explosion. There was an amnesty advertised in your paper and the gun was worrying me. You said yourself that if I could identify the killer he might come here. So I didn't want the gun in the house. I wouldn't use it, not on another human being, but he might. So I decided to give it in as part of the amnesty the police were running in Brimstone Hill – all over the Fens. I don't think it had been fired for thirty years. The police will have destroyed it by now. I've always wanted that.'

She opened the front door and Dryden took the

two steps down. 'I don't think you'd do that with the rifle, would you?' he said. 'It was your brother's gun, his prize. Which police station did you take it to? Did PC Powell take the gun?'

She ignored the question, closing the door, but decided to say more. She stepped out under the light from the single bulb. 'I lost my brothers *because* they were riflemen. It's a rank in the army, like private, or captain. Rifleman Davenport. In our house, before they went to Korea, that's who they were to Dad. Rifleman Peter, Rifleman Paul. I hated that. They were my brothers, not nursery rhyme characters. Later, after they'd brought the bodies back, or whatever was left of them back, Jock Donovan taught me to shoot. And yes, I used that gun. He set up a target out on the big field. But secretly I hated it, loathed it. And when Jock left I stopped. I just couldn't pull the trigger. I kept thinking that it was how they had died. That someone had pulled a trigger and death had screamed out of the night and taken them from me.'

She slammed the door. The sound bounced off the distant line of poplars, then the barn, then – faintly – off the facade of the house itself. A triple echo, like a gunshot.

THIRTY-EIGHT

Dryden rang DI Friday from the Capri, the four neat Georgian windows of the Calder place visible still across the shadowy fen. They weren't the only lights. Euximoor Drove was like an impossibly long trans-Atlantic liner in the night, a ribbon of lights a mile from start to finish: porch lights, barn lights, yard lights, floodlights, even the single green illuminated cross on the Methodist Chapel. A satellite crossed the sky and Dryden wondered if it was his celestial friend from that morning.

His call to DI Friday switched to an answerphone, then the detective cut in. 'Dryden?' In the background he could hear birdsong, and a dull, random thud. He imagined a garden in Ely, or perhaps a park, a ball being kicked around by streetlight.

He told DI Friday everything in a neat series of causal links: the original murder of Ronald Calder in 1999, the sighting of Will Brinks at Brimstone Hill, the Lee Enfield in its display cabinet, now an empty display cabinet. Muriel Calder's studied antagonism. Her skill with a rifle. And her alibi, or rather the *gun's* alibi.

'If she didn't give the gun in then she might be our killer,' said Dryden. 'I think she went out there to administer summary justice. I think she tried to shoot Brinks with the rifle. The bullet did the rest...'

'She's an old woman,' said Friday. 'It's a bit fanciful.'

'If she did give the gun over as part of Powell's amnesty, where will it be?'

'Standard procedure is clear,' said Friday. 'No overnight storage. So if she gave it in at Brimstone Hill, Powell would have taken it in to Wisbech to be locked up. Next stop would be the incinerator at Cambridge; they do a weekly burn for several police forces. Melt them down. Not just guns; knives, clubs, baseball bats. Then any drugs which have been seized, any contraband. Up goes the smoke, we get the scrap if there's anything left. It's three hundred degrees Celsius so it's mostly smoke. Let me call Powell. There may be a quick answer. Where are you?'

They arranged to meet at The Brook, the pub in the village, in forty minutes.

Humph dropped him in the centre of Brimstone Hill and went home to his mum's to see Grace. Dryden bought a pint of Pickled Pig in the bar of The Brook and went outside. He sat alone, at a picnic table, under the weak beam of a security light. The space around him – the empty streets, the sky above, the open fen – felt oppressive. He drank the cider, felt better, and got another pint.

Then he felt odd. He hadn't entirely recovered from the shock he'd suffered hauling Will Brinks from the river. The result was a very strong sense of dislocation: not physical, but

306

sensory. The idea that Muriel Calder was a killer suddenly seemed laughably improbable. But she was hiding something, he was certain of that. Then he had a bizarre thought, that she wasn't hiding something in the past, but something in the future. It was a surreal idea, so he put it down to the cider, which was stealing over his brain like an anaesthetic.

From the picnic table he could see all there was to see of downtown Brimstone Hill. There were seven streetlights, four this side of the level crossing, three on the far side. The lights left circles of amber on the pavement.

It was very quiet. A combination of the cider and the silence produced another line of thought. It was unsettling the degree to which PC Stokely Powell seemed to hover at the edge of events in Brimstone Hill. What if Muriel Calder had given him the gun and he *hadn't* taken it into the station at Wisbech? It was a thought which led to another suspicion. Powell's lifestyle hardly suited that of a lowly police constable. Had he been tempted, perhaps, to make sure his inquiry into the illicit trades in scrap metal and moonshine ran into the sand?

DI Friday had a black Ford and Dryden saw it a mile and a half away, turning the corner by The Jolly Farmers. The headlights got imperceptibly brighter and closer until the car slid in to the kerb by Christ Church.

Friday hauled his bad foot out of the nearside door and pointed at the church. The building looked cold and dead. Dryden downed his pint and walked steadily towards the graveyard

307

gates. The movement broke the spell he'd been under, and yet the sense that he was walking on to a stage was so real he could almost feel unseen eyes watching him, just out of sight, in the darkness beyond the church.

'Powell's inside,' said Friday. 'Someone saw kids hanging around. And there's been lights apparently, on and off. He's checking the place out. The station at Wisbech says he rang in half an hour ago.'

Friday checked his mobile. 'I'd ring him but the signal's dodgy.'

'What about Calder's gun?' asked Dryden.

'Wisbech will check tomorrow. Desk sergeant was off last week so he doesn't know if Powell took anything in for them. The amnesty has been a success, so maybe. Or she may have taken it to Peterborough, or Ely. But you know the terms: any police station, no names, no questions. So it could take some tracking down if she won't give us details. But it's not been incinerated, the date for that is next week. Nothing this week.'

'But there are police records?'

'You'd think,' said Friday. 'But of the guns. Not the owners. That's the whole point of an amnesty.'

They'd reached the porch. The inner door was just open.

'How's Will Brinks?' Dryden asked.

'Fine,' said Friday, adopting a whisper appropriate for a church. 'Given he's sharing his hospital room with three uniformed coppers. I'd have got one in his bed if they'd let me.'

Friday pushed open the door; it was oak, with

308

lozenge-shaped iron studs. A modern stone font stood under a functional chandelier inside, dead light bulbs on steel circles. Friday flicked a few switches but nothing happened. Then the lights came on, but went out immediately. He shouted Powell's name. There wasn't an echo; the space seemed to snuff out the sound like a candle.

The torchlight beam swung across the nave and caught the gilt on the frame of the Italian master. They walked down the aisle until they were opposite the canvas.

'Well, that's still here,' said Friday. 'That's something.'

Dryden thought there was a strange smell in the church, competing with the funereal reek of the lilies on either side of the altar: turps, perhaps? He saw that the workmen had finished creating Temple-Wright's new meeting room – the chipboard had been painted white; a door stood open.

Friday went down the aisle shouting Powell's name, then round the altar following the graceful curve of the outer wall of the apse. Dryden walked to the opposite side and through a door marked 'vestry' in copperplate gold script.

He'd been behind the door once before, to see the verger about a spate of vandalism in the graveyard – kids using a spray can on headstones. It wasn't really a room at all, just an area of the side-aisle partitioned off with wooden panels, black now with age.

'Stokely?' said Dryden. He took out his mobile and clicked on the torch beam.

He knew what to expect: a whitewashed wall

with three framed photographs of Victorian rectors, and a large colour shot of Temple-Wright. There was an old vestments holder, a kind of huge sideboard with narrow drawers. A tape deck. Some silver candlesticks they never used on the altar. A Sunday school table crammed with toys. A Baby Belling portable gas fire. On the wall an ugly circuit board with the switches for the lights. And the church chest, a copy of a medieval original, in wood, with brass hoops.

Friday shouted from the main body of the church: 'Dryden. Here.'

The sound came to Dryden easily, looping over the partition wall. There was a note of interest in the command, of brisk authority, but no sense of threat or danger.

But Dryden didn't move.

He was looking at the body of PC Stokely Powell on the parquet floor. His arms, legs and torso were twisted into a human knot. His head was thrown back so that it actually seemed to arch his spine off the floor. His eyes were wide open, as was his mouth, gaping to reveal back teeth. The torchlight caught a filling. His face was so different from his living expression that it added to the shock, as if he'd been physically desecrated, even mutilated. But his skin was untouched, smooth – almost ageless.

He was aware of DI Friday shouting again but the sound, this time, seemed to come from far away. There was a smell in the vestry, too. A gunshot?

But Dryden could see no blood. If he had been

able to see blood he would have felt less fear himself. Powell was dead, he could see that without touching that caramel skin, without feeling for the petrified pulse. The lack of a wound, the absence of cause, made the corpse seem surreal, almost supernatural. It was as if he'd fallen here, from another life. If Christ Church had boasted a medieval roof, supported by angels, Dryden would have looked up, searching for the gap.

Someone touched his shoulder and Dryden's entire nervous system seemed to short out so that he fell to his knees.

DI Friday knelt beside him and Dryden heard the air flooding out of the detective's lungs in a kind of reverse gasp. Friday's torch made the dead man's body spring to life, in stark black and white, transforming a scene-of-crime chalk outline into a three-dimensional corpse.

The detective edged forward, taking one of the thrown-back arms. He felt for the pulse, but he was looking at the eyes. They were both looking at the eyes. Dryden had always been haunted by the legend that a murder victim holds the image of the killer in their dead eyes, so he forced himself to look. The whites were clear, startling, the brown irises flat and lightless. Powell seemed to focus on a point in the air, as if his killer had been weightless, maybe even unseen. There was no picture in those eyes, just a look of dismal surprise that his life had ended here, like this.

THIRTY-NINE

A helicopter hung over Brimstone Hill like a night hawk, a single searchlight appearing to tether it to the shard-like miniature spire of Christ Church. The village had been 'locked down' within an hour of the discovery of PC Powell's corpse: three roadblocks, the freight trains – which had begun to run that day – halted. Powell had phoned his station sergeant twenty-eight minutes before his body had been found. The corpse was still warm, stiffening with the onset of rigor. If his killer was on foot he was within a few miles of Brimstone Hill. If. Further roadblocks had been set up out on the Fens along the radial routes leading out of Brimstone Hill towards Peterborough, Ely and Lynn.

Once the bare facts were released to radio and TV, Dryden's mobile was flooded with calls, which he didn't answer, setting the ringtone to silent. The TV companies were all trying to get footage on air for the ten o'clock local bulletins. Dryden's next paper, in contrast, was three days away. He didn't like to appear cynical, even to himself, but PC Powell's death couldn't have come at a worse moment in the journalistic week. He'd sent Vee Hilgay a text saying he was

312

in Brimstone Hill and could cover the story, then he'd shut down the mobile. The Press Association had someone on the ground with a camera, so they were covered for pictures. All Dryden could do was watch. He'd found the body, which might prove a valuable 'scoop' when his own deadline finally arrived. He was already framing an 'eyewitness' account, trying to consolidate the details of what he'd seen by listing them in his head: the shape of the body, the whiff of gun smoke, the discarded torch.

The rest of the press was being ferried in by squad car from the roadblocks and corralled under a cypress tree in the churchyard for a press conference, timed for nine fifteen. A few of the hacks smoked inside the roped area for press, a haze drifting from the scrum of figures, as if they were cattle sweating. A burst of laughter marked them out for what they were: professionals, dealing with death.

Dryden sat on the steps of the war memorial. The glare of floodlights obscured the stars.

DI Friday made his way towards him, picking his way between the graves. 'We need to talk,' he said.

'You're not going to dump me, are you? After all these years? Think of the kids.'

'Just shut up and listen. I've got the Regional Crime Squad en route. The Met's got an organized crime branch and they want reports on the hour. I've been asked at least three times by people above my pay grade to explain why I was looking for Powell in the company of a local journalist.'

313

Dryden went to protest. They were looking for Powell because they were on the trail of the gun. They were on the trail of the gun because Dryden had found a link between Barrowby Airfield and the Calder killing. Questioning Dryden's presence in Christ Church was a bit rich.

'I know,' said Friday, anticipating Dryden's response. 'I know. But I need to play this by the book. You're an eyewitness. I'm the investigating officer. I need to establish a bit of professional distance. OK?'

'I was there. What'd you want me to do, forget I found him?'

'No. Although it would be a smart move not to print too many details. I'm sure you know that for us this is family. Plus, he *has* a family.'

'Really? He never mentioned one. What kind of family?'

'Ex-wife, two kids. She's a PC too, so don't even go there.'

Dryden recalled Powell's penchant for bling, the gold watch, the low-slung sports car. None of that matched up to paying maintenance on two kids on a constable's salary.

'They know, do they?'

'Sure. They're being looked after.'

Dryden found the surge of emotion which gripped the police, or any of the emergency services, on hearing the words 'officer down' mildly irritating. It was as if they felt the need to re-enact a not very well-written episode of *Hill Street Blues*. The tribalism didn't do them any favours; it felt primitive, and knee-jerk. And for him it always begged the question: why don't

314

they go into overdrive when the victim is just a member of the public?

'How did Powell die?'

'What information I have will be given at the forthcoming press conference, Dryden. I'd recommend you come and listen to what I have to say. Some of it will be news to you.'

'Sir.' A uniformed PC stood at Friday's shoulder. 'The TV people are on their toes. They say they need to get something now...'

Friday straightened his tie and turned on his heels.

The press conference was businesslike. Friday said that PC Powell's death was almost certainly linked to the outbreak of gang warfare in the Fens which had been sparked by the murder of Sima Shuba. He revealed that Powell had transferred to Brimstone Hill specifically to track triad trade in both scrap metal and alcohol. He had begun his career with the Thames River Police. The force's serious crime squad believed large quantities of scrap metal were being moved out of the area by barge. Alcohol was being sold to intermediaries – shopkeepers, car boot sale traders, pubs. Powell's investigation was strictly undercover and would have culminated in a raid on the gang once its storage and production site had been identified. Events – in the form of the Barrowby Airfield explosion – had overtaken the inquiry. The results of a preliminary autopsy would be known within twenty-four hours.

Friday walked away without taking questions. The press dispersed to cars and vans, eager to get the details on to late evening broadcasts and into morning papers.

Dryden followed the detective back towards Christ Church. 'One question, because you do owe me,' said Dryden. 'Just before I found Powell's body you called out, like you'd found something. What was it?'

Friday straightened his back, then dropped his head back, holding the arc until there was a plastic click from his spine. 'There's a rear door, in the apse. Little wooden Victorian door, painted white. There was a handprint on it, in colour. Lots of colours. Vicar says it's workmen and it was there yesterday. The place reeks of paint. No big deal. We've taken pictures, we'll look for a match. But it's a sideshow.'

'Colours?'

'Forget it.' But Dryden couldn't forget it, because the workmen had used only white paint to build the vicar's partitions in the apse. So whose hand had made the print?

FORTY

DI Friday was halfway to the cypress tree and the pool of halogen-white lights when he stopped, wheeled round and walked back. Up close Dryden realized he had a brown envelope in his hand.

'I forgot. We did a quick check through

Powell's paperwork at the station. He kept a punctilious diary. But he was behind on a lot of routine stuff, because of the CID work. He was due to make a call on Meg Humphries, out on Euximoor Fen. Some business from Ely. A delivery. It's for your mate.'

'Humph.'

'The fat bloke.'

'That might be him.'

'Sorry. We had to read it, standard procedure. Give it to him, will you?'

It was an envelope with a long history. There was no stamp but a watermark in the top right corner which read: Ely Coroner's Court Office. And a crest of the Royal Arms.

The first address was a suburban street in Witchford, Grace's home. That had been scratched out and replaced with Humph's name and address. Then that had been crossed out and replaced with Humph's name again, but his mother's address on Euximoor Drove. Various scrawled signatures marked the front of the letter.

'Good job it's not urgent,' said Dryden, out loud, but Friday had gone.

Dryden walked to the wall of Christ Church so that he could stand in the splash of red and blue light coming out through the narrow stained-glass window. A white card, with the letterhead of the coroner, was attached to a page of A4.

Dear Mr Humphries,
I attach an email message left on the com-
puter of a seventeen-year-old boy at Ely's

317

Cromwell School. The young man, Julian Amhurst, died in the river at Ely this weekend. A tragic case. He took his own life. It was clear that he was largely motivated by stress over exams and trying to win a place at Cambridge University. Emotional problems had also begun to emerge. He left a whole series of messages for friends and family, but they were never sent, one of the details which persuaded me to record an open verdict, rather than one of suicide. This message is for your daughter, Grace. I know that anyone left behind after the death of a young person in these circumstances feels a certain amount of guilt. This is only natural. In this case it seemed it might be helpful to Grace if she was able to read the message. I thought I would, however, leave the final decision to you.

I enclose a printout of the message.

Yours sincerely,

Dr Digby Ryder

Her Majesty's Coroner

Dryden had no right to read on. He had the printout in his hand but he deliberately made his eyes focus on a point short of the paper so that he couldn't read the words.

A set of TV lights thudded on, then off, and caught his attention. When he looked back at the words they were in focus and he couldn't stop himself seeing the first sentence, which was like taking the bait on the hook, because it led to the second sentence, and so onwards to the end.

Grace,

Just a note. I'm sorry that other people will read this. I just didn't want you to think that what you'd said had upset me. I know it did, you saw that, but I would have just asked again, probably. It was just a trip to the cinema and I don't even like 3D films. It was Chris's idea. He said you'd like it. And he said it was what normal people did. So I needed help. That's one thing they'll say about me – that he did his homework.

I like you. I'm sorry you didn't like me, but it was cool that you said it straight. It is weird I got it wrong because I'm supposed to be good at chemistry. I really got upset because I'm not coping with the work, and the exams coming. I sit and look at pages in text books and I blink and then an hour's gone on the little clock in the top right of the computer screen and I don't remember anything. I can't link thoughts together any more, not like in a series. They're circular, and so they don't go anywhere, like they're trapped. Chemical symbols are a bit like that sometimes, but equations balance out. But this doesn't feel like that. It doesn't feel right. I should see someone, a doctor maybe, but the effort puts me off. Either way you might get this. It's just to say not to worry, that it's nobody's fault, and certainly not yours.

Jx

Dryden had an insight into the boy's mind. He

saw him sitting in front of a computer screen, the letter finished, then adding that final x.

When did Grace know he was missing? That evening she fled from home, perhaps. Maybe she did blame herself, maybe that explained everything. Humph said she'd been listening to the local radio so she'd know he was dead by now, but that was hardly a surprise, given he'd been missing for days. But the fact of it might be devastating.

Dryden wanted to go quickly and take the letter to her, but he needed to avoid the lights and his colleagues in the press. So he set out around Christ Church, going anti-clockwise. There was a splash of light beyond the apse, not from the pencil-thin stained-glass windows, but from the coffin-like apse door DI Friday had mentioned. A forensic officer in a white suit emerged with a camera and tripod and walked away towards a parked police van.

The door stood open, the light flooding out.

Dryden got within ten feet before a scene-of-crime tape stopped him in his tracks. He could see the handprint on the white paintwork, blue little finger, blue for the next and for the middle finger, but smudged with red, then the index finger – sharpest of all – in a kind of brown-black. It wasn't an ordinary hand that had left this mark. Either the index finger was shorter than the rest, an abnormality in itself, or the fingertip was missing.

FORTY-ONE

Grace's bedroom was at the back of the double bay-windowed bungalow. Humph's mother was watching TV as they came through the front door. Football, Europa League, although she had to admit she had no idea who was playing, but she liked men in shorts. There was a pot of tea beside her armchair and she was holding a catering-sized pack of cheese and onion crisps.

'Grace is in bed,' she said. 'Something's upset her. She was reading your paper, Philip. The *Ely Express*. Then we had more tears. But she wouldn't say why.'

She looked out the front door where the helicopter still held its position low over Christ Church.

'The radio said ... The neighbours called, too. A policeman? Did they really kill a policeman?'

Humph walked straight past her towards the bedroom door.

'Don't, Humph love, she's asleep. Leave her.'

Humph stood for a heartbeat on the threshold and knew it was too late, but he knocked once anyway, then threw the door back. They saw the window open, the net curtain turning in the breeze. The bed was empty but the sheets were swirled into a nest. A copy of the *Ely Express* lay

321

half-under the pillow.

Humph went to check which coat Grace was wearing.

'Don't worry,' said Dryden, helping Meg take a seat on the sofa. 'We know what's wrong now – we just have to find her. Ring the police...' He took the woman's hands. Like Humph's they were surprisingly small and nimble. 'Tell them she might harm herself. That we know why, that she might do this tonight. Then ring the neighbours, all of them. Tell them to put lights on everywhere and check outbuildings, and unlocked cars, and the nearest bus stops. We'll get out on the road.'

Dryden offered to drive but Humph took the wheel of the Capri. 'Where?' he asked, as if Dryden had an answer.

Dryden did have a picture in his head of the roads of Brimstone Hill. Grace had been 'asleep' an hour, so she could have got no further than five miles without a lift. There were no buses, and the road back into the township was blocked by the police. They drove first to the roadblock on the Ely Road and explained to the officers on duty that they were looking for a missing girl. Fifteen, fair, round face, in a red coat. They took a note but Dryden could see that they were still mesmerised by the emotional punch of those two words: officer down.

In an hour they were back at Euximoor Drove at the house. Across the fen neighbours had lit up everything they could. The darkness pulsated with electric light.

Humph stood outside with a mug of tea,

staring into those lights, as if one of them would give up his daughter, as if she'd emerge from the black velvet night carrying a star.

Dryden stood in Grace's bedroom. He felt that if he immersed himself in the room, in its random items, he'd somehow *see* her, and know where she was. But all he could recall was that last time he'd set eyes on her, in Dacey's auction room, moving between the stalls, in a trance. He ran the memory like a YouTube clip, back and forth, until a new set of images appeared on the end. He'd forgotten that last glimpse of her, walking to one of the fine art stalls, studying a lithograph on the wall, a view of Denver Sluice, the croquet-hoop superstructure against an evening sky, the high lock gates closed, holding back the water. She'd seemed to fall under some kind of spell as she studied the image.

'The car,' he said, making the decision to trust in intuition, and walking out the front door. 'I've got an idea.'

Denver was six miles north, then four south on the far side of the Bedford Levels. They drove at a steady thirty mph, the windows down, checking the fields under the moonlight, the bus shelters, the pumping stations. Meg rang to say there was no news and Dryden could see Humph struggling with his anger, and with the guilt, trying not to blame anyone but himself.

The sluice was a complex of floodgates spanning both the Ouse, and several of the artificial rivers built in the seventeenth century to drain the Fens. Beyond it, downstream, the river magically became two, each channel running the last

323

twenty miles to the sea side-by-side. But on the upriver side the landscape was criss-crossed with ditches, drains, meres and rivers. The sluice was the landscape's watery heart, regulating the flow of water off the land, and keeping back tidal seawater coming up from the coast.

Dryden had never liked it; there was something mechanical – steely – about its clockwork power. The old wooden sluices had long been replaced by two industrial steel sets of gates. Perhaps, secretly, it wasn't the aesthetics of the gates which unsettled him, more that he yearned for the water to come back and flood the land, to turn the landscape back into a waterscape.

There was a pub by the sluice and the car park was emptying. Lights played on a lawn which ran down to the towpath. A tinny loudspeaker played a Bee Gees track. They left the Capri on the verge and ran along the lane which climbed, then turned, crossing the sluice itself high above the water. Floodlights lit the whole structure, but the water below was in shadows, although the churning of white foam showed where the gates stood open a few inches, letting the water out to sea.

'Gracey.' He heard Humph shout the word but when he turned he found the roadway behind him deserted. It hadn't been a pleading call, but one of soft recognition. But where had Humph gone?

Black tarmac, a white line, nothing else. Everything was wet because the churning water had created a mist. A miniature rain forest micro-climate. It was a surreal scene in that

324

tinder-dry summer, and it was heightened by a sudden movement: a bright green frog on the road, jumping once, then freezing.

The thunderous vibration of the water below came up though Dryden's legs.

He ran to the parapet and looked down on to the top of one of the three sluice gates in the set. Grace's head was there, no body visible, except her legs and feet, hanging down. Looking along the narrow steel edge of the gate he saw Humph, moving out from a metal stairwell at the side, small, nimble feet shuffling sideways.

Humph stopped, held up the brown envelope, and said, 'Grace. You have to read this, OK? Do this for me, sweetheart. Read it.'

But the raising of one arm unbalanced the cabbie, and one of his feet slipped away from the steel edge. Dryden saw him begin to fall, so he turned away from the sight and ran, along the road, to the far end of the parapet to see if he could get down to the water.

He found the handrail of the steel staircase, and dropped down three corkscrew turns, to a small maintenance platform beside the sluice. Looking down he could see nothing of Humph. Then he looked back at the ledge and realized the cabbie was still there; somehow he'd avoided a fall, and sat down instead, winded. Grace had backed off, into the shadows at the edge of the gate, where the metal cogs dovetailed with iron runners, smeared with glinting grease. It was as if she was sinking back into the machine itself, a human cog.

Dryden stepped out on to the ledge and

reached his friend in three sideways strides.

'Sit tight,' he said, and took the envelope, stuffing it inside his shirt.

'I'll get help,' said Humph, and looked back at the bank, but didn't move.

Dryden looked down. The magnetic pull of the wavelike, boiling pool below was as real as if he'd felt the tug of ropes. But the paralysing fear he usually felt was absent. He felt afraid, but in a way which seemed proportional to the real world. He was – after all – on a narrow sluice gate above several thousand tonnes of churning water. He might fall. He might drown. What he had to do was reach Grace.

Breaking eye contact with the water, he looked at Grace's face, just visible in the shadows, and edged towards her.

The oily dark corner in which she hid was dry. Once out of the floodlights' glare, Dryden had to stand still, letting his eyes switch to night-time vision. Grace was crying, her knees drawn up to her chin. 'Your dad's upset,' he said. She could not have heard him because she didn't react, so he shouted it out.

He didn't think she'd jump but when he took an extra step she tried to stand, her legs scrabbling on the oily ledge.

He knelt quickly. 'It's OK. I just wanted you to have this.'

He gave her the envelope. The floodlight above cast a single rectangle of bright light into the dark corner. She held the A4 sheet within it, very close to her face, scanning the words.

She read it twice, then folded it all up without

putting it back in the envelope and gave it back. In taking it, Dryden edged closer.

'I'm glad he wrote that,' she said. 'He asked me out. I said no – he was a nerd really. So I don't know why I said no because I'm not a stranger to being a nerd, am I? He liked draughts, just like Dad. He said the strategy involved was much more complex than chess. That's what Dad says too. So we could have played draughts. But he wanted to go to the cinema so I thought I'd just say no. Not interested. It *was* a bit cruel.

'When I heard he'd gone missing, that he'd tried to kill himself, I did feel guilty. A bit. But like, I didn't know him. I think, like, he was one of those people who think that a relationship can *be* just by thinking it is. Like it's not about two people. That it can exist in just one head. It can't.'

She looked at her father, who had now reached the end of the floodgate and was winching himself over an iron railing on to the spiral stairs.

Dryden was breathing in ozone, and negative ions, from the water below, and it was making him light-headed, and almost euphoric. 'This isn't about the boy, is it?' he said. 'But the letter helps?'

'Yes. Thanks.' She looked down at the water.

'It's about you,' said Dryden.

'It's about Dad. And Mum. And now I'm fifteen it's going to be about me because I can't choose between them, and they want me to.' Grace laughed, which undid whatever emotional locks she'd put in place, so that she started to cry

327

again, pushing her face into her knees.

'You live with your mum, that's OK. He understands,' said Dryden.

'I live with Mum because I have to. Because the court said I had to. That's why he's OK with it. But when I'm sixteen I get to choose, and he won't understand it if I stay. And Mum wouldn't understand if I went. And I don't want to live in the back of a smelly cab with a dog. And I don't want to live with Barrie and his stepsons with their webbed feet. And I'm only fifteen, and I want to go to sixth form college, not get a job, so I can't live on my own. So there's no way out.'

The water thundered.

'And they won't say what *they* want. If I told them it was up to them they'd think I didn't care, about either of them.'

Dryden thought the more she talked the better she'd be so he didn't answer.

'I do care. I wouldn't have jumped because I know they'd never get over that. Dad's never got over the divorce. I thought he was going in just then...' She tried a smile. 'Big splash.'

Dryden leaned over and took her hand.

'I thought it would take him longer to find me anyway, that nobody would see me till it was light. I don't know why I did it. I thought I could tell Grandma, but I couldn't. It's cold, isn't it?'

They both stood, on the edge, and Dryden gave her a kind of stiff hug. 'I'll sort it out,' he said.

FORTY-TWO

Wednesday

Thunder rolled round Euximoor Fen like a bowling ball. Dryden had slept on the sofa at Meg Humphries' bungalow and the sound of a storm brewing only added to his sense of disorientation. The day threatened rain at last. The thunder ushered in lightning which crackled in the air. Dryden saw a single forked bolt through his closed eyes. He had the window open and the wind was steady and warm; a fenland sirocco. It blew under the door of the house and hit a note: woodwind section, a bassoon maybe, unwavering. Dryden tuned the radio on the mantelpiece to KLFM at Lynn and picked up the forecast for the day: soil and dust storms across the region, with the NFU warning farmers to pin down plastic fleece where they had it on the fields, and to postpone harvesting. Finally, by nightfall, rain. Real rain, a harbinger of autumn.

Dryden found Meg in the kitchen, and took Humph a cup of tea in the Capri. The cabbie was asleep, despite the thunder, wrapped in a full-length Ipswich Town picnic blanket. He got out of the cab to take his mug of tea. They'd talked the night before until nearly dawn about Grace, so the subject was exhausted. Neither of them had the energy to rerun the arguments in the light of day.

'Radio says there's a press conference on PC Powell's death at Wisbech mid-morning,' said Dryden. 'It'll be on the gang wars. That's Friday's big idea. Big city crime hits the Fens. And they'll have the forensics.'

'No problem,' said Humph, nodding. He patted the roof of the Capri as if the cab was a dog. The real dog was in the house on Grace's bed. The cabbie sipped his tea. He missed Boudicca, but he wasn't going to say so.

Dryden's mobile rang. 'Talk of the devil,' he said, as the phone displayed the caller's name.

It was DI Friday. Outdoors, because Dryden could hear traffic.

'Just so you know,' said Friday, 'we found your sodding gun. At Addenbrooke's Hospital, Cambridge, due to be melted down next week in the incinerator. It's engraved with the name of the kid who won it, so that helped. Hasn't been fired for twenty years, probably longer. So that's Muriel Calder out of the frame. Not that she was ever really in it, in my book. According to the paperwork, the gun was handed in at Brimstone Hill on the date she specified. So Powell played it by the book too, took it to Wisbech that night.'

'So who killed Powell?' asked Dryden.

'Presser later,' said Friday and rang off.

Dryden walked away from the cab and Humph followed. They could see Christ Church in the far distance.

'It's always felt as if the roots of this were

here, in the soil, even,' said Dryden. 'Right here. I don't trust the police when they're involved with these gangs. They spend months, years, not being able to lay a hand on them, but knowing they're responsible for a lot of crime. Then they get their chance and they jump in feet first. Nothing is going to stop DI Friday charging some of the gang members – one of the soldiers – with murder, or murders. But has he got the evidence? He's not telling me if he has.'

There was a double thunderclap and sheet lightning overhead and the wind, for the first time, gusted, rocking the car on its springs. On the bare field a miniature tornado sprang into life and whirled for a few seconds before blowing itself out.

Dryden felt tired, dried out. He searched for the right word: desiccated. 'Maybe Friday's right – maybe it is a gang killing,' he said. 'But there're so many loose ends. I'm still not convinced about Powell. He's got an ex-wife and two kids to keep, plus a fast car. Whatever Friday says, he could have been playing the easiest game of all. He was an expert in river crime. Why did he fail to track the barges full of stolen metal back to the source – along the Twenty Foot Drain to Barrowby Airfield? Was he really a gamekeeper, not a poacher?'

Dryden collected Humph's empty mug. 'And where did Vincent Haig get his £125,000 to buy Sexton Cottage? How many pictures have you got to frame to notch that up?' As he walked back to the bungalow, Dryden recalled the handprint he'd seen on the apse door at Christ

331

Church. A multi-coloured hand, with a fingertip missing.

The presser in Wisbech was at noon. He had an hour to kill.

After breakfast they left Grace with Boudicca and drove down to the Old Forge. As they parked Humph had one hand on the fluffy steering wheel cover, the other back between the seats, searching for the dog that wasn't there. He'd been planning his early morning exercise: three times round the cab with the dog, then a short stint with the green ball and the plastic thrower.

They sat in silence. The thunder was fading away. There was no helicopter now over Brimstone Hill, no roadblocks on the road in from Ely. In fact during the ten-minute drive they hadn't seen a single policeman. Dryden thought he could smell rain in the air.

Humph settled into his seat. 'I'll wait here then.'

'Why don't you spend some time with Grace, like you said you would? I'll call when I need you.'

'She'll be all right now...'

'No she bloody won't,' said Dryden, enjoying a rare flash of temper. He was out of the cab so he squatted down to look his friend in the eyes, trying to keep the loss of control alive – the freedom of it. 'You can't live in this little bubble world, Humph.' He put a hand on the cab's frame. 'She's fifteen, she'll be sixteen soon. Talk to her. About what you want, about what she wants.'

Humph started to whistle tunelessly, so Dryden walked away, up the track. On the field by the road another miniature red twister was dancing like a living scarecrow. When he got to the gate he looked back and saw the Capri trundling away.

The sliding wooden doors of the Old Forge stood open. Haig was inside, holding a painting up with arms wide, clasped on the frame. It was a picture of a group of shepherds walking through a ford, shades of Constable in the grey water ripples catching the light, and Turner in an evening sky full of light and clouds.

For a second Dryden saw his face, for once, not composed for effect. There was a genuine critical interest there, a kind of desperate focus, as if the picture was more important than the reality around him – the workshop, with its tool bench, the wall of gilt frames, his own work opposite, dominated by the landscapes with their blocked colour and mathematical edge, and his leitmotif – the little three-dimensional replica of Christ Church.

Haig heard Dryden's footstep and turned, his eyes narrowing.

'Sorry, you're busy,' said Dryden.

Haig put the picture down and his hands to his hips as if to make a judgement on the work. 'It's easy to despise the unoriginal,' he said.

There was a mug of tea on the bench; Dryden could see the deep-brown builders' colour of the liquid within.

'Too early for the Zabrowka? Or has the supply run dry? If you know anything about the operation out there, on the airfield, you should tell the police.'

Haig jinked his shoulders, a hand searching for his pocket. 'Thanks for the lecture. I didn't know it was illegal. They said they paid taxes, they said they had a licence.'

'Right. So you did work for them, or were you a customer, or a distributor?'

'I've told the police. I gave a statement. Your mate Friday not tell you that?' Again, the sneer.

There was a large set of wooden drawers by the workbench. He slid one out and took out a sheet of printed labels: the amber-yellow brand of the flavoured vodka, the woodcut of the reeds.

'My design. I've got a small hand press. HGOGNAV. That's the business name – Van Gogh backwards.'

So that was Vincent's Haig's little sideline. He printed the labels, and presumably got a free supply of the hooch in payment.

'I do Barrowby Oilseed as well.'

'Any cash for the job – or just booze?'

'They paid. Not much, but it all helps.'

'But you'd want more, a lot more. When Sexton Cottage came up you needed thousands.'

'Christ, not this again.' A look of sudden disbelief crossed Haig's face, as if he'd just seen the implications of Dryden's question. 'You think I did it, don't you? Took their money, then took a pot shot at the lock-up. Left them there, all of them, dead inside. You think I did that?'

Dryden was surprised how quickly Haig had jumped to self-accusation. 'No, I didn't. Now I'm wondering.'

The wind outside buffeted the old barn and the

334

beams creaked.

'You got the money from somewhere.'

'That it? You all done?'

He picked up the mug of tea but it shook as he lifted it to his lips, so he held it with both hands.

'Not quite,' said Dryden. 'I wondered what you'd been doing in Christ Church. You left a multi-coloured handprint on the apse door, the little coffin-shaped one. Easy to get in, of course, because Albe has a key.'

Haig's attempt to look innocent of any knowledge of Christ Church was almost comical. Dryden thought again that it was the man's face that gave him away – that if you couldn't see him, you might like him.

Dryden held up his own hand, the fingers splayed.

Haig held up his. The fingers were smeared with paint. 'Occupational hazard. There's been kids about, smoking, drinking, God knows what else in the porch. The place was locked because of the Masaccio. I went in a few times to check everything was OK. I actually care about the place, right? I don't want some idiot burning it down. And I don't really want a blind OAP checking up on a bunch of louts. Do I?'

'Paint would be dry by the time you got to the church,' said Dryden.

'I'm painting something for Grandad, of Sexton Cottage, at Sexton Cottage. You saw it. I do a little most evenings. It's a good excuse to keep an eye on the old man.'

Dryden had to nod.

'The paint's laid on with a trowel, thick, sticky

gouts of reds and greens in the garden, black for the roof tiles. When we thought he'd have to leave I started it, as a keepsake. When it dries he can touch it. Feel the shapes.'

It was such a bizarre explanation Dryden instantly believed him.

'I've never been in the church after dark,' said Haig. 'There's a safety light on an automatic switch but it's been cutting on and off; the wiring's probably rotten. I could have told Powell that, if that's why he went in.'

He put the landscape painting back on the wall.

Dryden walked to one of the canvases and turned it round. It was the portrait of Temple-Wright. 'I guess you're not a fan,' he said.

'She's got the cash from the sale of Sexton Cottage; she'll get the money for the Masaccio. I doubt it's an original, that's just greed talking, but even the copy's worth a bit. She'll have enough for her *virtual* church. It's like a rival to the real one. It's a war she's waging. She thinks virtual is spiritual. Does that make sense?'

Dryden, embarrassed by the question, looked away into the corner of the barn. He saw a statue there, in plaster, about four foot tall, a rough model of a soldier in a boot-length cape.

'That's the statue on the war memorial at Christ Church, for Jock Donovan's pals.'

'The Davenport boys. Sure. I've always known Jock.'

'You did it?'

Haig nodded, helping Dryden pull aside some lengths of framing board.

336

'How d'you know Jock?'

Haig shook his head, pulling a welding cylinder out on wheels. 'You've got to live out here to know what it's like. In the city people live in crowded streets, well, they did. Tenements. Back-to-backs. We're as close out here, it's just that there's space between us, but there's nothing in the space, so we're close. I've known Jock for years. He taught me and half the kids on the fen to shoot. Rabbits, muntjac, crow. He was a rifleman too.'

Dryden had reached the statue so he knelt down to look under the helmet at the soldier's face. 'It's good, isn't it?' he said, genuinely impressed.

For once Haig's eyes were on his. 'Yes. Jock's got pictures from the war. There's something about the cape, right? It's the shape, it kind of echoes. And both sides wore them, and Jock liked that, the idea that it was a memorial to the dead on both sides. He's not a bitter man at all. I like that.'

They both considered the statue for a moment.

'There's something about the way the cape hangs,' said Haig. 'I didn't know what it was until I'd finished. They look like angels, don't they?'

And that was right, Dryden could see. Angels, with folded wings.

He left him then, walking into Brimstone Hill. Haig had brought Jock Donovan back into Dryden's mind. He saw him that day of the explosion, standing outside his house just moments after the blast, disorientated, shocked. And he

337

thought about the cool interior of his art-deco home with its whitewashed walls, the neat office, the clock with its lettering in blue.

The single word: ORIENTO.

He'd emailed his friend on the *Financial Times* and asked him to track down the company, find out what it made, and where it sold what it made.

He punched in a text. *Oi! Where's my info on ORIENTO?*

He'd walked less than 100 yards before there was an answer. *Whoops. Busy here – you won't know what that means now you're out in the sticks. Info just sent to your inbox. Sorry. Love to L.*

Dryden thought he'd walk to his office and access the email on his desktop PC.

The centre of Brimstone Hill was busy, the level-crossing barrier down, a line of traffic waiting, a customer outside the café. His office was hot and stale so he threw open the windows. The Word document from the *FT* was not compatible so the computer had to convert the text, which took thirty seconds. He told himself later that he'd guessed the truth, or part of it, before the computer had finished. While he waited he went to his pictures file and found a snap he'd taken of the war memorial to the Davenport brothers. He read the lettering again, remembering what Donovan said: they'd all been brothers. *Brothers in arms*. Then he read the Word document and knew who had fired the bullet that killed three men.

338

FORTY-THREE

Wisbech General Hospital stood on the edge of the town, a former Victorian workhouse, perched on a high bank over the river. The tide was out, and a few boats sat, tilted over, in the silver mud. Humph did his usual circumnavigation of the rabbit roundabout: three times, notching up a total of twenty-one sightings. The rest of the town was suitably down-at-heel. All the pubs had Day-Glo stickers in the shape of starbursts in their windows advertising cut-price shots and happy hours. Dryden liked the place if only for the fact that he could always smell the unseen sea, six miles down the muddy channel to the Wash. Humph, who found almost nowhere interesting, slipped his earphones on as soon as they'd come to a stop. So Dryden stood outside, looking down into the deep cut in which the river lay, waiting for the clock on the town hall tower to reach noon, the appointed time for the press conference on the killing of Stokely Powell.

He studied the windows in the facade of the old hospital's main building. The General, as it was known, was humming like hospitals do: vents, heating systems, water towers all vibrating, creating a soundtrack. Steam dribbled from

339

various pipes and gratings all over the old building, making it look as if it was boiling on the inside. Behind one of those windows was Will Brinks, making a second attempt to recover from the blast on Barrowby Airfield, the injuries compounded by ditching his car in the New Bedford River. Pulling him out of the water felt like a page from history to Dryden, someone else's history.

PC Powell's body, and those of the three victims of the Barrowby Oilseed blast, and indeed Sima Shuba's corpse, would all be in the police morgue, a single storey concrete block to the rear of the main hospital. It was fifties in style, strictly utilitarian, with cracked tiles, and always reminded Dryden of a wholesale butchers.

The press conference was to be held in the hospital. Dryden thought he'd let Friday deliver his forensic results on Powell to the media before telling him what he knew about ORIENTO. The detective would resist Dryden's solution to the mystery of Barrowby Airfield, because it shattered his neat assumption that gang warfare lay at the root of all the murders. He'd have to follow the trail himself, piecing it together as Dryden had done. But there was little doubt where it would lead. Perhaps Friday would be able to find the last, missing link in the story: the motive.

The town hall clock struck noon. By the time Dryden got to the hospital's old dining room – the venue for the press conference – there were about twenty members of the press in the front

340

two rows. Everything echoed in this vast Victorian space beneath a wooden neo-Gothic roof. The place reeked of sadness and soup. There were no TV crews, and no national newspapers, a sure sign Friday had nothing interesting to say. CID tried to keep on the good side of the major news networks, and dragging them halfway across East Anglia for a 'no comment' was considered bad form. The press who had turned up were all local evenings and weeklies, plus local radio. Whatever preliminary advice had been given to the nationals – what in the trade was called a 'steer' – had clearly been withheld from the provincial press.

DI Friday sat behind a desk and drank a glass of water. The double wooden doors were shut behind the last reporter. Silence fell, and the detective began reading a prepared statement:

'The preliminary autopsy on PC Stokely Powell has revealed that in all probability he died of accidental electrocution.'

One of the reporters forgot himself. 'Shit,' he said, tossing a notebook into a shoulder bag.

Friday outlined the key facts: Powell's fingerprints had been found on the light switch by the door, and then his palm print on the switchboard in the vestry. His torch was found beside the body, the switch in the 'on' position, but the bulb shattered. It seemed clear that he had entered the church after dark to investigate reports that children had been seen hanging around the building and that the lights had been switching, erratically, from on to off. The light switch by the door did not work when tried by DI Friday,

341

the officer present when the body was discovered. It seemed likely that PC Powell therefore made his way to the vestry, by torchlight, where the main power switchboard was located. It seemed that he tried some of the switches. What he did not realize was that the church had been visited by metal thieves who had removed lengths of cabling and several pieces of electrical equipment, including earthing wires. As a result the switches in the vestry were 'live'. The full mains power had coursed through his body and killed him instantly. 'Death,' concluded Friday, 'would have been instantaneous.'

So that, thought Dryden, was Powell's unseen killer.

The church, reported Friday, had been locked for several days. It was possible, therefore, that the metal thieves responsible had died in the explosion at Barrowby Airfield and that Powell had simply been unlucky: the first person, in all probability, to try and use the lights since the wiring had been tampered with. The reckless crime had cost PC Powell his life. The force wished to express its condolences to his wife and children.

The hacks scrawled notes. It wasn't a bad story, just not as good as having a real live cop-killer manhunt. Now they knew why the TV crews were absent.

Friday began to outline the series of events which had occurred in the Erebus Street area of Lynn on Sunday. This had led to several arrests. But Dryden wasn't listening. The doors to the old hall opened briefly as one of the reporters

342

made an early exit and Dryden was able to glimpse the lift out in the reception area. He saw Muriel Calder standing, holding a pot plant which was partly obscured by wrapping paper, waiting for the lift doors to open.

Dryden slipped out of his seat and through the doors, his heartbeat picking up. Who was Muriel Calder intending to visit? There was one obvious possibility. Dryden doubted she was there to wish him a speedy recovery. So why was she there? The entry lobby was vast, a Victorian shrine of carved stone and mosaic. The lift doors had closed. There was a desk, but the woman behind it was speaking into a telephone headset. So he chose an elderly man behind a desk marked: VISITOR INFORMATION.

There was a charity box labelled TocH in front of him.

Dryden stuffed a fiver in the tin. 'Hi. Sorry to bother you. I've got to get a message to a couple of police officers...' He pointed at the lifts. 'They've got their mobiles off. They're guarding that bloke who got blown up out on the fen. Could you take it up...'

'I don't move,' said the man. 'That's not my job. Never has been. The kids do messages but they're not on till five.'

Dryden looked at the tin as if he might try and get the fiver out.

'It wouldn't take you a second,' added the old man. 'You've got young legs. Sixth floor, go on up.'

Dryden strolled over to the lift and got on with a patient in a bed being pushed by a porter.

When the doors opened on the sixth he saw a copper reading a paper by a coffee machine.

The corridor straight ahead ran the entire length of the hospital. One of those grand Victorian gestures – 200 yards of diminishing sight lines, a textbook lesson in the concept of the vanishing point. He saw Muriel Calder walking steadily away carrying the pot plant. She was lost, suddenly, in a gaggle of nurses, as a bed was wheeled across the corridor.

Dryden started to run. His boots slapped on lino. In retrospect he could have just raised the alarm then and there, but he doubted anyone would have believed what he had to say, and certainly not in time.

When he was just fifty yards behind her, he was so sure he knew what she was going to do he stopped and shouted her name. Just her first name: Muriel. She looked back, then sideways at the door she was level with, before stepping out of sight.

Dryden lifted his right leg to start running again when he heard the shot: a single percussion, which might, to bystanders, have been something else – a metal bed frame collapsing, perhaps, or a door slamming. A nurse, moving quickly but not in panic, went through the same door as Muriel, and then came out, back-pedalling, a hand to her mouth.

When Dryden got to the open door the scene inside was perfectly framed. The pot plant was on the floor, the earth spilt out. Muriel Calder had taken a chair as if she was a visitor. On the far side of the bed a woman PC sat looking back at Dryden, a very fine spray of blood across her face. She was in shock, and her mouth hung open like an old cutlery drawer. Most of the blood was on the pillow, a halo, around Will Brinks' shattered, bandaged face. The bullet had entered his skull almost exactly through his left eye. The wound had redefined his face, pulling it all in, as if he'd been nailed to the pillow with a red spike.

FORTY-FOUR

If Muriel Calder wasn't in shock, Dryden was. The sound was the first clue – a kind of deadened, underwater effect, through which everything was filtered and rebroadcast. A scream, shouting, an alarm over the tannoy. And he could hear his heart, lumbering, as if his body was somewhere else doing something draining, struggling uphill under a great weight. But he couldn't actually feel anything. It was as if his skin had stopped sending signals to his brain.

He stood by the bedside seat holding Muriel's hand. They couldn't see Will Brinks' body now, because some nurses were in their way, and then a pair of doctors, and then a machine. Someone gave Muriel a glass of water and Dryden saw that she held the glass with a steady hand and that rather than gulping it down she took a little, then considered the level she'd left, as if she'd have to make it last.

Then everyone left and they could see the body. There was a lot more blood now, so that the colour was impossible to cut out, as if Dryden's own eyeballs were tinted red. And there was a new sound, that of trickling, quite distinct, which might have been coming from under the bed.

'I'm sorry,' said Dryden, for a reason which must have existed but which escaped him immediately.

'I'm not,' she said. 'I've waited ten years to do that to one of them. Any one of them. I suppose I am sorry it was him, but only after the fact. That's what they say, isn't it? After the fact.'

The nurses slid a screen between them and the fact. The door was shut and a policeman stood guard. They were all alone with the young man's body behind the screen.

'I didn't know that it was him until you told me. And the picture confirmed it. Once I knew, I had to do something. Thank you for that.'

Not a trace of irony, thought Dryden.

He wondered how long they'd be left like this, just inches away from the corpse. It felt like hours already, but might be minutes, or seconds.

'Brinks' stepfather said he fell in with a gang when he was a teenager,' said Dryden, feeling he had to tell Will's story, because he was no longer able to defend himself. 'Then, one day, he just came home to Third Drove and stayed there. He told the family that he'd spent a night in the cells and that it had terrified him. That he couldn't live with the feeling of being locked up. He needed to be outside, under the sky. I think that was all true, as far as it went, but the real reason he came home was what happened in your kitchen that day. Fangor was there too. The difference was that Will's nerve didn't hold. It broke. So he hid himself away from the world. He was probably the best of them.'

She laughed through her nose. 'I've saved him from a life in a cell.'

Dryden let her hand slip out of his.

'I suppose he thought he was safe at Third Drove,' she said. 'He didn't know, did he, that I'd remember. So he would have felt no anxiety. My life's been unbearable.'

There was a sound from behind the screen, like a sigh. The body breathing, in its own after-life way, in death.

She laughed then and Dryden knew that it was time which had done this to her: time in that house, time in that kitchen, time around that table. A hollow, empty wilderness of a life she'd filled up with anger, and bitterness, but only silently, sharing it with no one.

'So I went into Ronald's room this morning,' she said. 'Not a bedroom, an office, where he did the farm accounts. I haven't been in that room for months. There was a red dust over everything. The windows are never open in that room but the dust still gets in. Over all his papers, and over the framed pictures of us. The happy couple on the beach, in the Lakes, our wedding. So I cleaned each one and put them back and then I took the pistol out of his top drawer, and a box of bullets, and I drove here. Then I sat in the car

347

and filled the chamber. I thought then: I can do this. I hid the gun in the pot plant. It's a hibiscus. I'd like to keep it.'

She looked at Dryden. 'When you shouted it was too late already. I'd done it really, a thousand times. This...' She gestured at the screen. 'This was inevitable.'

The door opened and DI Friday stood there.

'I'm looking forward to going home now,' she said. 'I really am.'

The detective's mobile trilled.

'You shouldn't have that on in here,' said Muriel Calder, standing, as if that was the crime that had brought them all to this, not a young man's blood draining away.

FORTY-FIVE

Shock held Dryden's mind imprisoned for an hour. He sat in an office he'd never remember looking out over the car park, watching the vehicles shuttle and crawl, executing devious U-turns, like counters on a game board. DI Friday came in, asked questions, and went out. Dryden was given water and coffee and a plate of biscuits. Another detective took a statement which he signed, the pen moving smoothly over the paper, but curiously without making any noise. Progressively he became aware of sound again, including a soft strain of music, and the ticking of an institutional clock, which he couldn't locate with his eyes. Then he saw a black four by four, with a BBC TV logo on the side, edge under the barrier and park beside a police squad car. Laura got out and talked to a policeman. After a moment she looked up at the facade of the hospital but she didn't see Dryden because the sight of her had broken the spell that held him, and he was already walking down that long, processional corridor towards the lifts.

In the car he held Eden and told Laura what had happened, listening to his own voice, as if it was on the radio. She told him that they'd been invited for food at Meg Humphries. Or they could go home, back to the boat. She'd brought a picnic too, so that was a third option. They could find somewhere green and cool and enjoy the last dry hours of summer. But they'd have to be quick. The police had broadcast warnings of dust storms, then rain, at dusk. So it might be best to go home? She concentrated on the road but flicked her eyes sideways to watch his profile, which was expressionless. They drove east, the red setting sun in the rear-view mirror.

'Let's eat,' he said eventually. 'A picnic, at Christ Church.' He turned to her, making a great effort to move the muscles of his face, to mimic a smile.

'You've had a shock. I wouldn't work if I was you.'

'It's OK. I need to talk to George Friday as well. I couldn't face it back there, and in a strange way it isn't really that urgent. But it must be said. I'll ring later, when we're home.'

349

The centre of Brimstone Hill was deserted. The sky, a strange watery blue-green, looked sick. The horizon, in all directions, was slightly fuzzy, as if the line had been drawn in charcoal and then smudged with a finger. There was very little wind, although the smell of rain was pungent.

He stood by the car as Laura unpacked Eden from the child seat and grabbed a picnic blanket, and the child's new ball.

'We'll be fine over there.' She pointed to the grass in the lee of the church. Laura poured red wine into tumblers and Dryden sat, his back against a tree bole. Eden lay on his front.

In the still air they heard a gate hinge. Looking through the trees, Dryden saw Jock Donovan walking quickly along the gravel path that led to the Clock Holt. For the old man it was the appointed hour.

Laura was setting out the food. 'I'll be back in a moment,' said Dryden, forcing himself up on to his feet. He circled the church and saw two figures in the distance: the soldier in stone, his cape wide and stiff, billowed out; and before him Jock Donovan, leaning forward, slightly bent at the ankles.

Dryden had been walking on the grass but he switched to the gravel path to give the old man warning of his approach.

Donovan's shoulders stiffened but he didn't turn round.

They stood together, side by side.

Dryden's eye jumped to the words on the memorial, seeking the familiar dedication to the

350

Davenport brothers. *Brothers in Arms*. And when he found the words, and the letters that made them up, he knew why Donovan had become a killer. Why he'd picked up his gun and gone back into battle one more time. There had to be a spark, an emotional jolt, which had set him on that path, on that day. And here it was. Exquisite, heart-breaking and cruel.

The memorial stone was as it had been the first day Dryden had seen it. But the lead letters, the words which stood as a testament to the comrades Donovan had lost that night in Korea, had been prized out of the stone. A few were scattered amongst the flowers at the base. Dryden bent down and picked one up: a Capital P. 'The metal thieves,' he said.

'It's the price of lead,' said Donovan.

Donovan let some of the letters fall from his hand. They reminded Dryden of 'jacks' – a toy from his childhood – and they made the same soft lead sound when they fell on stone.

Dryden knelt down and picked them up. 'I wondered why,' he said. 'There had to be a trigger.' He left it at that because it was the perfect metaphor.

'I've got a friend in the financial press,' he said. 'He traced ORIENTO for me. An import-export business, privately owned, slightly shadowy. Operating in the Far East, especially South Korea. It was guns, of course. High-performance rifles. And gun-sights, all the optics needed to see a target from several miles away. I traced the details on one model supplied to the British Army. It holds the record for the longest

351

kill. You'll know the numbers, but it is about three thousand yards. And that's a tiny target, of course, under battle conditions.'

Donovan rearranged his feet.

'In 2005 ORIENTO's export and import licences were revoked. There were two police inquiries – one in Singapore, one in Pretoria – into allegations that the company had been bribing government officials. Neither resulted in charges. You were struck off as a director here in the UK in 2007. I guess that explains the retirement to the Fens?'

'You can't do business in the Far East without paying bribes. Our crime was we didn't pay enough.'

'I presume you have one of the high-velocity rifles. And the house, of course, has a flat roof.'

One of the old man's knees gave way and Dryden thought he was going to fall over.

'I'll have to tell the police,' said Dryden.

'I'm not going to talk about it. Not again. They can do what they want.'

Dryden looked at Donovan's profile. 'So you decided to kill in revenge, for this, for a handful of lead letters?'

Donovan shook his head, his chin down. 'I saw their van the night they stole the lead off the roof, the night they killed that man and hung him on the cross, the night they did this.' He let a few more letters drop from his hand. 'I couldn't sleep and I'd gone up on the roof to see if I could see any muntjac or foxes with the night glasses. It was early morning, about three a.m., and as I came out on the roof I heard the van coming along the road, maybe twenty mph, less. And it stopped right opposite the house and a figure came out of the shadows opposite; he must have been there all the time, standing lookout. The driver got out of the van to open the tailgate. I saw them both clearly because they'd stopped under one of the street lights. One was ethnic Chinese. Then they were off. Just a white van, like all the rest.

'By the time I heard what they'd done at the church it was the next night. It was on the radio, and they said the police thought it was gangs fighting over territory. So I thought, I don't want any part of that, and what do I know anyway? I saw a white van. Big deal. So I kept quiet. Last thing I want is the police in my life again. They said arrests were being made, so what difference would it make? Then I went out to Barrowby Airfield with you to see the kites. The van went past and there he was, the Chinese driver. I recognized him. The police hadn't got him at all. That shook me. I thought then I should speak up, but I'd have to tell them why I didn't report it on the day. So I just waited.

'Thursday morning I came here to visit the memorial. The first time since the murder in the graveyard. I found this – that they'd torn the letters out – and I couldn't walk away, could I? It was personal, as if I'd been singled out. I told myself I hadn't. That they were just thieves. But I couldn't find the peace I always get here. It broke the spell. The magic of the place.'

He leaned forward and touched the stone.

'They never knew what they'd done,' he said.

'What they'd unleashed. I told you it was the explosion which unlocked the memory of that night in the trench in Korea. But it was this. Just a few metal letters in stone.' He heaved some air into old lungs. 'It's always been important to me, this place, because it meant I didn't have to remember. Didn't have to feel anything. All I had to do was touch the stone. Bear witness. Keep the rest of it inside here...'

Donovan put both hands to his head.

'When I saw this, it was over,' he said, swaying slightly. A sudden gust of wind cracked like a sheet. The pine trees began to sizzle. 'I saw everything again. And I can't stop seeing it.'

'We should get in the church, Jock. There's a dust storm brewing. Then rain. You could sit down. You need to sit down.'

'Everything was unlocked. The fear came out, and the guilt, and the loss – and then, what came out last but overshadowed everything, was the anger. I had to do something with the anger. I had to hit back. I nearly died of the tension, the bottled-up feeling that I had to hurt someone else. And then I knew. I knew who to blame. The people I'd never blamed. The enemy. All those years I hadn't hated. But that morning, standing here, it crowded around me, like these dust storms, blocking out the light.'

Dryden could taste dust on the wind now, on his lips.

Donovan stepped back. 'I'm not mad. I was for a while in the years after I got back. But I've been better. And I thought I could keep the good feeling...' He shrugged, struggling to put what he felt into words. 'Keep the *absence* of the bad feeling. I just wanted to feel nothing, as I've always felt nothing. I thought if I punished them I could have that back, my old life. Punished them the way that Peter and Paul would have done. So I took the rifle and went up on the roof. I saw someone in the telescopic sight but he had his back to me. He had that dark, black hair. Glossy. I thought, I'll kill one. One shot. Then the others will come out. And maybe, if I still feel the anger, I'll kill them as they come out, one by one. I pulled the trigger and in the same moment he bent down, touched his shoes. I'd have probably missed him anyway. My arms shake now I'm old.'

He rubbed a hand over his rough skin and stubble and Dryden saw he was crying.

'Life's a comedy sometimes.'

He stepped away from the edge of the memorial.

'The blast terrified me. I thought, it's God. It's His judgement.' Donovan raised his voice. 'When I got myself up on my feet there was this silence, and even if I screamed there was still silence. I just went outside and tried to find a noise, any noise. I saw you go by in the cab. Then I heard a siren. And that bell.' He twisted at the waist, looking back at Christ Church. 'It rang out of time.'

The old soldier stood to attention. 'I'm sorry now for what I did. I just wish they hadn't taken the letters. Because then I'd have died never having remembered, and that would have been a mercy. Now I've got to live with what I've done

– I've killed three men. But most of all I've got to live with what I didn't do that night in 1953. I didn't die with my friends. Did I? I didn't even fight alongside them.'

FORTY-SIX

He took Donovan's arm, a bone in a sleeve, as if his muscles had dissolved, and tried to lead him away from the memorial.

The churchyard around them was suddenly churning with leaves. Looking across the Clock Holt, Dryden could see the edge of the dust storm blotting out a line of poplars. Daylight was bleeding out of the sky.

And then he saw a ball rolling along one of the churchyard paths, blown by the wind. It was Donovan's present to Eden: small, multi-coloured, with the Korean script blurred as it spun.

And then he saw Eden, walking, with strange, staggering steps, in pursuit of the ball.

'Eden! Philip!' Laura's voice was clear above the sound of the wind. She came into sight around the apse of Christ Church, calling for her child.

'He's here!' Dryden ran towards the child. Eden was looking at the ball, not at his feet, which were set at odd angles with each step. The wind and the dust and the *whirl* of things made the child scream with joy. He stamped his feet as

356

the ball rolled away.

Dryden made himself stop a few feet short of his son, holding out his arms. Laura arrived, doubled over. 'I left him playing with the ball on the blanket,' she said. 'I just looked away and he was gone.' She was half laughing, half crying.

Eden walked into Dryden's arms. He picked up the child and turned him round so that he could see the ball, which was being blown towards the church porch.

The coming storm reached the pine trees round the vicarage and somewhere a door banged, wood splintering. A single car alarm began to pulse a warning.

'Inside,' said Dryden. Donovan had caught them up, so he shepherded the old man down the path towards shelter.

The door to the church was open so they went in, pulling it shut behind them. The light here was redder, darker. The dust storm hissed at the windows. Donovan took a seat in the back pew and looked around him. Dryden saw him differently then, as a figure from his own childhood in North London: a Catholic church, the confessional box, and the forgiven sitting quietly, mumbling their penance.

'I'm going to have to ring the police,' said Dryden. He felt he had to keep saying it in case he took the easy way out and just let the truth be a punishment in itself.

'After the storm,' said Donovan.

Laura rolled the ball down the nave and watched Eden follow.

The door of the vestry where they'd found

Stokely Powell's body swung open and Rev. Temple-Wright came out. Her head was down, her eyes on her feet, and Dryden guessed that she never looked up at the painted roof.

She met them halfway down the nave opposite the Masaccio, and smiled at the child. 'Take a last look,' she said, pointing at the painting. 'It's going away tomorrow. At last. They've got someone coming from Florence to see it in London, did I say? An expert. Everyone's excited.'

'You'll sell?' asked Dryden.

She laughed as if the question was outlandish. Then she noticed Donovan in the back pew and her neck straightened, as if she were drawing herself up.

'Of course. If it is Masaccio then I'm told we could be talking in excess of a quarter of a million. It probably won't be, but they'll sell a copy, too. It'll pay for a few tea mornings if nothing else.'

Dryden stepped a foot closer. 'There's been some vandalism in the churchyard. They've taken all the lead letters out of the memorial to the soldiers who fought in the Korean War.'

'Yes, I know. They were very methodical. Still, wars are best forgotten,' she said.

'What wars do you remember?' He struggled to keep the aggression out of his voice.

'I'm talking about the wars of men. The wars I'm interested in are more difficult to win. The war on ignorance, the war on greed...'

Dryden held up a hand to silence her and was deeply satisfied that the gesture worked, even here, in her own church. But then it wasn't really

358

her church at all.

She forced a smile for the child, reminding Dryden to make sure the door was locked when they left. Then she pulled a scarf up across her mouth and fled.

Laura was standing in front of the Masaccio. Eden was sitting on the carpet now, the ball in his hands, but captivated instead by the light, which shimmered as the dust storm passed, sudden beams of sunlight breaking through, cutting across the nave like strings of silver.

'I don't understand,' she said, as Dryden stood beside her. 'Look...'

He stood two feet from the canvas, studying the familiar landscape between Rome and the sea. Superimposed, in the foreground, the grassy Golgotha, with its three crosses. All the details suggested Italy: the Roman ruins, the Arcadian scenes, the villages and campanile. The tiny figures engaged in everyday life – the innkeeper on his doorstep, a washerwoman under white sheets, a beggar with one arm beside the road. And the peasant chopping wood. The peasant hc'd called 'Everyman' but Laura had christened Stefano after a man she'd known in her own village. And Stefano was turning from the woodpile because the wind had blown his hat off.

But there was no hat.

'That's impossible,' he said. He stood back, scanning the background.

Laura held both hands over her mouth. 'Tell me I'm not going mad,' she said.

And then Dryden knew. 'You're not going mad.' That one missing detail told the whole story.

Temple-Wright had said the other painting, this one's twin, had been destroyed by damp but they had sold the frame. Had Vincent Haig been the middle man, or offered an expert opinion? Or did he know someone who'd spotted that the frame *was* original, even if the picture was lost forever, and that therefore it was time to take a closer look at its twin? Then, perhaps, he'd looked at the work itself: the paint, the pigments, the frame. Had he seen the hallmarks of its master? And when Temple-Wright announced the painting was to go to London to be valued, had he taken his chance? Dryden saw again the multi-coloured handprint by the door to the apse, the intermittent lights at night in Christ Church. Did the heady smell of paints in Sexton Cottage mask a secret masterpiece, Vincent Haig's copy of Masaccio's Crucifixion? A copy to hang here, while the original was passed on for sale in the shadowy world of the European art market.

Dryden glimpsed the future: the Florentine expert smiling a sad smile. A copy after all. And Albe Haig, living out his last years in the security of Sexton Cottage. And then, after a decent passage of time, the original turning up on the market. Or perhaps it would never surface, hanging instead on an art lover's wall, a source of private delight.

He thought then that Brimstone Hill had seen many crimes since the day of its first miracle, the casting out of the Devil. This one, he felt, should remain a secret he would share only with Laura.

'What's happened?' she asked, her brown eyes wide.

'A miracle,' said Dryden. 'The second miracle of Brimstone Hill.'

The door closed with a bang and they realized Jock Donovan had fled. Then they heard the rain on the roof like a blessing.

FORTY-SEVEN

Barrowby Airfield was deserted. Laura lay on a picnic blanket in a white dress, her natural tan enhanced by ten days of unbroken clear skies since that one night of rain. Eden wore a sun hat and was covered in cream, although he'd inherited Italian skin – olive, dark already. Boudicca lay on the edge of the blanket, panting.

Dryden sat in the back of the Capri. A red letter L was attached to the rear bumper, another in front. Dryden didn't know why he'd volunteered to sit in on the driving lesson but it seemed like an act of solidarity, of support. He was frankly regretting it now, not because he didn't trust Grace, but because he suspected Humph's pedagogic powers were limited.

'OK,' said the cabbie, squirming slightly in the passenger seat. 'Let's start the engine.'

Grace glanced in the rear-view mirror and gave Dryden a look of infinite long-sufferance.

The Capri's engine coughed twice then caught.

'OK. Clutch down and into first gear.'

'What?'

Humph removed the sausage roll from his mouth and repeated the sentence. They edged forward over the wide expanse of grass. A few curious rabbits fled. Eden was up on his feet in pursuit, Laura ten feet behind, shepherding.

Dryden's mobile lit up on the back seat beside him.

Vee Hilgay was in the Magistrate's Court, Ely. The text was not a surprise. Muriel Calder had made her third appearance on a charge of manslaughter. She was remanded in custody for further psychiatric reports. DI Friday was uncertain if they would ever get the case into the Crown Court. Dryden was perfectly sure Calder was sane. But the calm premeditation of her killing seemed to defy some unwritten law of murder. It marked her out as a demon. Another devil of Brimstone Hill. The more she demanded her public trial – in her mind, the trial of Will Brinks for the murder of her husband – the more the experts wanted to study her mind. In the end, Dryden hoped, she'd get her day in court. Then the years that followed in gaol would at least offer some satisfaction.

The case that most definitely would come to the Crown Court involved the civil war which had broken out between the Erebus Street triad gang – 14K – and its breakaway rival – Sun Yee On. DI Friday had charged three men from 14K with the murder of Sima Shuba. Their case would be held in tandem with that of two men – related to the victims of the Barrowby Airfield

362

explosion and members of Sun Yee On – charged with the murder of the *master* of 14K in the burnt-out house on Erebus Street.

The Capri circled the airfield in first gear, then second, then third, then back down through the gears to one, and an orderly halt. Grace swapped seats with her father and they headed for the gates.

Dryden called through the open window to Laura: 'Ten minutes.'

They took the Ely Road to The Jolly Farmers and then turned down to Brimstone Hill. The cab notched up forty-five mph and slipped into third gear, then slipped back to thirty mph as they reached the lampposts in the town. They came to a stop outside Christ Church.

Grace got out to let Dryden free, then got back in to hear the latest lecture on the relationship between speed and gear selection. Grace was booked in for her test on her seventeenth birthday. She would have to sit through a lot of lectures about driving. It was her father's special subject. But if she passed, her life would be transformed. Humph had promised her a car for her birthday. She could drive to Humph's house, go and see her grandma, organize her own complicated life. It was just fourteen months away.

There were flowers on Jock Donovan's grave. There had been every day since the funeral. The police found his body on the flat roof of Brimstone House. He'd shot himself with a US handgun, very neatly, in the left temple. Vincent Haig had paid for the burial, and his grandfather changed the flowers each day with blooms from the cottage garden.

Dryden felt that Donovan's suicide had been a release the old man deserved. Not so much self-destruction as a preventative execution. No court could have contrived a punishment to match the one he'd faced: to remember, finally, and daily, that single night of incessant fear in 1953 at the Battle of the Hook; to be haunted by the very feeling itself, of standing in the blood of his brothers-in-arms.

Grace sounded the horn on the Capri.

Dryden climbed in and regained his seat in the back. He knew something had happened. Grace was crying, holding her father's hand.

She looked at Dryden in the rear-view mirror. 'Dad says – if it's OK with Mum – I can have Boudicca.'